A faint rattling noise attracted his attention. He remembered locking the door, and when he turned, he saw the doorknob rotate, then slowly fall back into place.

Roosevelt pulled the Colt out of his gun belt, where he'd placed it on his desk.

"Who's there?" he said in a sharp voice.

Footsteps pounded down the outside stairs. Roosevelt crossed the room, unlocking the door, and threw it open. He glimpsed the shadowy figure of a man jumping off the boardwalk into the street. He moved onto the stairwell landing.

"You there!" he shouted. "Halt!"

The man spun around, his arm raised. Too late, Roosevelt realized he was framed in a spill of lamplight from the room. The gun in the man's hand spat flame, and a slug splintered the doorjamb beside Roosevelt's head. He brought his Colt to bear, thumbing the hammer, and fired back . . .

DAKOTA

MATT BRAUN

St. Martin's Paperbacks

This is a work of fiction. All of the characters, organizations, and events portrayed in this novel are either products of the author's imagination or are used fictitiously.

DAKOTA

Copyright © 2005 by Winchester Productions, Ltd.

For information address St. Martin's Press, 175 Fifth Avenue, New York, NY 10010.

ISBN: 978-0-312-99783-0

Printed in the United States of America

St. Martin's Paperbacks edition / September 2005

St. Martin's Paperbacks are published by St. Martin's Press, 175 Fifth Avenue, New York, NY 10010.

10 9 8 7 6 5 4 3 2

To Bettiane,
Always

The credit belongs to the man who is actually in the arena, whose face is marred by dust and sweat and blood . . . who at the best knows in the end the triumph of high achievement, and who at the worst, if he fails, at least fails while daring greatly, so that his place will never be with those cold and timid souls who know neither victory nor defeat.

Theodore Roosevelt

DAKOTA

ONE

Roosevelt wouldn't allow himself to believe they were dying.

The night train from Albany rattled along through the darkened countryside. Dimmed lanterns swayed overhead, lighting the passenger coach, his features reflected in the grimy window. He looked exactly the way he felt, drained and stunned, his eyes rimmed with despair. He refused to yield to the terror that pulsed in his heart.

Five days ago, when he'd left New York City, Dr. Murdock, the attending physician, had assured him there was no reason for concern. His mother was bedridden with a severe cold, and his wife, expecting their first child, seemed normal. His responsibilities as an assemblyman in the state legislature and a leading voice in the Republican Party required his vote on impending legislation. He was loathe to leave, but the doctor had again reassured him that his anxiety was unwarranted. He'd caught the Sunday train for Albany, the state capital.

Just that morning, a crisp, snowy Thursday, he had received a telegram from his brother, Elliot. The message informed him that his wife, Alice, had given birth to a healthy baby girl and was doing fairly well, considering it was her first delivery. The date was February 14, 1884, and Roosevelt, euphoric with the news, thought it auspicious that his daughter had been born on St. Valentine's Day. His colleagues in the legislature, when he entered chambers for

a critical vote on civic reform, pummeled him with congratulations. He was proud as punch.

"Wonderful news, Theodore," one of his friends said,
pumping his arm. "How does it feel to be a father?"

"By Godfrey!" Roosevelt replied with a nutcracker
grin. "I never imagined it would be so grand."

But now, as he stared out the train window, the words
rang hollow. Late that afternoon, when the legislature adjourned for the day, he had returned to his office. His secretary handed him another telegram, and he'd fully
expected a glowing report on mother and child. Upon
opening the envelope, his face went ashen as he scanned
the message, and a chilling numbness struck at his very
core. The text was a death knell, short and brutal. Too
much to comprehend.

> Mother is dying, and Alice is dying too.
> Come quickly.
>
> Elliot

Even on the best of days, there was no quick way from
Albany to New York City. The train was slowed by snow
squalls in the north and thick ground fog to the south along
the Hudson River. The slow, tortuous journey was all but
unbearable, and mile-by-mile, alternating between prayers
and a sense of desolation, Roosevelt's thoughts skewed
wildly from hope to abject fear. One moment he believed
the God he worshipped would show infinite mercy, and the
next he dreaded he would be too late. He cursed himself
for not being there, for having left when he should have
stayed.

The train pulled into Grand Central Station shortly after
ten o'clock. Roosevelt was out the vestibule door before
the coaches stopped rolling, and hurried up the stairway to
the main terminal. The central chamber was a vast beaux
arts amphitheater, with vaulted arches, massive stained-
glass windows, and the constellations of the zodiac
wrought in gold against blue on a majestic ceiling. He

marched through the terminal as though blind to the airy marble colossus.

People invariably noticed Roosevelt and were quick not to block his path. He stood four inches shy of six feet and weighed perhaps 150 pounds when fully clothed. Yet he was unusually muscular, with a bull-like chest and a thick neck that strained against his shirt collar. His eyes were pale blue, pince-nez glasses squeezed onto his nose over a full mustache, and brushy side whiskers emphasized his hard, square jaw. His expression was offset by a mouthful of dazzling tombstone teeth and bordered on the snarl of a man peering directly into the sun. He looked like he could walk through granite.

Outside the terminal he caught a hansom cab on Forty Second Street. The broad thoroughfare and nearby buildings were all but invisible in a dense drizzling mist. For the past ten days the city had been enveloped in a fog so pervasive that there was little difference between dawn and dusk. The air smelled of sodden ashes, for homes and businesses were heated by coal, and street lamps appeared shrouded in a viscous gray gauze. The driver held his horse to a cautious walk in the soupy murk.

Roosevelt was reminded of a similar night, just six years ago. An undergraduate at Harvard, he'd taken the train from Boston after being notified his father was mortally ill. Theodore Senior was a partner in an importing firm, a millionaire several times over, and the Roosevelts were among the inner circle of New York aristocracy. Only forty-six, he had taken ill suddenly and died three days later of a malignant tumor of the bowel. A noted philanthropist, Theodore Senior had been a man of tireless vitality, whose love of family was matched by his compassion for the poor. Roosevelt still thought of him by the name he'd secretly invented as a child—Greatheart.

Three years later, in the summer of 1880, Roosevelt had graduated *magna cum laude* from Harvard. He and Alice had married that fall, shortly before he enrolled as a law student at New York's Columbia University. His father's

idealism led him to consider a career generally shunned by
the wealthier class but one that enabled him to champion
the rights of the downtrodden. In 1881 he joined the Republican Party, and at age twenty-three he was the youngest man ever elected to the New York State Legislature.
His meteoric rise was attributed to his combative stance
against the corrupt politics of Tammany Hall, and last November he had been elected to a third term in the legislature. *The New York Times,* in a recent article, hailed him as
"the most remarkable young politician of our day."

Tonight Roosevelt would have traded it all for a reversal
of what he feared awaited him at home. As the cab drew to
a halt before the mansion at 6 West Fifty Seventh Street, he
jumped out and handed a wad of bills to the driver.
Through the fog, Roosevelt saw the dull glow of lamps inside, and he hurried up the steps and rapped sharply on the
door. A moment elapsed, and he was about to knock again
when the door opened. Elliot, who was two years younger,
pulled him into the vestibule. Elliot's expression was stark.

"Thank God you're here," he said. "I prayed you would
make it in time."

"What's happened?" Roosevelt demanded. "Mother
and Alice were perfectly fine when I left for Albany."

"Dr. Murdock will have to explain it. I still find it all
so . . . incomprehensible."

Anna and Corinne, Roosevelt's sisters, rushed from the
parlor into the hallway. Anna, fondly known as "Bamie,"
was the oldest at twenty-nine and seemed destined for the
life of a spinster. Corinne was the baby of the family,
scarcely twenty-two, and already married. Bamie threw
herself into Roosevelt's arms.

"Oh, Teddy!" she cried in a shaky voice. "I can't bring
myself to believe we might lose them."

Roosevelt hugged her and drew Corinne into the embrace. The mansion was three stories, lavishly furnished
with Persian carpets in every room and an ornate hand-
carved staircase leading to the upper floors. Usually alive
with laughter and gaiety, the house was now eerily quiet.

Bamie sniffled, her eyes moist with tears, and Roosevelt patted her shoulder.

"Where is Dr. Murdock?" he said. "I must speak with him."

"In the parlor," Corinne said softly. "We've been waiting for you."

Dr. Harold Murdock was a short, stout man with a mane of white hair. He was standing before a blazing fireplace when they came through the doorway to the parlor. His features were dour as he moved forward to shake hands with Roosevelt. Watching them, Elliot was struck again by his brother's force of character. Whenever he entered a room, he radiated such a sense of voltage that he immediately became the central presence. Tonight he seemed somehow larger than life in a house of death.

"I require an explanation," he said with a perfunctory handshake. "On Sunday, you assured me there was no reason for concern. What has happened to change your diagnosis?"

"Your mother contracted pneumonia," Murdock said frankly. "Her condition deteriorated overnight, and the suddenness of it has no medical explanation. She was simply too frail to fight it off."

"Are you saying there's nothing to be done?"

"Nothing known to medical science, Mr. Roosevelt. Only the very strong of constitution survive pneumonia."

Bamie snuffled quietly while Corinne and Elliot averted their eyes. Roosevelt stared directly at the physician. "And what of my wife?"

"Bright's disease," Murdock informed him. "In layman's terms, irreversible failure of the kidneys. She's probably had it for some time, a dormant strain. Lying in wait."

"Lying in wait for what?"

"A stress to the system too grievous to endure. Quite likely, the rigors of childbirth unleashed toxins into her system. Her delivery was long, and difficult."

Roosevelt frowned. "You couch these terms in a certain vagary, Doctor. Perhaps we need another medical opinion."

"I felt so, too," Murdock said. "Dr. John Phelps, chief

surgeon at St. Luke's, was here this afternoon. He concurs with what is now my prognosis."

"Prognosis, as in final, if I understand the distinction. Are you convinced there's no hope?"

"I regret to say that is correct, Mr. Roosevelt."

"You've made no mention of the baby. Is she well?"

"Your daughter is quite healthy, perfectly fit. You needn't worry."

Roosevelt's gaze was drawn to the fireplace. He stood for a moment, staring into the flames, as if unwilling to accept the verdict on the women he loved most. Then, abruptly, he turned toward the doorway. "I must see them."

"Mr. Roosevelt," Murdock said gently.

"Yes." Roosevelt paused, unable to look back. "What is it, Doctor?"

"I suggest you see your mother first. In my judgment, she will not last the night."

"And my wife?"

"She has time yet, perhaps the morning."

"Thank you, Doctor."

Roosevelt went through the hall and mounted the sweeping staircase. His shoulders were squared, as though summoning courage. He willed himself to be strong.

The bedroom was lighted by lamps turned low. A fire flickered in the hearth, and a nurse, an older woman in a white uniform, sat in a chair beside the bed. When Roosevelt entered the room, she rose and stepped aside. Her expression revealed nothing.

"Good evening, sir," she said kindly. "I'll just wait outside till you finish your visit."

Roosevelt seated himself in the chair. His mother lay propped against a bank of pillows, her flannel nightdress open at the throat. Her face was flushed bright with fever, and her breathing was labored, hardly more than a wheezing rasp. Her dark hair was tinged with gray, upswept in the fashion she preferred, and her eyes were closed. He thought she looked as beautiful as ever.

Some of his fondest memories of childhood were of the woman endearingly called Little Motherling. Martha Bulloch Roosevelt was originally from Savannah, the youngest daughter of an aristocratic southern family. She was delicate, with vivid blue eyes and a creamy complexion, and after marrying Theodore Senior she had become the belle of New York society. She was known to her husband and closest friends as Mittie, and her gentle spirit, mixed with a buoyant serenity, made her almost angelic. She was the calm in the storm of an exuberant and oftentimes volcanic household.

Roosevelt found it impossible to reconcile that she was dying so soon after her fiftieth birthday. In January, when family and friends gathered for her birthday gala, she had been effervescent, the very picture of health and happiness. And now, only a month later, she lay fragile and withered on her deathbed. His mouth was suddenly thick with the taste of bile.

"Theodore."

The sound of her voice startled him. Her eyes were watery and she stared at him as though unable to bring him into focus. Her hand trembled when she tried to lift it from the bed.

"Mama." Roosevelt leaned closer, taking her hand in his own. "How well you look, absolutely in the pink."

"Always the fibber," she said with a wan smile. "I knew you would come. I waited for you."

"You mustn't tax yourself, Mama. Save your strength until you recover."

"I'm dying, Theodore, and you needn't pretend. I waited to tell you something."

"Yes, of course, what is it?"

"I am so very proud of you. . . ." Her face congested and she drew a ragged breath, gathering herself. "Your father would have been proud, too. I wish he had lived to see all you have accomplished."

Roosevelt was unable to speak. He swallowed hard, determined to control his emotions, holding them tight inside.

She squeezed his hand with the silken touch of a butterfly.

'Now, I have to rest. Run along and see Alice, Theodore. She needs you so."

"Yes, perhaps you're right, Mama. I'll look in on her and return before you know it. We'll talk some more."

"I will be . . ."

Her voice failed even as her eyes closed. Roosevelt stood, hesitating a moment, waiting until he heard the sibilant rasp of her breathing. He finally moved to the door, and when he went out, the nurse returned to the room. As the door closed, he paused to compose himself, dreading what came next. He steeled himself to take heart, hold it together.

Down the hall, he entered the suite of rooms he shared with Alice. Off to the left of the parlor, he saw a heavyset woman bending over a crib in the room redecorated some months ago as a nursery. Quickly, not yet ready to meet his daughter, he walked to the bedroom. A uniformed nurse moved away from the bed and crossed to where he stood in the doorway. She nodded to him with a look of heartfelt sympathy.

"Mr. Roosevelt," she said in a hushed tone. "We've been expecting you. Mrs. Roosevelt is resting quietly."

"Well, that's good," Roosevelt managed. "Is she awake?"

"No, sir, not at this time. She drifts in and out every hour or so. She's quite coherent when she's awake."

"Is she in pain?"

"Not all that much, no, sir. Dr. Murdock ordered laudanum to ease her discomfort. She's actually doing very well."

"Yes, I know you're doing everything possible. I believe I will sit with her for a while."

"I'll just wait in the parlor, then. Call if you need me."

She went out. Roosevelt walked to the bed, mentally prepared for the worst. Alice's features were pale, somewhat gaunt, and her auburn hair, long and loose, fanned down across her shoulders. Her breathing was shallow, her lips slightly parted, the lashes of her eyes still, as though she'd fallen into a deep sleep. He seated himself in a chair beside the bed and lightly stroked her cheek with his fingertips. He thought, even now, she was the loveliest woman he'd ever seen.

The memory of it, the day they'd first met, suddenly flooded his mind. Her name was Alice Hathaway Lee, and it was during his third year at Harvard. She was seventeen, the daughter of a wealthy businessman, the family prominent in Boston society. Roosevelt was bewitched from the moment he saw her and told friends she was the most enchanting creature he'd ever known. He courted her for two years, and four months after his graduation from Harvard they were married at Chestnut Hill, the Lees' family estate. He thought then, and had never doubted it since, that he was the luckiest man in the world.

Alice was vivacious and animated, with a sly humor that led him to call her his sunny little bride. After a honeymoon in Europe, they settled into the mansion on Fifty Seventh Street, and her vibrant gaiety quickly enchanted everyone in the Roosevelt family. They were soon the toast of New York's social elite, invited to a whirlwind of dinner parties and gala balls hosted by the Vanderbilts and the Rockefellers. They danced the nights away, carefree and laughing, while he spent his days in law school at Columbia University. Others were quick to comment that they'd never seen a couple so perfectly matched.

Ever his most ardent supporter, Alice reveled in whatever enterprise he undertook. His family, particularly an uncle who had assumed the helm of the Roosevelt & Company importing firm, had argued strenuously against Theodore's entering the political arena. Their social position and their sober Dutch heritage held that politics was suitable only for low-class Irishmen, certainly not for men of his status. But Alice, who was unwavering in her faith, insisted that he follow his dreams, wherever they might lead. Her pride in his accomplishments ultimately became the pride of the Roosevelt family.

"Pardon me, sir."

Roosevelt's reverie was broken by the nurse's voice. Alice was still fast asleep, and when he glanced at the wall clock he realized he'd been lost in rumination for almost an hour. He turned in his chair and saw the nurse waiting in the doorway. Her look was grave.

"Dr. Murdock asks that you come to your mother's room. He suggested you come right away."

"Yes, of course," Roosevelt said, pushing out of his chair. "You'll look after my wife?"

"Yes, sir. I'll be here when you return."

The family was gathered around the bed when Roosevelt hurried into the room. Bamie and Corinne were crying softly, and Elliot looked paralyzed with grief. Dr. Murdock stood apart, his features stoic, nodding to Roosevelt, as if to say it was time. Roosevelt moved past Elliot, joining Bamie and Corinne at the head of the bed.

Martha Bullock Roosevelt appeared strangely at peace. Her labored breathing of an hour ago was now little more than a gentle gasp, slow and irregular and fainter by the moment. Her face was composed, somehow less flushed, her high, patrician cheekbones rosy with color. The small clock on her writing desk lightly chimed midnight, and shortly afterward she drew her last breath. Her visage was serene in death.

Bamie and Corinne began sobbing, and Elliot mopped his face with a handkerchief. Roosevelt felt numb and cold, struggling against tears, afraid, once started, he might never stop. Dr. Murdock took his arm.

"Your place now is with your wife, Mr. Roosevelt. Your mother is at peace."

Roosevelt nodded, unable to speak, unable to console anyone, least of all himself. He walked back down the hall, entered the suite, and relieved the nurse in the bedroom. He dropped into the chair, searching Alice's face a moment, and found nothing to kindle any vestige of hope. His shoulders slumped, and he leaned forward, his head bowed.

Once, when he was a small boy, his father had told him that

you cannot bargain with God. Yet now, fresh from his mother's passing, he thought it unmerciful of God to take his wife at such a young age. She was only twenty-two, with a newborn daughter and a lifetime of promise before her. Surely there was mercy if he could somehow find the right words.

Hours later, his head still bowed in prayer, night slowly faded to the dinge of dawn. Throughout the night, he had wracked his mind for something he might offer God to spare her life. He repeated it now as a litany of his shortcomings, a benediction for blessing and mercy. He was vain and prideful, overly ambitious, sometimes arrogant in his swift, harsh judgment of these who opposed his will. He would renounce his wealth and social position, his political aspirations, even sacrifice his pride. He would impoverish himself, devote his life to charity and good works for the poor.

All that and more he would exchange to have her whole and well, to see again her sunny smile. He prayed, head bowed in supplication, offering all he had or would ever have for the miracle of life. Yet, after hours of humbling himself, even as he mouthed the words once again, he could not shake his father's admonition that bargaining, however well intentioned, fell on deaf ears. God would not hear.

"Teddy."

Her eyes were open and she was looking at him with a faint smile. Roosevelt took her hand and pressed it to his cheek. "My love," he said, thinking there were miracles after all. "Are you feeling better?"

"Yes, now that you're here."

"I came as quickly as I could."

"Of course. I knew you would." Her smile was limned in the dull light of day. "And you see, I've waited for you."

Roosevelt kissed her hand. "By thunder, we'll have you up and around in no time!"

A dim shape came swimming forward in her mind. She focused on the blurred image, watching it sputter and weave closer. The image suddenly took clarity, and she saw, so clearly now, that it was a flame. Not bright or fiery, somehow lessening in intensity, but nonetheless a flame.

"Sweet Teddy . . ."

Then, gathering itself in an ebbing spark, the flame flickered and died. Her eyes closed on a last soft breath.

"Alice?"

Roosevelt felt his heart lurch. Her fingers were loose in his hand, her features still, and he knew she was gone. His throat constricted, and he moved forward, tenderly taking her in his arms. His eyes welled with tears.

"Oh, my dear sunny Alice."

Unbidden, he heard again her final words, and he knew, however long he lived, they would remain with him forever. Her benediction as she went on alone.

Sweet Teddy . . .

TWO

"The Lord is my shepherd; I shall not want. He maketh me to lie down in green pastures; He leadeth me beside the still waters. He restoreth my . . ."

The Reverend Dr. Edward Hall, pastor of the Fifth Avenue Presbyterian Church, looked out over the assemblage. Before the altar were two rosewood caskets, the air heady with the scent of floral arrangements. The church was filled with mourners come to pay their respects.

The family was seated in the two front pews. Roosevelt and Bamie, Corinne and her husband, Douglas Robinson, Elliot and his family, Alice's parents, and a dozen or more relatives drawn by the tragic loss. They were all too aware that they had sat in these very pews six years ago for the funeral services of Theodore Senior.

Roosevelt scarcely heard the pastor. Four days had passed since the death of his wife and mother, time to arrange the funeral and extend invitations to those closest to the family. His expression impassive, Roosevelt was consumed by a fiery bitterness, charring everything that had once represented happiness and tranquillity, and hope. His outlook on life now rang false, as if heard through the tuning fork of death. A sinister tone that his world had gone dark forever.

The pews on either side of the aisle were crowded with distinguished guests. Among the social oligarchy were the Astors, the Harrimans, and the Vanderbilts. Sen. Warner

Miller, the statewide czar of the Republican Party, was there representing Gov. Grover Cleveland, and his entourage included a score of sober-faced assemblymen from the New York legislature. Henry Cabot Lodge, a fellow politician and Roosevelt's closest friend, had traveled by train from Boston for the services.

". . . With the certainty that we shall all meet again at the Resurrection, through Jesus Christ our Lord. Amen."

The Reverend Dr. Hall closed the services in a somber voice. He looked down from the pulpit at the family, his gaze lingering a moment longer on Theodore, whose loss was twice as hard to bear. Elliot, who had made the funeral arrangements, only yesterday had told Dr. Hall that Theodore showed little interest in his newborn daughter and seemed somehow disoriented by the condolences of those few friends he'd seen over the weekend. The family, Elliot confided, feared for his sanity.

The burial ceremony was to be held at Greenwood Cemetery. Outside the church, two regal black hearses, each drawn by four black horses, waited at curbside. A long line of carriages extended south on Fifth Avenue for three blocks, and uniformed police had closed off the intersecting streets. The drizzle and fog had been borne seaward on westerly winds just that morning, and a warm sun arced higher in a cloudless sky. Crowds gathered along Fifth Avenue to watch the procession.

There was a delay while attendants prepared to carry the caskets from the altar to the hearses. The family, followed by friends and mourners, came out of the church and slowly made their way to the waiting carriages. Roosevelt paused on the steps, his manner curiously abstract, and accepted condolences from Senator Miller and his colleagues in the legislature. As the others filed down the steps, Henry Cabot Lodge remained by Roosevelt's side. They stood wrapped in silence for several moments.

"Dr. Hall gave an excellent service," Lodge finally ventured. "His remarks about your mother and Alice were most commendable."

"Yes, very nice indeed," Roosevelt said absently. "I must remember to thank him."

"I'm sure no thanks are necessary. Your mother, as I recall, was one of his most devout parishioners."

"And Father as well. He and Dr. Hall were quite active in charitable causes. His eulogy when Father passed on was one I shall never forget."

"Need it be said, your loss is my loss, old friend. I greatly admired your mother and father, and like all who knew her, I adored Alice."

"Thank you, Cabot."

Henry Cabot Lodge, like Roosevelt, was a man of wealth who gloried in the political arena. He had served two terms in the Massachusetts House of Representatives and as chairman of the Massachusetts Republican Party and even now was campaigning as a candidate for the U.S. Congress. A Boston Brahmin, old money and elite among the elite, he shared with Roosevelt an aristocratic lineage of inherited wealth and unswerving ambition. No public office, they often joked, was beyond their grasp.

Yet their kindred spirit went beyond politics. They had met at Harvard, and their friendship was one of intellect and mutual respect. Despite their relatively young age, they had each made their mark and garnered praise, in the literary world. Lodge had authored biographies of Alexander Hamilton and Daniel Webster and published *A Short History of the American Colonies.* Roosevelt, while still at Harvard, had published *The Summer Birds of the Adirondacks,* and only last year he had published, to much critical acclaim, *The Naval War of 1812.* Their work was much sought after by publishers.

Lodge admired Roosevelt as well for his ability to quote Omar Khayyám, disclaim at length on German poetry, and discuss in esoteric terms naval strategy, forestry, Greek drama, and metaphysics. Roosevelt, in turn, held Lodge in great esteem for his integrity and his high-minded attitude about government. Unlike many politicians, Lodge's word truly was his bond, and his scathing attacks on graft and corruption often made national headlines. He and Roosevelt were men of breeding who shared the belief that honest government was the birthright of the people.

"Quite a turnout, hmmm?" Lodge said, trying to make conversation. "Wasn't it good of Senator Miller to come down from Albany? He's a fine man."

Roosevelt nodded. "Yesterday he called on me at home. We spoke at length about the future."

"The future?"

"I've requested a leave of absence from the legislature. He was reluctant, but in the end, he agreed."

"I confess I'm at a loss," Lodge said. "Why would you take a leave of absence?"

"Alice was . . ." Roosevelt hesitated, as though searching for words. "The light has gone out of my life, Cabot. I'm not at all sure I wish to continue in politics."

Lodge was taken aback. He fully appreciated the depth of his friend's bereavement. Yet Lodge understood as well the import of such a hasty decision. In the last election, Roosevelt had promised his constituents that he would break the power of the Tammany Hall political machine. On February 14, the day his daughter was born, he had pushed through legislation that appointed him chairman of a Special Committee to investigate corruption in New York City.

Immediately afterward, in the hallway outside chambers, a Tammany Hall politico had insulted him, questioning his personal motives in the affair. Roosevelt, who had been the welterweight boxing champion at Harvard, would not brook an insult to his honor, and he'd knocked the man unconscious with two swift blows. Only yesterday, in an article on his tragic loss, *The New York Times* had noted that "Theodore Roosevelt has the moral force of a crusader where individual honor and political reform are concerned."

"Have you considered the consequences?" Lodge asked. "Your future in public office might well be jeopardized."

"Perhaps," Roosevelt said with little interest. "I need time to come to terms with . . . my situation."

"How much time?"

"I really couldn't say."

"What will you do with yourself, Theodore? You've never been one to sit and watch the passing parade."

"I leave day after tomorrow for the ranch in Dakota Territory. All the arrangements have been made."

Not quite a year ago, in the spring of 1883, Roosevelt had traveled to Dakota Territory to hunt buffalo. He'd spent three weeks out West and discovered, apart from the thrill of the hunt, that the region was attracting ranchers from throughout the cattle industry. Always alert to investment opportunities, he had bought a ranch on the Little Missouri River, outside the town of Medora. The original owner, a man named Bill Merrifield, had been retained to manage the operation.

"I've never been more amazed," Lodge said with a bemused look. "Have you any idea how long you'll be away?"

"Until I find what I'm looking for."

"And what is that?"

"To be perfectly frank, I'm not quite sure, Cabot. I only know I won't find it in New York."

The doors to the church opened. The Reverend Dr. Hall stepped outside, his vestments colorful in the bright forenoon sunlight. He led the pallbearers carrying the caskets toward the waiting hearses.

Roosevelt and Lodge followed them down the steps.

A cheery fire burned in the grate. The study was paneled in dark wood, with bookshelves built into the walls and a large walnut desk positioned facing the fireplace. Late-afternoon sunlight spilled through windows looking westward on Fifty Seventh Street.

Roosevelt laid his pen aside. Two days had passed since the funeral services, and tonight he would depart for Dakota Territory. A good part of his time had been devoted to thinking through the memorial he planned to write. His purpose was to capture the spirit of his late wife in words, without being mundane or overly sentimental. He leaned forward and studied a single sheet of paper on the desk.

IN MEMORY OF MY DARLING WIFE

She was beautiful in face and form, and lovelier in spirit; as a flower she grew, and as a fair young flower she died. Her life had always been in the sunshine; there had never come to her a single great sorrow; and none ever knew her who did not love and revere her for her bright, sunny temper and her saintly unselfishness. Fair, pure, and joyous as a maiden; loving, tender, and happy as a young wife; when she had just become a mother, when her life seemed to be but just begun, and when the years seemed so bright before her—then, by a strange and terrible fate, death came to her.

And when my heart's dearest died, the light went from my life forever.

Theodore Roosevelt

Roosevelt folded the sheet of paper, satisfied with his effort. Once he had penned the memorial, it occurred to him once again that he was now a widower. A line from one of Tennyson's poems came to mind: "'Tis better to have loved and lost / Than never to have loved at all." He took comfort from the thought and felt it quite likely he would remain a widower the rest of his life. In his view, which was rigidly moral, the mystical union between man and wife simply didn't exist outside marriage. He resigned himself to a lifetime of celibacy.

Tonight, he reflected, would place him on a journey to an uncertain future. His gaze wandered around the room, touching on the bookshelves and the marble fireplace, and he was reminded that it had once been his father's study. As a child, his physique frail and suffering from asthma, he had spent many evenings in this very room with the man he thought of as Greatheart. He recalled one evening in particular, perhaps the turning point in his life, when he was wracked by a severe attack of asthma. His father had said to him, "Theodore, you have the mind but not the body. You must work to *make* your body."

Theodore Senior, to emphasize the lesson, installed a gymnasium in the house. Young Roosevelt, with his father's supervision, undertook a daily regimen of weight lifting and calisthenics. His physique slowly developed muscle and strength, and by his early teens the debilitating effects of asthma had all but disappeared. A few years later, at the family's summer home in upstate New York, he was so fit that he routinely paddled a canoe back and forth across the lake and rode his horse at breakneck speeds over the countryside. His sturdy growth enabled him to excel at boxing and wrestling during his years at Harvard.

All through his formative years, his father stressed the need for a sound mind as well as a sound body. Roosevelt was coached by private tutors in English, French, German, and Latin and became a voracious reader, consuming books of history, literature, and philosophy. At fifteen he was sent on the Grand Tour, traveling for three months through Great Britain and the rest of Europe, North Africa, and the Middle East. By the time he sailed back across the Atlantic, he'd seen the world's noblest art and architecture, haggled with merchants in Arab bazaars, and rode to the hounds in England. His education was exhaustive long before he entered Harvard.

A spark in the fireplace broke his ruminations of boyhood. He rose from the desk, collecting the memorial, and went in search of Bamie. Over the weekend, after solitary hours of thought, he'd made the decision to travel to Dakota Territory. Then, in an emotional discussion with Bamie, he had explained his reasons and asked her to care for the baby in his absence. He had named the child Alice Lee, in honor of his wife, and revised his will to appoint Bamie executrix in the event of misfortune. She happily accepted the responsibility of surrogate mother, for it seemed unlikely she would ever have children of her own. She felt far less sanguine about his leaving New York.

Bamie was in the drawing room, working on an elaborate embroidery of flowers. She looked up as he came through the door. "There you are," she said. "I began to wonder if you had lost track of time."

"Hardly," Roosevelt replied. "The train departs at seven, and I fully intend to be aboard. I've reserved a berth in the sleeping coach."

"How I wish you wouldn't go, Teddy. I shudder to think of you off alone in the Wild West."

"I shan't be alone; never fear for that. I daresay the ranch will occupy my time."

"You belong here," she said, glancing at him, "with your daughter and those who love you. Why must you go?"

"You know my reasons." Roosevelt handed her the memorial and another sheet with a list of more than a hundred names. "I've written a remembrance of Alice and what she brought to our lives. Would you have it printed on a fine vellum and delivered to those I've indicated?"

"Yes, of course I will. I'll speak with the printer in the morning. Shall I mail you a copy?"

"No, that won't be necessary. I have committed it to memory."

"I feel certain everyone will treasure it. We all loved Alice so dearly."

"Your love was returned, as you well know. Now, if you'll excuse me, I believe I'll look in on the baby. I must leave the house by six."

"Elliot and Corinne will be here shortly. They wanted to see you off."

"I shouldn't be too long."

Roosevelt turned back into the hall and took the stairway to the second floor. When he entered the upstairs suite, he walked directly to the nursery. The nanny who was caring for the baby, like the other household servants, knew he was leaving New York. He asked her to step out a moment, and she smiled shyly, moving into the parlor. He closed the door.

Alice Lee was asleep, one tiny hand curled beneath her

chin. She was chubby, with rosebud cheeks, wisps of downy hair covering her head. A light blanket was drawn up to her waist, and her expression was one of almost angelic contentment. Roosevelt stood by the crib, looking down at her, and his eyes suddenly glistened with tears. He thought she was the perfect image of her mother.

The resemblance brought a hard lump to his throat. He removed his pince-nez, took a handkerchief from his pocket, and wiped his eyes. Over the past several days he had struggled with his decision to leave her in the care of Bamie. Yet his heart was barren with loss, and he could not abide another night in a house so crowded with memories. He felt he might go mad if he stayed.

Gently, fearful of waking Alice, he took her little hand in his own and held it a moment. Then he clipped his glasses on his nose, turning away, and nodded to the nanny as he hurried through the parlor. Downstairs he found Bamie waiting in the vestibule with Elliot and Corinne. Elliot was an officer at a bank, shrewd with investments, and Theodore knew Bamie would not lack for advice. Corinne, so generous at heart, would lend moral support.

The door to the street was open. A manservant carried out the last of Roosevelt's luggage and stowed it in a hansom cab waiting at curbside. As Roosevelt descended the stairs, he thought his timing was perfect. He hated prolonged good-byes.

"Corinne. Elliot," he said, moving into the vestibule. "How nice of you to see me off."

"How could we not?" Corinne said. "We're very concerned about you, Teddy."

Roosevelt took his coat and hat from a hall tree. "Your concern is appreciated, but unnecessary. I shall be fine."

"All this seems so hurried," Elliot observed. "You haven't said how long you'll be gone. Do you have some idea of when you will return?"

"No, at the moment I do not. I only know there's no peace for me here."

Roosevelt found it difficult to hold his emotions in

check. One moment he seemed to himself quite rational, and the next he feared he might lose all control. He felt he was standing on the edge of the abyss of insanity.

"We know you're distressed," Elliot said. "But how could you not find peace here? This is your home."

"No longer," Roosevelt said in an uneven voice. "When I buried Alice, I buried the best part of myself. There is a curse on this house."

"Surely you're not serious?"

"I have to go or I'll miss my train."

Roosevelt hugged Bamie and Corinne and quickly shook hands with Elliot. He clapped on his hat and shrugged into his overcoat as he went down the steps and climbed into the cab. A pulse pounded in his temple as the cab pulled away from the curb.

There was a sense of flight in his urgency to be gone. A part of him running, fleeing headlong, from a house he looked upon as cursed. Then, in a moment that seemed almost revelation, another thought crossed his mind. Perhaps something closer to the truth.

He wondered if it wasn't himself who was cursed.

THREE

The terrain was hostile and alien, desolate at first sight. Centuries ago, wary of evil spirits, the Sioux had named it *Mako Shika,* Bad Land. Today, inhabited mostly by white men, it was called the Badlands.

Roosevelt sat staring out the window. A midmorning sun glinted off patches of snow as the train hurtled westward. His journey had taken five days, with layovers in Chicago and St. Paul to change trains. He was now some two thousand miles from New York, and yet distance seemed to have little effect. He still felt the drag of what he was trying to outrun.

The Badlands was located in the western reaches of Dakota Territory. A place of vast spaces, the terrain was a convoluted tangle of peaks and buttes, broken by narrow ravines and silver streams coursing through deep chasms. There was a sense of volcanic upheaval, with veins of subterranean lignite, bright with heat, ignited aeons ago by wayward bolts of lightning. The smoke seeping skyward hung wraithlike beneath the morning sun.

Gen. Alfred Sully, campaigning against the Sioux in 1864, had called it "hell with the fires out." Yet amid the chaos of the landscape there were rolling prairies of grass, and square buttes, flat as a billiard table at the summit, rich with graze. The sheer cliffs and steep hillsides, the jutting ridges of sandstone, were a grotesque mask that obscured a land hospitable to buffalo and other wild things for thousands of years. A land seemingly sculpted for scattered herds of cattle.

The train rattled across a trestle over the Little Missouri River. Groves of cottonwoods lined the river along sagebrush flats walled by lavender and scarlet buttes. A few hundred yards downrail was the settlement of Medora, with a population of six hundred and a hodgepodge of some eighty buildings. The town's main street was crowded with several shops and stores, a bank and a newspaper office, and a hotel with a wide veranda. The tall brick chimney of a slaughterhouse stood like a monolith at the end of the street.

The engineer set the brakes, and the train ground to a halt before a whitewashed depot with a peaked roof. Roosevelt shrugged into his overcoat, squared his hat on his head, and collected his traveling valise from the overhead rack. As the passengers stepped off the coaches, the door of the express car opened and the stationmaster began unloading luggage. A man in range clothes with a high-crowned Stetson, a pistol strapped to his hip, waited on the platform.

"Mr. Roosevelt!" he called, hurrying forward with an outstretched hand. "Glad to see you again."

Roosevelt accepted the handshake. "Very good to see you, too, Bill."

"How was your trip?"

"For the most part, it was quite pleasant. Although I haven't had a decent meal since we left St. Paul."

Bill Merrifield laughed. "Well, sir, we can fix that in a hurry. You got any other baggage?"

"One suitcase." Roosevelt glanced at the express car. "There it is now."

"Lemme take care of that for you. We'll put 'er in the buckboard."

A buckboard drawn by a sorrel gelding waited at the side of the depot. Merrifield stowed the suitcase and valise in the back, and they walked upstreet to the Metropolitan Hotel. The noon hour was approaching, but the dining room was all but empty, and they took a table by the window. Roosevelt had forgotten how much he enjoyed simple western fare, hearty and filling rather than gourmet in nature. He ordered steak and eggs, with fried potatoes and buttermilk biscuits.

After the waitress brought mugs of coffee, Merrifield rolled a cigarette. "Sorry to hear about your loss," he said, popping a match on his thumbnail. "Guess the story must've come out on the telegraph. The paper ran it couple days ago."

"Thank you," Roosevelt said without inflection. "Now, if you will, please don't mention it again. I've no wish to discuss the matter."

"Whatever you say goes with me, Mr. Roosevelt."

Merrifield was tall and broad through the shoulders, four years older than Roosevelt. But there was a quality of command about the younger man that instantly demanded respect from those in his employ. His manner made it apparent that he was never to be addressed by his Christian name. Although he was generous and friendly, there was nonetheless something military in his bearing. Familiarity simply wasn't to be tolerated.

A Canadian by birth, Merrifield had drifted into Dakota Territory some years ago. He'd worked as a mule skinner, a buffalo hunter, and a section boss on the railroad. With the money he saved he had then bought land south of Medora, and stocked it with cattle and horses. Last year, on his trip West, Roosevelt had purchased the ranch, known as the Maltese Cross for the shape of its brand. Afterward, never one to stint on an investment, he had Merrifield buy an additional thousand head of cattle. Merrifield was paid a salary and 10 percent of the profits to manage the operation.

The waitress brought Roosevelt a platter of beefsteak, sunny-side up eggs, and fried potatoes heaped beside steaming biscuits. He lathered butter and jam on a biscuit and attacked the steak and eggs as though he hadn't eaten in a week. Merrifield, who hadn't seen Roosevelt in almost a year, was impressed all over again by his quality of vitalizing any situation. He seemed to radiate vigor, a sense of galvanic energy in motion.

Roosevelt paused with a chunk of steak speared on his fork. He peered through his owlish spectacles. "Tell, Bill," he said, "how are affairs at the Maltese Cross? Are we to have a banner year?"

"Yessir, looks to be," Merrifield said. "'Course, we won't know for certain till spring roundup. Wasn't all that bad a winter, so I reckon we're in good shape."

"Bully!" Roosevelt said, as though fortified by the news. "I have high hopes for our endeavor."

"Well, you dang sure got into it at the right time, Mr. Roosevelt. Beef prices oughta be mighty fine come summer market."

"Excellent."

Roosevelt resumed his attack on the platter of food. After he finished, he paid the check and they walked back through the hotel lobby. As they stepped outside, a dapper man in a fur-collared greatcoat came rushing along the veranda. He abruptly stopped when he saw them.

"M'sieur Roosevelt!" he said, beaming. "What a grand surprise."

"Marquis de Mores." Roosevelt and the man exchanged handshakes. "A pleasure to see you so soon upon my arrival."

The man in the natty coat was Antoine-Amedee-Marie-Vincent-Amat Manca de Vallombrosa, Marquis de Mores. A French nobleman immigrated to the West, he had built the slaughterhouse on the edge of town and shipped beef by railroad on refrigerated cars to eastern markets. He was two years older than Roosevelt, unbearably handsome, with black hair, striking green eyes, and a waxed mustache. The people of Medora, unable to contend with his full name, simply called him Marquis.

"I read of your misfortune in the newspaper," de Mores said with a sympathetic expression. "Permit me to extend my most sincere condolences for such a tragic loss."

"Your sentiment is appreciated," Roosevelt replied. "However, I've come West to put all that behind. I have no wish to live in the past."

"A most commendable attitude, and certainly understandable. How long do you plan to stay?"

"For the immediate future, perhaps indefinitely. I may well make Medora my home."

"*Bon, mon ami!* You must come for dinner quite soon."

On his last visit to Medora, Roosevelt had accepted an invitation to dinner at de Mores' home. He found the Marquis and his wife to be pleasant company, for their aristocratic backgrounds gave them much in common. He thought de Mores sometimes put on airs, but that was to be expected. He was, after all, a Frenchman.

"Allow me to decline for the moment," Roosevelt said. "I plan to be on an extended hunt for the next few weeks."

"Hunt?" de Mores repeated. "What is it you plan to hunt?"

"Why, anything that comes into my sights. Assuming, of course, that it has four legs."

"How very witty of you to put it in that light. I presume your prey will not include cattle."

"No, no cows," Roosevelt said with an amused smile. "Has your business prospered since last we met? I recall you were quite optimistic."

"*Mon Dieu!*" de Mores exclaimed. "I pride myself on having a natural instinct for affairs of business. I shall soon become a financier without rival!"

"I daresay you have prospered. Now, if you will excuse me, I must be on to the ranch."

"As ever, M'sieur Roosevelt, a distinct honor to have you in our little community. I look forward to the pleasure of your company."

"Dee—*lighted*!" Roosevelt often spoke with dental snaps, biting off words in an audible click of his teeth. "I shall call on you upon my return."

A short while later Merrifield drove the buckboard through the ford by the railroad trestle. The Little Missouri was at low ebb during late winter, and the sure-footed gelding found a path across the rocky streambed. Merrifield debated whether or not to say anything about the Marquis and how things had changed in Medora. But then on second thought he decided Roosevelt had enough on his mind. Today was not the day for more bad news.

They drove south toward the Maltese Cross.

The mansion stood on a high terrace overlooking Medora and the Little Missouri River. A two-story structure, with cupolas and turrets, it had twenty-seven rooms, all furnished as lavishly as a palace. The locals referred to it as the Chateau de Mores.

The Marquis, with no irony intended, thought of himself as the *grand seigneur.* From his palatial home on the hilltop he looked down on those he regarded as vassals, commoners whose only role was to serve his interests and his vision. He never for a moment forgot that he was a nobleman in a land of peasants.

At noontime every day, barring imperative business matters, he went home to lunch with his wife. A partner in his ambitious enterprises, Medora de Mores was an attractive redhead, svelte and sophisticated, and shared his imperious view of Westerners. The lord of all he surveyed, he had named the town he'd built in her honor. She was, apart from business, the sole passion in his life.

Medora always set a beautiful table. The household was staffed by a butler, four maids, and a cook, and their mistress was a demanding taskmaster. Today, in a dining room that would seat twelve, the luncheon prepared was vegetable bisque, delicate braised squab, and *crème fraiche* over berries to satisfy her husband's sweet tooth. She was dressed in a fetching blue gown that accentuated her tiny waist and sumptuous figure.

"How lovely you look," de Mores said, bussing her on the cheek as he entered the dining room. "And what a wonderful repast! All my favorites."

"You may thank the cook," Medora said with a demure smile. "I merely suggest what she creates."

"You are, as always, my dear, too modest."

De Mores seated her at one end of the table and took his chair at the opposite end. The butler, who might have been invisible for all they noticed, began serving. After tasting the bisque, de Mores rolled his eyes in exaggerated rapture and nodded to her in approval. He paused, dabbing his mouth with a napkin.

"I have a bit of news," he said. "Theodore Roosevelt has returned to town."

"Has he?" Medora said with some interest. "You saw him?"

"Yes, outside the hotel not ten minutes ago. He apparently just arrived on the morning train."

"I do hope you expressed our condolences. The poor man, to have lost his wife and mother so suddenly. How terrible."

"Indeed," de Mores said. "Although I must say he appeared quite fit for the ordeal. He remarked that he might stay on here indefinitely."

"Then we must invite him to dinner!"

"I have already done so. M'sieur Roosevelt is off on a hunting excursion of some duration. He will contact me upon his return."

"How I miss New York," Medora said, her voice wistful. "It would be so nice to have someone of breeding at our table. I long for intelligent conversation."

"I sometimes regret having brought you to this wilderness outpost. I might have made my fortune elsewhere."

"Have no regrets for me, my sweet. I have faith you will succeed beyond all expectations."

De Mores was descended from Orléans royalty. Under threat of the guillotine, during the bloody years of the Revolution, the family had renounced its claim to the throne of France. Some generations later, as the son of a duke, de Mores had graduated from Saint-Cyr, the French

military academy, and served briefly in the army. He resigned from the military in 1881, determined to restore his
family's fortune.

Medora von Hoffman was the daughter of a wealthy
New York investment banker. While vacationing in Paris
the summer of 1882 she met de Mores, and they were married after a whirlwind courtship. De Mores, sensing opportunity, returned with her to New York and worked for a
short time in her father's bank. Yet he found little appeal in
the drudgery of Wall Street, for it lacked adventure, the
promise of conquest. He began searching for some greater
opportunity, a challenge.

Late in the fall of 1882, a cousin of de Mores returned
from a buffalo hunt in Dakota Territory. He told fanciful
stories of the Badlands and the booming cattle industry, all
of which fired de Mores' imagination. An innovator, bold
with ambiltion, he envisioned a way to marry an outdated
cattle trade with modern technology. With Medora's support, he persuaded her father to become a partner in the
venture and thereby secured a million-dollar line of credit.
They entrained for Dakota Territory.

In 1882, the town was a ramshackle affair on the opposite side of the river and was called, with languid simplic-
ity, Little Missouri. De Mores promptly bought the flat
land on the west side of the river and set about building
the town he would name Medora. Having already formed the
Northern Pacific Refrigerator Car Company, he then convinced the railroad to construct a spur line into his new
town. His plan was practical and cost-efficient, and he pro-
claimed that it would revolutionize the western cattle industry. Instead of shipping cows on the hoof by freight car,
he processed steers in his slaughterhouse and shipped
dressed beef by refrigerator car to eastern markets. The
end result, he contended, was cheaper beef prices for the
public.

By the spring of 1883, the town of Little Missouri was
virtually deserted. All the merchants had moved across the
river and opened shops in the bustling new community of

Medora. But a year into the project, de Mores discovered that not every rancher was a convert to modern technology. The prices he paid were necessarily lower, owing to the cost of operating a slaughterhouse and maintaining refrigerator cars. Many cattlemen felt their profits were greater with the traditional method, shipping steers to the packing plants in Chicago. He was still working on the problem.

"Well, however enjoyable, I must be off," de Mores said after finishing his *crème fraiche* over berries. "I have a meeting with our dear friend Paddock."

Medora wrinkled her nose. "I cringe every time you mention his name. What a detestable man!"

"Yes, but essential to our endeavor. Any business requires at least one man without conscience."

"Antoine, do be careful in your dealings with him. He is not to be trusted."

"Trust, my dear, may often be purchased. His loyalty is that of a mercenary—ever for sale."

"Mercenaries have been known to turn on their masters."

"True, but don't you see, I am the highest bidder. His avarice makes him mine."

De Mores kissed her on his way out the door. To the west of his hilltop mansion, smoke billowed out of the slaughterhouse chimney, and he was reminded again that the plant seldom operated at full capacity. His father-in-law, Louis von Hoffman, routinely peppered him with letters demanding to know when the venture would become profitable. There was the implicit threat of cutting off further funds, but thus far Medora had been able to pacify her father. Her appeals were couched in the language of a loving daughter, his only daughter. The line of credit, though depleted by three-quarters of a million, was still in place.

Downtown, de Mores proceeded along the boardwalk fronting stores in the business district. Headquarters for the Northern Pacific Refrigerator Car Company was in a building located between the hotel and the office of the newspaper, the *Badlands Cowboy*. When de Mores entered the door, he found Jake Paddock waiting for him in the outer office. The staff consisted of a secretary, two accountants and a clerk, and a general manager who was generally at the slaughterhouse. De Mores led Paddock to his private office at the rear of the room.

The office was expensively decorated, with a broad mahogany desk, walls paneled in hardwood, and leather furniture. De Mores motioned Paddock to a chair as he seated himself behind the desk. "I am displeased with your progress," he said without ceremony. "You gave me to believe that matters would be handled in a more expeditious manner."

"Things like this take time," Paddock said evenly. "You didn't want nobody killed, and that puts a hitch in my gait. Hard to scare folks off when their lives ain't in danger."

"Be that as it may, you assured me you were up to the task."

"Hell, lemme kill a couple or three and things'll change pronto. Nothin' like dead men to make an argument stick."

"I will not countenance killing."

"Then you'd best get used to a long road and a slow haul. I ain't no magician."

Jake Paddock was one of the original settlers of Little Missouri. A taciturn man, lithe and muscular, his eyes were cold and pale and his manner iron hard. He was reputed to have killed, or murdered, nine men, and his cronies included gamblers, whoremasters, and horse thieves. The common wisdom was that he had fled Texas to escape a hangman's noose.

De Mores was a product of European nobility. As a foreigner, he cared nothing for the overall betterment of Dakota Territory or any interests but his own. Nor was he concerned about laws or legality in a strange land, for he saw himself as above the law. His business enterprise was stalled because too few ranchers were willing to sell him cattle at wholesale prices. And his father-in-law, barring a turnaround in profits, might well sever the financial cord. A month ago he'd sent for Jake Paddock.

The plan was a Machiavellian invention concocted by

de Mores. He couldn't force the larger cattlemen to deal with him, but there were a dozen or more small ranchers scattered throughout the Badlands. His intent was to frighten them off or, failing that, to buy their spreads for pennies on the dollar. He would, in effect, become a rancher himself and provide the herds necessary to fuel his slaughterhouse. Though he saw it as a short-term solution, it would buy time to convince large cattlemen that their outdated methods had been overtaken by technology. The legality of the scheme never once entered his mind.

Jake Paddock saw the Frenchman as the new patron saint of the lawless element. De Mores was a man of wealth and influence, and once he was drawn into a web of crooked deals, that influence might be used as a buffer for any manner of shady enterprises. The fly in the ointment was that the Marquis would not condone outright violence, particularly murder. One small rancher, a man with no backbone, had been terrorized by threats alone and had sold out. But it was not much to show for a month's work.

"How about this?" Paddock suggested. "Suppose me and the boys put the torch to a couple cabins. Might just scare the bejesus outta some of them shit kickers."

"Definitely not," de Mores said sternly. "Someone might be killed in a fire, or fight back, and result in more killing. I will not have it."

"Well, Marquis, you've pretty much got my hands tied. How am I gonna run 'em off if I can't bust a few heads?"

"I thought your reputation as a gunman would have been sufficient to the task, Mr. Paddock. Am I now to believe otherwise?"

"No, I'll come up with a new twist of some sort. There's more'n one way to spook a man."

"See that you do before next we meet. I'm paying you for results, not excuses."

"Lemme ask you something," Paddock said, ignoring the brusque tone. "I heard that Roosevelt feller's back in town. Heard he might stay on a spell. Anything to it?"

"Yes. I spoke with him this morning," de Mores said. "What is your interest in Mr. Roosevelt?"

"Read in the paper he's a big auger back East, politician of some sort. And his foreman, Bill Merrifield, ain't exactly one of your admirers."

"I fail to see the connection."

"Always found it pays to be leery of politicians and lawmen. Roosevelt hangs around too long, he might figure things need a little civilizin'."

De Mores stared at him. "Are you a prognosticator, Mr. Paddock?"

"Can't say," Paddock allowed. "What's it mean?"

"One who foretells the future."

"No, I haven't got no crystal ball. Just call it a hunch."

"And what does your hunch tell you?"

"This Roosevelt feller could be trouble. He ain't like you and me."

"Too civilized?" de Mores said, faintly amused. "Is that the idea?"

Paddock shrugged. "Don't trust a man that holds with the law."

De Mores almost laughed. Though he would never admit it, he was in complete agreement. Laws were made for those who believed in convention and rules. Whereas he believed the end justifies the means.

Perhaps Roosevelt *would* bear watching.

FOUR

The Little Missouri meandered in a serpentine path through the southern Badlands. The wagon trail they followed zigzagged here and there across the river to skirt outcroppings and steep grades. Four miles south of Medora they forded the river for the ninth time.

A midafternoon sun drifted westward, streaking the terrain in vibrant hues of gold and vermilion. The landscape was a forbidding montage of cliffs and ravines, gnarled cedars caught in the looming shadows of buttresses framed against an azure sky. The bottoms along the river were timbered with tall groves of cottonwoods.

Roosevelt remembered that the winding path along the river was called the Custer Trail. In years past, it had been the mail route between Fort Keogh in the south and Fort Abraham Lincoln to the north. The summer of 1876, George Armstrong Custer and the Seventh Cavalry Regiment had camped on the river in pursuit of hostile Sioux bands. A few weeks later, to the west in Montana Territory, Custer and his troops met their fate on the Little Bighorn.

Three miles farther on, Merrifield popped the reins as the sorrel gelding hauled the buckboard to the crest of a wide butte. On the opposite side, at the foot of a rocky downslope, they forded the river yet again. To the west, silhouetted against a cloudless sky, was a towering landmark known as Chimney Butte. Beyond a stand of cottonwoods, a level valley of tall grass stretched southward for thirty miles. The verdant plain, some four miles broad, was the Maltese Cross range.

The valley gave Roosevelt a small sense of comfort. Far removed from towns and cities, absent of people apart from cowhands, it seemed to him a sanctuary from all he'd left behind. Hardly more than five years ago, the Sioux had roamed the land at will, a place where wild game could survive winter and grow fat on lush summer graze. Cattle, though less hardy than buffalo, nonetheless endured the harsh winters and thrived when spring again brought tall grass to the prairie. The valley was broad, watered by tributary streams, and bountiful

Off in the distance, Roosevelt saw a small herd of cattle. The cows appeared no worse for the winter and were marked on the flank with a distinct ✠, the Maltese Cross brand. His investment in the ranch was sixty thousand dollars, and some two thousand head of cattle were scattered over the coulees and ridges of the valley. He prided himself on being an astute judge of character, and he thought he'd done well to place his trust in Bill Merrifield. The Maltese Cross was in good hands.

"Those cows"—Roosevelt motioned to the distant herd—"appear to be in fine condition. Will we do so well with all our stock?"

"Wouldn't be surprised," Merrifield said. "This year was one of the easiest winters we've had in a long time. Course, roundup's what'll tell the tale."

"When do you plan to begin roundup?"

"Likely the first or second week in May. Winter runoff and rain makes things a little boggy till then."

"Excellent," Roosevelt said. "That allows adequate time for my hunt."

Merrifield glanced at him. "Where was you aimin' to hunt?"

"Jolly good question, Bill. I had in mind antelope and deer, perhaps a buffalo, if one is to be found. Where would you suggest?"

"Well, sir, the hide hunters pretty much cleaned out the

buffalo. I was you, I'd head west, over into the rough country. Lots of game in them parts."

"West it is, then."

"When you reckon to leave?"

"Tomorrow morning," Roosevelt informed him. "I presume you can provision me from the ranch commissary?"

"Shore can." Merrifield was silent a moment. "You figger to take somebody along? I could spare one of the hands."

"No, I shan't need a guide."

"That's wild country out there, Mr. Roosevelt. Man gets lost, he's in a heap of trouble."

"I'll have my compass, and I much prefer to go it alone. Solitude rather than company."

"You're the boss," Merrifield said, clearly not in agreement. "When should we expect you back?"

"Why, when I return, I imagine. I've no particular schedule and no particular destination. Follow the stars wherever they lead."

Merrifield thought it fanciful, even reckless. The Badlands were hostile at best and sometimes dangerous to those who'd spent years in the trackless wild country. There were accounts of men who had ridden off alone into the unmapped western reaches and never been heard from again. A year ago, Roosevelt had wisely taken a guide on a buffalo hunt that lasted nearly a fortnight. Today, he seemed determined to fend for himself, and Merrifield sensed that further argument would be taken as an insult. He let it pass.

Headquarters for the Maltese Cross was located near a stately row of cottonwoods. The ranch compound consisted of a main cabin, a bunkhouse constructed of logs, a large corral, and a roofed equipment shed. The main cabin looked out across the valley, where the river curled in a lazy dogleg over the rocky streambed. To the east and west, massive buttes rose from the valley floor, awash in a spectrum of sunlight. Tendrils of smoke drifted from the chimneys of the buildings.

Merrifield brought the luggage in from the buckboard. The interior of the cabin was rough-hewn, a fireplace and small cookstove in the living area and two bedrooms forming the north wall. One of the bedrooms was occupied by Merrifield, and the other, vacant for almost a year, belonged to Roosevelt. When he'd bought the ranch, he had left all his gear from the buffalo hunt stored in the bedroom. Merrifield placed the valise and the suitcase on the floor.

"All your stuff's in here," he said. "Just the way you left it last time."

"Thank you, Bill," Roosevelt said, looking around the cabin. "How has my horse fared over the winter?"

"Done real good, Mr. Roosevelt. Had him brought to the corral before I took off this mornin'. Figgered you'd want to see him."

"Yes, most certainly. And what of the men on the payroll? Any changes from last year?"

"Cowhands tend to drift," Merrifield said. "George Myers stayed on, and I managed to keep the cook by braggin' on his grub. The other five are new to the outfit."

"Perhaps you'll introduce me to the men before dinner. After I say hello to Manitou, of course."

Merrifield led the way back outside. Last year, the guide on the buffalo hunt had provided a mount, and Roosevelt, who knew horseflesh, had bought him after the hunt. The corral was a log enclosure, some fifty feet in diameter, halfway between the bunkhouse and the river. The horse herd, five mounts for every man on the payroll, was normally kept in a fenced pasture a quarter mile south of the compound. Today only one horse, a sleek gelding, stood in the center of the corral. Roosevelt stopped in front of the gate.

"Hello, old fellow," he said loudly. "Do you remember me?"

Manitou was barrel-chested, all sinew and muscle, fifteen hands high, and almost a thousand pounds in weight. A blood bay, with black mane and tail, his hide glistened in

the sun like dark mercury on polished redwood. He held
his ground, watching Roosevelt, and pawed the earth with
a gusty snort.

The horse possessed the stamina and catlike agility of
his noble ancestors, the Barbs. His spirit was evident in his
glittering eyes, and yet he had an even disposition, rarely
given to bucking. He suddenly whinnied a shrill blast of
greeting and charged across the corral, skidding to a halt
before the gate. He stood, nostrils flared, like an ebony
statue bronzed by the sun.

Roosevelt patted his velvety muzzle. "By Jove, I believe
he does remember me!"

"Yessir, I think you're right," Merrifield said. "Acts like
he's plumb glad to see you."

George Myers, one of the cowhands, ambled over to the
corral. He'd been with the Maltese Cross for three seasons,
and Roosevelt recalled meeting him last year. He was a
lanky towhead, with a soup-strainer mustache and hands
gnarled from a lifetime of hard work. He nodded amiably.

"Howdy, Mr. Roosevelt," he said. "Mighty good to to
see you again."

"George," Roosevelt said pleasantly. "I understand
you're the only man remaining from last year's crew."

"Well, sir, I ain't fiddle-footed like most hands. I just
'spect I've found me a home here at Maltese."

"Bully for you!"

Roosevelt's strange expressions and his Harvard accent
were a subject of discussion among the cowhands. That
night, he had dinner with them, what they called supper,
and they listened to him with the curiosity of men watching a carnival barker. The cookshack was attached to the
west end of the bunkhouse, with a blazing woodstove and a
rough, planked table. The fare was steak and beans, with
sourdough biscuits, and dried-apple pie for dessert. The
hands were impressed that the boss evidenced an appetite
for workingman's grub.

Later, in his bedroom, Roosevelt prepared for his hunting expedition. From a standing wardrobe with drawers he

took out wool pants and a soft buckskin shirt he'd had tailored in Medora. Next he selected a tall-crowned Stetson, high cowhide boots, and spurs with blunt rowels. His arsenal, oiled and stored from last year's hunt, included a .45 Colt Peacemaker, a .44-40 Winchester rifle, and a 10-gauge Winchester double-barreled shotgun. He carried the pistol in a crossdraw holster.

The last item was reading material. Roosevelt's lust for literature was insatiable, and most of the space in his suitcase was devoted to books. He'd brought from New York the collected works of Dickens and Milton, Longfellow and Poe, Tolstoy and Shakespeare. The conundrum was what he might enjoy reading by a campfire.

He decided to take *A Tale of Two Cities*.

The southwestern corner of the Badlands was a maze of sawtoothed spires, rocky gorges, and sheer cliffs. Millions of years of torrential rains and wind erosion had carved through clay and limestone to leave castlelike formations streaked with bizarre colors. The landscape was as though painted by a demented artist.

Yet more than half the baroque phantasm of stone was tallgrass prairie. Scattered among the thousands of square miles of canyons and starkly barren mountains were vast expanses of flat, treeless plains. Thick black slabs of lignite jutted from the cliffs, and the earth appeared to have been shaped aeons ago by some titanic upheaval. There was an aura of bleak emptiness about it all.

Roosevelt had been on the hunt for nearly a week. Before him, the plains swept onward to the horizon, flat and featureless, evoking a sense of something lost forever. The trackless barrens seemed as if nature had flung together earth and sky, mixed it with deafening silence, and then simply forgotten about it. A gentle breeze, like the wispy breath of a ghost, rippled through grass still blanched by winter.

Seated astride Manitou, Roosevelt felt himself an intruder here. He had the odd sensation that he was looking upon something no mortal was meant to see. About the windswept plains there was an awesome quality, as though some wild and brutally magnificent force had fashioned something visible yet beyond the ken of man. A hostile land, waiting with eternal patience to claim the bones of those who violated its harsh serenity. A land where man must forever walk as an alien.

Over the course of his hunt, Roosevelt had nonetheless become aware that the Badlands teemed with wildlife. He'd seen coyotes and gray wolves, mule deer and white-tailed deer, soaring hawks, and even a black-footed ferret. Once, in a layer of shale beneath a cliff, he had found fossils of lizards, giant turtles, and other marine creatures that had perished in some ancient saltwater sea. The ravines and grasslands were alive as well with all manner of birds, among them his favorite songster, the meadowlark.

The solitude of a lone man roaming among wild creatures was exactly what Roosevelt sought. Though he could not outrun the past, there was a certain peace to be found in the harsh, strangely beautiful barrens. Ahead on the plains, he saw a prairie-dog town, mounds of dirt piled up before the entrances to their burrows. They were social little rodents, living in colonies that sometimes stretched for miles, a population of ten thousand or more snug in their dens. Their light brown fur blended almost perfectly with their earthy mounds.

A high-pitched bark sounded in warning. Roosevelt watched as a badger trundled into the prairie-dog town in search of a meal. A carnivore, the badger was built low to the ground, with long claws and sharp teeth, and often feasted on the furry little rodents. Several more squeaky barks went up as the sentry male voiced the alarm, and prairie dogs scattered in a frantic rush for their dens. The badger, relying on determination rather than stealth, went to work digging out a burrow. His powerful claws flung earth in a rhythmic spray.

Manitou's ears flickered. Roosevelt followed the direction of his gaze and saw three pronghorn antelope edge over a low knoll on the prairie. They were cropping tawny grass, their eyes fixed on the ground, distinctive in their reddish tan hides with white striations looping the neck and belly. Roosevelt knew an antelope was the fastest animal on the plains, easily doubling the speed of a horse in short bursts. There was small likelihood that he could ride one down.

Still, as he watched them, he recalled that antelope possessed a fatal flaw. Their keen eyesight and bounding speed sometimes fell victim to their unwitting curiosity. He estimated the range at four hundred yards, too long a shot for a certain kill with his Winchester. Slowly, wary of sudden movement, he swung his right leg over Manitou's rump and stepped down out of the saddle. He gingerly pulled the Winchester from the saddle scabbard.

Manitou, schooled by a hunting guide, was trained not to move once he was ground-reined. Roosevelt inched a step to the left, seated himself in the tall grass, and braced the Winchester across his knees. He took a handkerchief from his pocket, raised it overhead, and let the breeze take it like a small flag. The pronghorns instantly stopped grazing, heads alert, their eyes drawn to the fluttering speck of white. Roosevelt remained motionless, the handkerchief trailing from his fingers in the wind. Fascinated, their curiosity aroused, the antelope drifted a step at a time in his direction.

The stratagem consumed the better part of an hour. After moving a bit closer, the antelope would pause to graze awhile and then move a few steps more. Roosevelt was a seasoned hunter, and he waited with the patience of a spider luring prey into its web. In all that time he sat like a stone Buddha, and Manitou, as though an interested spectator, stood perfectly still. Finally, their curiosity piqued by the fluttering white streamer, the pronghorns closed the distance to perhaps two hundred yards. They were within range.

Roosevelt gripped the forestock of the Winchester with his left hand, the handkerchief trailing from his fingers. He snugged the butt of the rifle into his shoulder, calculating wind drift by the rippling motion of the handkerchief. Squinting through his pince-nez, he saw that one of the antelope was a buck and the other two were does. Elbows propped on his knees, locked into a solid shooting position, he thumbed the hammer and centered the sights on the white of the buck's chest. His finger gently feathered the trigger.

The roar of the Winchester echoed like a small thunderclap. Across the way, the buck collapsed as though struck by a scythe and the does bounded back over the knoll. Roosevelt ejected the spent shell, lowering the hammer on a fresh round, and rose to his feet. He was pleased that he'd outwitted his prey with the handkerchief trick, a story he might consider writing for a New York publication. As he walked to Manitou and shoved the rifle into the saddle scabbard, he was no less pleased with his marksmanship. He mounted and rode across the prairie.

The buck was slumped on its side in the tawny grass. Larger than the does, perhaps 120 pounds in weight, the buck's horns were two feet in length and curved inward with a spiked hook at the top. The wound was centered on the chest, and from the amount of blood Roosevelt knew his shot had found the heart. He dismounted, drawing a skinner's knife from the sheath at his belt, and went to work dressing the buck. He made a deep incision over the left hindquarter.

Earlier in the week Roosevelt had shot a white-tailed deer watering at a creek. Today, as he'd done with the deer, he removed only a haunch with quick surgical strokes of the blade. A haunch provided sufficient meat for two or three days, and he felt no compunctions about leaving most of the carcass on the grassy plain. By nightfall, wolves and coyotes would devour the remains and the bones would be picked clean by buzzards. Taught to hunt in the forests of Maine, he'd learned as a boy that it was all part of nature's cycle. Man often shared his kill with other predators.

The haunch was wrapped in a length of heavy canvas.

Manitou was not skittish to the smell of blood, and the haunch was secured with rawhide thongs behind the saddle. Even as he rode off, Roosevelt saw a lone coyote watching from a distance and a flock of vultures turning lazy circles in the sky. Within the hour the coyote and the vultures would be snarling over the carcass, and by twilight a pack of wolves, canines snapping, would drive them away from the feast. The cycle of life and death on the windswept plains would be complete.

Not quite an hour later, Roosevelt approached a craggy ridge to the north. His campsite was situated at the base of the cliff, within a row of cottonwoods along the grassy banks of a clear stream. His packhorse was tied to a tree and stood hip-shot in dappled light as the sun steadily slipped westward. There were patches of snow still dotting the countryside, but adequate grass covered the banks along the creek. After dismounting, he untied the antelope haunch and dropped it on the ground by the fire pit. Then he unsaddled Manitou, hobbled both horses, and put them out to graze. He next turned to camp chores.

Before long, he had a low blaze kindled in the fire pit, which was surrounded by large stones. The victuals brought by packhorse—coffee, sugar, salt pork, and flour with sourdough starter—were suspended by rope over a tree branch to keep them from varmints. His bedroll was wool blankets wrapped in heavy canvas; though it was early March, the night still hovered around freezing. That morning, he'd baked biscuits in a small Dutch oven, and he soon had a steak from the haunch sizzling in a frying pan. His dessert would be strictly rationed pieces of horehound candy.

Roosevelt thrived on the outdoor life. His face was bronzed and ruddy from the sun, and his body was hardened from a week in the saddle. He estimated he'd traveled two hundred miles or more, making three camps along the way, and he still wasn't certain when he would return to the Maltese Cross. He thought about his solitary journey into the wilderness as he ate juicy antelope steak and dipped cold biscuits in hot grease from the frying pan. There was something to be said for free, unfettered days, and nights in his bedroll staring into a starry sky. He found some degree of comfort in living among wild things.

A full moon rose in the east an hour or so after sunset. By the light of the fire, his mackinaw buttoned to the throat, he read a chapter from *A Tale of Two Cities*. Then, though he admired Dickens's way with words, he put the book aside lest he finish it before his journey was complete. One of the horses whiffled, and he looked in their direction, judging it was almost time to secure them to the picket line in the trees. His gaze strayed back to the fire, and out of the corner of his eye he caught movement. His hand went to his pistol as he turned.

The vision before him almost stopped his heart. There, along the streambed, shapes moved beneath the tree line. The images hovered above the water, drifted closer, slowly separated into two figures, distinct in the moonlight. Their arms were outstretched, their long hair rippling in the wind. Their mouths were parted in silence.

Alice and his mother.

The universe seemed to pause as their forms floated between water and earth. The moonlight shone on their hair, the gentle movement of their arms, their nightdresses fluttering above the stream. They tried to speak, their mouths moving in a soundless whisper.

Roosevelt felt their suffering. Unbidden, in some dark corner of his mind, he sensed alternate worlds where the dead sought communion with the living. He strained to hear what they were trying to say, reached out to them. Their words were lost on the wind.

Their features were loving, peaceful, and as quickly as they had appeared, they faded back into the moonglow. One moment they were there and the next they were gone, streamers of silty light sparkling on the water. The wind moaned softly through the trees.

Unnerved, his heart racing, Roosevelt wondered if it was some form of madness, a macabre chimera born of grief and guilt. But then, though it questioned his sanity, he knew it was real, a brief echo from the beyond. He hadn't imagined it.

They were trying to tell him something.

FIVE

Twilight settled over the land as the sun dropped below the horizon. Dusk rapidly gave way to darkness, stars sprinkled like diamond dust across an indigo sky. A coyote yipped a mournful howl somewhere in the distance.

Roosevelt followed the winding course of the Little Missouri. His hunt was ended, lasting two weeks and traversing more than four hundred miles through the Badlands. He had killed deer and antelope and spent several days in a futile search for buffalo. He was somehow weary of shooting game.

All in all, he had not found the solace he sought in the barrens. The solitude, living off the land, had restored his physical health but done nothing to temper his inner conflict. A week ago, when Alice and his mother had appeared in the form of apparitions, he'd thought a door might have been opened to the beyond. Every night, seated by the campfire, he waited for them to return and speak in voices that might be heard. Yet they had not appeared again.

Whether it had been an aberrant illusion, some self-induced hallucination, troubled him still. Always the omnivorous reader, he'd once delved into the world of mystics and shamans and clairvoyants. He knew there were people in every culture who claimed the gift of entering into a trancelike state and speaking with the dead. But the idea that he possessed supernatural powers and had unwittingly summoned Alice and his mother from the grave was one he

found difficult to accept. He thought it more likely that
they had come on their own. If they had come at all. . . .

The road he followed was faintly visible in the starlight.
From last year's buffalo hunt he recalled an inn and stagecoach station off in a remote stretch of the Badlands. The
stage line ran from Medora to Deadwood, almost two hundred miles to the south, and the road was used by freighters
as well. His hunt ended, he'd planned to spend the night at
the inn and have a solid meal for the first time in two
weeks. But as the night deepened, he began to wonder if he
had misjudged the distance. He might have no choice but
to camp yet again by the river.

Overhead, he saw the Big Dipper and off to the outer
edge of the Dipper's cup, the North Star. The stage-line
road ran almost true north and south, and for no particular
reason, his mind turned to the southern terminus. Though
he'd never traveled to Deadwood, stories abounded that it
was the deadliest mining camp in the West. A place that attracted the likes of Doc Holliday, Wyatt Earp, and Wild
Bill Hickok, who had been killed there the summer Custer
went under at the Little Bighorn. As Roosevelt stared into
the starry sky, he told himself a trip to Deadwood might be
worth the while. A diversion for a man with no timetable
and lots of time. Perhaps sometime in the spring. . . .

Off to the north, he saw a twinkle of light. He gigged
Manitou into a slow trot, and the packhorse reluctantly
took up the pace. Before long, the light grew brighter, the
windows of the inn suffused with the glow of coal-oil
lamps. The building was two stories, constructed of weathered clapboard, a beacon in the seeming emptiness of the
hinterlands. Several freight wagons were parked around
the inn, and a corral for stage horses was positioned off to
one side. He reined to a halt and dismounted, tying Manitou and the packhorse to the hitchrack. He hoped the
innkeeper served decent fare.

A gunshot rang out from inside. Roosevelt hesitated,
listening intently, concerned he might walk into a barroom
altercation. The Deadwood road was traveled by freighters

and men of rough persuasion, and arguments, particularly
fueled by liquor, often led to gunfights. He heard a voice
raised in anger, though the words were indistinct, and then
a long, unsettling silence. But there were no more gun-
shots, and the sudden quiet very likely meant the dispute
had ended. He fully expected to find a dead man laid out on
the floor.

The door opened onto a large, crudely furnished room.
Roosevelt eased through, closing the door as he stepped inside, and positioned himself against the wall. There was a
battered mahogany bar along the north wall, the back bar
stocked with bottles and a cloudy mirror flanked by paint-
ings of voluptuous women in the nude. Opposite the bar
was a scattering of tables and chairs; and beyond, a stairway that led to the upper floor. The tables were crowded
with men who appeared frozen in time, their features flat
and watchful. They were staring at the bar.

A man dressed in mule skinner's garb stood propped
against the counter. He was large as a bear, wobbling
drunk, with a matted beard and a pistol dangling from his
right hand. He ignored the bartender, who stood motionless by the mirror, and glowered at the crowd through eyes
bloodshot with whiskey. He waved his pistol in a threatening gesture.

"You lousy sonsabitches," he growled. "Somebody's
gonna stand drinks for the house, and no two ways about it.
How many times I gotta tell you?"

No one moved or spoke. The man stared at them a moment, then flung his arm around, the pistol cocked, and fired.
The bartender ducked, head cradled in his arms, as the mirror
exploded in shards of glass. While everyone was distracted,
Roosevelt took the opportunity to lose himself in the crowd.
He walked to an empty table near a large potbellied stove in
the center of the room. He seated himself in a rickety chair.

The man turned from the bar just as Roosevelt settled
into the creaky chair. His mouth twisted in a crooked grin.
"Well, looky here," he said. "Goddamn four-eyes done
joined the party."

The crowd followed his gaze, focused now on Roosevelt's spectacles. In the West, particularly among the rougher element, a man who wore glasses was thought to be of defective character and quite probably a coward. Roosevelt sat perfectly still, all too aware he was the center of attention.

The gunman crossed the room, teetering as he stopped at the table. His features quirked in a drunken leer and he fixed Roosevelt with an ugly glare. "Four-eyes," he said in a coarse voice, "I just changed my mind. You're gonna buy the drinks."

Roosevelt pegged the man as a bully. A dangerous bully, in that he'd already cowed a room filled with armed men. The situation might well go wrong unless handled with some degree of finesse. And duplicity.

"Do I understand correctly?" Roosevelt asked. "You wish me to buy a round of drinks?"

"Lissen that fancy talk! Didn't I just say you was buyin'?"

"Well, if I must, I must."

Roosevelt rose from his chair. He smiled weakly and motioned in the direction of the bartender. The gesture distracted the gunman, and when he glanced toward the bar Roosevelt lashed out with a hard, clubbing blow to the jaw. He set himself, then followed instantly with a splintering left hook and a right cross to the nose. The gunman went down, firing his pistol by reflex into the floor, his face smeared with blood. He was out cold.

There was a moment of stunned silence. The last thing anyone expected was that "Four-eyes" would fight, and the crowd stared at the fallen gunman with amazed disbelief. Roosevelt knelt down, scooped up the pistol, and placed it on the table. He looked around the room.

"Gentlemen," he said to no one in particular. "Have we properly settled the matter?"

The crowd suddenly broke out in cheers. A man at the end of the bar walked forward and stopped at the table. His features were florid and his style of dress was somewhat better than that of the other men in the barroom. He shook his head with a confounded look.

"I'm Harry Baxter," he said. "For what it's worth, I own this place. Do you know who you just whipped?"

"No, sir, I do not."

"Black Jack Perkins, that's who. Meanest sonovabitch in these parts."

"Well, then, I daresay he was overdue."

"You don't mind my askin', who the hell are you, anyway?"

"Theodore Roosevelt," Roosevelt said. "I thought to stay the night with you. Do you have a vacant room?"

"Hell, I'll vacate one," Baxter said. "Nothin's too good for a man with your grit."

"I'll require supper as well. Do you have someone who could attend to my horses?"

"I'll look after everything, Mr. Roosevelt. How do you like your steak?"

"Rare will be fine."

Black Jack Perkins was carried to a storeroom to sleep it off. Several men stopped by Roosevelt's table to shake his hand and inquire his name. In conversation, he discovered Perkins was a mean drunk but seldom recalled anything the morning after. He was a teamster, working out of Deadwood, and showed up about once a month looking for trouble. No one had called his bluff until tonight.

One of the men offered to buy Roosevelt a drink. He declined, quick not to give insult, tactfully explaining that he never took liquor with food. In truth, he was a teetotaler and had been since his days at Harvard. As a student, he'd found that he had little tolerance for alcohol; even a few glasses of wine tended to cloud his judgment. Sobriety and a clear head were more important to him than the zestful buzz of spirits. He simply never drank.

Baxter returned shortly. He carried a platter heaped with a slab of bloodred steak, greasy potatoes, winter turnips, and chunks of crusty bread. He waited while Roosevelt wielded a knife and fork and cut into the steak. Baxter's curiosity was clearly not yet satisfied.

"You don't mind my askin'," he said, "where you from, Mr. Roosevelt? Gentlemen like you don't come in here too often."

"I own the Maltese Cross ranch," Roosevelt said around a mouthful of steak. "A few miles south of Medora, near Chimney Butte."

"For a rancher, you handle your dukes pretty good. You could've been a prizefighter."

"Hardly in the league, Mr. Baxter. I learned a bit about boxing while in college."

"Way you laid Perkins out, you learned more'n a little. Could I get you something to drink?"

"A cup of coffee would be most appreciated."

Baxter walked off toward the kitchen. Roosevelt was amused by the conversation and found the whole affair somewhat droll. He had never before been mistaken for a prizefighter. Nor had he been involved in a barroom brawl.

He thought he'd come a long way since Harvard.

The wind moaned through the prairie grasses with a sound like that of a sobbing child. Roosevelt rode over the crest of a butte as sunset washed the landscape in a brilliant patchwork of red and gold. His mood was one of dark reflection.

All day, as he rode north, his mind was filled with images of Alice and his mother. But late that afternoon, when the wind rose out of the southwest, the keening rustle of the grass somehow reminded him of his daughter. He imagined he heard her crying, and he was overcome with guilt. He tried not to listen to the wind.

Cannonball Creek wound around the base of the slope and emptied into the Little Missouri. A tall stand of cottonwoods arched skyward where the creek intersected the river. Smoke filtered through the trees from the chimney of a sprawling log house some fifty yards beyond the juncture of the streams. The compound was headquarters for the Yule ranch.

The manager of the outfit was a man named Gregor Lang. He was a Scotsman, transplanted to America, and oversaw the operation for the owner, a wealthy English lord. Like many ranches in the Badlands, the Yule was the property of an absentee owner, one of many foreigners who seldom crossed the Atlantic. Cattle were considered a prime investment, and the owners, after hiring responsible managers, conducted business by mail. Their interest was in the profits, not the details.

Last year, on his buffalo hunt, Roosevelt had stayed a night at Lang's spread. The Scotsman was from Edinburgh, intelligent and well educated, with an abiding interest in politics and literature. The two men found they had much in common and had talked far into the night on a wide variety of subjects. Lang had expressed the belief that as a business proposition, cattle were an exceedingly profitable venture. A week later Roosevelt bought the Maltese Cross.

Lang emerged from the house as Roosevelt rode through the trees. "Theodore!" he called out, his voice thick with a Scottish burr. "How wonderful to see you again!"

"And you as well, Gregor." Roosevelt dismounted, exchanging a warm handshake. "I've anticipated our next meeting with great relish."

"Bill Merrifield told me you were off on a hunting expedition. I hoped you might come by and give us the pleasure of your company. Will you stay the night?"

"By Godfrey, nothing would please me more. I've grown weary talking to myself these last two weeks."

"Come inside and say hello to Edith and Lincoln. I'll have someone take care of your horses."

Lang led the way into the log house. The entrance opened onto a large room with the parlor at the front, the dining area in the center, and the kitchen at the rear. There were three bedrooms on the south side of the house, one reserved for Sir Percy Nevin, who had visited only once, and then hastily, since purchasing the ranch in 1882. The interior evidenced a woman's touch, with lacy curtains, a carpet in the parlor, and along one wall a piano shipped all the way from St. Louis. A stone fireplace warmed the room with a merry blaze.

Edith Lang was a plain dumpling of a woman, short and stout like her husband, with quick, bright eyes and a sunny disposition. Their son, Lincoln, towered over them at age fifteen, a gangly lad with handsome features and a shock of red hair. Roosevelt recalled wondering how two people of such unremarkable stature had produced a boy who would top six feet long before he was grown. He stood by shyly as his mother rushed from the kitchen.

"Home is the hunter!" she said gaily, clasping Roosevelt's hand. "We heard you were off in the wilderness."

"Dee-*lighted* to see you both," Roosevelt said, glancing at the boy. "Lincoln, I do believe you've sprouted like a sapling since last I was here."

"Yessir," Lincoln replied, ducking his head. "I keep outgrowing my clothes, boots especially. Wish it'd stop."

"No, no, Linc," Lang insisted. "You've a ways to go, and thankful for it. The Lord meant you to be tall."

"Well, now," Edith chimed in, "supper will burn unless I tend the stove. You are a pleasant addition to our table, Theodore."

Roosevelt smiled. "I confess I timed it perfectly. I've not forgotten your cooking."

Lang led them in prayer before the meal was served. Edith loaded Roosevelt's plate with pot roast smothered in gravy, corn and snap beans from her summer canning jars, and rolls fresh from the oven. Their conversation was general, centering on Roosevelt's hunting trip, and he noted that they were at some pains not to mention his family tragedy. Sympathy was expressed in many ways, and entertaining conversation was the best of antidotes. He knew before he departed that Lang would quietly offer a word of solace.

After dinner, Lang and Roosevelt retired to the parlor

while Lincoln helped his mother clear the table. Watching the boy, Roosevelt was reminded that the father was something of an idealist. Gregor Lang was the oldest child of an archconservative family and contrary in his views. He detested any form of government that was based on class distinctions and rewarded the gentry at the expense of the people. His convictions had brought him to America, where free institutions and the rule of the ballot prevailed. His son was named after the Great Emancipator, Abraham Lincoln.

Lang fired up his pipe when he and Roosevelt were seated in the parlor. He puffed a thick wad of smoke and inquired as to the state of public affairs in New York. Roosevelt hadn't given a thought to politics in almost a month, but he responded like an old warhorse to the sound of cannon. Ever the reformer, eloquent in his opinions, he denounced "boss rule" and the corruption that permeated Tammany Hall. In the same breath, he reviled "fireside moralists" who decried bad government but never actually joined in the fight for reform. The duty of every American, he declared, was not just to vote but also to actively work to overthrow unscrupulous politicians in either party. Honest people, by virtue of the Constitution, held the power to reclaim their government.

"We are freeborn," he concluded. "We must acknowledge no man our superior, except by his moral worth. All too few politicians possess that particular attribute."

"The Badlands are much the same," Lang said. "Has Merrifield spoken to you of the Marquis de Mores?"

"No, we discussed little but ranch business before I departed for the hunt. What of de Mores?"

"The Marquis apparently believes he has some sort of divine right to rule the whole of the Little Missouri. The Lord made the earth for all of us, not the chosen few. Certainly not for one man."

"I agree," Roosevelt said. "What is it he's done?"

"Aligned himself with outlaws," Lang observed. "He formed an alliance with Jake Paddock, perhaps the most despicable man in Dakota Territory. His reputation is that of a mankiller. A common murderer."

"I am not familiar with the name. Are you saying he has murdered someone at de Mores' order?"

"No, not as yet anyway. Paddock and his henchmen are terrorizing small ranchers, in an effort to force them to sell out. De Mores clearly intends to dominate the cattle trade in the Badlands."

"And what of the large ranchers?" Roosevelt asked. "Has he attempted to threaten them?"

Lang shook his head. "De Mores is a shrewd strategist. First he will consolidate power by taking over the smaller outfits. Then he will come after the larger ones."

"Have you spoken of this with other cattlemen?"

"Yes, on any number of occasions. They condemn de Mores' methods, but none of them seem willing to take action. We are very much in need of a leader."

Roosevelt thought it a subtle probe to enlist his services. He let the remark pass. "I must say I'm disappointed in the Marquis. He has assumed aspects of the Artful Dodger, eh?"

"Rather an apt comparison," Lang said. "I see you know your Dickens."

"Indeed, he is one of my favorite authors."

"I favor English writers myself, and of course the Scots. Robert Burns has few peers."

"Now, there we differ, Gregor. Though I enjoy poets, nothing compares to solid prose. Tolstoy, if I may say so, rivals the best of Shakespeare."

"Why, I wouldn't have thought it of you, Theodore. The Russians cannot hold a candle to the Bard."

Roosevelt enjoyed nothing quite so much as a stimulating debate. Tossing out Tolstoy was meant to divert Lang, and he'd succeeded admirably. He would gladly have taken the opposite view, for he privately agreed that Shakespeare was without equal. But he was delighted to have provoked his host on the matter of literature. For the moment, the Marquis de Mores was brushed aside. They fell to arguing the merits of various writers.

Their discussion ranged late into the night. But life on a ranch begins at dawn, and the following morning Roosevelt prepared to leave shortly after breakfast. He made his good-byes to Edith and Lincoln, and they watched from the door as Lang walked him to the corral. Manitou and his packhorse stood hitched to a fence post.

"Theodore, a parting thought," Lang said, suddenly solemn. "I can only imagine what you must be going through with the loss of your wife and mother. Last night, when we were discussing Shakespeare, I was reminded of another poet. John Milton."

"Milton?" Roosevelt said, curious but almost afraid to ask. "What about him?"

"Something he wrote in *Paradise Lost*: 'The mind is its own place, and in itself can make a heav'n of hell, a hell of heav'n.' Perhaps his words will help guide you in the days ahead."

"Thank you for the thought, Gregor. You are most kind."

"Do not be a stranger, old friend. Come back and see us often."

"I shall."

Roosevelt rode north from the Yule compound. The first rays of sunlight skittered over the waters of the Little Missouri as he crossed a ford in the rocky streambed. Gregor Lang's comment still echoed through his mind, and he tried to take solace from the wisdom of the words. Yet a poem, in the end, was just a poem.

So far, he'd found little heaven in his hell on earth.

SIX

Late that afternoon, Roosevelt forded the river beneath the shadow of Chimney Butte. All day, riding north, he'd seen herds of Maltese Cross cattle but no cowhands. He hadn't thought anything of it until now.

The headquarters compound was eerily quiet. So close to sundown, the men usually began drifting in from the tasks assigned to them for the day. The corral was empty, and he saw no one around the main house or the bunkhouse. A wisp of smoke spiraled from the chimney over the cookshack.

Roosevelt dismounted outside the corral. He unsaddled Manitou and slung the saddle over the top rail. The diamond hitches on the packhorse took a little longer, and when he finished, he dropped the packs on the ground. Then he led the horses into the corral, removed their bridles, and turned them loose for a roll in the dust. As he closed and latched the gate, he thought he might have a talk with the cook. Something wasn't right.

The sound of hoofbeats attracted his attention. He turned from the gate and saw Merrifield and all six of the Maltese Cross hands crossing the ford from the west. As they rode closer, he noted that their horses were worn down, covered with a film of dried sweat. The men themselves looked exhausted, and their features were set in a hard cast. Merrifield stepped out of the saddle and asked

one of the men to take care of his horse. He walked toward
Roosevelt.

"Afternoon, Mr. Roosevelt," he said in a weary voice.
"Back from your hunt?"

"I've just returned," Roosevelt said. "What's going on
here, Bill?"

"Horse thieves raided our herd last night. Got off with
the whole damn bunch, 'cept what was in the corral. We
didn't tumble to it till a little after sunup."

"How many were stolen?"

"Fifty-one head," Merrifield said. "We took off trackin'
the bastards soon as we got squared away. Trailed 'em over
into the wild country."

"I see," Roosevelt said. "And were you able to recover
the horses?"

"Yessir, we just dropped off our own and three extra
down in the pasture. You might say we come out ahead on
the deal."

"What happened to the horse thieves?"

"Rascals put up a fight," Merrfield said, his expression
rigid. "One got shot and the other two quit when things
turned sour. We hung 'em."

Roosevelt frowned. "Was that necessary?"

"The sonsabitches fired on us, Mr. Roosevelt. Lucky
we're not buryin' one of our own."

"Yes, but from what you say, they surrendered. Why not
turn them over to the law?"

"What law?" Merrifield said bitterly. "These ain't no
lawmen within five days' ride of here."

Roosevelt knew the statement was meant in earnest.
Billings County was not yet organized, and the nearest
sheriff was in Mandan, 150 miles to the east. The nearest
Deputy U.S. Marshal was two hundred miles to the south,
in the mining camp of Deadwood. The remoteness of the
Badlands stacked the odds in favor of the lawless element.

"I understand your concern," Roosevelt said. "However,
in the future, any lawbreakers captured will be transported

to the proper authority and held for trial. I will not condone summary justice."

"What if they're shootin' at us?" Merrifield said stubbornly. "What if they kill one of our men? What'd we do then?"

"If you kill someone in self-defense, that is perfectly acceptable. Anyone captured will be prosecuted in a court of law, whatever his offense. Let us be clear on the distinction."

"We've acted as our own law for a long time, Mr. Roosevelt. You go changin' the rules and these toughnuts are gonna have the edge. They know it ain't too likely they'll be convicted in Mandan or somewheres else."

"Be that as it may," Roosevelt said firmly, "you will follow my instructions. Summarily hanging men is no longer an option."

Merrifield kicked at a clod of dirt. "You're the boss and I'll follow orders. But horse thieves are gonna catch on real quick that it ain't so risky anymore. We'll lose lots of stock . . . regular as clockwork."

Roosevelt understood that it might become an expensive proposition. Herds of wild horses ran free on the vast plateaus in the southeast quadrant of the Badlands. Ranchers sometimes organized a hunt to capture mustangs and then expended considerable effort in breaking the horses to saddle stock. The alternative was to buy horses from livestock dealers, who commanded exorbitant prices for animals broken to saddle. Either way, whether the cost was in time or hard cash, raids by horse thieves represented a substantial loss. Roosevelt was nonetheless determined that the Maltese Cross would no longer operate by lynch law.

"We will conduct ourselves in a civilized manner," Roosevelt said. "Please inform the men of my decision."

"Whatever you say, Mr. Roosevelt."

"Thank you, Bill. Now, if you will excuse me, I've had a long trip. We'll talk more after dinner."

Roosevelt collected his gear and walked to the house. He stoked the stove with firewood and put a bucket of water to heating. By the time he'd oiled his rifle and shotgun and stripped out of his buckskins, the water was boiling. He carried the bucket to his room and gave himself a good scrubbing with a washcloth. Then he shaved and changed into fresh clothes from the wardrobe. He felt clean for the first time in two weeks.

Some while later, he walked over to the cookshack for supper. The mood at the table was sober, and it appeared obvious Merrifield had already relayed his instructions. The men merely nodded, avoiding his eyes, as he greeted them and took a chair. He ignored their sullen manner and proceeded to regale them with stories of the deer and antelope he'd brought down on his hunt. A change of mood occurred only when he told them of the fossils he'd found and expressed the belief that the Badlands had once been submerged in a saltwater sea. The men exchanged amused glances, not at all sure he wasn't spinning a tall tale. The Badlands under water seemed to them fanciful talk.

After supper, Merrifield followed him back to the house. Roosevelt chunked a log into the fireplace and soon had a blaze that warmed the room. Once they were seated, he explained that he'd stopped over last night at the Yule ranch. He asked Merrifield's opinion of Gregor Lang.

"Honest as the day is long," Merrifield said. "You could take his word to the bank."

"And the Marquis de Mores?"

"Wouldn't trust him any farther'n I can spit."

"Mr. Lang shares your view," Roosevelt said. "He told me de Mores is in league with an unsavory character named Paddock. Do you know the man?"

Merrifield nodded. "Paddock wandered in when the first Texans brought herds up this way. He's got a reputation as a gunman."

"Lang says he and his cohorts are attempting to intimidate small ranchers. All at the direction of de Mores. Anything to it?"

"Yessir, it's a fact. A man by the name of Wittaker had a little spread over by Painted Canyon. Paddock and his boys scared him so bad he sold out and took off like a scalded cat. Word has it de Mores bought his outfit for a song."

"I see." Roosevelt was silent a moment. "All of that is a rather drastic change from last year, quite disturbing. Why didn't you tell me when I arrived from New York? After we met de Mores outside the hotel?"

"Well, I thought about it," Merrifield admitted. "But I figgered you had all the troubles you could handle just then. More bad news didn't seem called for."

"I appreciate your consideration, Bill. And I daresay you were right not to mention it."

"Now that we're talkin', there's something else you ought to know. The horse thieves we hung today?"

"Yes."

"They're part and parcel of Paddock's operation. He's thick with every outlaw in the Territory. That's why de Mores hired him."

"Is that conjecture, or do you have proof?"

"Whatever you call it, everybody knows it. Gets back to there not being any lawmen in these parts."

"Perhaps . . ." Roosevelt hesitated, as though weighing what he'd heard. "We will speak of this again, but enough for now. I have another matter I wish to discuss."

"Yessir." Merrifield looked attentive. "What's on your mind?"

"Everything I've seen reaffirms my belief that cattle are an excellent investment. You've done quite well with the Maltese Cross, and Gregor Lang informs me that Yule is very profitable. I have decided to organize another ranch."

"You talkin' about buying somebody out?"

"Actually, I was thinking of purchasing land and building a house of my own design. Would you have any suggestions as to a suitable piece of land?"

Merrifield considered a moment. "There's a stretch on the Little Missouri, maybe thirty miles or so north of Medora. Always thought it'd make a fine spread."

"Does someone own the land?"

"Heard a wolf hunter staked out a claim. Course, that's by way of the grapevine. He might be long gone."

"How would I find the parcel?" Roosevelt said. "Would it be possible for you to draw me a map?"

"Glad to," Merrifield said. "You understand there's no way I could manage Maltese Cross and another spread. Specially one that far downriver."

"Oh, that's quite all right, Bill. I have a man in mind for the job."

Roosevelt didn't elaborate, and Merrifield felt reluctant to ask the man's name. Instead, at Roosevelt's request, Merrifield laboriously sketched a map with pencil and paper. The map was crude but accurate, identifying landmarks along a stretch of river that ran almost due north and south. High buttes to the east and west further pinpointed the location.

Later, in his bedroom, Roosevelt collected gear for the trip downriver. A new venture always preoccupied his interest, and he saw no reason to delay. He would depart in the morning and allow two days for the journey north. Once he'd finished packing, his thoughts turned to his faraway family. He hadn't written since leaving New York and he knew they would be concerned. He penned a jolly letter to Bamie:

Well, I have been having a glorious time. For the last two weeks, I played at frontier hunter in earnest, off entirely alone, with my horse and rifle, on the prairie. I knew I could do perfectly well without a guide, and I enjoyed the expedition to the utmost. I felt as absolutely free as a man could feel.

A pause came over him as he studied the last line. He thought it was a partial truth, bordering on a white lie. To say that he felt free intimated that he felt at peace, which was not the case. The letter was nonetheless meant for their benefit, not his own.

He continued writing.

. . .

The trail from Medora skirted the Little Missouri for five
or six miles. There it turned west into rugged terrain, broken by steep ridges and sheer ravines. Cattle grazed on the
tableland atop the crests of wide buttes.

Some ten miles north of town the trail crossed a broad
plateau, then dropped again into the valley along the river.
Merrifield had marked a spot on the map, locating a ranch
in the valley owned by the Eaton brothers. Roosevelt spent
his first night on the trail with them and found them to be
excellent company. There were three brothers: John, the
eldest; Paul, in his late twenties; and Charles, about Roosevelt's age. He learned they were originally from Pittsburgh
and had migrated West three years ago to enter the cattle
trade. Their herds now exceeded three thousand head, and
the ranch was profitable beyond their expectations.

Roosevelt told them nothing of his own plans. He
thought it best to secure rights to the land before discussing
his bold vision for the future. Nor had he been entirely
forthcoming with Merrifield about his reasons for expanding his landholdings and organizing a new ranch. On his
two-week hunt he had experienced the wondrous inner joy
of solitude and isolation. Upon his return to the Maltese
Cross, he'd felt burdened by the matter of horse thieves
and the Marquis de Mores' sinister ambition. He wanted to
separate himself from the world to the extent possible, live
the simple life in search of peace. A remote ranch on the
upper Little Missouri seemed the answer.

On the second day, he rode north from the Eaton ranch.
The trail crossed the serpentine path of the river, time and
again, winding through flats of sagebrush and immense
natural parks of grazeland. Here and there, as though the
earth had erupted skyward, the trail narrowed where forbidding walls of limestone towered on either side of the
river. The farther he rode, the land became increasingly
wilder, and he spotted wolves and coyotes watching alertly
in the distance. Deer abounded, and once, watering at the
edge of the river, he saw a bull elk, standing nearly ten feet

tall, with a magnificent rack of antlers. He thought the abundance of game made it a hunter's paradise.

Early that afternoon Roosevelt rounded a bend in the Little Missouri. Before him was a long valley with groves of cottonwoods along the river and a vast meadow carpeted with grass still tawny from winter. To the east and west, sheer cliffs rose abruptly from the valley floor into a range of lavender buttes that rolled onward toward infinity. The vista was one of singular grandeur, spectacular even for the Badlands, and he knew he's found the spot marked on Merrifield's map. He told himself it was indeed remote, a primeval wilderness removed from the outside world. Perfect.

Under a stand of cottonwoods Roosevelt saw a small cabin. Though stoutly built, the cabin was low to the ground, scarcely ten by ten, constructed of unbarked logs. Off to one side, a slat-ribbed dun horse, restrained by hobbles, looked up from cropping grass. A man ducked through the doorway of the cabin, a Winchester carbine in his hands, and stopped in the dappled sunlight. He was wiry, with weathered features and a tangled beard, dressed in greasy buckskins and mule-eared boots. His expression was wary, his eyes guarded. He offered no welcome.

Roosevelt reined Manitou to a halt. "Good afternoon," he said with an amiable nod. "Are you the owner of the property?"

"Nate Blackburn," the man said. "Who might you be?"

"My name is Theodore Roosevelt. I was informed you are a wolf hunter, Mr. Blackburn."

Wolves preyed on cattle, particularly during the hard winter months. Ranchers paid a bounty for the pelts, and men such as Blackburn earned their livelihood by baiting meat with strychnine or running traps. A skilled wolf hunter might earn five hundred dollars in a year.

"I hunt some," Blackburn allowed. "You don't mind my askin', you talk kinda funny. Where you from?"

"New York," Roosevelt said. "I've recently come west to start a ranching enterprise. May I inquire if you are interested in selling your property?"

"You want to buy my claim?"

"Yes, assuming the title is free of encumbrances. When did you file for homestead, Mr. Blackburn?"

"Sight more'n six years past. Hunted buffalo a good while, but there ain't many left now. So I turned wolfer."

The Homestead Act was passed by Congress in 1862. Under the terms of the law a man could file claim on 160 acres of government land anywhere in the West. He was required to live on the land for five years and make improvements such as a house or a cabin. Having fulfilled the obligation, he was granted title to the homestead.

"Well, then," Roosevelt said. "Would you be interested in selling?"

"Depends on the price," Blackburn said in a cagey voice. "What d'you got in mind?"

"Before we talk price, I first have to know how you staked the property. Where are your markers?"

Blackburn gestured with a thorny finger. He'd staked his homestead entirely in the valley, shrewdly marking the claim to cover the grassy bottomland on the west side of the Little Missouri. The back of the homestead abutted the steep buttes to the west and extended north and south almost a mile on the river. He grinned as he looked around at Roosevelt.

"Laid'er out so's it's all bottomland, knee high in grass come summer. Cabin ain't big, but it's solid."

"Yes, very commendable," Roosevelt said. "I am not a man to dicker, Mr. Blackburn. I will offer you a fair price, take it or leave it."

"What might that be?"

"A thousand dollars."

Blackburn blinked. Land was cheap as dirt in Dakota, and a thousand dollars was more than he made in two years trapping wolves. His mouth crooked in a sly smile.

"Mister, you done made yourself a deal."

Roosevelt always carried a writing kit in his saddlebags. The kit was comprised of a pen, a small bottle of ink, and a sheaf of paper. He wrote out a quitclaim deed and watched as Blackburn signed over the homestead. Then he loosened a money belt beneath his shirt and counted out a thousand dollars in greenbacks. He offered his hand to seal the bargain.

"Most pleasant doing business with you, Mr. Blackburn."

"Hell, that ain't the half of it," Blackburn cackled. "You done made me a rich man."

"You are welcome to stay the night. I wouldn't put you out of your cabin on such short notice."

"Won't take ten minutes to pack my gear. I aim to hit them saloons in town and stay drunk for a week. What'd you say your name was again?"

"Theodore Roosevelt."

Blackburn was saddled and gone in less than ten minutes. Roosevelt waited until he was out of sight and then inspected the cabin. When he opened the door, a foul odor not unlike that of a bear's den forced him to step back. Cedar boughs covered one side of the dirt floor to make a bed, and a small stone fireplace occupied the end wall. The rancid smell was such that he knew he would never spend a night in the cabin. He left the door open to let it air out.

After unsaddling Manitou, he walked the riverbank to the north. The valley stretched onward for at least two miles, with a meadow of equal proportions on the opposite side of the river. The Eaton brothers were his nearest neighbors, almost twenty miles upstream, and he quickly calculated that he had thousands of acres of open range for grazing cattle. He thought he might start with a thousand head.

On the riverbank he happened across the interlocked antlers of two elk. The antlers were bleached from time and exposure, and he surmised the elk had died in mortal combat during rutting season. Their mighty struggle sparked his imagination, and he decided to name his new ranch Elkhorn. A low bluff overlooking the river seemed to him a perfect site to build on, for it provided a sweeping view of the valley. He began designing the house in his head.

By dusk, he had walked the land north and south for two miles or more. He secured Manitou to a picket line in the

trees and found a spot on the riverbank to camp. After
gathering wood for a fire, he made supper of deer jerky and
water heated in a tin cup for tea. He spread his bedroll by
the fire, lulled by the plaintive cooing of mourning doves
in the trees. The sky was now dark as pitch, and as he
searched for the Big Dipper he saw a shooting star flash in
a brilliant arc across the heavens. He felt the strange sensation that he'd somehow come home.

The hair suddenly prickled on the nape of his neck. He
turned from the fire and saw Alice and his mother on the
verge of the riverbank. Their forms wavered in a luminous
spectral aura, and they were shrouded in gossamer gowns
riffling on the breeze. Their eyes were vividly haunting,
holding him mesmerized and still, scarcely able to breathe.
They were trying to speak, first one, then the other, but
there was no sound, even though he strained to hear their
words. The effort brought distress to their features, and as
if undone by the silence of their voices, they drifted away
over the dark waters of the river. One moment there,
limned in ebbing light, the next moment they were gone.

Roosevelt stared into the darkness, his heart thudding
against his chest. There was no trace of uncertainty that
what he'd seen might be some dreamlike stirring of his
imagination. He knew he hadn't conjured them from the
beyond, but rather, though they were dead, they were yet
real. As before, when they had appeared on a moonlit
night, he realized they were attempting to communicate
with him. Desperately trying to tell him . . . what?

He willed them to return, to speak, to pierce the void
separating his world from theirs. He fell into a troubled, fit-
ful sleep, still waiting.

SEVEN

Roosevelt rode into Medora late the next afternoon. He was vitalized by plans for the new ranch, though still bothered by the uncanny spiritual ordeal of last night. He tried not to think of it but couldn't put it from his mind for any length of time. Some visceral instinct told him they were never far away.

The date was March 22, a Saturday. The street was jammed with wagons and buckboards, the hitchracks lined with saddle horses. On Saturday ranchers came to town to conduct business and replenish supplies, and cowboys squandered their wages on rotgut whiskey and saloon girls who doubled as whores. Saturday night was the busiest night of the week for the sporting crowd.

The Dakota Bank & Trust was one of the few brick structures in town. Roosevelt reined in at the hitchrack, stepped out of the saddle, and slapped the dust from his mackinaw. He looped the reins around the rack, mounted the boardwalk, and brushed past cowhands wandering the street. Whenever he was enthused by a project and intent on business, his manner of entering a room was to bolt through the door as if ejected from a catapult. Customers and tellers looked around as he walked to a man seated at a desk toward the rear.

"Good afternoon," he said. "Who is the president of your establishment?"

The clerk inspected his scruffy clothes. "Mr. Daniel Gilmore owns the bank."

"Excellent," Roosevelt said, peering through his spectacles. "Inform Mr. Gilmore that I am here on a matter of the utmost importance. The name is Theodore Roosevelt."

"I'll see if he's busy."

The clerk went through a door with a frosted-glass window and returned a moment later. He ushered Roosevelt into a spacious office with a broad desk and several file cabinets. The man behind the desk was portly, with salt-and-pepper hair, attired in a vested suit. He rose with a cordial smile.

"Mr. Roosevelt," he said, hand outstretched. "The Marquis de Mores told me you'd returned to our fair town. I've looked forward to meeting you."

"Dee-*lighted*," Roosevelt said, accepting his handshake. "I wish to avail myself of your services."

Gilmore motioned him to a chair. "How may I assist you?"

"I've just purchased land some distance north of Medora. I plan to establish a ranch and stock it with cattle. I'll need to open an account to conduct my affairs."

"I understand you own the Maltese Cross outfit. Will this be a new venture?"

"Yes, altogether separate, some twenty miles north of the Eaton ranch. Splendid location for raising cattle."

"If I may ask, who did you purchase the land from?"

"A rather eccentric wolf hunter by the name of Nate Blackburn."

"I'm not familiar with him," Gilmore said. "Do you wish to make a deposit today?"

"Indeed," Roosevelt replied. "I'll write a draft for fifty thousand dollars on my brother's bank in New York. You may telegraph him to clear the funds."

Gilmore was visibly impressed. "You certainly think on a grand scale, Mr. Roosevelt. Fifty thousand is no small sum."

"Only small men think in small terms, Mr. Gilmore. Wouldn't you agree?"

"Of course, very much so."

Roosevelt penned a blank draft for fifty thousand and provided the details for telegraphing Elliot. Gilmore walked him to the door with a smile all the wider by virtue of the bank's sudden increase in assets. They exchanged a parting handshake at the office door.

Outside, Roosevelt turned downstreet. The boardwalk was packed with cowhands, wandering from saloon to saloon, out to "see the elephant." The term was cowboy parlance for liquor, games of chance such as poker and faro, and fast women. Roosevelt knew they would be broke by the end of the night, and he particularly frowned on the thriving industry of prostitution. Still, he never attempted to impose his own rigid code of morality on other men. Ambrosia rather than abstinence was the cowhands' motto.

A few doors west of the hotel, Roosevelt turned into the Medora Hardware & Emporium. The store was owned by Joe Ferris, who had acted as Roosevelt's guide on last year's buffalo hunt. Some months following the hunt, Ferris had married a local woman, who convinced him to settle down. He'd bought the store with his lifetime savings and built a house in the residential area south of town. For five years he had been a buffalo hunter and a guide for wealthy Easterners. He was now a respectable storekeeper.

The store was stocked with all manner of goods, hardware as well as clothing and foodstuffs. Saturday usually accounted for most of the week's business, and two clerks were scurrying about waiting on customers. Ferris was at the cash register, having just finished with a customer, when Roosevelt came through the door. He spotted Roosevelt and hurried around the counter with a broad grin. He extended his hand in greeting.

"Mr. Roosevelt!" he said, pumping Roosevelt's arm. "By golly, it's good to see you again."

"A pleasure, Joe," Roosevelt said. "Quite a change from hunter to merchant. Does business agree with you?"

"Yessir, the store's real prosperous, and my wife's expectin' our firstborn in May. I'm happier than a pig in mud."

"Congratulations are indeed in order. Please convey my regards to Mrs. Ferris."

"I sure will."

Ferris was a muscular man, with dark hair and a droopy handlebar mustache. Though he was five years older, he immediately reverted to the habit of addressing Roosevelt in a formal manner. Something in Roosevelt's bearing dissuaded him from doing otherwise.

"Heard you was back," he said. "You aimin' to stay awhile?"

"Yes, I believe so," Roosevelt remarked. "In fact, I've just purchased land for a new ranch. North of the Eaton brothers'."

"Why, you'll turn out to be a cattle baron, Mr. Roosevelt. Don't know anybody else that owns two outfits."

"Hardly operational as yet, Joe. I'll be needing a good many supplies for the house I plan to build."

Roosevelt handed him a list. The order included a cookstove, axes, hammers and nails, furnishings for eight rooms, and all manner of household goods. Ferris scanned the list, then read it again. He whistled softly.

"That's gonna set you back a pretty penny. You want me to price it out for you?"

"Charge whatever you think fair," Roosevelt said. "Aside from the furniture, I would like to have the supplies on hand within two weeks. I'll have bought a wagon and team by then."

"Yessir, whatever you say," Ferris agreed. "You mind me askin' you a personal question?"

"Certainly not."

"Word travels on the moccasin telegraph. Heard you whipped Black Jack Perkins out at the stage station. Any truth to it?"

"I take no pride in fisticuffs. The man was drunk and

threatening, and I merely put him in his place. There seemed no other recourse."

"Well, don't that beat all," Ferris said in an awed tone. "Your fisticuffs have earned you a nickname, Mr. Roosevelt. Course, nobody's gonna say it to your face."

"Perhaps you would be so kind as to tell me, Joe. I've never before had an alias."

"Folks are callin' you Ol' Four-eyes."

Roosevelt was amused. "I recall Mr. Black Jack Perkins made a similar remark. He seemed rather fixated on my glasses."

"Yessir, that's why nobody's likely to say anything. They know you whipped him 'cause of what he said."

Roosevelt let the subject drop. He mentioned that he needed a residence in Medora, somewhere to spend the night during trips between the Maltese Cross and the new ranch, Elkhorn. He felt the cost of a permanent room at the hotel would be prohibitive and asked if Ferris had any suggestions. Ferris noted that he had a furnished room above the store, where he and his wife had lived until their house was built. The room was comfortable, though not richly furnished, and he was willing to rent it for fifteen dollars a month. There was an outside stairway to the second floor, which afforded both convenience and privacy. Roosevelt took the room sight unseen and paid him a month in advance.

Ferris gave him the key, and after another handshake, Roosevelt turned to leave. On his way out the door, he ran into Merrifield. "Well, Bill," he said. "Just the man I wanted to see. I was on my way to the Maltese Cross."

"Saturday's my day in town," Merrifield said. "What can I do for you, Mr. Roosevelt?"

"I've purchased the land you recommended. Splendid location, I might add. Just splendid."

"So you'll be startin' another ranch?"

"Indeed so."

Roosevelt explained that he planned to start with a thousand head of cattle. The nearest market for shorthorn cows, usually of the Hereford breed, was in St. Paul, Minnesota. He wanted Merrifield to travel there and purchase the herd.

"Longhorns are lots cheaper," Merrifield said. "Might be able to put together a herd from some of the Texas outfits."

"You stocked the Maltese Cross with shorthorns because they produce more beef than longhorns. Isn't that so?"

"Yessir, that's a fact."

"Then I see no reason to change now," Roosevelt said. "Have you some estimate of what the herd will cost?"

"You'd want breeder cows and enough bulls to service them. You're likely lookin' at somewheres in the neighborhood of twenty thousand. Depends on the market."

Roosevelt nodded. "I will write a check for twenty-five thousand to cover any eventuality."

"When you want 'em here?" Merrifield asked. "I need to get this done before we start spring roundup."

"Leave as soon as practical, Bill. And while you're at it, hire four or five cowhands for the new ranch. I'm calling it Elkhorn."

"Now that you're serious, I guess it wouldn't hurt to ask who's gonna run the operation. You said you had a man in mind."

"His name is Adam Sewall," Roosevelt said. "I've known him since I was a youngster. He's from Maine."

"*Maine?*" Merrifield said, as though he hadn't heard correctly. "Thought them folks was all fishermen. What's he know about cows?"

"What he doesn't know, he will learn quickly enough. I have great confidence in Sewall."

Merrifield looked skeptical but restrained himself from voicing an opinion. Roosevelt left him there and walked off toward the train station. He had no idea whether Adam Sewall would accept his offer to move West. Yet there was never a moment's doubt as to who was right for the job. Sewall was the man for Elkhorn.

Roosevelt began composing the telegram as he crossed the street.

• • •

"Kings bet twenty."

Paddock studied the dealer's hand. On the table were an eight-king-nine-king. He figured it two pair, kings and eights or kings and nines. They were playing five-card stud, and the dealer's hole card gave him pause. All afternoon he'd had rotten luck, pulling decent cards only to have them topped by better cards. He pondered a moment longer.

The other players had dropped out. Jess Hogue, the dealer, was watching him with a blank expression. Paddock's own hand revealed a four-ace-king-four. In the hole he had another ace, but it was the king that impressed him most. With three on the board, Hogue would have to hold the case king in order to win. The odds dictated otherwise.

"Your twenty"—Paddock counted out greenbacks and tossed them into the center of the table—"and raise fifty."

Hogue consider briefly, then shrugged. "I think you're bluffin', Jake. Up another fifty."

"It's gonna cost you to find out. I'll take the last raise— fifty more."

"You're called." Hogue quickly matched the bet. "What've you got?"

"Read 'em and weep." Paddock flipped his hole card. "Aces and fours."

"I'll be goddamned!" Hogue turned his hole card to reveal a nine. "How the hell's kings and nines suck hind tit? Where'd you get an ace?"

"You tell me," Paddock said, dragging in the pot. "You're the dealer."

The poker game was at a back table in the Alhambra Saloon. Jess Hogue was the owner and Paddock's partner in various schemes, all of them shady and some illegal. Hogue was a stocky man, bald as a bullet, with a brushy red mustache and eyes the color of carpenter's chalk. He was brutish, quick with his fists, and no less feared than Paddock. He prided himself on acting as his own bouncer.

The Alhambra, a two-story frame structure, was the

largest saloon in town. The bar was on the ground floor, positioned opposite faro layouts and a roulette wheel, with poker tables toward the rear. The place was gearing up for Saturday night, and cowhands lined the bar while others stood ganged around the gaming tables. Four saloon girls circulated through the crowd, their peekaboo gowns cut low on top and short at the bottom. Their rooms on the second floor were for entertaining customers with quick and energetic love for sale. The standard tariff was two dollars a pop.

Apart from cowhands and local workingmen, the Alhambra was frequented by horse thieves, cattle rustlers, and the occasional stagecoach robber. Paddock and Hogue were rumored to be the ringleaders, but in a community that had yet to elect a town marshal no one had stepped forward with proof. Nor was anyone bold enough to say it out loud. Live and let live was thought to be the best motto,

Jess Hogue presided over the only high-stakes poker table in the Alhambra. The other players in the game included a rancher, a notions drummer who fancied himself a card slick, and a horse thief who volunteered nothing about his occupation. The deal passed to the notions drummer, and he began shuffling with the showboat technique of someone who practiced in his spare time. A man edged through the crowd and stopped beside Paddock. He stooped down, whispering something.

"Now?" Paddock flared. "Won't it wait?"

The man winced, taking a step back. Except for the notions drummer, everyone at the table knew he was a clerk for the Marquis de Mores. He shook his head in answer to Paddock's outburst and turned from the table. He disappeared into the crowd.

"Helluva note!" Paddock rose, stuffing a wad of greenbacks into his pocket. "Just when I got started on a winnin' streak."

Hogue laughed. "Don't worry, the game'll be here when you get back. We're liable to play all night."

"Make sure you save me a seat."

Paddock walked off. He carried a Colt .45 with rose-wood grips, and he hitched distractedly at his gun belt as he pushed through the crowd. The abrupt summons from de Mores nettled him, for he felt like a servant being ordered to report for duty. But then, in a sense, that's exactly what he was. Hired help.

Outside, he crossed the street and moved along the boardwalk. A short while later he entered the office and found the mousy-looking clerk again seated at his desk. He stalked past without a word and went through the door of the Marquis' private office. De Mores looked up from his desk with a tight, irritated expression. John Goodall, the manager of the slaughterhouse, and Otto Driesche, the chief accountant, were seated in leather armchairs. They appeared somehow uncomfortable in Paddock's presence.

"Gentlemen, you must excuse me," de Mores said. "We will continue our discussion on Monday."

Goodall and Driesche eased past Paddock. He closed the door and dropped into one of the armchairs. "You must learn to knock," de Mores said in a testy voice. "I do not appreciate being interrupted."

"You're the one that sent that pissant to fetch me. He said it wouldn't wait."

"Yes, perhaps you are right. Prompt is preferable to tardy."

"So what's the big rush?"

"Theodore Roosevelt," de Mores said. "Daniel Gilmore came to see me not an hour ago. Roosevelt has purchased land for another ranch."

"Yeah, I know," Paddock said. "He bought it from Nate Blackburn, feller who hunts wolves for bounty. Blackburn's been on a drunk all over town. Braggin' how he skinned the Eastern dude."

"Why have you not informed me of this?"

"Didn't see any reason to fly off the handle. Buying land's a long ways from startin' a ranch."

"You are wrong," de Mores countered. "Roosevelt has deposited fifty thousand dollars in Gilmore's bank. He obviously intends to move with dispatch."

Paddock wasn't surprised that Gilmore had hurried to report the news. De Mores was the bank's largest depositor, not to mention the owner and landlord of the bank building. One hand washed the other.

"Fifty thousand," Paddock repeated in a musing tone. "I reckon that'll buy lots of cows. *Muy pronto,* too."

"Precisely," de Mores said. "And Roosevelt still owns the Maltese Cross, which now makes him one of the largest ranchers in the Badlands. I do not like it."

"Well, you'll recollect I told you he was trouble. Never pays to trust an honest man."

"Or a man so versed in politics. He might well rally the other ranchers into a cohesive faction."

"That'd put a helluva kink in our plans, wouldn't it?"

De Mores thought it was an understatement. He operated on the theory that a man's reach should always exceed his grasp and already envisioned the next step in his refrigerated beef business. He intended to cut out the middleman and open his own wholesale plants in Kansas City and Chicago. The success of those ventures would enable him to establish wholesale operations throughout an even larger market, New York and the Atlantic Seaboard. He planned to become nothing less than the Beef King of America.

Roosevelt suddenly appeared to be a potential threat to those plans. De Mores needed large quantities of beef to supply his expansion program into Kansas City and Chicago. Nothing would derail him quicker than to have the Badlands ranchers join forces and present a united front in dealing with his company. And Theodore Roosevelt, who possessed the gift of leadership, was entirely capable of organizing the ranchers into a cohesive, and adversarial, faction. De Mores saw it as a risk he could not afford or tolerate.

"Roosevelt must be neutralized," he said sternly. "I cannot allow him the opportunity to disrupt my plans."

Paddock grunted. "Why not lemme kill him? Wouldn't be much of a chore."

"I prefer discreet measures whenever possible. We must cause him to lose the respect of the other ranchers. Destroy his influence."

"How you figure to do that?"

"We will wait until he has this new ranch in operation. Let him build a house and stock it with cattle. Then we will act."

"Yeah?" Paddock said, interested. "What sort of 'act' you got in mind?"

"You will force him to abandon his ranch."

"Well now, I like the sound of that. How much force we talkin' about?"

De Mores smiled. "Never fear, I have a plan."

EIGHT

The platform outside the train depot was crowded. A fortnight had passed since Roosevelt wired Adam Sewall, and the offer had been accepted. He was there to meet the new foreman of Elkhorn.

Roosevelt was accompanied by Bob Hallett, a wiry man with bowed legs and a feisty disposition. Hallett was a top hand, seasoned in the ways of cattle and horses, and he'd been hired as something of a tutor. The new foreman had a lot to learn about the cow business.

The noon train, almost an hour late, chuffed to a halt before the depot. Passengers filed out of the coaches while those on the platform waited to board. Sewall was in his late thirties, a tall man with craggy features, thick though the shoulders. He was followed by his nephew, Will Dow, who was somewhat taller and built along the same lines. The younger man had been hired as a general assistant.

"Adam! Will!" Roosevelt rushed forward with an ebullient handshake. "How was your journey?"

"Long," Sewall said succinctly. "Never knew this country was so big. We're a far piece from Maine."

"Don't mind him, Mr. Roosevelt," Dow said. "He's been glued to the window the whole trip. Didn't once stop talkin' about the sights."

"Indeed, the mountains and plains are natural wonders."

Roosevelt introduced them to Hallett. The cowboy inspected their backwoods clothes and heavy boots with an expression normally reserved for pig farmers. After a round of handshakes, Roosevelt had Sewall and Dow collect their luggage and led the way uptown. As they walked along, he told them that supplies for the ranch were even now being loaded into a wagon. He explained that Elkhorn was some thirty miles north of Medora, too far to travel before dark. They would camp for the night on the trail.

There was an easy camaraderie between Roosevelt and the two newcomers. Their relationship was born of long treks into the backcountry and nights lounging around a campfire. From age sixteen until he graduated from Harvard, Roosevelt had spent two weeks every summer in Maine. Sewall was a woodsman and guide, as was Dow, and they had taught Roosevelt how to hunt deer and moose, how to forage off the land in the wilderness. After Harvard, he had returned once in the fall and again in the winter, as much for their company as the lure of the hunt. He considered them two of the most competent men he'd ever met.

The deal Roosevelt made with them by telegraph was one they could hardly refuse. They were to be paid a generous salary and split 10 percent of the profits; if there were no profits, Roosevelt would absorb the loss. Sewall wired back that it was something of a one-sided arrangement, particularly since neither he nor his nephew had any experience in the cattle trade. But they knew fortunes were being made in the West, and they were willing to uproot from Maine and try their hand at ranching. The contract for their services was the deal made through an exchange of telegrams. They trusted Roosevelt implicitly.

Long ago, when Roosevelt first traveled to Maine, they had called him Theodore. Their time together in the woods, tracking game and camping out, engendered a kinship that was very close to family. But in later years, when Roosevelt returned as a grown man and a member of the New York legislature, there was something in his bearing, his force of character, that gave pause to the old familiarity. Sewall was fifteen years his senior and Dow was four years older, but Roosevelt seemed to them a man of the world, matured beyond their limited experience. They addressed him now, as they had for some years, as Mr. Roosevelt.

Their walk uptown brought them to the Medora Hardware & Emporium. A wagon with a team of draft horses was parked out front, with Manitou and three saddle horses tied to the hitchrack. Joe Ferris stood on the boardwalk, supervising his clerks as they loaded the last of the supplies into the wagon. He looked around as Roosevelt and Sewall, followed by Dow and Hallett, approached the store. He motioned to the wagon with an amiable smile.

"Ready to roll, Mr. Roosevelt," he said. "Got enough there to last you a couple weeks, maybe more."

"Bully!" Roosevelt said exuberantly. "Joe, I would like you to meet Adam Sewall and Will Dow. This is Joe Ferris, our town's leading merchant."

The men shook hands. Ferris nodded to Dow, then looked at Sewall. "Heard a lot about you fellows. Mr. Roosevelt thinks you're made-to-order for the cow business."

"Hope he's right," Sewall said. "What we don't know about cows would fill a bushel basket. Guess we'll learn as we go."

Ferris laughed. "Half the cowmen in these parts didn't know tail from horn when they started. You'll catch on fast enough."

"Well, sir, I don't suppose there's any choice in the matter. Mr. Roosevelt moves things right along."

"Now that you mention it," Roosevelt said. "We might as well put our little caravan on the trail. Who would like to drive the wagon?"

"I'll drive," Sewall said. "A wagon's more my speed."

Hallett chuckled. "You mean to tell me you can't ride a horse?"

"I doubt I'm the horseman you are, Mr. Hallett. But I'll learn."

"You'd better learn purty quick. Hard to rope cows from a wagon seat."

"Horses first, roping next. Maybe you'll give me lessons."

"Boy howdy," Hallett said, stepping aboard his horse. "Looks to be a long summer."

The spare horse was tied to the tailgate of the wagon. Sewall climbed into the seat, popped the reins, and the team leaned into the traces. Dow mounted with a nimbleness that belied his bulk, and Roosevelt, astride Manitou, led the way out of town. Hallett brought up the rear.

A mile or so north of Medora the trail ascended a steep grade onto a butte. The weather was warm for the first week in April, and the draft horses were huffing by the time the heavily laden wagon topped the crest. To all points of the compass, a broken landscape of ridges and canyons stretched into the distance. There was no longer any snow on the ground, and the tabletop on the butte was just turning green with grass. The vista was one of chaotic splendor.

Roosevelt was riding beside the wagon. Sewall gazed around at the rugged terrain and shook his head. "You've brought me to a strange land," he said. "God must've been in a fury when He made it."

"Yes, perhaps so," Roosevelt commented. "But I must say it grows on you, Adam. There is no place like it in all the world."

"You'll get no argument from me on that score. How is it cows can thrive on such land?"

"Wait until you see Elkhorn! Miles and miles of valley, and of course, the tablelands on the buttes are rich with grass. No finer spot for a ranch."

"Sounds good to me," Sewall said. "How many cows will we have on Elkhorn?"

"A thousand to start," Roosevelt replied. "Bill Merrifield, the foreman of my other ranch, is off buying them now. I expect the herd to arrive next week."

"And what are we to do in the meantime?"

"I want you and Will to build a grand house overlooking the river. I've designed it myself."

"Maybe I don't know much about cows, but I'm an old hand at felling trees. How big a house?"

"Eight rooms," Roosevelt said. "Large enough for you and Will to bring your wives West. If that is your wish, of course."

Sewall was quiet a moment. "Back there in town, I saw only one church. What denomination is it?"

Roosevelt knew it was no idle question. Sewall was a deeply religious man, as was Will Dow. The remark about their wives had clearly prompted thoughts about the church. A church Sewall and Dow, who were Methodists, would never enter.

"It is a Catholic church," Roosevelt said. "The slaughter-house and most of Medora are owned by a Frenchman, the Marquis de Mores. He built a monument to his own faith."

"Or the pope," Sewall added. "Where do other people worship?"

"Itinerant preachers occasionally travel to Medora. Services are held in the train depot, or outside in good weather, but there is no particular denomination. You have to understand that cowboys, and most cattlemen, feel no great need of spiritual instruction."

"Are you sayin' they don't believe in God?"

"Not at all," Roosevelt observed. "Cowboys live by the plainsman's code of religion. I've heard it expressed in rather poetic fashion."

"What sort of poem?"

" 'My books are the brook, and my sermons the stones; / My parson a wolf on a pulpit of bones'."

"Sounds a little heathen," Sewall said. "Did they adopt it from the Indians?"

"Perhaps," Roosevelt said. "I've always thought it a fundamental expression of belief in a God who created earth and sky. I rather fancy it does well for white men or red."

"Well, one thing's for sure, Mr. Roosevelt. There's lots of sky out here."

"Yes, a cathedral of open space measured by sunup and sundown. Not at all like New York or Maine, is it?"

"Couldn't be any different." Sewall hesitated, considering at length. "You plannin' on bringing your daughter out here?"

"No, I am not," Roosevelt said in a stolid voice. "My sister can care for her far better than I ever could. She will be just as well off without me."

"You won't always feel that way. Time heals things."

"I've picked a grand place to camp tonight. A clear-water brook surrounded by aspen and elms. You'll think you are back in Maine."

Sewall understood that a door had been closed. Roosevelt's daughter was not a topic for discussion, not now and, from the sound of it, not anytime soon. The memorial written by Roosevelt to his wife, so full of imagery and emotion, had been mailed to Sewall shortly after the funeral. He saw now that the wound was still fresh, grief a mere scratch beneath the surface. He sensed as well that he might be wrong.

Not all things were healed by time.

The sun was high in the sky, shafts of light like warm syrup over the land. Wooded bottoms were green with leaves, and the river sparkled brightly as it coursed through the valley. The jagged buttes to the west cast deep shadows beneath the sheer limestone walls.

Adam Sewall was soaked with sweat. He swung the ax with practiced ease, the *thunk* of the blade meaty as it ripped into the base of a tree. His arms moved in a steady rhythm, chunks of wood flying with every strike of the ax. One last blow severed the trunk in a sharp snap and the tree slowly toppled to the earth. He began trimming branches off with methodical precision.

Hallett was seldom more than a tree behind. As the branches were trimmed, he hooked the trunk into the claws of a drag chain, which in turn was attached to the harness of one of the draft horses. Then, leading the horse by the halter, he dragged the log from the grove of trees to where the house was being erected. For the past week he'd been work-

ing with the others on the house, and his curses got darker
with every log he hauled across the clearing. He thought it a
blasphemy that a top hand was reduced to manual labor.

Dow and Roosevelt were trimming a log to the proper
length with a crosscut saw. Hallett brought the horse to a
halt and unhooked his load from the drag chain. He removed his Stetson and mopped his face with a bandanna.

"Be damned glad when we're through," he said in a
grumpy tone. "I didn't hire on to be no teamster or such."

"Look on the bright side," Roosevelt said cheerfully.
"You're gaining valuable experience in the field of construction. You might have a whole new career, Bob."

"That'll be the day!"

Hallett turned and led the horse back toward the grove.
Dow dropped the crosscut saw on the ground. "Mighty
touchy fellow," he said. "Acts like he's too good for regular
work."

"In a manner of speaking, he is," Roosevelt said. "No
self-respecting cowboy would ever willingly stoop to common labor. His place is in the saddle."

"Guess it takes all kinds."

Will Dow was an artisan with an ax. He began notching
the log at both ends with surgical strokes. The notches
were roughly the width of the ax blade and hewn out to
dovetail with notches in other logs they cut. The dressed
logs were then winched upward with pulleys mounted on
two stout tripods, and joined to form the walls of the house.
One log at a time, the structure rose from the ground.

Roosevelt was something of an apprentice. He possessed no skills whatever with an ax, and his role was to
provide muscle on the crosscut saw and the winch. The
walls of the house were halfway up, and he was pleased
with the progress they'd made in a week. When completed,
the walls would be chinked to seal the gaps, and adzed
boards would be laid for the flooring. Three stone chimneys were planned, one in the parlor, another in the kitchen,
and a third in the room Roosevelt intended to use as a
study. The roof would be the last step in the construction.

Until then, the men were living in tents. Sewall and Dow shared one tent, and Roosevelt had the other to himself. Hallett, who disdained such civilized amenities, pitched his bedroll on the ground. The campsite was on a flat near the riverbank, beneath a tall stand of cottonwoods. A large fire pit, ringed with stones, had been constructed by Sewall, and Roosevelt kept them in fresh meat by stalking deer farther upriver. Dow was handy with skillets and a Dutch oven, and he'd volunteered to act as cook. Hallett, forced to suffer yet another indignity, was assigned to scrub the utensils and tinware.

Later, when the main house was completed, work would start on a bunkhouse for the cowhands. As Dow continued to notch the log, Roosevelt imagined how it would all look when it was finished. The house would be large but compact, with a central parlor, a dining room adjoined to the kitchen, three bedrooms, a private study, and a storage room for supplies and assorted gear. Three weeks ago Roosevelt had written Bamie and asked her to ship a small library of books to fill the shelves in his study. He had also queried his New York publisher about a book he intended to write.

A meadowlark trilled a flutelike song from the trees near the house. Distracted, Roosevelt watched as it preened, the black V distinctive on its yellow breast. His eyes strayed to the western buttes, where bluebirds, wrens, rosy finches, and white-throated swallows built their nests in the cliffs. Yesterday he'd seen a golden eagle soar majestically on a seven-foot wingspan across the valley and light in a tree downriver. Grouse and killdeer and magpies flitted about the land, their warbling a constant calliope of birdsong. He often thought Elkhorn was an ornithologist's dream come to life.

A different sound attracted his attention. He turned, looking south along the valley, and the bawling of cattle suddenly became louder. Then, as though appearing through a mirage, a herd of cows simply materialized on the grassy prairie. He saw a horseman riding point wave his arm in a circular motion, and other riders galloped forward to turn the lead elements of the herd and bring it to a halt. As if a genie had been uncorked from a bottle, a thousand cows abruptly stopped and began grazing across the valley. The sight seemed to him somehow magical, the very creation of Elkhorn.

Bill Merrifield rode forward at a trot. He reined smartly to a halt and stepped down out of the saddle. "Afternoon, Mr. Roosevelt," he said. "We've brought your herd."

"By Jove!" Roosevelt said with a jack-o'-lantern grin. "I've never seen anything quite like it. Splendid work!"

"Trained 'em in three days ago. Figgered we'd make better time, but the trail from Medora gets steep here and there. Them cows ain't used to climbing buttes."

"I trust they are no worse for wear?"

"Fit as a fiddle," Merrifield said. "Bought you nearly a thousand mama cows and some fine bulls. Got a remuda of horses, too."

"Excellent!" Roosevelt was galvanized with excitement. "Were you able to purchase the cattle at a fair price?"

"Took a little hagglin', but things finally worked out. Got 'em for twenty-one a head."

Merrifield handed him a piece of scrap paper. The penciled list indicated $21 a head for cows, $30 each for six bulls, and $40 a head for thirty cow ponies. The freight charges were $500 for shipping the stock by train from Minnesota to Medora. The total came to $22,880.

"Stopped by the bank in town," Merrifield said, handing him a receipt. "Deposited the balance of the twenty-five thousand you gave me to your account. Figgered you wouldn't want all that cash money out here."

"Very thoughtful of you," Roosevelt said. "You've done a marvelous job, and it deserves a bonus. Add three hundred to your wages this month."

"Well, that's mighty generous of you, Mr. Roosevelt."

"Good work merits a reward, Bill. You have earned it."

Merrifield seemed embarrassed by the praise. He studied the house construction a moment. "Looks like things are comin' right along. How many rooms?"

"Eight here, and a bunkhouse, of course. I want you to meet Adam Sewall and Will Dow, who will run Elkhorn. I'll depend on them as I do you at the Maltese Cross."

Roosevelt introduced Dow and hailed Sewall up from the grove of trees. Between handshakes Merrifield looked them over, as though weighing his competition for Roosevelt's patronage. He clearly wasn't impressed by their woodsmen's clothing and their flat-heeled lace-up hunting boots. His attitude was that of a cowman talking to farmers. Polite but somewhat standoffish.

The crew Merrifield had hired for Elkhorn consisted of Hallett and four other cowhands. He'd also hired a cook for the outfit, a heavyset, loquacious man named Bud Ledbetter. Dow helped him unload his battery of pots and skillets and showed him where the victuals were stored in the old cabin by the river. Working together, they began preparing supper for the crew.

Ledbetter proved to be a master of simple but hearty food. He set about cooking deer steaks, fried potatoes, sourdough biscuits, and the staple of every cowboy's meal, a pot of beans. He even whipped up a dessert he called Spotted Pup Pudding, rice heavily laced with raisins and flavored with brown sugar. His one fault was that he evidenced a propensity for one-way conversations. He talked a blue streak the entire time he cooked.

The sun teetered above the western buttes in a wash of scarlet and gold as supper was served. The men sat around the fire, tin plates balanced on their crossed legs, listening to Ledbetter launch into another soliloquy as they ate. Roosevelt, Sewall, and Merrifield seated themselves somewhat apart, for Roosevelt wanted his two foremen to become friends rather than rivals. He sensed Merrifield was envious of the bigger house and all the money being spent on Elkhorn. He prompted Sewall to play the role of a greenhorn.

"No two ways about it," Sewall admitted, nodding to Merrifield. "Any advice you've got, I'd be obliged to hear it. Anything a'tall."

Marrifield took a swig of coffee. "Bob Hallett is a good man with cows, what we call a top hand. Hired him so's he could show you the ropes." He paused, peering over the rim of his tin cup. "Course Bob tends to be a little cantankerous now and then. You gotta let him know who's boss."

"I noticed he's a mite cocky," Sewall said. "One way or another, we'll come to terms. Anything else?"

"Yeah, if you're open to some personal advice. Wouldn't want to hurt your feelin's."

"I've got a thicker skin than most. Have away."

"You don't look nothing like a cowman," Merrifield said. "Get shed of them Eastern duds, specially them clodhopper boots. Buy yourself some cowboy boots and a Stetson, maybe even a set of spurs. Dress like your men dress."

"I take your point," Sewall said with a trace of humor. "Although I'll have to get accustomed to those high-heeled boots. I'm liable to wobble at first."

Merrifield laughed. "You'll get over it soon enough. Just takes a little practice."

Roosevelt was pleased with the tone of the conversation. He wanted Sewall to succeed and felt that Merrifield's advice was on the mark. He was reminded of Shakespeare's observation that "all the world's a stage."

A man first had to look the part.

NINE

Hallett tugged his hat down tight. Roosevelt was standing outside the corral, and no matter how many times he watched, he thought it was like a monkey leaping nimbly to the back of a circus pony. One moment the cowboy was on the ground, and the next he was seated firmly in the saddle.

Leaning forward, Hallett jerked the blindfold loose. The day was bright and sunny, and for perhaps ten seconds the buckskin gelding remained perfectly still, blinking in the sudden glare of light. Hallett sat loose and easy, waiting a moment longer, then thrust his boots deeper into the stirrups. The jinglebobs on his spurs, in the quiet of the corral, gave off the chime of cathedral bells.

The buckskin exploded at both ends. All four hooves left the ground as the horse bowed its back and in the same instant came unglued in a bone-jarring snap. Then it swapped ends in midair and sunfished across the corral in a series of bounding, catlike leaps. Hallett was all over the buckskin, bouncing from side to side and back and forth, never twice in the same spot. The bronc whirled and kicked, slamming him front to rear in the saddle. His hat went spinning skyward in a lazy arc.

Hallett gave a whooping shout and raked hard across the shoulders with his spurs. The buckskin roared a great squeal of outrage, leaped straight up in the air, and humped its back. A moment later it hit on all four hooves with a jolt that shook the earth and popped Hallett's neck. Then, as if berserk and intent on killing the rider, the buckskin erupted in a pounding beeline toward the corral fence. Hallett saw it coming and effortlessly swung out of the saddle at the exact instant the bronc collided with the springy cross timber. The gelding staggered, buckled at the knees, and fell back on its rump.

Hallett casually stepped into the saddle as the buckskin righted itself. He rammed his spurs into the flank, and now there was less fight in the horse, ending in three or four stiff-legged crowhops that lacked punch. A firm hand on the reins, Hallett turned the horse in a few simple maneuvers, then eased to a halt and climbed down out of the saddle. The buckskin stood head bowed and sides heaving as it gasped for air.

"Guess that oughta do it," Hallett said, dusting off his hat. "Hammerhead won't be so sassy next time."

Three of the hands were sitting on the top rail of the fence. One of them jumped down, crossed the corral, and began unsaddling the buckskin. Roosevelt nodded approvingly. "Very nice job," he said to Hallett. "There for a moment I thought he had you."

"Mr. Roosevelt, there ain't a horse born that could punch my ticket."

Hallett had volunteered as chief broncbuster for Elkhorn. The date was April 26, and spring roundup was scheduled to start in two weeks. Of the thirty horses in the remuda, over half were green broke, cowman's parlance for a horse broken to saddle but still determined to fight a rider. The hammerheads, as Hallett called them, were being taught to accept the inevitable. Fight or not, they would be ridden.

Four horses were tethered outside the corral. These were the worst of the lot and, along with the buckskin, had been selected for today's lesson in manners. Roosevelt reveled in the hardship and challenge of breaking horses, and he sensed the pride the cowhands felt in a job well done. In his view, they possessed the qualities he deemed fundamental in manhood: courage, independence, bold hardiness, and integrity. He had known many men whose lives had not been as fortunate as his own, workingmen, servants, and common laborers. But he had never before lived with them on a daily basis, and the last few weeks at Elkhorn had altered his outlook on the men he employed. He admired their rugged spirit, and he found them to be excellent companions. Even more, he enjoyed working beside them.

The progress at Elkhorn was a matter of pride as well. The spacious main house was completed, a solid log structure with a covered porch overlooking the river. Roosevelt's bedroom was on the southwest corner, adjoining his study, with a panoramic view of the valley and the towering buttes to the west. The bunkhouse and cookshack, located fifty yards north of the main house, were in the final stages of construction. Even now, Sewall and Dow were completing the roof, laying shingles split by hand from squared logs. Their last project would be an enclosed shed, for all manner of gear necessary to operating a ranch. Sewall expected to have it built before spring roundup.

Roosevelt watched as another horse was brought to the corral. All morning he'd been an observer, studying with interest the way the men handled difficult horses and how Hallett rode them to a standstill. Three of the five horses had been ridden, and as the fourth was led forward, Roosevelt was struck by an urge to try it himself. He knew bronc-busting required skills acquired over a lifetime and there was always the danger of being injured or worse. Yet he felt some odd compulsion, however foolhardy, to test himself. A rite of passage having less to do with reason than with respect.

"Hold on there, Bob," he called out to Hallett. "I believe I might try this one myself."

Hallett looked astounded. "Mr. Roosevelt, you don't wanna ride these hammerheads. They're plumb rank."

"Yes, they certainly kick up their heels. I think it looks like good sport."

"Take my word for it, they're not gonna give you a sportin' chance. You're liable to get stomped."

"Nonetheless, I believe I'll try."

"You're sure I can't talk you out of it?"

"Quite sure, Bob."

Sam Jeeter, one of the other hands, yelled out across the compound, "Mr. Roosevelt's gonna ride a *bronc*!"

Everyone turned at the sound of his voice. Sewall and Dow scrambled down off the roof of the bunkhouse, and Bud Ledbetter came out of the cookshack. They fell in together and trooped across the clearing to the corral. Sewall gave Roosevelt a concerned look but didn't say anything. He knew better than to question the "boss" in front of the men.

Jeeter led a sorrel gelding into the corral. He turned it loose as the other men closed the gate and Hallett uncoiled a lariat. The horse was a raw bronc, not yet thoroughly broken to saddle, and required somewhat harsher measures than used on the rest of the remuda. The men knew their jobs and there was little lost motion in their actions.

The sorrel started racing around the far side of the corral as they walked forward. Hallett's arm suddenly moved and the lariat snaked out, catching the gelding's front legs in a loop just as its hooves left the ground. Hauling back, Hallett set his weight into the rope, and the horse went down with a jarring thud. The men swarmed over him in a cloud of dust and flailing arms.

Jeeter wrapped himself around the sorrel's neck, grabbing an ear in each hand, and jerked it back to earth as it started to rise. One of the men darted in with a length of braided rawhide and lashed the animal's hind legs together. Another man quickly clamped hobbles around the front legs and Hallett released the lariat with a flick of his wrist. Tugging and shoving, sometimes rolling the sorrel up on its withers, the men managed to cinch a saddle in place. Hallett jerked the latigo taut as Jeeter tied a blindfold around the gelding's eyes.

The entire operation had taken less than a minute.

Quickly the rawhide lash was removed from the hind legs and the sorrel stumbled to its feet. Blinded and dazed, still winded from the fall, the horse stood absolutely motionless. The hobbles on its front legs kept it from rearing or jumping away, and the blindfold calmed it into a numbed stupor. The bronc was ready to ride.

Jeeter and the other men hurried through the gate. Hallett, his brow wrinkled in a frown, motioned Roosevelt forward. "Wish you'd change your mind," he said. "This here's rough business, Mr. Roosevelt."

"Thank you for your concern, Bob. Hold him while I mount."

Roosevelt stepped into the saddle, reins in hand, as Hallett removed the hobbles and retreated to the fence. The men gathered outside the corral watched intently as Roosevelt leaned forward and jerked the blindfold loose. The sorrel shook its head, blinking in the sunlight, and went from a standing start into a soaring leap. All four hooves left the ground and Roosevelt sailed over the horse's head, landing on his rump in the dirt. He managed to hold on to the reins.

Hallett flung himself around the gelding's neck until Roosevelt regained the saddle. The sorrel whirled away, arching its back, and kicked high in the air with its rear hooves. Roosevelt was left hanging in midair and dropped to the ground with a dusty *thump*. Twice more, hardly before Roosevelt had swung into the saddle, the horse pitched and bucked and dumped Roosevelt sprawling in the dirt. Yet he wouldn't quit, and the men realized it had become a contest between man and animal. They thought the horse was winning.

The fifth time, as Hallett clung to the gelding's neck, Roosevelt clipped his spectacles tighter and yelled to Jeeter. "Open that gate—*now!*"

Jeeter jumped to obey the command. The sorrel saw daylight and took off at a headlong lope through the gate. Roosevelt sawed the reins, bent low in the saddle, and gigged the horse into a gallop toward the river. A moment later the gelding cleared the riverbank in a crazed leap and struck the water with the force of a cannonball. The current

of the Little Missouri all but immobilized the horse, and
the harder he fought, the quicker his energy was sapped.
After several minutes of wild-eyed thrashing, Roosevelt
reined the exhausted gelding onto dry land. He rode back
to the corral.

"Gawdalmighty!" Hallett shouted. "That's the damnedest
thing I ever seen. Where'd you get that idea?"

"The old axiom," Roosevelt said, stepping out of the
saddle. "Necessity is the mother of all invention. I couldn't
beat him on land, so I took him to water."

The men crowded around, shaking his hand and clapping him on the back. Roosevelt grinned at their praise,
though he was bruised and scratched and felt as though
he'd been run through an ore crusher. Hallett seemed particularly elated until his gaze fell on Sewall. His mouth
crooked in a sardonic smile.

"How about it, Mr. Foreman?" Hallett said. "You ready
to fork a bronc?"

Sewall shook his head. "I'm not horseman enough just
yet. Maybe another time."

"You might be a helluva carpenter, but you ain't much
of a ramrod. Haven't you got no guts?"

Roosevelt refused to interfere, for he could not *order* the
men to respect the foreman he'd chosen. Sewall would
have to win their respect himself.

"Listen to me, Hallett," Sewall said in an ominous
voice. "Maybe you can ride broncs, but you can't ride me.
If you think I'm short on guts, just give it a try."

"What?" Hallett said with a wiseacre grin. "You figger I
couldn't whip you in a fistfight?"

"I'll give you the first blow, and after that, it's no-holds-
barred. Go ahead, take a swing."

The men waited for Hallett to swing, for he was a barroom scrapper of some reputation. But instead, as though
calculating the odds, he eyed Sewall with a cautious look.
He finally spread his hands in a lame gesture.

"Tell you what," he said. "You try a bronc and I'll try
you. How's that sound?"

"Like you're begging off," Sewall said bluntly. "Don't you ever again speak to me in a smart-aleck way. You do and we'll finish this. Got it?"

Hallett shrugged "No need to get your nose outta joint."

"You've got horses to break and I've got a roof to finish. Let's get back to work."

Sewall walked off toward the bunkhouse, trailed by Dow. The men stared at Hallett a moment, and then, with a hollow laugh, he turned back into the corral. Roosevelt, watching them, thought a question had been answered in their minds. One put to rest by Adam Sewall.

No longer was there any doubt as to who gave the orders on Elkhorn.

Spring suddenly burst upon the Badlands. A Chinook wind out of the northwest brought warm weather and sunny skies that melted the last of the high-country snow. The valley was ablaze with wildflowers.

Roosevelt sat at the desk in his study. The window was open and the merry warbling of birds came to him on a soft afternoon breeze. He stopped, pen in hand, listening a moment as he formulated the image in his mind into words. His pen abruptly scratched as he put the thought on paper.

The working title of the book was *Hunting Trips of a Ranchman.* His New York publisher was ecstatic about the idea and requested that Roosevelt complete the manuscript by Christmas. The book would cover his many forays into the Badlands, his oneness with nature, and his deep admiration for the wild things he killed. Today's chapter was devoted to his stalk of pronghorn antelope.

The study was everything he'd envisioned, a solitary retreat, sacrosanct in its privacy. The desk was polished walnut and his chair was burgundy leather, ordered from a furniture dealer in Chicago. One wall was floor-to-ceiling bookshelves, lined with the works of Hawthorne and Cooper, Milton and Poe, and a hundred other authors. A small fireplace occupied another wall, and the window before Roosevelt's desk afforded a vista of the buttes to the west. He considered the study the perfect sanctum for a man alone with his thoughts.

The date on his desk calendar was April 30. As it was the end of the month and payday, the men had ridden into Medora to squander their wages on liquor and women. Over the past few weeks, they had performed a prodigious feat of labor, searing a thousand cows with Elkhorn's unmistakable ✠ brand. Spring roundup was scheduled to start early in May, consuming the better part of a month, and Roosevelt felt the men deserved a reward for past and future labors. He'd given them three days off.

Sewall and Dow had declined the offer. They were, like Roosevelt, men who adhered to a strict moral code. Their wives might be two thousand miles away, but for them, out of sight was not out of mind. Despite the distance, they were as faithful as if their village in Maine were just downriver from Elkhorn. As payday approached, they'd overheard the men talking zestfully of cards and busthead whiskey and whores who performed shameless acts of lust. Some of the acts of lust sounded unusual, fascinating if depraved, yet Sewall and Dow were not tempted. They stayed behind at Elkhorn.

Construction at the ranch compound was completed. The main house, the bunkhouse, and the equipment shed had been built solid enough to last a hundred years. All the furniture had been freighted from Medora, with a divan and chairs for the parlor, beds and nightstands and armoires, and an oak dining table. The bunkhouse was more sparsely furnished, with single beds, washstands, and a two-hole privy out back. Dug wells, engineered by Sewall and walled with stone, provided freshwater for both buildings. Elkhorn, once raw land, was now a home.

Roosevelt was justifiably proud of what he and his men had accomplished in so short a period of time. Today, however, as he wrote furiously of antelope, his mind was off in the wild country. He searched for words to convey the stark beauty of the southwestern Badlands, the singular curiosity of antelope, and how he'd used a fluttering handkerchief to draw them within range. He was about to pen the climactic moment—the shot that downed the buck—when he heard the drum of hoofbeats through the open window. He couldn't imagine that the men had returned from town so quickly.

Laying his pen aside, Roosevelt walked through the house. Sewall was in the kitchen pouring a cup of coffee, and Dow was seated in the parlor, reading *The Last of the Mohicans.* As he crossed the room, Roosevelt looked out the window and saw Jake Paddock and six other horsemen approaching from the trail along the river. His first thought was that Paddock worked for the Marquis de Mores, and his second was that the men had no business on Elkhorn. He motioned Sewall and Dow to stay put.

Roosevelt routinely went armed with his Colt Peacemaker. He unconsciously checked the holstered pistol as he went through the door and stepped onto the porch. Paddock and the horsemen rode across the clearing, fanning out in a line, and reined to a halt before the house. One day in town, when Roosevelt was ordering supplies from Joe Ferris, the storekeeper had pointed out Paddock on the street. At the time, Roosevelt thought Paddock looked the quintessential villain from a dime novel of Western rogues. He thought now that the men with Paddock were of the same stripe.

"Good afternoon," Roosevelt said. "How may I help you gentlemen?"

"Roosevelt," Paddock said with a curt nod. "You know who I am?"

"Unless I'm mistaken, your name is Jake Paddock. I understand you are associated with the Marquis de Mores."

"Well now, that gets us off to a good start. The Marquis sent me to deliver a message. You're squattin' on his land."

"I beg your pardon?"

"Get the wax outta your ears," Paddock said roughly. "The Marquis owns this land and you're trespassin'. You and your whole outfit."

"Indeed?" Roosevelt said. "How may I inquire does the Marquis lay claim to my property?"

"Ain't your property," Paddock countered. "The Marquis run a herd of cows on this land last year. That makes it his."

"I purchased the property from a man named Blackburn. The deed has been recorded at the courthouse in Mandan."

"That deed ain't worth the paper it's written on. Nate Blackburn played you for a sucker, pure and simple."

Roosevelt thought it was all too coincidental. For Paddock and his gang to show up today—when the Elkhorn crew was in town—meant the gunmen had planned to catch him alone. He recalled Gregor Lang's allegation, later confirmed by Merrifield, that the Marquis employed Paddock to frighten small ranchers off their land. He was by no means a small rancher, but he saw now that he'd been targeted by the Marquis. The reason, though unclear, seemed almost beside the point.

"You may inform the Marquis," Roosevelt said, "that my deed is valid under law. His recourse, if he wishes to contest it, is to file suit in court."

"Don't work that way," Paddock said in a surly voice. "The Marquis told me to offer you five thousand for the place. That's a fair price, considerin' you ain't nothin' but a squatter. He wants you outta here by tomorrow night."

"And if I refuse the offer?"

"Then we'll burn you out right goddamn now! You might even get yourself killed."

"*Paddock.*"

Adam Sewall appeared in the doorway with a Winchester rifle. In the same instant, Will Dow thrust the muzzle of a double-barreled shotgun through an open window. Sewall raised the rifle to his shoulder, sighted on Paddock. "Anybody gets killed," he said, "it'll be you. Give me an excuse and I'll blow you off that horse."

There was a moment of strained silence. Roosevelt pulled his Colt and waved it at Paddock. "Take your men and leave," he said. "And I strongly advise you not to come back. You are not welcome here."

"This ain't the end of it," Paddock grated. "There'll be another day."

"Perhaps so, but today is not your day. Get off Elkhorn."

Paddock wheeled his horse away from the house. His men fell in behind and they rode south through the valley. Roosevelt watched them for a time, then holstered his pistol. He turned to Sewall.

"I rather doubt that is the last of it," he said. "Greed and arrogance are opposite sides of the same coin. The Marquis has an abundance of both."

Sewall knuckled his mustache. "Well, sir, we took the wind out of their sails today. Paddock didn't much like the odds."

"Nonetheless, we must be on the lookout. The gravest error would be to underestimate such men."

"Don't you worry, we'll keep a sharp eye."

Roosevelt stared out across the river. The peaceful setting seemed somehow violated by the incident, and he heard again Paddock's final words. He told himself it was no idle threat.

There would indeed be another day.

TEN

Spring roundup began on May 7. The men representing various ranches met on Box Elder Creek in the Killdeer Mountains, thirty miles northeast of Elkhorn. In three weeks, the crews would work their way south along the Little Missouri River for more than a hundred miles. Thousands of cattle would be flushed from the canyons and buttes of the Badlands.

The foremen for each of the crews reported to Frank Osterhaut, the man selected as captain of the roundup. The encampment, which usually moved south every other day, stretched for a half mile along the river. There were chuck wagons from the larger outfits, and a remuda of horses for each crew, all spread out within the encampment. Nearly a hundred cowhands labored from dawn to dusk gathering cattle.

Roosevelt worked at the branding fires. He was all but useless with a lariat, and roping from a horse was a skill he'd yet to master. Three days ago, when roundup started, he had reported to the captain and confessed his deficiency as a cowhand. The owners of the ranches were expected to work beside their men, and Roosevelt, after explaining his limitations, was assigned to the branding fires. His job, which required muscle rather than skill, was to wrestle calves.

The workday began an hour before first light. A yell from the cook signaled the start of another day, and the men assembled at the chuck wagon for a hasty breakfast. Afterward, the night wrangler brought in the remuda and the men roped the horses they would use for the morning gather. Every cowhand had eight horses in his string and rotated them over four days, since the work was tougher on ponies than men. One horse was used in the morning, and following the midday meal another was selected for the afternoon. A third horse, always well rested, was held aside for those who rode night guard.

The crews from the various ranches rode out at dawn. Captain Osterhaut assigned each crew to broad sectors covering a swath of river bottomlands and high country laced with gorges and plateaus. By sunrise, the crews were ten miles or more from camp, and the foremen dropped off their men at scattered points to hunt cows. The men drove the cattle they gathered back toward the encampment.

The law of open range still prevailed in Dakota Territory. Ranchers owned their homestead sites and claimed vast expanses of unfenced government land, the boundaries identified by natural landmarks. Some cattlemen bought range outright from the Northern Pacific, which had been awarded miles of land on either side of the railroad right-of-way. Over the winter, cows drifted from range to range, mixing with the herds of neighboring ranchers. A central part of roundup was to unmix the scrambled herds.

The morning gather usually lasted five or six hours. By midday cowboys appeared from every point of the compass, driving bunches of cows and calves, steers and bulls, collected throughout the morning. The branded cattle, including cows with newborn calves, were then cut out and separated into individual herds spread along the river. The cowhands afterward took a short break for the noon meal, collecting once again around the chuck wagon assigned to their crew. Having eaten, they selected horses from the remuda to finish out the day's work.

The afternoon was devoted to branding calves. Elkhorn was the exception among the ranches represented, in that its recently purchased herd was already branded and had no calves. Roosevelt nonetheless felt obligated to be there personally, for the southern swing of the roundup could cover the Maltese Cross. He had brought along Bob Hallett and Sam Jeeter from Elkhorn, and the crew he worked with included his nearest neighbors, the Eaton brothers, and the Hash Knife outfit, owned by a former Texan. Bill Merrifield was there as well, with George Myers and another cowhand from the Maltese Cross.

Merrifield and Hallett, along with other expert ropers, lassoed the calves and dragged them bleating from the herd. At the fires, a crew of five men, one handling a white-hot branding iron, swarmed over the calves. Roosevelt's job was to grab the legs, upend the calf by brute force, and pin it to the ground with his knee. Within a couple of minutes, the stunned critters were branded and earmarked, and a veteran hand, wielding a sharp knife, castrated the bull calves. Afterward, somewhat altered in appearance but no worse for wear, the calves scooted off searching for their mama cows. The operation was swift, every man to his task.

Capt. Frank Osterhaut, who routinely inspected the camps, rode by that afternoon during a lull in the action. He was the foreman of the Hash Knife spread, somewhere in his early forties, and generally regarded as the most knowledgeable cattleman in the Badlands. In years past, while working out of Texas, he had driven herds up the Chisholm Trail to Abilene and Dodge City and other Kansas railheads. He reined to a halt by the branding fire, nodding to Roosevelt.

"Mr. Roosevelt," he said amiably. "How's things for your first roundup?"

Roosevelt was covered in sweat and grime. "Quite well," he said, adjusting his pince-nez. "I've discovered an aptitude for throwing calves. Somewhat like Greco-Roman wrestling."

Osterhaut nodded as though he knew what the term

meant. "Well, you've got the build for it," he said. "Stout does better'n skinny where calves are concerned."

"I daresay I'm perfectly suited for the job. I might well become the champion calf wrestler of the Badlands."

"Down in Texas we had men called bulldoggers. They'd jump off a horse going lickety-split, grab a steer by the horns, and dump him on the ground. You'd likely been good at it."

"Are you referring to longhorns?" Roosevelt asked. "I rather doubt it would be practical with shorthorn cows."

"I just suspect you're right," Osterhaut allowed. "Never saw it tried with Herefords or such. Fact is, I haven't seen it a'tall since I left Texas."

Osterhaut worked for Jack Simpson, who owned the Hash Knife. Three years ago, Simpson and Osterhaut, with a crew of seven cowhands, had trailed a herd of two thousand longhorns from Texas to Dakota Territory. A year later, another Texas outfit, the O.X. brand, had established a spread in the Badlands. All of the other ranches were stocked with shorthorns.

"Do you like it here in Dakota?" Roosevelt inquired. "I would imagine it's a good deal different than Texas."

"Tell you the truth, I'd never seen snow till we come up here. Jack Simpson fooled me six ways to Sunday on that one. Never said boo about the tough winters."

"Have you ever considered returning to Texas?"

"Yessir, when it gets colder'n a witch's tit, I consider it a lot. Course, I been ridin' with the Hash Knife nigh on to ten years. Guess I'll stick a while longer."

"Look out there!" Hallett yelled, dragging a bull calf toward the fire. "Got a little feller that wants his nuts cut off."

Osterhaut laughed. "Bob, you're slicker'n greased owlshit with a rope. Sure you ain't a Texan?"

"Watch who you're insultin'," Hallett retorted with mock indignation. "My mama didn't whelp no blue-assed idjits. I'm a Montana boy."

Roosevelt grabbed the squalling calf. As Osterhaut and

Hallett rode off, it occurred to him that cowmen were the most inventive cursers in the world. He'd heard sailors and Egyptian camel drivers and workingmen on three continents utter vulgarities in as many languages. Yet he thought "slicker'n greased owlshit" was in a league all its own. Cowboys were masters of the profane.

Toward dusk, the branding fires were smothered for the day. The men on foot headed for the chuck wagon, and the mounted hands turned their horses over to the wrangler. Before supper, the men selected their night horses from the remuda, and after being saddled the animals were picketed near the camp. Every man in the crew rode night guard on the cattle herd, two men at a time posted from eight in the evening until first light the next day. Roosevelt found the two-hour stint on night guard the most relaxing part of the roundup.

The area around the chuck wagon was the domain of the cook, ruled by a tyrant. Even the owners and foremen watched their manners, for cooks were a notoriously capricious lot and easily offended. There were absolutes, never to be profaned, or the crew would rapidly find themselves on meager rations. The cardinal rule was that there were to be no complaints, spoken or otherwise implied, about the quality of the cooking. Those who didn't like it were welcome to go hungry.

A happy cook was considered a treasure on roundup. Tonight, with a crew that appreciated his efforts, the cook concocted a favorite among cowmen. When the hands lined up with their tin plates, he served son-of-bitch stew, a mix of loins, sweetbreads, liver, and heart simmered in a spicy gravy. The stew and Dutch oven biscuits were washed down with what was commonly referred to as six-shooter coffee. The name derived from the fact that most cooks considered coffee passable only when it was thick enough to float a loaded six-gun. Whether it would grow hair on a man's tonsils was a subject for discussion only away from the chuck wagon.

Roosevelt usually sat with Merrifield, the Eaton brothers, and Jack Simpson, owner of the Hash Knife. The fire cast a rosy glow over the camp, and the men fell to talking about events of their workday over a second cup of coffee. Merrifield remarked that he'd run across Frank Osterhaut late that afternoon and the roundup captain had commented favorably on Roosevelt's work around the branding fire. Everyone agreed it was high praise from a man of Osterhaut's experience.

"Nothing really," Roosevelt said modestly. "I've still a great deal to learn."

"Bet your rusty butt on that? Any piss-willie I ever seen could throw calves."

Wally Klaberg was seated on the opposite side of the fire. He was a lean man, all gristle and sinew, a former Texan and a top hand for the Hash Knife outfit. For the past two nights he had baited Roosevelt with personal gibes that bordered on insults. Tonight Klaberg took it a step further.

"Who the hell you lookin' at?" he bristled, glowering at Roosevelt. "Goddamn rich dude tryin' to act like a man. You ain't foolin' nobody."

The men around the fire fell silent. Jack Simpson, hadn't attempted to intervene before, and he made no effort now to restrain Klaberg. Roosevelt had fobbed off the previous remarks with humor, but he sensed that tonight's goad had crossed the line. The other men were watching, as if he'd been put to the test; unless he responded in a forceful manner, he would be marked a coward. He got to his feet.

"Klaberg, you have a big mouth," he said. "I accepted your remarks in jest, but you've gone too far. Put up or shut up."

"You offerin' to fight me?"

"If you insist," Roosevelt said, removing his spectacles.

Klaberg scrambled to his feet. He moved around the fire as Roosevelt assumed a boxer's stance. His face twisted in an ugly grin, Klaberg lunged forward, throwing haymakers with both fists. Roosevelt dodged the blows, belting him in the mouth with two snapping left jabs. Spitting blood, the

cowhand landed a murderous roundhouse right that opened
a cut over Roosevelt's eyebrow. He followed with a looping
left meant to end the fight.

Roosevelt ducked, sliding under the punch, and struck
him in the pit of the stomach. Klaberg's mouth popped
open in a whoosh of breath, and before he could recover,
Roosevelt hit him with a jolting left-right combination. His
eyes went glassy and Roosevelt walloped him with a searing left hook. His legs buckled and he went down hard, flat
on his back. He was out cold.

A moment slipped past as everyone stared at the fallen
cowhand. Roosevelt inspected his skinned knuckles, then
poured himself another cup of coffee. He knew Jack Simpson could have stopped the fight, and his curiosity, now
tinged with anger, was aroused. He looked directly at the
Texan.

"What have we proved here tonight, Mr. Simpson?"

Simpson averted his gaze. "Well, like you said, Wally's
got a big mouth. Guess he'll keep it shut from now on."

"That's it, nothing more?"

"Nope, I reckon not."

Roosevelt thought he'd heard something less than the
truth. Yet there was nothing to be gained in pressing it further. Simpson clearly preferred to let it drop.

He wondered why.

The night wrangler brought the remuda to the edge of the
camp. Four cowhands, working on foot, strung lariats
around the horses and formed a boxlike enclosure. Other
hands stepped into the enclosure one at a time, lariats
whistling over their heads. They began roping their mounts
for the morning gather.

The sky was like dull pewter, dawn breaking over the
land. Some of the horses were frisky, fighting the saddle
and fighting harder once a man swung into the saddle. A
chestnut gelding brought a chorus of laughter when he
bucked off his rider and headed back to the remuda. The
rider grinned good-naturedly and took a bow.

Bob Hallett stepped into the makeshift corral. Roosevelt was so inept with a rope that Hallett had volunteered to catch his horse every morning. The arrangement at first amused the other cowhands, but after the fight with Wally Klaberg it was no longer a laughing matter. Hallett's lariat zinged through the air and the loop settled neatly over the neck of a dun gelding. He led the horse to where Roosevelt stood waiting with a saddle.

"Thank you, Bob," Roosevelt said. "I'll take it from here."

Hallett nodded. "Glad to help."

The dun was the gentlest horse in Roosevelt's string. He'd left Manitou at Elkhorn, for the blood bay was trained as a hunter rather than a cow pony. Sewall and Dow had been left behind as well, for neither of them was yet horseman enough to work a roundup. As he began saddling the dun, Roosevelt idly wondered how things were at Elkhorn. The roundup encampment would pass through there tomorrow on the way to the Eaton brothers' Slash E range. He thought he might take supper with Sewall and Dow.

A group of horsemen appeared in the dingy light. As he pulled the cinch tight, Roosevelt saw Gregor Lang in the vanguard. The Scotsman was accompanied by Harry Gorringe of the Circle G and Mike Boyce of the Three Seven, two of the largest cattlemen in the Badlands. John Eaton and Jack Simpson walked forward from the chuck wagon as the riders reined to a halt. Roosevelt hadn't seen them all together since the first day of roundup.

"Good morning, Theodore," Lang said, stepping out of the saddle. "We've come to requisition you from the gather."

Roosevelt sensed something strange in their manner. "Gentlemen," he said, nodding around at the group. "How may I assist you?"

"Let's have some coffee," Lang suggested. "We wish to discuss a matter in private."

The camp suddenly emptied as the cowhands rode out for the morning gather. A moment later, the wrangler choused the remuda back onto a spot of grazeland along the river. The group of cattlemen walked to the chuck wagon, where the cook scurried to provide clean cups and pour them coffee. He had no idea what the conclave was about and at a look from Simpson wisely chose to absent himself. He walked off in search of firewood.

The men stood blowing steam off their coffee. "Theodore, we have a problem," Lang finally said. "We've talked it over and hoped to avail ourselves of your counsel."

"Of course," Roosevelt replied. "What is the nature of the problem?"

"Horse thieves and cattle rustlers."

Lang went on to elaborate. After the first week of roundup it had become apparent that far too many cattle were missing. The number exceeded what any rancher might reasonably expect to lose from winter storms and predators, mainly wolves. There was no question that rustlers were responsible for the losses.

The problem was compounded by horse thieves. Lang nodded to Harry Gorringe, who explained that horses were stolen on a regular basis, whatever the season. There were gangs of thieves who raided throughout western Dakota, eastern Montana, and northwestern Wyoming. The thieves operated what amounted to an underground railway for stolen livestock.

"It's called the Outlaw Trail," Gorringe concluded. "They swap horses, alter the brands, and sell 'em off the home range. Lots of folks turn a blind eye when the price is right."

"Even run 'em into Canada," John Eaton added. "Ranchers up there don't give two hoots in hell that they're stolen. Hard to track stock once it's crossed the border."

"This Outlaw Trail?" Roosevelt asked. "What do you mean when you say they sell horses off the 'home range'?"

Gorringe wagged his head. "They're tricky devils. Horses stolen in the Badlands are sold in Montana, and stock from Montana gets sold here, or maybe Wyoming. Bastards swap herds and sell 'em somewheres else."

"Rather ingenious, isn't it?" Roosevelt said. "These thieves appear to be quite organized."

"No doubt about it," Eaton agreed. "Jake Paddock's most likely the head wolf around these parts. We heard you backed him down when he came callin' at Elkhorn."

"Oh?" Roosevelt looked surprised. "How did you hear that?"

"Bob Hallett's been braggin' about it to anybody that'd listen. Your man Sewall evidently told him the whole story."

"Took sand to brace Paddock," Gorringe interjected. "The story's also around how you whipped Wally Klaberg the other night."

Roosevelt turned his gaze on Jack Simpson. "A mystery solved," he said. "You had Klaberg challenge me to fight. May I ask why?"

"These boys weren't in on it," Simpson said, gesturing to the other ranchers. "I heard about Paddock and wanted to see if you really was a scrapper. Figured it was the thing to do before we asked you to volunteer."

"Jack, that's a helluva note," Gorringe said indignantly. "You had no call to go off on your own like that. We'd already agreed to ask Roosevelt."

"Ask me what?" Roosevelt demanded. "Why do you need a volunteer?"

Lang cleared his throat. "There is a rancher in Montana by the name of Granville Stuart. Have you heard of him?"

"No, Gregor, I am not familiar with the name."

"Stuart is a man of some influence. He has called a convention of cattlemen to be held the first week in June. His purpose is to form a coalition to combat rustlers and horse thieves."

"Quite commendable," Roosevelt said. "How does that involve me?"

"We want you to represent us," Lang said earnestly. "Someone has to be there, and we think you're the man. We took a vote on it."

Roosevelt suspected that Lang was the moving force be-

hind the vote. He recalled Lang once saying that the Badlands ranchers desperately needed a leader in their opposi-
tion to the Marquis de Mores. He saw now that Lang had
come at it another way.

"Why me?" he protested. "I'm rather new to the cattle
business. You need someone more experienced."

"We discussed that," Lang admitted. "But none of us
have your experience in dealing with complex issues, or
with men of power. And Granville Stuart is the most powerful cattleman in this part of the country."

"What is the source of his power?"

"Theodore, he runs some fifty thousand head of cattle.
No one but Stuart would have the audacity to convene a
convention of cattlemen . . . and know they will attend."

Roosevelt was intrigued despite himself. He'd heard of
Richard King and Charles Goodnight, Texans who owned
herds numbering more than one hundred thousand cows.
Granville Stuart sounded like a man of similar ambition
and unquestionably a man of forceful character. Perhaps a
man worth meeting.

"Where is the convention being held?"

"Miles City," Lang said. "One of the larger towns in
Montana."

"And you're quite certain of this, all of you? I wouldn't
otherwise presume to represent your views."

The men bobbed their heads in unison. Lang smiled
with genuine sincerity. "The vote was unanimous," he said.
"You are our only choice, Theodore."

"Very well," Roosevelt told them. "I will accept on two
conditions."

"What d'you mean?" Simpson said skeptically. "What
sort of conditions?"

"Gentlemen, in a convention of this nature, I will be
called upon to make decisions that affect us all. The first
condition is that you accept my judgment in the matter—
regardless of what I decide."

"Hell, that's fair," Simpson said. "We wouldn't have voted
for you unless we trust you. What's your other condition?"

"A supernumerary," Roosevelt replied. "I require a rancher of broader experience to accompany me to Miles City. I may well need the benefit of his advice."

"Good idea," Gorringe said. "Who'd you have in mind?"

"I believe that requires some consideration. I will let you know when I decide."

"So it's settled then?" Simpson insisted. "You'll take on the job?"

Roosevelt smiled. "I do believe I will."

Gregor Lang thought he was watching a master politician at work. All in a matter of minutes, a group of hard-headed ranchers had yielded their collective will to the judgment of one man. Then, with no debate whatever, they had agreed to let him select his own confidant. A coup of no small proportions.

Roosevelt was definitely the man for Miles City.

ELEVEN

The roundup crews steadily worked their way southward. Day by day the encampment was moved farther upriver, passing through Medora on a Sunday. The men looked longingly at the saloons, but Capt. Frank Osterhaut allowed no one to stop. The last week of roundup still lay ahead of them.

On May 20, eight miles south of Medora, the encampment moved onto the Maltese Cross range. Bill Merrifield took over as foreman of Roosevelt's crew as they camped in the shadow of Chimney Butte. Roosevelt was the owner and the Eaton brothers and Jack Simpson were still part of the crew, but Merrifield was nonetheless in charge. The Maltese Cross was his home spread.

The gather that morning collected almost a thousand cows of various brands. Over the winter cattle had drifted from range to range, and by noontime three separate herds were scattered along the river. The afternoon was devoted to roping calves and dragging them to the branding fires, where the men worked on them with swift efficiency. By now, after two weeks together, the teamwork among the men was almost rote.

Shortly before dusk the crew wandered back to the chuck wagon. Those who were mounted turned their ponies into the remuda, and every man selected a horse for night guard. Merrifield rode into camp just as Roosevelt finished saddling his night horse and tied the reins to the picket line. They were both caked in dust and grime, their shirts sticky with sweat. Roosevelt crossed the clearing as Merrifield stepped out of the saddle.

"A fine day's work," Roosevelt said. "I counted well over a hundred Maltese Cross calves."

"Things are lookin' good," Merrifield said, loosening the cinch on his horse. "I rode by the other camps this afternoon and took a rough count. Least three hundred calves, maybe a little more."

"Well, that is bully!"

"Yessir, I'd have to say I'm mighty pleased. Still got a day to go on Maltese and we're already in clover. Think we're gonna have a bumper crop this year."

Merrifield dropped his saddle on the ground. He swatted his horse on the rump, hazing it into the remuda, and roped a piebald gelding for his night horse. Roosevelt held the rope while Merrifield attached the bit and bridle and then reached for the saddle blanket. As he swung the saddle in place, he stopped and looked out at the westward skies. His features creased in a frown.

"What is it?" Roosevelt asked. "Something wrong?"

"Dunno yet." Merrifield tightened the cinch, his gaze still westward. "We might be in for a storm tonight."

"How can you tell?"

"Take a look at the sky."

The air was still and sultry, and dark clouds were massing beyond the buttes to the west. A brewing storm might move in any direction, for spring weather in the Badlands was unpredictable, clear one moment and raining the next. Yet the warm, fetid air gave Merrifield an uneasy feeling, since it often heralded the approach of a storm. He tied his horse to the picket line.

"Guess it wouldn't hurt to put the boys on notice."

Roosevelt nodded. "I subscribe to better safe than sorry."

"Yessir, specially with three herds in the valley. Be hell to pay if they took off runnin'."

The men were congregated around the chuck wagon.

Merrifield pointed out the darkening skies to the west and the faint scent of ozone in the air. "Have to wait and see," he said. "Wind might change and it'll turn out to be nothin'. Course it could just as easy keep headed our way."

"That'd be my bet," Simpson said. "Them clouds are comin' right along."

Merrifield scratched his jaw. "Think we're gonna double the night guard and hope for the best. Last thing we want's a bunch of spooked cows."

"Amen to that," Bob Hallett said. "I ain't one to borrow trouble."

"Me, neither," the cook added. "You boys quit your jaw-bonin' about the weather. Come and get it while it's hot."

The men needed no coaxing after a hard day's work. They formed a line, collecting plates and utensils from the end of the wagon, and filed past the fire. The cook loaded their plates with beefsteak, beans, sourdough biscuits, and glops of dried-apple cobbler from a small Dutch oven. The men helped themselves to coffee and took their usual places around the campfire. There was little conversation as they wolfed down the food.

Dark settled over the land by the time they finished supper. Merrifield was still sniffing the wind, and he decided to post the night guard earlier than usual. He picked four men for the first round, and they wearily trooped off toward the picket line. They were tired from fourteen hours in the saddle, and to stay awake during guard rounds some of them used a home remedy called rouser. A man first worked his chaw into a moist cud and then dabbed a touch of tobacco juice under his eyelid. One dose of rouser cured any thought of drowsiness.

The men left in camp stuck close to the fire. Those who smoked, fashioned roll-your-owns, and everyone helped themselves to a second cup of coffee. By now there was a camaraderie among the men, born of shared hardship, mishaps working cattle, and grueling days in the saddle. At night, lounging around the fire, they'd fallen into the habit of entertaining themselves by spinning tall tales. Over time it had become an ongoing contest, the idea being to concoct the biggest whopper. No lie was considered too audacious.

Tonight, Sam Jeeter spun a windy about roping a coyote, taming him of his wild ways, and training him to catch cottontail rabbits for supper. The men guffawed loudly, questioning Jeeter at length on how he'd trained a coyote to fetch. Not to be outdone, one of the Hash Knife hands unraveled a tale of trapping a rattlesnake and teaching him to shake his rattles in tune with the melody on a harmonica. The very idea of it brought snorts of laughter and a round of praise. Everyone declared his snake topped Jeeter's coyote.

Roosevelt laughed as loud as anyone. He'd never before entered into the competition, but tonight he decided to try a story of his own. "Let me tell you a true tale," he said when the laughter died down. "Are you men familiar with Andrew Jackson, the seventh president of the United States?"

"Why, sure," Hallett said. "He won some big battle or another down at New Orleans."

"Indeed he did," Roosevelt acknowledged. "Jackson was noted as a cantankerous man, ever in search of an argument. While serving as president, he hosted a dinner party one night at the White House."

The men exchanged glances, wondering where the tale was headed. "The wife of the English ambassador," Roosevelt went on, "was never one of Jackson's favorites. They got into a squabble and she became so upset that she said, 'Mr. President, if you were my husband I would poison your brandy.' Jackson looked her over and said, 'Madam, if you were my wife I would drink it.'"

The punch line didn't register for a moment. Simpson was the first to get it and broke out laughing, followed by Merrifield and the Eatons. The men liked their humor coarse rather than subtle, but one by one their tentative smiles turned to spirited laughter. The story was all the more amusing because until now everyone thought Roosevelt was as solemn as a church deacon. Jeeter cackled with high glee.

"By God, that's rich!" he said. "Ol' Andy Jackson would've drunk it if he had to bunk with her. Woman must've been a bitch on wheels."

"Knew one like that myself," Hallett said with a grin. "Ugliest whore ever worked a cathouse, warts and all. One look and your pecker went limp."

The men hooted and jeered, all of them familiar with ugly whores. The talk became general, centering on saloon girls in Medora, for no one felt they could top Roosevelt's story. Within the hour, with the men exhausted by their day's labors, the talk dwindled off and they began spreading their bedrolls. Roosevelt was pleased that his story had amused them, and as he crawled into his blankets he searched his mind for one he might tell tomorrow night. He went to sleep thinking of a wartime tale about Ulysses S. Grant.

Shortly before ten o'clock a sudden gust of wind swept through camp. The rush of air was like a gentle slap in the face, and every man in the crew was awake in an instant. A few seconds elapsed, and the herd of cows, already restless, turned their heads to the west, scenting the breeze. Then a dead calm settled over the valley and a crushing blast of heat buffeted the men.

"Get to your horses!" Merrifield shouted. "Head 'em off before they run!"

Roosevelt and the other men hurried toward the picket line. But even as they climbed aboard their horses, the herd started drifting south at a fast walk. The air abruptly went cool, ripe with the smell of ozone and rain, and the atmosphere was charged with electricity. The darkened sky came alive with a blinding light that turned the whole of the valley an eerie blue-white. A great streak of lightning flashed from the clouds and struck the ground, gathering itself into a ball of fire. The tumbling sunburst rolled across the prairie only to vanish in an explosion that shook the earth.

The herd stampeded as a clap of thunder reverberated over the land. Sparkling balls of static fire played across the tips of their horns and, as they ran, a wave of scorching heat clung in their wake. The drum of their hooves, and their terrified bellows, sent a quaking tremor ripping through the valley. Bolts of lightning lit the sky, and the roar of the wind swelled to a deafening pitch. With it came the rain, tearing and slashing as torrents of water deluged men and animals. Along the flanks of the seething mass of cattle the cowhands savagely quirted their horses, riding in a blind, mindless fury. Their one hope was to keep the herd in sight.

Before them, the other herds gathered on the holding ground were in full stampede. Roosevelt gigged his horse into a gallop, bending low in the saddle, only a short distance behind Merrifield. The storm, as quickly as it had started, was blown eastward on the wind; the jagged lightning bolts faded and the torrent of rain slowed to a misty drizzle. Merrifield and Roosevelt, joined by Hallett, passed the rear of the column, steadily gaining ground as the cattle hurtled through the valley. The sky suddenly cleared, as though wiped clean of clouds, and starlight bathed the land.

Some ten minutes later, the three men overtook the night guards. Still at a gallop, Merrifield loosened his lariat, edged his horse into the herd, and began popping the steers leading the charge. Close behind, Roosevelt and Hallett shouted and slashed with their lariats, crowding the cows to Merrifield's rear. The steers at the point began a sweeping curve to the west, forced to slow their pace as Merrifield pressed them into a tighter turn. The column curled, doubling back on itself, and the stampede dropped off to a shuffling turnabout. The herd milled into a mass of bawling, wild-eyed cows.

Merrifield quickly stationed the other hands around the herd. He turned to Roosevelt, who reined to a halt beside him. "We got lucky," he said. "We'd still be runnin' if that storm hadn't blown over."

"By Jove!" Roosevelt said, bristling with excitement. "I've never seen anything like it."

"You did good, Mr. Roosevelt. Anybody'd think you was a top hand."

"Oh, I seriously doubt that, Bill. I've yet to rope a cow, or a horse, either."

"Yeah, but you were damn sure here when we turned a stampede. Don't short yourself."

Roosevelt thought it was the laconic praise so typical of cattlemen. He made a mental note to include it in the book he was writing. Nothing stalwart or overly bold.

Perhaps a footnote on the hazards of a stampede.

Roundup ended on a prairie called Teepee Bottom, twenty miles south of the Maltese Cross. Over three weeks something more than thirty thousand cattle had been gathered from the basins and ravines of the Badlands. Everyone agreed it marked a banner year along the Little Missouri.

Teepee Bottom was at the southern edge of the Yule range. Lots were drawn to determine who would trail the remudas and the chuck wagons back to their respective home ranches. The losers moaned and cursed their misfortune, and the winners thanked their lucky stars. Forty men galloped off for Medora, awarded three days to guzzle whiskey and frolic with whores. None of them expected to be sober by nightfall.

Gregor Lang invited Roosevelt to stay the night at Yule headquarters. The other ranchers were anxious to return to their spreads, but Roosevelt was in no particular hurry. He felt confident Sewall and Dow could manage well enough at Elkhorn, and another day or so hardly seemed to matter. There was no pressing business at the Maltese Cross, but he told Merrifield he would stop by tomorrow and planned to spend the night. That left him free to accept Lang's invitation.

The sun quartered over into the western sky as they rode into Yule headquarters. Edith Lang and Lincoln, the Langs' son, greeted Roosevelt as though he were family. The vast distances separating neighbors in the Badlands made ranching life a lonely existence for women. Edith sometimes saw other ranchers' wives on the occasional shopping trip to Medora. But the visits were necessarily brief, and she was usually starved for social events of any nature. She welcomed Roosevelt into her home with a joy normally reserved for holidays.

Roosevelt and Lang hadn't bathed in three weeks. Edith playfully wrinkled her nose at their overripe odor and organized a battery of boiling pots on her cookstove. Linc, under his mother's supervision, spent the next hour ferrying buckets of hot water to the men's bedrooms. Lang changed into fresh clothes, and Roosevelt, who carried a clean shirt in his saddlebags, looked presentable after a sponge bath and a shave. Lang humorously remarked that most cowboys prided themselves on taking a bath only when it rained.

By the time the men returned to the parlor, Edith had whipped together a meal worthy of a celebration. The dining table was covered with white linen, and the place settings sparkled with crystal and china. She served a tender shoulder roast and an array of steaming vegetables from her summer canning. After three weeks of chuck wagon food, Roosevelt and Lang fell to it like trenchermen at an unexpected feast. Edith glowed under their compliments.

"Fit for kings!" Roosevelt declared, popping a slice of beet into his mouth. "Cuisine in every sense of the word."

"And quite fitting," Edith said with a smile. "After everything you two have been through on roundup. That terrible storm and the stampede. It must have been horrid."

"In all candor," Roosevelt confessed, "I must say it was one of the most exhilarating experiences of my life. A stampede has its dangers, to be sure. Nonetheless, it was absolutely stimulating."

Lang chuckled. "Bill Merrifield told us Theodore took to it like a wild Indian. He was quite high in his praise."

"Nothing really," Roosevelt said modestly. "I simply followed Bill to the front of the herd. He deserves all the credit."

Linc listened with rapt attention. "Wish I'd been there," he said, darting a glance at his father. "Dad wouldn't let me come along."

"Maybe next year, laddie," Lang said. "There's time enough being a man when you are grown. Enjoy your youth while it lasts."

"I'm sixteen," Linc said stubbornly. "Lots of boys go on roundup when they're my age. Mr. Gudgell's son was there!"

"Yes, that's true," Lang conceded. "But the Gudgell boy cannot quote Shelley or Keats, nor do his numbers. Your studies are more important than a roundup."

Roosevelt couldn't resist a pearl of advice. "When I was a boy," he said, "my father often remarked that nine-tenths of wisdom is to be wise in time, and at the right time." He paused, nodding to the boy. "Listen to your father, Linc. He's wise to insist on your education."

"Yessir, I guess so," Linc relented. "Just wish I'd been there for the stampede."

"Well, as your father said, there's always next year. You've time yet to be a cowboy. But first, be a scholar."

"Yeah, you're right; that Gudgell kid's thick as a brick. He thinks the *Iliad* is a river in Oregon."

The meal ended on a note of laughter. While Linc helped his mother wash the dishes, Lang and Roosevelt retired to the parlor. Once they were seated, Lang fired up his pipe in a blue cloud of smoke. He puffed a moment, then glanced at Roosevelt.

"Thank you, Theodore," he said. "Boys sometimes need reminding that their fathers are not tyrants. Linc respects you very much."

Roosevelt waved it off. "You're done a fine job schooling him, Gregor. Perhaps you could school me in another matter."

"Of course, anything at all."

"I leave for Miles City the end of the month. What can you tell me of Granville Stuart?"

"He's something of a legend," Lang said. "By all reports, he started with little more than a dream and built a cattle empire. The ranchers in Montana look to him for leadership."

"Which says a good deal," Roosevelt commented. "You've said he plans to form an alliance of cattlemen to combat the outlaw element. Do you think he intends to govern the alliance?"

"I wouldn't be at all surprised. From what I've heard, Stuart follows no star but his own."

"Men of influence often believe they are destined for the greater good. I look forward to meeting him."

"Have you decided who to take with you?"

"Jack Simpson," Roosevelt said without hesitation. "Of all the ranchers in the Badlands, I believe he is the most knowledgeable. Driving a herd from Texas speaks well of his credentials."

"Quite so," Lang agreed. "How do you feel he will be of assistance in Miles City?"

"Simpson has been a cattleman all of his life. I daresay there will be no surprises for him at this convention. I may well seek his advice."

"And if you shouldn't agree with his advice?"

"That will depend entirely on the situation. A river to be crossed, so to speak."

Lang smiled. "Spoken like a true diplomat."

"Hardly," Roosevelt said. "When I was a boy, my father taught me an axiom I've lived by. 'Speak softly and carry a big stick.'"

"That sounds somewhat philosophical, Theodore. What does it mean?"

"Never be overbearing to other men, and require the same courtesy of them. But if someone attempts to intimidate you, or wrongly impose his will on you, use the big stick with dispatch—and with a strong hand."

"Interesting," Lang said, puffing his pipe. "You are indeed the man to deal with Granville Stuart. You may find yourself two peas of the same pod."

"Nothing would please me more, Gregor. If so, we may well think alike."

Edith and Linc came in from the kitchen. Lang turned the conversation from business affairs and suggested that

Edith play something on the piano. Roosevelt was delighted, listening attentively, not at all surprised by her virtuosity. She played Bach and Chopin, then deftly sequed into popular tunes of the day. She ended with a haunting rendition of *"Beautiful Dreamer."* The men applauded her performance as though an audience of three at a concert. She smiled graciously and curtsied with old-world charm.

Later that night, as he was preparing for bed, Roosevelt's chipper mood suddenly deserted him. In a moment of dark reflection, he went back over the evening, from the dinner to the pleasant strains of the piano. The Langs had something he'd lost, the joy of family, the closeness of shared memory. A life so easily taken for granted . . . until it was gone.

Once he was in bed, Roosevelt lay staring at the ceiling. Elkhorn, the new house, the camaraderie of roundup, none of it was enough. For all his labors, despite the many projects, grief somehow reveled in catching him unawares. He thought he had it suppressed, under control; then it leaped out of nowhere, resurgent pain that stripped away any pretense of normalcy. He was reminded of something from *King Richard II,* the infinity of loss:

> *These external manners of laments*
> *Are merely shadows to the unseen grief*
> *That swells with silence in the tortur'd soul . . .*

Shakespeare knew too well the emptiness of a dead heart.

TWELVE

Miles City was something more than a hundred miles west of Medora. Roosevelt and Simpson stepped off the train on June 1, just as dusk settled over the town. They were traveling light, carrying warbags with shaving gear and a change of clothes. The convention was scheduled to last only one day.

A porter gave them directions from the depot to the hotel. As they turned uptown, a lamplighter moved from one post to the next, bathing the business district in a flickering glow. The street was lined with shops and stores, and a horse-drawn trolley car clanged along steel tracks. The first impression was one of a bustling plains community.

The town was located on the banks of the Yellowstone River. On the south side of the railroad line, saloons and gambling dens, dance halls and bawdy houses, composed a thriving vice district. Fort Keogh was two miles west, and on a summer evening soldiers and cowhands were routinely fleeced by the sporting crowd. Farther uptown, the business district was packed with stores and hotels, restaurants and banks, and two daily newspapers. The railroad had transformed a frontier outpost into a hub of trade.

Yet for all its citified elegance, Miles City was still very much a cowtown. Every summer, herds were trailed to the railhead from eastern Montana's vast cattle industry. A great deal of money exchanged hands with cattle brokers from Chicago, and in the process the town prospered. However progressive their outlook, everyone from store-keepers to whorehouse madams catered to cattlemen for the most basic of reasons. Cows were big business, the mainstay of Miles City's economic growth.

Roosevelt and Simpson turned into the Macqueen House, the largest hotel in town. The lobby was furnished with a couch and armchairs, and several men dressed in range clothes were huddled in conversation. The desk clerk was sallow and balding, with bottle-thick spectacles and a pinched expression. He looked up from a newspaper.

"Good evening," Roosevelt said. "We wired ahead for reservations. Theodore Roosevelt and Jack Simpson."

"Yessir," the clerk said. "Holding rooms for you on the second floor. Need your John Hancock in the ledger."

Roosevelt signed, waited for Simpson to scrawl his name, then nodded to the clerk. "We are here for the Montana Stockgrowers Association convention. Where will the meeting be held?"

"Main ballroom," the clerk replied. "Down the hall past the dining room. Set to start at eight tomorrow morning."

"How may I contact Mr. Granville Stuart? I wish to introduce myself this evening."

"Well, sir, I'm afraid you'll have to wait till tomorrow. Mr. Stuart left orders he wasn't to be disturbed."

"Nonetheless, please inform him we are in the hotel. Theodore Roosevelt and Jack Simpson, of Dakota Territory."

"Yessir, I'll see he gets the message."

The clerk gave them keys and they took the stairs to the second floor. After settling into their rooms, they came back downstairs and entered the dining room. Roosevelt was surprised to find braised pheasant on the menu, even more surprised that it was prepared with wild cherry sauce. Simpson ordered a blood-rare steak.

"Stuart's playin' the big man," Simpson said as the waiter moved away. "You'd think he'd make time to meet folks."

Roosevelt shrugged. "Perhaps he is preparing for the convention. We have a good deal of ground to cover in one day."

"Any idea what he's gonna say?"

"I've had no communication except what you and Gregor Lang told me. A unified front of some nature against rustlers and horse thieves."

"Well, he's done got my vote," Simpson noted. "What is it you want of me in this conflab? You haven't exactly said."

"I am a relative neophyte," Roosevelt informed him. "Something may arise which involves brand registration or cross-territorial roundups. I would value the benefit of your experience."

"Have you changed your mind about who makes the decisions? Do I get an equal vote?"

"The conditions of our agreement still stand. I will, however, consult with you on all decisions."

"Thought so," Simpson said in a dry voice. "Way I hear it, you're still callin' the shots. That about it?"

Roosevelt smiled humorously. "I couldn't have put it better myself."

After supper, Simpson suggested a drink in the hotel bar. Roosevelt begged off, saying he preferred a good night's sleep and a clear head for the convention. Simpson wryly observed that liquor never dulled his wits and he always slept better with a couple under his belt. Roosevelt bade him good night in the lobby and retired to his room. Simpson went on to the bar.

The next morning, they met for breakfast in the dining room. Simpson looked like a man bursting with news, and over bacon and eggs he related his night in the bar. He'd fallen in with a group of Montana ranchers, who were pleased to learn that Dakota Territory would be represented at the convention. When he asked them about Granville Stuart, it was as though he'd opened a spout. They bragged well into the night.

Granville Stuart had come west in 1849, one of many to join the California gold rush. Unlike many, he made a respectable fortune and worked the fields for five years. When the pay dirt played out, he drifted east, prospecting through Utah, and in 1858 he struck gold in Montana. For the next several years he followed the ore to various mining camps, and then settled in the town of Deer Lodge in 1867. He invested his money in what he envisioned as the new bonanza—beef.

The Bar S, over the next sixteen years, became the largest ranch in Montana. Apart from running fifty thousand cows, Stuart also branched out into mercantile stores, lumberyards, and politics. He was first elected to the territorial legislature in 1879, and only last year, in 1883, he was elevated to president of the legislature. The territorial governor, a political appointee with friends in Washington, soon discovered that the power broker in Montana was a cattleman turned politician. Such was the legend of Granville Stuart.

"Talk about the top dog," Simpson concluded. "When he barks, they all howl at the moon."

"I daresay," Roosevelt remarked. "Your trip to the bar paid rather handsome dividends."

"Whiskey makes men gabby, specially when they're in a braggin' mood."

"So it would appear."

Roosevelt felt it was valuable information. Money and politics, as he'd learned from years in public life, was a powerful combination. He understood now why Stuart's reputation was known even to ranchers in Dakota Territory. Perhaps more to the point, he understood that Stuart would prevail in any discussion at today's convention. The Montana Stockgrowers Association would follow where it was led.

The convention was something less than advertised. Though there were thirty or more members of the Montana Stockgrowers Association, there were only eight ranchers in the hotel ballroom. Granville Stuart was in his late fifties, clearly a man of iron nerve, with piercing eyes and the bearing of someone accustomed to being obeyed. He greeted each of the ranchers with a firm handshake and a square-jawed smile, addressing them on a first-name basis. He seemed particularly pleased to see Roosevelt and Simpson.

"Mr. Roosevelt. Mr. Simpson," he said affably. "We're certainly glad to have Dakota represented. You're most welcome here."

"Thank you," Roosevelt said. "On behalf of our fellow ranchers, we are delighted to be here. We appreciate the invitation."

"Well, come right in and find yourselves a seat. We'll get the meeting started."

Four tables, draped with dark cloth, were joined to form a rectangle. Roosevelt and Simpson took chairs at the end table, nearest the door. Stuart walked to the head table and remained standing, facing the ranchers. His expression was somber.

"We've got serious business to discuss," he said. "You men are here at my personal invitation, and whatever's said here stays in this room. Anybody who can't abide by the rules is free to leave now."

None of the men opted to leave. Stuart launched into an impassioned review of depredations by the outlaw element. He noted that losses of livestock were crippling cattlemen in both Montana and Dakota and the losses grew heavier every year. Horse thieves and cattle rustlers, he observed, conducted their raids with virtual impunity. The chances of getting caught were practically nil.

The Outlaw Trail, he went on, stretched from southern Dakota to the Canadian border. The thieves held the advantage because they were organized, large gangs that operated in force and they were willing to fight to avoid capture. Law enforcement officers, on the other hand, were few in number, separated by long distances, and hesitant to tangle with gangs of killers. The end result was that cattlemen suffered intolerable losses.

"Here's what I propose," Stuart told them. "We organize a band of vigilantes that will operate in absolute secrecy. Only the men in this room will know the details."

Cal Nutt, one of the ranchers, leaned back in his chair. "Granville, there'd have to be more men brought into it. We can't carry the fight all by our lonesome."

"Everyone here has men on their payroll they can trust. We will enlist their services and pay them a bonus for rough work. We'll have no trouble raising forty or fifty men who can keep their mouths shut."

"Awright, lemme ask you this," Nutt said. "What happens when we catch a horse thief or rustler? Do we turn 'em over to the law?"

"We do not," Stuart said shortly. "We shoot first and ask questions about stolen stock later. Any outlaw captured alive will be hung on the spot."

There were murmurs of assent from the men around the tables. Roosevelt waited until the buzz dropped off. "Mr. Stuart, I cannot agree," he said. "You are advocating taking the law into your own hands. The ranchers of Dakota Territory will not be party to such action."

Simpson started to speak, but Roosevelt silenced him with a look. Stuart stared at them for a long moment. "Think about this, Mr. Roosevelt," he said. "Unless we stamp out these outlaws, the situation will only grow worse. We have no choice but to act."

"Everyone has choices, Mr. Stuart. Outlaws who are captured could just as easily be turned over to the proper authorities."

"And I say to you that horse thieves and rustlers fear nothing but the rope. They will not stop until we've hanged a goodly number from the nearest tree. The law cannot solve our problem."

"On the contrary," Roosevelt countered. "Summary justice is little short of anarchy. The law must prevail."

The room fell silent. Stuart's eyes hooded in a look of menace. "We are at an impasse," he said in a measured voice. "You agreed to keep our discussion here today private and confidential. Will you honor your word?"

"You have no need for concern, Mr. Stuart. I am duty bound to report to my fellow ranchers in Dakota. But I tell you now, they will not be happy with my decision. They may well vote to join your vigilantes."

Roosevelt stood. He nodded curtly to Stuart and walked out of the room. Simpson hurried after him and fell in alongside as they headed for the lobby. He darted a glance back over his shoulder.

"Lucky you didn't get us shot. Those boys weren't whistlin' in the dark. They're dead serious."

"Jack, you may well have a point. I think the next train out of town would be highly prudent."

Later, as the train pulled out of Miles City, Roosevelt was struck by the irony of the situation. Granville Stuart was the most powerful man in Montana and, by virtue of his position in the legislature, the chief lawmaker. Yet he was perfectly willing to break the law when it suited his own ends.

Somehow, and there was the irony, it sounded like a medieval tale penned by an embittered monk. One law for the king and another for the people.

Streamers of sunlight flooded the room. The windows were open, and noise from street traffic drifted on a warm summer breeze. The town was always a hubbub of activity on a Saturday.

Roosevelt stood at the washstand. His face was lathered with soap and he peered at himself in the mirror. He carefully shaved around his mustache and side-whiskers with a bone-handled straight razor. When he finished, he rinsed the razor in a porcelain bowl and dried his face, He began trimming his mustache with a set of small, curved scissors.

The room over the Medora Hardware & Emporium was comfortably furnished. There was a bed against the rear wall, a dresser and wardrobe along another wall, and a modest desk he'd ordered through the store. He kept a suitable change of clothes for when he was in town, and Manitou was stalled at the livery stable. A local widow woman came in once a week to clean the room.

On June 2, eight days ago, Roosevelt and Simpson had returned from Miles City. Roosevelt had visited the Maltese Cross and Elkhorn in the interim and dispatched riders across the Badlands. The message they carried was a summons to ranchers to attend a meeting in Medora this afternoon. Apart from reporting on his decision about Granville Stuart, he intended to put before them a far-reaching proposal. He still wasn't entirely comfortable with what he planned.

On the train back to Medora, Roosevelt had deliberated the matter at length. He arrived at the conclusion that the Badlands ranchers didn't need Granville Stuart or the Montana Stockgrowers Association. By forming their own association, they could better contend with rustlers and horse thieves who preyed on their herds. Yet simply by offering the proposal he went against his determination to live a secluded life at Elkhorn. He rationalized by telling himself that a man was bound to work toward the common good. Duty would permit nothing less.

Still, if he was to do it, he meant to have all the pieces in place. As he trimmed his mustache, he considered his decision to invite the Marquis de Mores to the meeting. De Mores owned a ranch, albeit one he'd virtually stolen, and to exclude him would merely antagonize the town's leading citizen. Roosevelt's ulterior motive was somewhat more Machiavellian, for he believed in the axiom that it was wiser to stay close to one's enemies. He intended to use de Mores as a conduit to Jake Paddock and the lawless element. The theft of livestock was about to become a risky proposition.

Roosevelt left the room shortly after nine o'clock. He ate in a café across the street and then proceeded on to the Metropolitan Hotel. Earlier in the week he'd hired the hotel dining room for the morning lull between breakfast and lunch. The dining room would be used for his meeting, with the doors closed to the public and the waiters banished to the kitchen. The ranchers had been notified in advance by his riders as to time and place, and he sent a written invitation to de Mores. He was ready to present his argument.

The dining room was already full when he arrived. There were some twenty ranchers, most of them men he'd met on spring roundup. De Mores was at one of the tables, and seated nearby were Lang, Simpson, the Eaton brothers, and Harry Gorringe. Roosevelt was pleased to see as well Mike Boyce of the Three Seven outfit, Arthur Huidekoper of the Box H, and Luther Gudgell of the O.X. He exchanged nods with several of the men, noting that the small ranchers were at some pains to keep their distance from de Mores. He halted in the middle of the room.

"Thank you for coming," he said, turning to look at everyone in the group. "By now most of you know that Jack Simpson and I traveled to Miles City to meet with Granville Stuart. The result of our meeting was not positive."

Roosevelt went on to elaborate. He related that Stuart was organizing a band of vigilantes, their purpose to track down and hang livestock thieves. In a forceful voice, he explained that summary justice—lynch law—was the resort of those who believed the end justified the means. He told them he had refused to enlist the Badlands ranchers in Stuart's cause.

There was a dark muttering among some of the men. "You may vote to overturn my decision," Roosevelt said, silencing them with an upraised hand. "But before it comes to that, I wish to propose an association of our own. A joint effort to rid the Badlands of outlaws and thieves."

The boldness of the proposal claimed their attention. In the past, some of the ranchers had bandied about the idea of forming a cattllemen's association. But it was loose talk, idle conversation, and no one had stepped forward to lead them in a spirit of unity. They waited to hear if Roosevelt was that man.

For the next half hour, Roosevelt hammered home the points. He envisioned an organization that would formulate and enforce laws for the regulation of the cattle industry. He spoke of the organization as a cohesive rallying point for law and order in a sparsely settled country where outlaws roamed at will. In hard terms, he argued that vigilantism was mob rule, beneath civilized men, and that outlaws should be brought to trial in a court of law. His eyes burning, he smacked a fist into his palm.

"Unite and govern ourselves!" he said vigorously. "I propose we call it the Little Missouri Stockgrowers Association."

Jack Simpson, surprisingly, was the first man on his feet. "I tell you boys," he said earnestly, "I thought Roosevelt was dead wrong in Miles City. But he's brought me around to seein' things his way. We gotta have law and order or we're no better'n horse thieves."

"Exactly so!" Lang said in his thick Scottish burr. "And I nominate Theodore Roosevelt for president of our new association. Let us be guided by a voice of reason."

"Gregor, I must decline," Roosevelt said quickly. "There are men far better suited than I to such work. I have no experience in pursuing lawbreakers."

Lang wagged his head. "None of us here are lawmen. If not you, then who's to lead us?"

"Allow me to volunteer." De Mores rose from his chair, shoulders squared. "A military background will serve our cause well, and I am a graduate of Saint-Cyr. I will lead the fight against these thieving brigands."

No one jumped to second his self-nomination. The general feeling in the room was that de Mores, through his connection with Paddock, was aligned with the thieves. Lang again put Roosevelt's name forth, and Simpson, backed by others, voiced their approval. Roosevelt adamantly protested, but the men laughingly shouted him down, and he finally shrugged acceptance. By acclamation, they voted him president of the Little Missouri Stockgrowers Association.

De Mores appeared disgruntled by the defeat. Yet he nonetheless brought the first motion to the floor before the assembled ranchers. He argued strenuously that the fledgling association still needed a stock inspector, someone to check the brands of cows being shipped by rail from Medora. He went on to say that Joe Morrill, who currently held the job, should be retained because he worked on behalf of all cattlemen. There was little discussion, for the ranchers seemed generally satisfied with Morrill's performance. The motion carried by a vote of 18–3.

The meeting ended with Lang, Simpson, Gudgell, and John Eaton being elected to the board of directors. They were charged with drafting bylaws and formulating plans for a campaign against cattle rustlers and horse thieves. Lang stayed behind when the other ranchers, along with de Mores, drifted off to conduct their usual Saturday business. Roosevelt gave him a bemused look.

"Gregor, I have every reason to be displeased with you. I hardly sought a position of such responsibility."

"I can think of no one better suited for the job, Theodore. You inspire confidence in men, and that quality is essential to leadership. We've done well here today."

Lang reflected that Roosevelt represented all that was good in progress and reform. De Mores, on the other hand, was an aristocratic schemer without moral compass. One advocated privilege for the few while the other championed the equality of all men. Lang sensed a struggle for supremacy had begun here today.

"Who is Joe Morrill?" Roosevelt asked. "I wasn't aware Medora has a stock inspector."

Lang pulled a face. "Morrill was once the deputy town marshal of Deadwood. A year or so ago, de Mores convinced everyone to hire him as our stock inspector." He paused, arched an eyebrow. "I voted against him today because I do not trust him. He owes his job to de Mores."

"A year certainly makes a difference," Roosevelt said. "When I was last here, de Mores wasn't involved with Paddock or the criminal element. Are you saying Morrill is part of their enterprise?"

"I have no proof of any wrongdoing. I'm simply saying his allegiance is to de Mores."

"Well, then, forewarned is forearmed. We must keep an eye on the fellow."

Roosevelt led the way out of the dining room. As they moved into the lobby, a gangly young man with a mop of ginger hair rushed through the door. He spotted Lang and skidded to a halt, pulling a pad and pencil from his coat pocket. He was the editor and publisher of the *Badlands Cowboy* and his name was Amos Packard. Lang performed the introductions.

"Pleasure to meet you, Mr. Roosevelt," Packard said with the look of a reporter hot on a story. "I've just heard that you've formed a cattlemen's association. I was hoping you might give me a quote."

"Very well," Roosevelt replied. "You may quote me as saying justice will be meted out to badmen and desperadoes. The law will henceforth be enforced."

"Our readers will love that! When do you plan to move against the outlaws?"

"Within the fortnight, perhaps sooner."

"What is your attitude toward lawbreakers?"

"No quarter asked, none given."

"Do you intend to hang them?"

"I intend to put them behind bars."

"What have you got against hanging?"

"It ends too quickly," Roosevelt said with a smile. "Prison is far closer to Hades."

"Great stuff!"

Packard hurried out, scribbling furiously in his notepad. Roosevelt turned to Lang. "Tell me," he said. "Does that eager beaver also work for de Mores?"

"No, Theodore," Lang said. "Amos Packard is the bravest man in Medora, or the most foolhardy. He reports the truth."

"Bully!" Roosevelt woofed. "Small wonder I liked him."

Lang thought it was only the first of many quotes in the *Badlands Cowboy*. Theodore Roosevelt was about to become big news.

THIRTEEN

Dawn broke over the cottonwoods and limned the camp in a dusky blue halo. The night damp, strongest at first light, filled the air with a crisp earthen smell. The sky slowly brightened as the last vestiges of dark fled the day.

Roosevelt sat up in his bedroll. He tossed the blanket aside and stood, stretching with a wide yawn. Around him the other men awakened, scratching and grumbling as the camp stirred to life. Their horses dozed at a picket line in the trees.

The men were some twenty miles west of Medora. Two days ago Mike Boyce had sent a rider to summon Roosevelt from Elkhorn. Horse thieves had raided the Three Seven outfit, and one of Boyce's cowhands had tracked them to a remote cabin in the western Badlands. Boyce was inclined to hang them but then remembered he was now part of an association. He waited instead for Roosevelt.

Their camp was along a wooded stream. The thieves' cabin was a mile or so farther on, located where the stream emptied into a broad canyon. Late yesterday, Roosevelt, Boyce, and five cowhands had ridden west from the Three Seven headquarters, halting just before sundown. The risk of a raid in the dark was too great, and they'd made a cold camp for the night. They planned to strike shortly after sunrise.

Roosevelt was in high spirits. The Little Missouri Stockgrowers Association had been formed five days ago, and to-day marked the first assault on the outlaw gangs. He was particularly pleased that Mike Boyce had delayed taking action until he could make his way west from Elkhorn. He thought it important that the head of the association take part in the first raid and even more important that the operation result in arrests. He wanted to send a strong message to thieves thoughout the Badlands.

Last night Roosevelt had ordered a cold camp. Wind shifts were unpredictable, and smoke from a fire might easily drift downstream and alert the gang. He rummaged inside his saddlebags and, like the other men, made a hasty breakfast on beef jerky and creek water. His nerves were on edge, which served to sharpen his wits, and it occurred to him that a manhunt was similar to a hunt for wild creatures. The element of surprise was key, particularly when the quarry could shoot back. He meant to take them unawares.

Roosevelt gathered the men for a final war council. The cowhands were on Boyce's payroll, but everyone understood who was in charge of the operation. Roosevelt looked around at them in the pale light.

"I thought about it overnight," he said. "I've decided we will proceed on foot. Surprise is our most vital ally."

"What if they run?" Boyce asked. "Them mounted and us on foot would make a damn poor race. We'd lose 'em for sure."

"No matter how careful, the sound of hooves carries on a quiet morning. Even more risky, one of our horses might whinny and alert their horses. We cannot afford to lose the element of surprise."

"Are you plannin' to storm their cabin?"

Roosevelt nodded to Ned Adair, the cowhand who had tracked the stolen horses. "Ned, if you will," he said, "review the situation one last time. Where is their cabin located?"

Adair took a stick and began drawing in the dirt. "The creek runs into the canyon," he said, scratching a line. "The cabin's 'bout fifty yards from where we come into the canyon, and the corral's this side of the cabin. There's trees all along the creek."

"All working to our advantage." Roosevelt sketched in the dirt with his finger. "We will assume positions on the south side of the stream, facing the cabin. I believe you said there were four men."

"Yessir, that's all I seen."

"We will wait until they are outside, on open ground. I prefer not to rush the cabin if at all possible."

"And when they come outside?" Boyce said. "What's your plan then?"

"The situation will dictate our actions," Roosevelt said. "Follow my command, and remember that I wish to take them alive. Our purpose is to deliver them to the authorities."

"And if they start shootin'?"

"Protect yourselves at all costs."

Roosevelt pulled his Winchester from the saddle scabbard. Boyce nodded to the men, and they collected their carbines from where their saddles were scattered around the campsite. Ned Adair led the way since he had scouted the terrain while tracking the stolen horses. Roosevelt followed him, with Boyce and the men strung out behind, and they moved past the horses into the trees. The only sound was the soft jingle of their spurs.

Some twenty minutes later they sighted the canyon. Overhead, a hawk floated past on smothered wings, veered into the wind, and settled high on a cottonwood beside the stream. The bird sat perfectly still, a feathered sculpture flecked with burnt amber and bronzed ebony in the flare of a fiery sunrise. Then, with the lordly hauteur of taloned killers, it cocked its head in a fierce glare and looked down upon the intruders.

Roosevelt signaled a halt where the creek emptied into the canyon. The cabin was a crude log structure, one window glittering in the sunlight, a wisp of smoke spiraling from the chimney. Yet the first thing the men noticed was the corral, where only four horses stood rather than the nineteen stolen

from the Three Seven ranch. There was a whispered conference, with Ned Adair assuring Roosevelt and Boyce he'd led
them to the right place. Which left the question of the horses.

"Swear to Christ!" Adair muttered. "This here's where I
tracked 'em."

"That was two days ago," Boyce said angrily. "Looks to
me like somebody's been here and gone and our horses are
somewheres on the Outlaw Trail. We've come up short."

"Not altogether," Roosevelt said. "There are four horses
in the corral, which means our thieves are in the cabin. I intend to capture them."

Boyce snorted. "What're we gonna charge 'em with?
Don't see none of my stock down there."

"I'll think of something."

Roosevelt took the lead. The men ghosted through the
trees as the sun cleared the horizon in an orange ball of
fire. They skirted the creek along the southern bank, taking
cover behind the trunks of cottonwoods, and spread out in
line. Their carbines were trained on the cabin.

Nothing happened for perhaps a half hour. Then, just as
the wait seemed interminable, a wad of smoke spouted
from the chimney. A moment later the door opened and a
man with a soup-strainer mustache stepped from the
cabin. He was dressed in boots and pants, filthy long johns
covering his chest and a pistol strapped to his hip. He
walked to the creek, unbuttoned his pants, and pulled out
his pud. He began relieving himself with a look of wolfish
bliss.

A second man emerged from the cabin. He was followed by a third and fourth, all of them half-dressed and
armed with pistols. Roosevelt watched from behind a tree,
somehow intrigued that outlaws went armed even when attending to their morning toilet. The three men joined the
first at the creek, their mouths working in jaw-cracking
yawns as they stood at the edge of the grassy bank. One of
them loosed a loud fart in the morning stillness.

"Hands up!"

Roosevelt stepped from behind the tree. His sharp command froze the four men directly across the creek. For a moment the tinkling sound went on, water splashing water, then died with the suddenness of a faucet cut off. In the next instant, the man with the sweeping mustache let go his pud and grabbed for his holstered pistol. Boyce appeared beneath the leafy overhang of a cottonwood, a Winchester carbine at his shoulder, and fired. The heavy slug struck the outlaw in the chest, his dirty long johns bright with blood. He pitched face forward into the creek.

"Stand steady!" Roosevelt ordered. "We've no wish to kill you!"

The men stood motionless, their pants still unbuttoned. Boyce and the cowhands emerged from the trees, their carbines at the ready. Roosevelt motioned them forward and they waded through the stream, water lapping at the top of their boots. They surrounded the three outlaws.

"Drop your gun belts," Roosevelt said sharply. "And make yourselves decent."

The men hastened to obey. They carefully unbuckled their gun belts and dropped them on the ground. Then, like naughty schoolboys, they sheepishly tucked themselves away and buttoned their pants. Boyce inspected the man lying facedown in the creek, confirming with a nod that he was dead. Roosevelt wagged the snout of his Winchester at the other men.

"You are under arrest," he said. "The charge is stealing horses."

"You're off your rocker," one of the men said sullenly. "We ain't stole nothin'."

"What is your name?"

"Smith."

"A likely sobriquet," Roosevelt said skeptically. "In any case, Mr. Smith, we tracked the horses to your doorstep. I believe that will suffice."

"Won't hold water," Smith retorted. "Only four horses in that corral, and they're ours. You ain't got shit for proof."

"Hate to say it," Boyce interjected, "but he's right, Mr. Roosevelt. We'd play hell gettin' a conviction in a court of law. I vote we hang 'em and be done with it."

Roosevelt feigned a thoughtful expression, as though weighing the idea. Smith and the other two men knew the penalty for horse stealing was a knotted rope over a stout limb. They sensed Roosevelt was the leader here, and they watched him, their features taut, as he deliberated their fate. His gaze finally settled on them.

"You have a choice," he said. "Leave the Badlands forever, or we will hang you now."

"No choice about it," Smith said, faint with relief. "We'll clear out quick as we saddle our horses."

"Your saddles are forfeit, Mr. Smith. You will leave here bareback and barefoot. Off with your boots."

"What the hell you talkin' about?"

"Your destination," Roosevelt said. "I understand Deadwood is overrun with thieves and robbers. You will be among your own kind."

"Whoa now!" Smith protested. "Deadwood's a couple hundred miles from here, and bareback's bad enough. How we gonna ride all that way without boots?"

"I would recommend you be careful where you dismount. Avoid rough ground."

"No gawddamn way we're gonna do that. Ain't civilized to make a man go barefoot."

Roosevelt stared at him. "I suggest you reconsider, Mr. Smith. The alternative would be most unpleasant."

"Roy, shut your trap," one of the other men muttered. "Let's get while the gettin's good."

Ten minutes later, barefoot and bareback, the three outlaws rode south into the Badlands. Boyce and the cowhands were of mixed emotions, amused by the unusual punishment but saddened they'd missed a hanging. Roosevelt seemed quite satisfied with the outcome.

Boyce shook his head. "Them boys are gonna be crippled by the time they hit Deadwood. Hell, it's almost worse'n being hung."

"Indeed," Roosevelt said. "Do you approve?"

"Well, sir, I think it's gonna make one helluva fine story. Horse thieves are liable to get lots more careful."

Roosevelt smiled. "Yes, I daresay they will."

ELEVEN MEN HANGED IN MONTANA

The *Badlands Cowboy* carried the story on the front page. The article was reprinted from the *Daily Gazette*, of Billings, Montana, and reported that eleven men, accused of livestock theft, had been hanged within the past two weeks. The identity of the vigilantes was unknown.

Roosevelt rode into Medora on Friday evening. He was still elated with events of the day, having exiled the horse thieves to Deadwood just that morning. After leaving Manitou at the livery stable, he walked uptown to the hotel for supper. Newspapers were available at the desk, and the headline caught his eye as he moved through the lobby. He bought a copy.

The dining room was almost empty. He seated himself at a table and ordered the blue-plate special: meat loaf with potatoes and gravy. When the waiter turned away, Roosevelt unfolded the paper and began reading. The eleven men had been hanged in three separate incidents, with no witnesses, notes left pinned to the bodies identifying them as cattle rustlers and horse thieves. The hangings had occurred on roadside telegraph poles near towns.

The identity of the vigilantes was no mystery to Roosevelt. Yet he was shocked that Granville Stuart and the Montana ranchers had moved with such dispatch, for he had met with them hardly a fortnight past. The fact that the hanged men had been executed near towns seemed to Roosevelt diabolically calculated, designed to attract the attention of newspapers and publicize a warning to livestock thieves. With no witnesses, he thought it probable that the hangings had taken place at night. Deadly business conducted in the dark.

The waiter returned with his meat loaf. As he ate, Roosevelt pondered what might have happened if he'd joined in Stuart's conspiracy. He had no doubt that Badlands ranchers, left to their own devices, would gladly hang every thief they caught. Gregor Lang and a few others might prove the exception, but the majority subscribed to the atavistic belief that livestock thieves, along with murderers and rapists, deserved the rope. There was always the chance that members of the Little Missouri Stockgrowers Association might be infected by the mentality of Stuart's vigilantes. He cautioned himself to be wary of dissension.

Over a second cup of coffee Roosevelt glanced through the newspaper. On the fourth page a headline caught his attention: COWBOY CHARGED WITH RUSTLING. The article reported that Joe Morrill, the association's stock inspector, had brought charges of cattle rustling against George Myers, a cowhand who worked for the Maltese Cross. According to Morrill, the cowboy had shipped eight steers by rail to a Chicago slaughterhouse and two of the steers were unbranded, which meant ownership could not be established. Morrill had filed papers at the courthouse in Mandan for an arrest warrant on Myers.

Roosevelt was surprised that a cowhand in the employ of any ranch was allowed to own cattle. The conflict of interest was obvious, and he was even more surprised that Bill Merrifield permitted such a practice. But he found it stranger still that an article on cattle rustling, alleged or otherwise, had been buried on page 4 rather than being bannered on the front page. The reason became evident when he read further and saw that Amos Packard, the editor, had openly excoriated Morrill, insinuating that the stock inspector had an ulterior motive, as yet unknown. Otherwise, why hadn't Morrill quarantined the steers rather than allowing them to be loaded on a boxcar? Why had he waited to file charges until the evidence—the two unbranded steers—had been shipped to Chicago?

The questions, Roosevelt told himself, were the crux of the matter. To people in cattle country, an accusation charging a man with rustling carried a stigma almost as onerous as a conviction. There was suspicion as well about the ranch that employed an accused rustler, for if a man was stealing cows, the outfit he worked for might be in the same business. The outfit in this case was the Maltese Cross, which made it all the more personal for Roosevelt. He decided he needed to have a talk with Merrifield, though the central question still nagged at him as he paid the bill and walked from the dining room. Why hadn't Morrill brought the charges *before* the steers were shipped?

Merrifield always came into town on Saturday to order supplies for the ranch. Early the next morning, Roosevelt left word with Joe Ferris to send Merrifield to his room over the store. An hour or so later, while he was trying to finish a chapter for his new book, someone knocked on the door. He opened it to find Merrifield on the landing.

"Come in, Bill," he said. "We need to have a word about something."

"Wouldn't doubt it," Merrifield said, moving into the room. "Guess you heard about George Myers?"

"Yes, I read the article in the newspaper. I wasn't aware our men were permitted to own stock."

"Well, it's sort of an unwritten rule here in the Badlands. A man's been on the payroll two years, he's allowed to run twenty cows. Course, he's gotta have his own brand."

"I see," Roosevelt said. "Is this a common practice?"

"Hardly ever happens," Merrifield noted. "Cowboys are a fiddle-footed bunch, mostly drift from spread to spread. Them that sticks two years get to own a few cows."

"A reward for loyalty?"

"Yessir, that's about the size of it."

Roosevelt nodded. "What do you know of this charge against Myers?"

"Joe Morrill's a black liar," Merrifield said pointedly. "The two steers he's talking about came wanderin' in after we finished roundup, and that's why they weren't branded. They belong to Myers."

"Then why would Morrill lodge a complaint?"

"You want my personal opinion?"

"Yes, of course."

"The Marquis," Merrifield said flatly. "First he tried to run you off Elkhorn, and then you beat him out for head of the Stockgrowers Association. Morrill's his man, and it's payback time."

"How so?" Roosevelt asked. "What does de Mores have to gain?"

"Hell's bells and little fishes, Mr. Roosevelt! He's tryin' to dirty your name with trumped-up charges against George Myers. Old story of guilt by association."

Roosevelt made a mental note to remember the inventive curse. *Hell's bells and little fishes* had a certain ring to it. He brought his attention back to Merrifield. "Do you really believe de Mores would stoop so low?"

"Everybody in town believes it, includin' Amos Packard. That's why he wrote what he did in the newspaper—about Morrill's motive."

"Gregor Lang warned me about Morrill."

"The Marquis says 'frog' and Morrill squats. Ain't no doubt about it."

Roosevelt considered a moment. "Bill, I want you to circulate through town. Find Lang, Simpson, Gudgell, and John Eaton. Inform them that I am holding a board meeting at three this afternoon, in the hotel dining room." He paused, thoughtful. "And one other thing."

"Yessir?"

"Inform Morrill that I have ordered him to appear. I would like you there as well."

"What're you aimin' to do?"

"I intend to weed out the riffraff."

Merrifield was able to find only Lang and Eaton. But with Roosevelt present, three out of five board members constituted a quorum. By three o'clock they were seated in the hotel dining room, empty now of customers and the waiters confined to the kitchen. Merrifield was seated off to one side.

The door opened and de Mores entered, followed by Joe Morrill. De Mores glanced from Roosevelt to Merrifield, then walked to where the board members were gathered around a table. He nodded pleasantly.

"Gentlemen," he said. "I understand you have convened an emergency board meeting. May I inquire the purpose?"

"No, sir, you may not," Roosevelt said levelly. "You are not a member of the board."

"Even so, I am a member of the Stockgrowers Association. I have every right to know your purpose."

"You will be duly advised when the board has acted. Now, you will please leave the room. This is a closed meeting."

"You cannot order me from here."

"I have just done so."

De Mores glowered at him a moment, then turned and stalked out of the room. Morrill seemed uncertain whether to stay or go and finally removed his hat. He was a lean man, with beady eyes and a reputation for being quick with a gun. Roosevelt motioned him to a chair.

"We are here," Roosevelt said, "to inquire into the allegations you've brought against George Myers. Would you care to explain yourself?"

"Nothin' to explain," Morrill said. "Myers shipped two unbranded steers, and I filed for an arrest warrant. They weren't his cows."

"How did you establish that fact?"

"Well, it didn't take a whole lot of brains. Like I said, they weren't branded."

Roosevelt looked across the room. "Mr. Merrifield, what have you to say about this?"

"Load of hogwash," Merrifield replied. "I saw Myers cut those cows out myself. I'm here to swear they were his."

"Thank you." Roosevelt turned back to Morrill. "Before acting so precipitously, why didn't you make inquiry at the Maltese Cross? Why didn't you quarantine the steers and wait to talk with Mr. Merrifield?"

"Didn't see no need," Morrill said. "Man sells unbranded stock, he's dealin' in stolen goods. Anybody knows that."

"If so, why did you wait until he had shipped the steers to request an arrest warrant? Your evidence, Mr. Morrill, is now in a Chicago slaughterhouse."

"What, you're gonna take Merrifield's word over mine? I'm your stock inspector."

"You, sir, are a blackguard," Roosevelt said evenly. "And as of now, you are no longer the stock inspector. You are herewith discharged."

"Watch yourself," Morrill said coldly. "You fire me and you're lookin' for trouble. Damn fast, too."

John Eaton shifted forward in his chair. "Listen to me real close, Morrill. Anything happens to Roosevelt and you ain't safe nowhere. We'll stretch your goddamn neck."

"In point of fact," Lang added, "you are posted from Medora and the Badlands, effective immediately. Leave town today."

Morrill's features twisted in an ugly scowl. He knew it was no idle threat, that they would hunt him down and kill him if he harmed Roosevelt. Nor could he expect more than a payoff from de Mores, even though he'd simply followed orders. Any way he sliced it, he was finished in Medora. He shoved his chair aside and walked from the room.

"Good riddance," Eaton said. "And the best part, it's a black eye for the Marquis. This was all his doing."

Lang chuckled. "You've had quite a week, Theodore. First the horse thieves and now Morrill. You're a busy man."

"Oh?" Roosevelt said. "How did you hear of the horse thieves?"

"Word gets around," Lang replied. "Mike Boyce has been bragging on you to anyone who passes his place. You've made a believer of him."

"Barefoot and bareback!" Eaton snorted a laugh. "By God, that's rich."

"And judicious," Lang remarked. "Far better than hanging men from telegraph poles. Granville Stuart might learn something from you, Theodore."

Roosevelt thought it unlikely that an old dog could be taught new tricks. But he was less concerned with Granville Stuart than with the opinion of the Badlands ranchers. He felt vindicated that they approved his methods.

Barefoot and bareback was indeed preferable to a rope.

FOURTEEN

The valley was ablaze with wildflowers. From the window of his study Roosevelt could see violets, bluebells, primrose, and goldenrod spread across the verdant grassland. The buttes to the west loomed like sentinels over a riot of color.

The scene was one he hoped to describe in a letter to Bamie. His pen paused as he considered the content of her letter, collected from the post last Saturday in Medora. She wrote that Alice Lee was growing and in perfect health, a happy little doll of a baby. She went on to say that Elliot, ever the banker, was concerned about all the money Theodore had invested in yet another ranch. They feared he might never return from Dakota.

Roosevelt thought his latest news would only heighten their fears. Today was June 20, and he marked it as a most auspicious date for Elkhorn. Sewall and Dow had gone into town yesterday, traveling by wagon, to meet the westbound train. Their wives were to arrive from Maine and would take up permanent residence at the ranch. Roosevelt had encouraged the move, and he was enthused by the prospect of women in the house. Three bachelors under one roof had long since lost its novelty.

Still, he decided to say nothing of this in the letter to Bamie. He felt guilty enough about having so little to say about his daughter, apart from professing thanks that she was in good health and in good hands. The longer he stayed in Dakota, the more it seemed he would never leave, and he couldn't bring himself to dishearten Bamie with such news. So he wrote instead of bluebells and violets and lightly related his "merry escapade" with a band of horse thieves. He ended the letter with a brotherly admonishment to Elliot. Ranching, he noted, was just as profitable as Wall Street.

The letter finished, Roosevelt turned to *Hunting Trips of a Ranchman.* His subject today was the stalk of bighorn sheep and the large ram he'd shot in a range of cliffs west of the ranch. The head was magnificent, with curling corkscrew horns, and was even now being mounted by a part-time taxidermist in Medora. Roosevelt wanted to include a chapter on grizzly bears, but he'd been told the best place for a hunt was in Wyoming. What with the Association just formed and his duties as president, he didn't foresee a trip anytime soon. Perhaps before the book was completed.

A commotion from out front distracted him from the bighorn ram. He set his pen aside, hurried through the house, and stepped onto the porch. Sewall was just climbing down from the wagon, his wife and daughter in the front seat. Dow was in the back with his wife and what looked to be a ton of trunks and valises. Roosevelt knew the women and the girl from his many hunting trips to Maine, though he hadn't seen them in almost a year. He stepped off the porch as they were helped from the wagon.

"By thunder!" he said ebulliently. "Dee-*lighted* to see all of you again. Welcome to Elkhorn."

Erma Sewall was in her late thirties, a plump woman with rosy checks and a cheerful disposition. Amy, her daughter, was thirteen, tall for her age, and the mirror image of her mother. Irene Dow was an attractive young woman, scarcely twenty, with hair the color of wheat, They moved forward from the wagon.

"We are happy to be here, Mr. Roosevelt," Erma said warmly. "We've never been much of anywhere, you know. This is quite an adventure."

"Wonderful country," Roosevelt said, nodding to Dow's wife. "Irene, you are as fair as I remember. How did Will get so lucky?"

"Thank you, sir," she said with a winsome smile. "You're looking very well."

"Never better!" Roosevelt turned his gaze on the girl. "Good heavens, could this be our little Amy? You've become a woman."

Amy blushed beet red. "Ma says I just keep sprouting." She ducked her head shyly. "Are you a cowboy now, Mr. Roosevelt?"

"I do believe I've earned my spurs," Roosevelt said with his nutcracker grin. "Of course, we've been living the rough life here. You ladies will have to civilize us all over again."

"You have a beautiful home," Erma said, staring past him at the house. "I never expected to see anything so nice in the wilderness."

"Adam and Will are master builders, and I must say we are quite comfortable here. Come inside and see for yourselves."

Roosevelt led them on a tour of the house. The women marveled at the furnishings in the parlor and the bedrooms and seemed particularly taken with the kitchen. The storage room had been refurbished with a wall added, half of the old space turned into a small bedroom for Amy. When they came to his study, Roosevelt gently cautioned the girl that it was his private hideaway, never to be entered alone. As though sharing a secret, he told her his books and his papers were his prize possessions. She looked into the study as if viewing a museum.

By the time the tour was finshed, Sewall and Dow had carried all the luggage to the bedrooms. The women, after their long trip west, were famished for their own cooking and immediately went to work in the kitchen. Sewall went outside to attend to the team and wagon, and Dow remained behind to butcher a deer Roosevelt had shot that morning. Amy was at odds with all the activity, so Roose-

velt invited her to see something of the ranch. Their first
stop was the corral.

Manitou greeted them at the gate. Amy rubbed his velvety muzzle and he nuzzled her hand. "Oh, he's wonderful," she said on an indrawn breath. "Could I ever have a
horse of my own?"

"Possibly," Roosevelt said, surprised by the directness
of her question. "Perhaps you should ask your father. He
will know best."

"Does Pa have his own horse?"

"On a ranch every man has several horses. Working cattle is more taxing on the horse than on the rider."

The statement was somewhat evasive, for Sewall was
not yet an accomplished horseman. Roosevelt thought it
best to let her discover that fact for herself. She gazed
around the compound.

"Where are all the cowboys, Mr. Roosevelt?"

"Off tending to the cattle. The men work from sunup to
sundown on a ranch. Never a dull moment."

"Do they do their own cooking?"

"As a matter of fact, they have their own cook. Come
along, I'll introduce you."

Roosevelt led her to the bunkhouse. The cookshack and
mess hall was cobbled onto one end, and they found Bud
Ledbetter preparing sourdough biscuits for supper. His
hands were caked with flour and he greeted Amy with a
gap-toothed smile. She inspected the kitchen with a femi-
nine eye and asked him all manner of questions. Ledbetter
patiently explained how he fed so many men so many
meals with only one stove.

Outside again, Amy looked dubious. "I'm glad we have
Ma," she whispered. "I don't think I'd like his cooking."

"Quite frankly, I am thrilled to have your mother and
Irene at Elkhorn. Women have no equal in a kitchen."

A wayward thought surfaced in Roosevelt's mind.
Holding a conversation with a young girl somehow made
him think of his own daughter. He wondered if Alice Lee,
years from now, would be a girl of lively curiosity and in-

nocent trust. Even more, he wondered if he would ever hold such a conversation with her. He damned himself and ruthlessly suppressed the thought.

Late afternoon shadows dappled the valley as they returned from their tour. The house was suffused with pleasant aromas from the kitchen, and Erma and Irene were carrying steaming dishes into the dining room. The centerpiece was a haunch of venison, roasted to perfection, with a savory sauce served on the side. Roosevelt stuffed himself, as did Sewall and Dow, and praised the women on their cooking. The conversation was lighthearted, everyone talking at once, a family gathered for the evening meal.

After supper, the men retired to the front porch. Blood gold shafts of light hovered beyond the western buttes as twilight crept slowly across the valley. There was a stillness on the land, a time when the earth and all its creatures awaited the coming of night. A soft breeze feathered the leaves of cottonwoods along the river.

"Women make a home," Roosevelt said with a contented sigh. "I do believe Elkhorn is now complete."

Dow chuckled. "You should've heard them talking in the kitchen. They've already got plans to redecorate the whole house."

"Nothing like a woman's touch," Roosevelt said. "We are most fortunate, don't you agree, Adam?"

"Yessir, I do," Sewall said, his features suddenly solemn. "While they're busy with the dishes, I've got something to tell you. It's not good."

"Oh, what's happened now?"

"Talked with Joe Ferris when we were in town. He says there's a story going around, and from what he hears, it's true. Jake Paddock's threatened to kill you."

"Has he indeed?" Roosevelt said calmly. "Did Joe by chance hear the reason?"

"Just saloon talk and rumors," Sewall said. "But it's likely got something to do with you runnin' Morrill out of town. Paddock's making it his fight."

"I detect the hand of the Marquis de Mores in all this. He was personally offended by my actions against Morrill."

"You figure he ordered Paddock to kill you?"

"Yes, I just imagine he did. Paddock is his good little soldier."

"More like his hired gun," Sewall said. "You'd best steer clear of town for a while."

"On the contrary," Roosevelt said quickly. "Mr. Paddock must be disabused of such notions. I will leave first thing in the morning."

"Wait a minute now! You're no match for a gunman like Paddock. You need to think that over."

Through the window Sewall saw the women and Amy come into the parlor. He motioned for Dow to join them and hung back for one last try. He stared hard at Roosevelt.

"I've known you long enough to talk plain. Don't act the fool just to prove you're a man."

"Thank you for your concern, Adam. I will sleep on it."

Sewall grunted harshly and went inside. Dark had fallen over the land, and Roosevelt stepped off the porch, walking toward the river. The news of the threat disturbed him, and something churned in his stomach at the thought of facing Paddock. Yet even as he confronted his own mortality, he wasn't convinced that discretion was the better part of valor. A man could outrun many things but never himself.

The sky was purest indigo, flecked through with stars. Roosevelt stopped on the riverbank, leaned against a tall cottonwood, and stared into the heavens. A movement startled him, and he pushed off the tree, his gaze drawn from the sky to their forms. Alice and his mother hovered over the water, sheathed as before in gossamer and illumined by a faint aura. Their arms reached out to him.

Roosevelt moved to the edge of the riverbank. The water lapped at his boots, and he watched as they tried to speak, their voices silent. Their features shone in the starlight, and he saw their anguish, felt their distress, as they struggled to summon words. He reached out to them and their anguish became greater, their faces contorted,

their voices still mute. Then, as though unable to bear it
longer, they dissolved before his eyes, faded away across
the darkened water. He stood alone.

Yet he was not alone. Somewhere between his world
and theirs, they waited, and he knew they would return
again. There would be no end to it, for they must return . . .
and speak . . . and speak again . . .

Until he heard their voices.

The sun was lodged high in the sky. Roosevelt rode into
town the next day shortly after the noon hour. The boardwalk was crowded with shoppers as he reined to a halt before the store and stepped out of the saddle. He left
Manitou tied to the hitchrack.

On the way into town he'd decided to talk with Joe Ferris
before taking the matter further. He trusted Sewall's account but it was secondhand information and therefore open
to interpretation. He wanted it straight from the source.

Ferris was waiting on a customer when Roosevelt entered the store. He glanced around as Roosevelt stopped by
the counter and his face first registered surprise, then
shock. He excused himself and quickly turned the customer over to one of his clerks. He hurried forward.

"Mr. Roosevelt," he said anxiously. "What are you doing in town?"

"I spoke with Adam Sewall," Roosevelt said. "He relayed your message about Jake Paddock."

"Well, sir, I think maybe he didn't relay the whole message. I told him to tell you to stay out of town for a while."

"Under the circumstances, I do not see that as an option.
Assuming, of course, that the circumstances are as Sewall
reported."

"We need to talk about this in private."

Ferris led him to a door along the rear wall. The door
opened onto a storeroom jammed with boxes and crates
and an assortment of hardware. They had the room to
themselves, and Ferris quickly closed the door. His features were etched with alarm.

"You're not safe in Medora," he said. "I thought I made that clear to Sewall. Didn't he tell you?"

"Yes, he was quite adamant," Roosevelt said. "As a matter of fact, we had an argument before I left Elkhorn this morning. He accused me of playing the fool."

"Then if you don't mind my asking, what the devil are you doing here? Why didn't you listen to Sewall?"

Roosevelt waved it off with an indulgent smile. "I am here because I wished to speak with you personally. Is it true Paddock has threatened my life?"

"Of course it's true," Ferris said tightly. "Why else would I've sent you a warning?"

"How did you learn of this threat?"

"Last Saturday, after you fired Morrill, word spread all over town. The next night, Paddock swore he was gonna kill you."

"Do you know if Morrill left town?"

Ferris nodded. "He caught the stage Sunday mornin' for Deadwood."

"Hardly a coincidence," Roosevelt said. "Morrill departs Sunday morning and Paddock threatens me that night. I suspect one was linked to the other."

"No doubt about it. Paddock was raisin' holy hell about the way you posted Morrill out of town. Said you was gettin' too big for your britches."

"Where did this occur?"

"Down at the Alhambra Saloon," Ferris said. "That's Paddock's regular hangout, and he was talkin' to Jess Hogue, the owner. Didn't care who heard him, either."

"How do you know?" Roosevelt asked. "Do you have personal knowledge of all this?"

"Lots of folks know we're friends, Mr. Roosevelt. I heard about it bright and early Monday mornin'. One of the fellows that told me was in the Alhambra."

"Did he repeat the exact nature of the threat?"

"Yessir, he did," Ferris replied soberly. "Paddock said, 'I'm gonna kill that son of a bitch deader'n hell.' I was told those were his very words."

"I see," Roosevelt said, nodding to himself. "Well, Joe, that rather limits my alternatives. I have no choice but to confront Paddock."

"Mr. Roosevelt, lemme ask you something. Have you ever been in a gunfight? Have you ever killed a man?"

"No, I have not."

"Then what in tarnation makes you think you've got a chance against Paddock? You brace him and you'll just get yourself killed."

"Perhaps," Roosevelt conceded. "But a man must first live with himself, Joe. I cannot do otherwise."

"Are you talkin' about honor?" Ferris demanded. "'Cause if you are, nobody writes epitaphs to a man that got himself killed defending his honor. He's just dead, that's all."

"Where do you think I might find Paddock?"

"You won't listen to reason?"

"Not today."

Ferris sighed heavily. "You'll likely find him at the Alhambra. I've heard he plays poker there every afternoon."

"Thank you, Joe."

"Mr. Roosevelt."

"Yes?"

"Do yourself a favor and don't give him an even break. Shoot him down like you would a mad dog. Nobody'll blame you."

"I shall bear your advice in mind."

Roosevelt moved to the door. He went through the store, leaving Manitou at the hitchrack, and turned downtown. He never frequented saloons, but he remembered that the Alhambra was in the next block. As he crossed the street, he briefly considered Ferris's advice and just as quickly discarded it. Whatever the protocol of gunfights, he felt sure it didn't include murder. Shooting a man without warning seemed to him nothing less.

The Alhambra was all but empty. A man stood at the bar sipping whiskey, a saloon girl at his elbow. Four men were seated around a poker table at the rear, talking in low tones.

Roosevelt confirmed at a glance that Paddock was not among them. He nodded to the bartender.

"I'm looking for Jake Paddock. Has he been in today?"

The man at the bar lowered his glass. "Aren't you Roosevelt?"

"You have the advantage of me."

"The name's Jess Hogue. I own the joint."

"Yes, I've heard of you."

"Mutual." Hogue's mouth crooked in a smile. "Have to say, you've got brass balls comin' in here. Not the safest place in town."

Roosevelt returned his gaze. "Do you know where I might find Paddock?"

"Stick around, Jake'll be here directly. He's lookin' for you, too."

"So I've been told."

"Hell, I'll even buy you a drink, while you're waitin'."

"Thank you, but I prefer to wait outside."

Hogue laughed. "Why not? It's your funeral."

Roosevelt ignored the gibe. He went through the door, and as he halted outside he saw Paddock coming along the boardwalk. The expression on Paddock's face was one of raw disbelief. He stopped not a yard away.

"Where'd you spring from, Roosevelt?"

"I understand you have threatened to kill me."

"Who told you that?"

'Let us say I have it on good authority."

"Just bet you do," Paddock said. "So you're here to call me out, that the idea?"

Roosevelt stared at him. "I am here to settle the matter."

"Way it smells, there's something fishy about this. I could drill you before you cleared leather. Why're you so anxious to get killed?"

"You may kill me, but before I die, I will kill you. Have no doubt of it, Paddock."

Paddock's eyes narrowed. "Think you're that good, huh?"

"No, not that good," Roosevelt said. "Just stubborn enough to outlast you."

A moment of tomblike silence slipped past as they stared at each other. Paddock finally shook his head with a satiric smile. "I think I'll pick my own time to kill you, Roosevelt. You got lucky today."

"Why do I suspect you plan to bushwhack me?"

"Well, you never know, do you? Just keep lookin' over your shoulder."

Paddock laughed and pushed through the door of the Alhambra. Roosevelt felt his heart thudding in his chest and for a moment he was unable to move. He realized that his nerves were badly shaken, despite all his bold talk and cool manner. Even more, he realized that today had ended nothing. He would forever be looking over his shoulder.

Ten minutes later he barged into the office of the Marquis de Mores. He slammed the door and planted himself in front of the desk. "You, sir, are a scoundrel of the first order. I am here to settle accounts."

De Mores rose from behind his desk. "What are you talking about? What accounts?"

"I have just come from a most unpleasant conversation with Jake Paddock. I am quite aware that you ordered him to kill me."

"You are mistaken, m'sieur. I issued no such orders."

"I cannot prove it," Roosevelt said, "but I believe you seek retribution over the matter of Joe Morrill. Paddock would not act except on your order."

"Enough!" de Mores snapped. "I killed two men in honorable duels while an officer of the French army. I do not require another man to do my killing."

"If that is true, I suggest you take an advertisement in the newspaper and so inform the public. Everyone in town is of the opinion that you employ others to do your dirty work."

"I do not believe you."

"Then you need only ask someone who will tell you the truth. Your name has been sullied by your own actions."

De Mores frowned. "You say you accosted Paddock. How is it you are still alive?"

"I think you overrate Paddock," Roosevelt said. "He does not care for a face-to-face showdown. He promised, instead, that he would ambush me from behind."

"Then you have nothing to fear, M'sieur Roosevelt. I assure you that will not happen."

"And if it does, I assure you the Stockgrowers Association will hold you accountable. I intend to file a full report."

Roosevelt walked out. He thought he'd rather nicely maneuvered de Mores into an untenable position. There was every likelihood that the Marquis, fearful of the Stockgrowers Association, would call off Paddock. All of which, Roosevelt told himself, vastly improved his odds of survival. Life insurance of sorts.

He went to his room to write the report.

FIFTEEN

The Alhambra was quiet the next afternoon. There was no one at the bar, and four men were seated at a poker table. The bartender stood polishing glasses.

Paddock was dealing draw poker. The other men at the table were Jess Hogue, Frank Miller, and Quincy Moore. Miller and Moore were horse thieves, and whenever their services were needed they worked as hired guns for Paddock and Hogue. They were, in the finest sense of the word, assassins.

"Everybody ante," Paddock said. "Open on guts or whatever strikes your fancy."

The ante was a dollar, and bets were limited to three dollars. Miller and Moore had sold a herd of stolen horses only last week, and they were flush with an impressive bankroll. But the men kept the stakes low, merely killing time, waiting until they could lure a sucker into the game. Moore, seated to the left of the dealer, opened for two dollars.

Hogue called and Miller raised three dollars. Paddock studied his cards a moment, then folded. Moore and Hogue just called the raise, and both of them took three cards on the draw. Miller took only two cards, and when they checked to the raiser he bet three dollars. Moore folded and Hogue slowly spread the cards in his hand. He shrugged.

"Gotta call," he said, tossing three dollars into the pot. "You trying to buy it or you got 'em?"

"Got 'em." Miller flopped his cards. "Three little fours."

Hogue nodded. "Beats a pair of queens."

Moore began shuffling the cards. Hogue poured himself a drink from a bottle of bourbon on the table. He tossed off the shot, grimacing slightly, and smacked his lips. His gaze shuttled around the table, settling on Paddock.

"Aren't we a pack of he-wolves?" he said derisively. "Playin' penny-ante poker and couldn't kill a goddamn four-eyed dude. We're slippin' fast."

"Don't start that shit again," Paddock bristled. "I've done heard enough from the Marquis."

"Well, hell, Jake, why shouldn't he be pissed? You had your chance at Roosevelt and muffed it. I'm a little pissed myself."

"Told you why I let him go. Way it was, I would've had to let him draw first. Otherwise, I'd wind up charged with murder."

"C'mon, admit it, you just got spooked."

Miller and Moore exchanged a quick glance. They had never seen Hogue and Paddock at cross-purposes and were troubled they might get caught in the middle. Moore finished shuffling and put the deck out for Paddock to cut. Hogue poured himself another drink.

"Whole thing's a washout," he grumped, watching Paddock cut the cards. "You was supposed to get the Marquis up to his neck in shit, and then we'd put the squeeze on him. We're a day late and a dollar short."

"Not my fault," Paddock said sourly. "The bastard wouldn't let me kill nobody till he sicced me on Roosevelt. And that just didn't pan out the way it should've."

"Tell you one damn thing! You'd better figure out somebody to kill, and when you do, make sure it can be laid on the Marquis. Christ, I never thought it'd strain your brain."

"Watch your mouth there, Jess. You got no call to talk to me thataway."

"Ante up," Moore said, dealing the cards. "Game's five-card stud."

Hogue reached for the bottle. As he started to pour, his eyes went to the front of the saloon and his mustache lifted in a tight smile. "Look who we got here."

Three men walked to the bar. The one in the middle, a tall rawboned man with jug ears, ordered drinks. He shot a glance at the poker table, then looked away as the bartender brought a bottle. He dropped a silver dollar on the counter.

"What d'you make of that?" Hogue said. "Why would O'Donald come waltzin' in here?"

Paddock grunted. "I think we're gonna find out."

Tom O'Donald, the man with jug ears, owned a ranch west of Medora. The outfit was small, with perhaps two hundred head of cattle, located on a tributary that fed into the Little Missouri. The other men at the bar were George Luffsey and Dutch Wannegan, cowhands who worked for O'Donald. They kept their eyes fixed on the back-bar mirror.

O'Donald was one of the small ranchers Paddock had targeted for takeover. Over the past few months he had first tried to buy the outfit, and when that failed, he'd sent Miller and Moore to burn down an equipment shed in the middle of the night. O'Donald refused to be intimidated, and two nights ago Paddock had pushed it a step further. Shortly after midnight, under a dark and moonless sky, Miller and Moore had bombarded O'Donald's cabin with rifle fire. They rode away only after every window in the place had been reduced to shards.

The three men at the bar finished their drinks. O'Donald slammed his shot glass on the counter, and the report echoed through the saloon. When he spoke, he looked directly at the bartender, as if making conversation. No one doubted his remarks were addressed to the men at the poker table.

"Couple nights ago," he said, "some sonovbitch shot out

all my windows. Next time he sets foot on my land, I'm gonna bury him. Already got the grave dug."

The bartender seemed paralyzed, his eyes darting from O'Donald to the back of the room. O'Donald went on in a conversational tone. "Course there's another way," he said. "I'm fixin' to get a bite to eat at Murphy's Café"—he paused, checked his pocket watch—"and I'll be on the street at two sharp. I'd be happy to meet the cocksucker man-to-man—if'n he's got the guts for it."

Paddock started out of his chair. Hogue grabbed his arm and signaled him to stay put. There was a long moment of strained silence, then O'Donald wheeled away from the bar. He walked to the door, his spurs chiming in the stillness, and his men followed him outside. Paddock glared across the table at Hogue.

"Why'd you stop me?" he said. "I could've killed that shitkicker right here."

"There's a smarter way," Hogue said with a crafty grin. "We've got a chance to put the Marquis right where we want him. Let's sucker him into gettin' his hands dirty."

"How you figure to do that?"

"Tell him O'Donald threatened to kill him."

Paddock nodded, his eyes alert. "One thing about the Marquis, he's a prideful man. Might just work."

Hogue laughed. "Goddamn right it'll work."

Paddock kicked his chair aside. He crossed the saloon, cautiously opened the door, and checked outside the Alhambra. Tom O'Donald was nowhere in sight.

He hurried uptown to the Marquis' office.

The wagon trail zigzagged through a craggy ravine. Beyond the gorge, to the west, the trail ascended onto the grasslands of a lofty butte. The sun slowly tilted over toward the horizon.

De Mores and Paddock waited below a rocky outcropping near the bottom of the ravine. Directly above them, thirty feet or higher on the rugged cliff, Miller and Moore

were stationed behind stunted boulders. All of the men
were armed with rifles.

"Where are they?" de Mores asked impatiently. "Do
you think they are still waiting for me in town?"

"Not too likely," Paddock said. "O'Donald would want
to make it home by dark. They'll be along directly."

"I have no taste for lying in wait like bandits. I should
have confronted him in town."

"We done talked that out, Marquis. You start slingin'
lead on the street and innocent people are liable to get
killed. This here's lots better."

"Yes, but I ask again, where are they?"

Paddock was wondering the same thing. They had se-
creted themselves in the rocks over an hour ago, hiding
their horses beyond the western reaches of the ravine. By
the angle of the sun Paddock estimated it was approaching
four o'clock, and he doubted that O'Donald was still waiting outside Murphy's Café. Nobody waited that long when
the other man failed to show.

All things considered, Paddock thought he'd done a
nifty job. He had gone straight from the Alhambra and delivered the warning in a voice laced with concern. O'Donald, he said, had walked into the Alhambra bold as brass
and threatened to kill the Marquis. O'Donald had even
brought two men along—Paddock had called them
gunmen—probably in the hope of drawing Paddock into
the fight as well. There was nothing secret about the fact
that Paddock worked for the Marquis.

The story was all the more credible because it required
so little fabrication. De Mores knew that Paddock and his
men had tried to intimidate O'Donald, even riddled his
cabin with rifle slugs. So it was easy to believe that
O'Donald's anger was directed at the man behind his troubles, the Marquis himself. From there, Paddock easily convinced de Mores that the problem was best solved away
from the busy streets of Medora. Paddock, Miller, and
Moore would cover O'Donald's "gunmen" and disarm

them. The Marquis could then challenge O'Donald to an honorable fight.

The difficult part had been in rushing de Mores out of town. O'Donald had boasted he would be outside Murphy's Café at two o'clock, and the timing was critical. Paddock had hurried back to the Alhambra, collected Miller and Moore, and assured Hogue the plan would work. From there the three men walked to the livery stable, where their horses were stalled, and Paddock rented a horse for the Marquis. They then took the alley south of Main Street, where they found de Mores waiting behind his office, armed with a pistol and a Remington hunting rifle. On the way back through the alley, one of the clerks from Ferris's store came out with a container of trash and stood watching as they rode past. They cleared the edge of Medora shortly before two o'clock.

The ravine was a mile west of the slaughterhouse. At first, when Paddock positioned the men, de Mores seemed almost glacially calm. Yet as time wore on, he became increasingly edgy and introspective. He wasn't overly concerned about Tom O'Donald, for he had killed two men in *affaires d'honneur* in France and acquitted himself well. But today, on the verge of another deadly situation, de Mores regretted ordering Paddock to kill Roosevelt. He had done it out of envy and spite, angered by the erosion of his power over ranchers in the Badlands. In hindsight, he thought Roosevelt's assessment was all too correct. He had sullied his name by his own actions.

Today, he told himself, he would reclaim his honor. Roosevelt and the other ranchers would learn that he needed no one, least of all Jake Paddock, to defend his reputation. He would kill O'Donald in an honorable manner, and as the offended party he was completely within his rights. O'Donald had, after all, threatened his life, and there was no graver insult. He thought pistols at twenty paces would do nicely and restore his name. A gentleman, in the end, always found the proper solution.

The clatter of hooves sounded at the east end of the

ravine. De Mores, every sense alert, turned to Paddock. "Do as I ordered," he said. "You and your men disarm them without incident. I will then challenge O'Donald to a duel."

"Just like we talked about," Paddock agreed. "The boys and me will be your witnesses. Don't you worry."

"I am always calmest in a moment of stress."

"That's the ticket."

O'Donald rode into view first. He was followed by Luffsey and Wannegan, slouched in their saddles. None of them spoke, and they appeared somehow listless, as though the day's events had sapped their energy. They stared into the westering sun at the end of the ravine.

"Halt!" De Mores stepped into the clear, his arm raised. "Do not resist!"

Paddock rose from below the outcropping. A Winchester was at his shoulder, the sights centered on O'Donald, and he fired. O'Donald screamed, clutching at his shoulder, and fell backward out of the saddle. Miller and Moore fired almost simultaneously, the hammering tattoo of their rifles echoing through the ravine. Wannegan grabbed his leg, toppling sideways off his horse, and Luffsey jerked erect, his throat scarlet from a gaping wound. His horse bolted, throwing him, and he dropped dead on the ground.

"Hold your fire! Hold your fire!"

De Mores leaped forward, arms spread wide to shield the fallen men. His features were contorted in a frantic grimace, his eyes wide with a look of horror. He shook a fist at Paddock.

"You imbecile!" he railed. "Why did you fire? Why?"

"Had to, Marquis," Paddock said, walking forward. "O'Donald was fixin' to shoot you."

"His gun is still in the holster!"

"Well, he was reachin'." Paddock turned to his men. "Wasn't he reachin', boys?"

"Shore was," Moore agreed, bobbing his head. "So was them other two jaspers. That's why we shot 'em."

"Oughta finish 'em off," Paddock said impassively. "We don't, they're gonna cause us trouble down the road."

"Bind their wounds!" de Mores ordered. "We must take them to the doctor. Do it now!"

O'Donald and Wannegan were moaning, hands clasped to their wounds. Paddock reluctantly waved Miller and Moore forward, then bent to inspect Luffsey. The cowhand's eyes were open and blank, sightless.

"No hurry here," Paddock said. "He's done gone."

De Mores looked down at the dead man. His face went ashen and he seemed staggered by the sight of so much blood. He turned away.

"Mon Dieu."

Five days later Roosevelt went down the stairs from his room. On the street he turned east, the boardwalks crowded with forenoon shoppers. He kept his eyes straight ahead as he passed the Northern Pacific Refrigerator Car Company.

The train from Mandan was due to arrive at noon. Roosevelt entered the depot through the street-side door and walked to the ticket window. Fred Overton, the stationmaster, turned from the telegrapher's desk and saw him waiting at the counter. He hurried forward with a telegram form in hand.

"Good morning," Roosevelt said pleasantly. "Will the train from Mandan arrive on time?"

"Yessir, expect it will," Overton said, extending the form. "Telegram just came in for you. Saved my boy a trip uptown."

"Thank you."

Roosevelt moved away from the counter. He opened the form and scanned the message, then read it again. The dateline was August 18, the origin New York City. The telegram was signed by John Abernathy, Republican Chairman.

> Republican Committee wishes to place
> your name in nomination for fourth term
> in legislature. Senator Warner Miller urges
> you to accept. Please advise your decision
> soonest.

The decision was already made. Roosevelt immediately sent a return wire, informing Abernathy to withdraw his name from nomination. Elections were in the offing, and he'd decided only last week not to seek a fourth term in office. His reply was tardy, but his mind had been occupied with other matters. He knew it would end his career in politics and he felt no great regret. His life was now in Dakota Territory.

Everything about his former life seemed oddly distant. A month ago, he'd learned that Grover Cleveland, governor of New York, had received the Democratic nomination for president of the United States. Yesterday, in the newspaper, he read that Cleveland had been accused of fathering an illegitimate child. Cleveland was a married man, and though the charge was salacious, there was no great outcry from the public. Roosevelt considered it a sad commentary on the moral climate of the country. He told himself he was well out of politics.

The noon train arrived seven minutes late. There were three coaches, all full, and Roosevelt waited on the platform as passengers began deboarding. A burly man with a badge pinned on his shirt stepped off the last coach. Roosevelt moved forward.

"Sheriff Bullard?"

"That's me," Bullard said, exchanging a handshake. "You must be Roosevelt."

"Yes, I received your wire."

"Hope you can make this thing stick, Mr. Roosevelt. Murder's a mighty serious charge."

"I believe you will be convinced by the witnesses."

Sheriff Seth Bullard was headquartered in Mandan, the county seat with jurisdiction over Medora. Roosevelt had written him the day after the shooting, identifying himself as the head of the Stockgrowers Association. In the letter, he outlined the complicity of de Mores and Paddock and formally requested their arrest. Yesterday he had received a telegram announcing Bullard's arrival in Medora.

"Let's talk to your witnesses," Bullard said. "Your letter indicated two of them are survivors of the shootout."

"Hardly a shootout," Roosevelt replied. "They were ambushed and fired upon in cold blood."

"What's the general feeling here in Medora?"

"Our newspaper published a story on the affair. Everyone is quite aware that the Marquis de Mores is responsible."

"What about the others?" Bullard asked. "Are they here in town?"

"Paddock is still here," Roosevelt said. "I understand Frank Miller and Quincy Moore have taken flight. They disappeared the day after the shooting."

"You've already buried the dead man?"

"Yes, in the town cemetery."

"Well, let's get to it."

On the way uptown, Bullard remarked on Roosevelt's policy of dealing with rustlers and horse thieves. The story from the *Badlands Cowboy* reporting on the "barefoot and bareback" incident had been reprinted in the Mandan newspaper. Bullard went on to contrast it with the rash of hangings in Montana.

The newspaper stories had received wide circulation. The Montana vigilantes, dubbed The Stranglers by reporters, had hanged thirty-two men in slightly more than two months. Roosevelt made no mention of Granville Stuart, or his knowledge of the vigilantes. But he thought it ironic that the work of The Stranglers had spilled over into Dakota. Horse thieves and rustlers were suddenly less active in the Badlands.

A short while later, Roosevelt and Bullard entered the office of Dr. Horace Stickney. He was the only physician in the Badlands and considered something of a saint among townspeople and cattlemen alike. Tom O'Donald and Dutch Wannegan were still confined to bed, quartered in a room Dr. Stickney used as an infirmary. O'Donald's left arm was in a sling, and Wannegan's left leg was heavily bandaged.

Sheriff Bullard questioned them at length. O'Donald admitted making threats against Paddock as a result of the raids on his ranch. He and Wannegan related how they were ambushed, fired upon without warning, and George Luffsey killed. They reluctantly admitted that de Mores had ordered a cease-fire and stopped Paddock from turning it into a slaughter. They were nonetheless adamant that de Mores was the leader of the ambush.

Afterward, Bullard questioned Dr. Stickney in his office. "Anything to add?" Bullard asked. "Apart from what we've already heard?"

"Yes, there is," Stickney said. "I can confirm that they were ambushed."

"How's that?"

"After I treated them, I took the opportunity to inspect their weapons. None of their guns were fired, and I'll swear to it in court."

"How did you get hold of their guns?"

"Paddock and his men brought them here and dumped them. Their guns were still in the holsters."

Bullard nodded. "Was de Mores with them?"

"Yes, he was," Stickney said. "De Mores waited on the street until O'Donald and Wannegan were carried inside. Then he rode off."

"Obliged for your help, Doc."

Outside the office, Bullard shook his head. "Sounds like de Mores tried to save these men's lives."

Roosevelt laughed bitterly. "Only after he attempted to murder them, and killed Luffsey. Any mercy involved was too little, too late."

Uptown again, Roosevelt introduced Bullard to Orville Kelton, the clerk in Ferris's store. Kelton recounted that he'd seen de Mores ride through the alley with Paddock, Miller, and Moore. He placed the time at about two o'clock on the day of the shooting and went on to say de Mores was carrying a rifle across the horn of his saddle. Kelton agreed to testify in any court trial.

"All right, I'm convinced," Bullard said as they emerged from the store. "Who do you think we ought to arrest first?"

"Jake Paddock," Roosevelt observed. "He is the most likely to resist. He fancies himself a gunman."

"In that case, you're hereby deputized. Anything goes haywire, you back my play."

A few minutes later they walked into the Alhambra. The saloon was empty, and Paddock was seated with Hogue at a poker table. Roosevelt identified Paddock and followed the lawman to the rear of the room. Bullard stopped at the table.

"Paddock, you're under arrest," he said, one hand on his pistol. "You're charged with murder, and two counts of attempted murder. Come along peaceable or I'll kill you where you sit."

There was a beat of silence while Paddock debated his chances. He finally rose, surrendering his pistol, and allowed Bullard to cuff his wrists with manacles. His gaze fixed on Roosevelt with a look of cold venom.

"You're always stickin' your nose in things, Roosevelt. One of these days, somebody's gonna cut it off."

"Let's go," Bullard said roughly, "and don't be threatenin' my deputy. I take it unkindly."

Uptown, shortly after the noon hour, they led Paddock into the Marquis de Mores' office. De Mores rose from behind his desk, glancing from Paddock's manacled hands to Bullard's badge. His features went slack.

"What is the meaning of this?" he demanded. "You cannot arrest me without a warrant."

"Save it for the judge," Bullard said. "I got a pair of bracelets for you, too, de Mores."

De Mores glowered at Roosevelt. "This is all your doing, isn't it? How dare you!"

"No, how dare you," Roosevelt said. "A man is dead and two are grievously wounded. You have much to answer for."

Early that evening, Roosevelt saw Bullard and his prisoners off on the eastbound train. As the engine pulled away, chuffing sparks like seething fireflies, he turned from the depot. He knew he'd done the right thing, performed his duty, but he was weary of men and their shabby affairs. Tired by the very thought of another night in town.

He longed to return to the solitude of Elkhorn.

SIXTEEN

A hazy sun stood framed against scudding clouds. The weather moderated in early September and the afternoon was warm but pleasant. Wildflowers still bloomed across the emerald grasslands.

Roosevelt and Dutch Wannagan were some five miles south of Elkhorn headquarters. Fall roundup was scheduled to start in two weeks, and Adam Sewall had assigned men to scout the range. He wanted a preliminary report on where the herds had drifted over the summer.

Fall roundup was a critical time for every rancher in the Badlands. Outfits gathered the cattle to be sold from their herds and drove them to the railhead in Medora. The sale to Chicago cattle buyers determined a rancher's profits for the entire year and his operating funds for the next. Elkhorn hadn't yet had its first calf crop, but Roosevelt expected a banner year for the Maltese Cross. He planned to use the profits to purchase even more cows.

Over the past two days it had rained almost constantly. The glades around tributary streams had become waterlogged and marshy, much like quicksand. As Roosevelt and Wannegan approached a creek, they heard bawling and saw a cow mired to its shoulders in a bog. The cow thrashed, struggling to break free from the muddy trap, and sank a little deeper. Some cows, unable to break loose, were simply sucked into the earth.

"Would you looky there?" Wannagan said. "Another hour and she'd be a goner."

"Indeed," Roosevelt said. "Fortunate we happened along."

"Well, I'll just get a rope on her. We'll have her out in a jiffy."

Roosevelt still hadn't acquired the knack of spinning a rope. On those days he wasn't off hunting or working on his book, he rode out with one of the cowhands. But unless it involved herding cows from one spot to another, he was largely a spectator.

He watched now as Wannegan uncoiled his lariat, built a loop, and cast it over the cow's stubby horns. Wannegan snugged the end of the lariat around his saddle horn and reined his horse backward. The cow popped out of the bog and was dragged to firm ground.

"Well done," Roosevelt said admiringly. "I think I shall never master the art of roping."

"Yeah, but you saved my bacon," Wannegan said. "Not many men could've put a loop on Jake Paddock. You just rope a different way."

De Mores and Paddock had been arraigned on charges of murder. To Roosevelt's astonishment, the judge in Mandan set bail at twenty-five thousand dollars each, and de Mores promptly posted bond. He and Paddock were back in Medora three days after being arrested, with the trial set for March 1885, seven long months away. Allowing bond on a murder charge was highly irregular, and many people thought de Mores had bought himself a judge. Others were of the opinion that political influence had been exerted in Bismarck by the Northern Pacific. The railroad had a large stake in de Mores' refrigerator car company, and the territorial capital was its playground. Keeping the Marquis out of jail was simply good business.

There was also widespread speculation that the witnesses would never live to testify in court. Jake Paddock, if not the Marquis, would kill anyone who could put his neck in a hangman's noose. Frank Miller and Quincy Moore had vanished from the Badlands, which left Tom O'Donald and Wannegan as the only witnesses. O'Donald, who was still recovering from his wound, rightfully feared another assassination attempt. He sold his ranch to Mike Boyce of the Three Seven outfit and hopped an eastbound train out of Medora. No one knew where he had gone.

Dutch Wannegan was the only remaining eyewitness to the shooting. Roosevelt, as head of the Stockgrowers Association, was determined that the murder trial would go forward. He convinced Wannegan to come to work for Elkhorn and then let it be known that the cowhand was under his personal protection. The upshot was a clear warning to the lawless element that the association would enforce the law in the Badlands. With Paddock effectively neutered, horse thieves and rustlers took the message to heart. Livestock theft had fallen off by a third over the past month.

After dragging the cow from the bog, Roosevelt and Wannegan turned toward the ramparts of the westward buttes. They planned to ride a circle in the lee of the buttes, checking for cattle as they went, and return to the headquarters compound by sundown. A mile or so north, they spotted tendrils of smoke spiraling skyward from a brushy gully. As they rode closer, they saw Pete Sturgis, one of the Elkhorn cowhands, working over a hogtied steer. He was using a piece of stiff wire heated cherry-red in the fire.

Wannegan knew instantly what was afoot. The length of wire, sometimes known as a running iron, was used to alter brands. Pete Sturgis was wielding a hot wire to change the Eatons' brand, a ⊣E into a crude TR for Elkhorn. The altered brand was so misshapen that even a cursory glance would detect the difference. Roosevelt saw it the moment he reined to a halt.

"Hold on there!" he barked. "You are putting my brand on an Eaton steer."

"Wandered onto our range, Mr. Roosevelt." Sturgis waved

the hot wire like a wand. "Just figgered I'd make him one of yours."

"Have you done this before?"

"Well, yeah, a few times."

"Do you understand that this is a form of rustling?"

"Most folks wouldn't see it that way."

"I do," Roosevelt said bluntly. "A man who will steal *for* me will steal *from* me. You're fired."

"Wait a minute now!" Sturgis protested. "I'm puttin' money in your pocket. Ain't nothin' wrong with that."

"Report to Sewall and draw your pay. I want you off Elkhorn by nightfall."

"Christ, don't fire me, Mr. Roosevelt. I won't do it again."

"Once is enough," Roosevelt said. "You no longer work for me, Sturgis. Get off my ranch."

Sturgis dropped the wire on the ground. He swung into the saddle, spurred his horse hard, and rode off at a gallop. Wannegan dismounted, untied the steer, and hazed it back up the draw. Roosevelt also stepped down, kicking dirt over the fire to smother the flames. He looked around at Wannegan.

"Do you think the other men have done this sort of thing?"

"I'd reckon not," Wannegan said. "Sturgis always struck me as an odd duck, anyway. Good thing you caught him."

Roosevelt nodded. "I will not tolerate a thief."

"Well, sir, once the story gets around, you won't need to worry. There'll be nothin' but honest men on Elkhorn."

"Yes, but it's still a vexing situation, most awkward. I'll have to tell John Eaton I owe him a steer."

Shortly before sundown they rode into the headquarters compound. Wannegan took the horses, and Roosevelt hurried off to make sure Pete Sturgis had left Elkhorn. In the house, Sewall confirmed that Sturgis was gone and said he planned to have a talk with the other hands that night. Over the summer Sewall had developed as a horseman and educated himself in the finer points of raising cattle. The men could still outride him and outrope him, but no one questioned his authority. His word was now law on Elkhorn.

Roosevelt was quite pleased with the arrangement. Sewall ran the ranch, and the women, who never seemed short of projects, ran the house. Every room was now decorated with curtains they'd sewn, the bed linens were changed weekly, and the house was neat as a pin. A garden flourished near the equipment shed, and the women were canning all manner of vegetables for the winter ahead. They washed and scrubbed and cooked, and Roosevelt often felt like a rajah in a log palace. He was free to write and hunt and watch his cows grow fat. He thought himself a lucky man.

Supper that evening was very much a family affair. Erma and Irene served a variety of dishes, and Amy chattered away about riding the pony her father had given her on her fourteenth birthday. The women had insisted that Roosevelt buy them a milch cow, and he listened to Amy with a humorous grin and buttermilk on his mustache. Over a dessert of chokecherry pie, Will Dow related the latest news from Medora. He'd returned that afternoon with a wagonload of supplies, and the talk in town was only incidentally related to fall roundup. Everyone was talking about the fires.

"Fires started three days ago," he said. "So far, it's burned off graze about ten miles on both sides of the railroad line. No end in sight, either."

"That is serious," Roosevelt said, his brow furrowed. "Every rancher in the Badlands will be affected."

"Yessir, no two ways about it. Folks are sayin' it could play hob with beef sales."

A broad strip of grassland some fifty miles wide in spots, lay between the railroad line and ranches to the north and south. Herds had to be trailed across the land to Medora, the nearest railhead for shipment to Chicago. Cattle driven over such distances with the natural graze burned to the ground shed weight at an alarming rate. Starved cows brought low prices, and trailing season was only a month away. The fires could cost ranchers tens of thousands of dollars.

"Are these wildfires?" Roosevelt asked. "We've had rain here the last few days, but no lightning storms. Was there lightning to the south?"

"Dry as tinder down that way," Dow said. "No rain, no lightning, nothing that'd start wildfires. Folks think it's the Indians."

"Why would the Indians set fires?"

"Everybody's saying they're tryin' to spoil the cattle season. Get a little revenge by hurtin' ranchers."

The Lakota branch of the Sioux tribe was confined to a reservation in the southeast quadrant of Dakota Territory. Following Custer's defeat at the Little Big Horn, the army had campaigned relentlessly against the Sioux, ultimately forcing them onto scattered reservations. The decimation of the buffalo herds by hide hunters had eliminated the Indians' key source of food and sustenance and opened the land to settlement by cattlemen. The Lakota were understandably hostile to ranchers.

"We live in a curious time," Roosevelt said philosophically. "For thousands of years buffalo roamed the Badlands in countless numbers. We killed them off to make way for cattle."

"Well, didn't we have to?" Sewall said. "The government encouraged hide hunters in order to rid the Indians of their food supply. How else would we have settled the country?"

"Yes, but suppose you were a Sioux, Adam. How would you feel toward ranchers?"

"I guess I wouldn't be any too friendly."

"Which may well explain these fires."

After supper Roosevelt retired to his study. He usually spent a few hours each evening working on *Hunting Trips of a Ranchman.* But the writing came hard tonight, for he was preoccupied with the matter of the fires. As president of the Stockgrowers Association, he felt he should take action of some sort. Perhaps investigate the fires, determine if the Lakota were to blame. Somehow protect the interests of his fellow ranchers.

Then, suddenly, his eyes misted with tears. He was overcome by a melancholy so intense that it was never far from the surface of his emotions. Usually, he could control it with iron discipline; other times, it simply swamped him with abrupt and unbearable anguish. Day by day, he tried to distract himself with building Elkhorn, his duties to the association, his efforts to write a book. Yet emotions sometimes won out.

Seven months now and he still hadn't subdued his grief. Alice and his mother were always in his thoughts, and he exhausted himself waiting for them to appear again from the vale, to speak to him. But he detested what he perceived as weakness, and he struggled to check his sudden fit of tears. He removed his pince-nez and roughly wiped his eyes with a handkerchief. Deal with it, he told himself. Take solace in . . .

He picked up his pen and went back to writing.

The earth was barren of vegetation. Where before tallgrass prairies rippled in the wind, there were now blackened stubs burned to the ground. The desolation stretched westward beyond sight.

Roosevelt crossed the ford by Chimney Butte shortly before sundown. He had spent the last three days inspecting the charred grasslands north and west of Medora. Today, on a wide swing southeast, he'd circled back to the Little Missouri. He rode into the Maltese Cross just before supper.

The men were waiting outside the cookshack. Roosevelt waved as he reined to a halt by the corral, then dismounted and began unsaddling Manitou. Merrifield walked down from the main house, exchanging a greeting, and stood watching as Roosevelt turned the horse into the corral. He motioned to the soot on the gelding's legs.

"Looks like you've been ridin' burnt land."

"Yes, for three days," Roosevelt said. "I wanted to inspect the damage for myself."

"Seen any Injuns?"

"No, not a one."

"Neither have we," Merrifield said. "I've had the boys keep a sharp lookout the last week or so. Nobody's spotted a redskin yet."

Roosevelt rubbed his jaw. "Wherever they are, I must say they're doing a fine job. There isn't a blade of grass for miles to the west."

"Maybe it ain't the Sioux."

"Who else could it be?"

"The Marquis," Merrifield said, one eyebrow cocked. "He could've sent Paddock and his boys out at night to start the fires. That'd account for why nobody's run across any Injuns."

"To what purpose?" Roosevelt asked. "Why would de Mores turn arsonist?"

"Well, think about it, Mr. Roosevelt. The Marquis needs beef for his refrigerated car company. If everybody's losin' their shirt, maybe his prices won't look so bad."

"That seems a little diabolical, even for de Mores."

"Does it?" Merrifield persisted. "Ain't no secret he's scramblin' to turn a profit. That's why he was trying to buy out small ranchers."

"Yes, but that's a far cry from firing the land."

"Maybe so, maybe not. Gaunt cows are gonna fetch low prices from the Chicago cattle buyers. Folks might do just as well sellin' to the Marquis."

Roosevelt was thoughtful a moment. "I think not, Bill," he finally said. "I would be the last one to defend de Mores. However, setting these fires would not be in his best interests."

"How you figure that?"

"The more pressing matter of a murder trail. Were he discovered to be an arsonist, no jury in Dakota would give him a fair hearing. In a land of cattlemen, he would be convicted out of hand."

Merrifield nodded despite himself. "Hadn't thought of that," he said. "Him and Paddock wouldn't have the chance of a snowball in hell. Not if they was caught settin' fires."

"My point exactly," Roosevelt said. "Now, let me ask you a question, Bill. Why do you think our range hasn't been fired?"

"Way it looks, whoever's behind it started up to the northwest and they're workin' their way southeast. Guess they just ain't got to us yet."

"And what lies to the southeast?"

"I'll be damned," Merrifield said with sudden understanding. "The Sioux reservation."

The Standing Rock Reservation was located some 120 miles southeast of Medora. Before being herded onto a reservation, the Lakota had fought tenaciously against white encroachment on their ancestral lands. Their animosity toward white cattlemen was particularly virulent.

"They'll likely hit us next," Merrifield said. "I'll tell the boys to keep their eyes peeled."

"Excellent idea," Roosevelt agreed. "Send someone to warn Gregor Lang as well."

"Yeah, it'd be lots rougher on Lang and ranchers to the south. Even on burnt land, our trail herd will make it to railhead in good shape. Guess we're lucky we're so close to Medora."

"Tomorrow I shall continue on southwest. I hope to establish firsthand the identity of these marauders."

Merrifield frowned. "Maybe you ought to take a couple of the boys, Mr. Roosevelt. You run across Injuns by yourself, you're liable to get scalped."

"Just a routine scout," Roosevelt said confidently. "If I happen across raiders, I shall run, and run quickly. I do not intend to fight them."

"Sometimes there ain't no choice but to fight. You'd be wise not to travel about all by your lonesome."

"I've been out three days now, Bill. You needn't be concerned for my safety."

Merrifield sensed it wasn't open to debate. Over the past seven months he'd watched as Roosevelt took on the Marquis, braced Jake Paddock and Joe Morrill, and tackled assorted rustlers and horse thieves. He told himself a band of Sioux renegades wasn't all that much worse. Roosevelt would probably talk them into surrendering.

They walked over to the cookshack for supper. The cowhands greeted Roosevelt with the deference accorded a man who was quickly becoming something of a legend in the Badlands. All the more so when they learned he'd been on scout for three days and planned to resume in the morning. They thought it admirable, if not particularly prudent.

The next morning, as Roosevelt forded the river, he wasn't altogether sanguine himself. Talk at the dinner table last night had turned to an incident not quite a year ago, when a small war party had raided through the Badlands. The Lakota had killed and scalped a teamster on the trail to Deadwood and wounded a cowhand who escaped only because he was mounted on a fast horse. A man caught alone was fair game for hostile warriors.

Roosevelt was aware of the risk. He knew that Indian reservations were operated by agents who had little control over their wards. The army seldom patrolled reservations, and young bucks seeking glory, sometimes led by older warriors, occasionally went on a rampage. The borders of a reservation were porous as a sieve; warriors could slip out, conduct a raid, and return before the army was alerted. The renegades were rarely caught or punished.

The situation was aggravated by corruption on the reservations. Agents were political appointees, and though some were devoted to the welfare of their wards, all too many were devoted to graft. The monthly ration allotments were often substandard—weevilly flour, rancid beans, and scrub cattle—or shorted by as much as half. The agents lined their pockets, Indian children went hungry, and warriors took out their hostility by stealing the white man's cattle or killing white men. White men, in turn, regularly shot any Indian caught off the reservation.

Toward noon, Roosevelt was some ten miles southwest of the Maltese Cross. The plains undulated into the distance, and as he topped a low rise he saw five Lakota braves riding in his direction. Farther away, perhaps a mile or so to the northwest, he spotted smoke and flames from a prairie fire rapidly gaining strength. There was no question in his mind that the Indians had only just set the fire and were now running before the flames. Their intent toward him was apparent in the next instant.

The warriors flogged their horses with their rifles and charged across the plain. Roosevelt grabbed his Winchester from the scabbard and swung down out of the saddle. Manitou was a seasoned hunter, alert but calm, trained to stand steady in the face of gunfire. As the Lakota pounded forward, Roosevelt thumbed the hammer on his Winchester and laid the barrel over the top of the saddle. The distance had closed to less than a hundred yards and he centered the sights on the brave in the lead. He waited to fire until they were within fifty yards.

The charge suddenly split apart. Roosevelt was shielded by his horse, clearly willing to fight, and the Lakota abruptly changed tactics. They reversed directions, whipping their ponies into headlong retreat, and halted at a range of perhaps a hundred yards. For several minutes they jabbered among themselves, gesturing angrily at him, plainly arguing their next move. After a time the oldest of the warriors, a man in his thirties, held his carbine overhead and rode forward across the prairie. He halted twenty yards away, slowly placing his carbine on his knees. He extended his upraised hand in the peace sign.

"How!" he called out. "Me good Injun!"

Roosevelt was surprised to be addressed in English. "That's fine," he yelled back. "Now ride on."

"No!" the warrior insisted. "White man not hear. Me *good* Injun!"

"Good Injun ride on and do so now. I will not tell you again."

"White man give good Injun tobac. Mebbe nuff for smoke."

"I have no tobacco."

In the distance, one of the Lakota split from the others and began circling to the west. A moment later another brave gigged his horse and trotted off to the east. Roosevelt immediately grasped that the older warrior meant to keep him talking while the other riders flanked him from opposite directions. He rose from behind the saddle, the Winchester at his shoulder, glowering through his spectacles. He drew a bead on the warrior.

"Ride on!" he commanded in a hard bellow. "Ride on or I will shoot!"

The warrior stared into the bore of the Winchester. "Sumbitch!" he shouted "White dog sumbitch!"

Roosevelt almost laughed at being cursed in pidgin English. The Lakota suddenly wheeled his pony, yipping something in a loud voice, and circled Roosevelt at a distance. His yipping apparently communicated an order, for the other braves gigged their ponies and fell in behind. They rode south across the tawny plain.

Watching them, Roosevelt realized that by taking a stand he'd saved his life. Had he attempted to outrun them, they would have ridden him down and lifted his scalp. Yet he now had proof as to who was setting the fires and no doubt whatever that they were renegades from the Standing Rock Reservation. Merrifield would be sad to learn that it wasn't the Marquis de Mores.

Late that night Roosevelt walked into the Medora train station. He wrote out a telegram to Gen. Philip Sheridan, commander of the Division of the Missouri, headquartered in St. Louis. The agent behind the counter looked up after reading the message.

"Uh-huh," he said. "Sure you want to send that, Mr. Roosevelt?"

"Quite sure," Roosevelt informed him. "Just as you read it."

> Sioux from Standing Rock agency firing
> graze of ranchers in Dakota Badlands.
> Post patrols around reservation and halt
> depredations or I shall report your derelic-
> tion of duty to General of the Army
> William T. Sherman.
>
>   Theodore Roosevelt
>   President
>   Stockgrowers Association

SEVENTEEN

The cattle buyers arrived in Medora on October 10. There were four buyers in all, representing slaughterhouses and processing plants in Chicago. They were rivals in a business where every man tried to undercut or overbid the other. Cattle season lasted a week, and they made the Metropolitan Hotel their headquarters.

Roosevelt came into town the day of the buyers' arrival. He was a novice at the game, having never taken part in the haggling common to the trade. Yet he was bursting with excitement, for it was his introduction to a vital aspect of ranching, the dollars and cents of profit. He meant to observe and learn from Bill Merrifield.

Every rancher approached cattle season with different tactics. Some trailed their herds into town the first day, thinking the early sellers would receive the highest prices. Others waited a few days, letting market prices stabilize, and still others waited until the end of the week. Bill Merrifield was of the opinion that the early bird gets the worm. He trailed the Maltese Cross herd in on October 11.

Merrifield, like many cattlemen, dealt with the buyer who had treated him fairly in the past. Hiram Tuttle was the longtime representative for the Armour Meat Packing Company, one of the largest plants in the industry. A portly man, with florid features and sharp eyes, he possessed the bonhomie of a snake-oil salesman. His company processed meat for markets in the Midwest and the East, and he was known as a shrewd trader. He knew more about cattle than most ranchers.

The Maltese Cross herd was being held along the river south of town. Early the next morning, Merrifield and Roosevelt brought a buckboard around and collected Tuttle in front of the hotel. They drove out to the herd, which was being held on grassy bottomland by three cowhands from the ranch. Merrifield circled the holding ground at a sedate walk, allowing Tuttle time to inspect the mixed herd of steers and older cows. Tuttle was silent until they completed the circle.

"Nice stock," he finally said. "Although those old cows aren't as prime as the steers. I tally five hundred twenty-nine head."

"You missed two," Merrifield said. "There's five hundred thirty-one. You want me to go around again?"

Tuttle laughed good-naturedly. "Just checking on you, Bill. Never hurts to see if our count matches."

"By Godfrey!" Roosevelt said, thoroughly intrigued. "I would have been off by fifty head or more. How do you count so quickly?"

"Twenty years' experience," Tuttle said genially. "You might say I run an abacus in my head. Simply a trick of memory, Mr. Roosevelt."

"And does it work for larger herds as well?"

"In their heyday, I traveled to all the Kansas cowtowns. I've tallied herds of two thousand or more any number of times. The mental abacus never fails."

"Hiram, you're a wizard," Merrifield said. "So what are you gonna offer me for the herd?"

Tuttle smiled. "Let me think about it on the way back to town."

A short while later Merrifield parked the buckboard in front of the hotel. As they moved through the lobby, they saw Gregor Lang and Jack Simpson huddled with cattle buyers. Tuttle led the way into the dining room and they took a table by the window. The breakfast hour was over, and except for a single late diner, they had the room to themselves. The waiter brought them coffee.

"Let's get to it," Merrifield said as the waiter turned away. "I'd sooner not sit around and dicker all day. Just give me your best price."

"Fair enough." Tuttle stirred sugar into his coffee cup. "If it was anybody else, I wouldn't start with my top bid. I'll give you twenty-seven fifty a head."

"Hell, Hiram, that ain't your top. Sounds more like the bottom to me. I gotta have at least thirty-two."

"Impossible! For old times' sake I'll go . . . twenty-eight."

"Them cows are fat as hogs, and you know it. Thirty-one fifty."

"Twenty-eight fifty."

"Thirty-one, and I won't go no lower."

"Let me *make* a nickel," Tuttle said woefully. "Twenty-nine, and that's my last offer. I can't do any better."

Roosevelt sensed that Merrifield was on the verge of accepting the deal. He'd thought there was some arcane science to dickering cattle prices. But he saw now that it was something closer to a bluffing game. Abruptly, before Merrifield could respond, he rose from his chair. He nodded crisply to Tuttle.

"Sorry we couldn't do business," he said, then nodded to Merrifield. "Come along, Bill, we'll talk with the buyers in the lobby. Good day, Mr. Tuttle."

Tuttle appeared momentarily confounded. "Hold on," he said. "Why spoil an old friendship? I'll go twenty-nine seventy-five."

"A pity," Roosevelt said, stepping back from the table. "Bill believes we will obtain thirty-one a head. I trust his judgment."

"All right, all right," Tuttle said, spreading his arms. "I'm losing money, but you've got a deal. Thirty-one."

"Bully!"

Roosevelt's teeth flashed in a jawbuster grin. He performed a quick mental calculation and arrived at $16,461 for the herd. The profit, he estimated, would allow him to buy another six hundred breeder cows and fund the Maltese Cross for the coming year. He sat back down and allowed Merrifield to work out the details. Tuttle, in the end, wrote a bank draft for the full amount.

Afterward, when Tuttle wandered into the lobby, Merrifield wagged his head. "Mr. Roosevelt, how'd you know he'd go thirty-one? He could've walked away."

"I wasn't absolutely certain," Roosevelt confessed. "But with three other buyers in town, the odds were in our favor. I simply bluffed him."

"You learn that playin' poker?"

"No, I am not a gambler, Bill."

"Hiram Tuttle wouldn't never believe it."

"Then we've done well here today."

The day's work was not yet done. Part of the deal was that the Maltese Cross would load the herd for shipment to Chicago. An hour or so later, Merrifield and his crew drove the herd into the stockyards south of the train depot. Loading chutes were dropped into place, and the men began shouting and prodding, hazing cows up the ramp into boxcars. The cows either balked at the head of the chute, refusing to budge, or spooked halfway up the ramp and started a stampede in the wrong direction. As the morning wore on, the men became soaked with sweat, skinned and bruised from scrambling to safety atop fences. Their curses turned viler with each new mishap.

Roosevelt watched from a perch on the fence. He fidgeted, hardly able to restrain himself, wanting in the worst way to join in the action. But he stayed put, content to learn how men outsmarted cows at close quarters. As the sun rose higher, nearing the noon hour, the last boxcar was loaded. Merrifield slammed the door shut, threw the retaining latch into place, and jumped to the ground. It had required a full train to handle the herd, and he was relieved to see them safely loaded and ready to pull out. Wiping his face with a filthy bandanna, he walked along the tracks to the north end of the cow pens. He grinned at Roosevelt.

"Only good thing about cows is that they're not sheep. Course, they fetch higher prices, too."

Roosevelt hopped down off the fence. "All in all an excellent year, and much to your credit, Bill. You may expect a bonus for your efforts."

"Well, hot damn!" Merrifield's grin broadened. "Look here, I'm fixin' to buy the boys a drink. You care to join us?"

"Thank you, but I have an association meeting scheduled. Enjoy your celebration."

Later that afternoon the Stockgrowers Association met in the hotel dining room. Many of the ranchers were in town for cattle transactions, and Roosevelt was able to convene a full board-of-directors meeting. The first item on the agenda was the series of prairie fires set by Sioux renegades in September. By now everyone knew of Roosevelt's standoff with the band of warriors and his sharply worded telegram to Gen. Philip Sheridan. He presented for the board's appraisal a letter from Sheridan noteworthy for its apologetic tone. The reservation would henceforth be patrolled by cavalry detachments.

"Gawdalmighty!" Simpson crowed. "I'd like to have seen Sheridan's face when he read that telegram."

"Bet he could've chewed nails," Luther Gudgell said. "Them army boys aren't used to being told how to and what for."

Roosevelt next raised the subject of livestock theft. In the past four months, the association had conducted five raids on outlaw camps, arresting twelve men and killing three in shootouts. Sheriff Seth Bullard had appointed Roosevelt a permanent deputy, and the arrested men had been transported to Mandan. All twelve had been tried, convicted, and sentenced to prison in short order. Livestock theft had fallen off by half since the association was founded.

"A fifty percent reduction," Roosevelt announced, "hardly seems sufficient. We must eradicate theft by our constant vigilance."

"That's a tall order," John Eaton said skeptically. "How the hell we gonna eliminate stealing altogether?"

"I propose we form a squad of stock detectives, one man from each of the larger outfits. Their assignment will be to root out thieves with regular patrols through the Badlands. We will strike anywhere, anytime—without warning!"

Gudgell seconded the motion and it carried by unanimous vote. The board further levied large ranchers one hundred dollars a month, to compensate the stock detectives for hazardous duty. There was general discussion of who to recruit and how the detective squad would be organized. The talk finally petered out, and as Roosevelt was about to adjourn the meeting several of the ranchers hastily glanced at Lang. He loudly cleared his throat.

"One further matter," he said. "We are all aware of the movement to bring Dakota Territory into the Union as a state. Last week Luther and I traveled to Bismarck for a conference with our new governor."

Pres. Chester A. Arthur had recently appointed Gilbert Pierce to the post of territorial governor. Over the past six years more than 24 million acres had been homesteaded through the public land office. The population had boomed to 102,000 in the same period; most of the homesteaders had settled in southern Dakota and north of the Badlands, and they were turning out bumper crops of wheat. President Arthur had charged Governor Pierce with the mission of leading Dakota into the Union.

"Statehood is not far away," Lang went on. "When it happens, Governor Pierce will appoint our first senator to the U.S. Congress. The purpose of our meeting was to convince him of the right man for the position."

"Wasn't hard, either," Gudgell added. "He jumped on the bandwagon quick as you please."

"It required no great salesmanship," Lang said. "He knew a good deal about the Badlands, and who has provided the leadership here. He was also quite familiar with our candidate's record in the New York legislature."

"Wait now—" Roosevelt tried to interrupt.

Lang hurried on. "Theodore, you will be the first senator from Dakota. You have Governor Pierce's support."

Roosevelt was humbled by the gesture. Less than eight months ago he was a stranger to most of these men, and now they were offering him one of the most coveted public offices in America. Yet he could not accept.

"I must decline," he said in a low voice. "I cannot tell you how much I appreciate your vote of confidence. But my life is no longer in the political arena. I am, like all of you here, a simple rancher."

"Theodore, you are anything but simple," Lang countered. "You belong in Washington, where you can work for the good of everyone in Dakota. We will not take 'no' for an answer."

"I'm afraid you must," Roosevelt said. "I came here to put all that behind me, and I have no aspirations for public office. I will not change my mind."

The men seated around the table knew him well enough by now to know that the matter was closed. They exchanged looks of profound disappointment, but none of them said anything more. For he had said it all.

Roosevelt, by his own word, would never leave the Badlands.

Yellow leaves glittered like a sea of golden coins in the trees. There was a nip in the air, a promise of frost, with brisk sunny days and cool sparkling nights. Autumn was upon the land.

A late afternoon sun flooded the study. Roosevelt stood by the window, watching as a V of geese winged their way southward against a muslin sky. On the crests of the westward buttes quaking aspens fluttered in a rainbow of saffron and bright rouge. He thought winter was not far away.

After a time, he moved to his desk. He had finished a chapter in the book that afternoon, and his attention turned now to a matter he'd avoided for almost a week. He had remained in Medora until the conclusion of cattle season,

and a letter had arrived from Henry Cabot Lodge. He took
out pen and paper for what his old friend would consider
an unsatisfactory reply.

October 18, 1884

My Dear Cabot,
The cheery optimism of your recent letter was most
welcome. As ever, I wish you grand good fortune in the
November election. The people of Massachusetts could
hardly hope for a more esteemed representative in
Congress.

We have only just concluded cattle season, the time
of year when our cows are sold for market. I must say it
has been a most rewarding experience; the profits real-
ized were quite substantial, and will underwrite my
ranching enterprise for the upcoming year. I may yet be-
come a cattle baron.

Autumn is upon us in all its splendid hues. I am re-
minded that Christmas follows shortly, and as of now, I
plan to spend the holiday season in New York. Bamie
has been quite insistent in her letters, and after so long
a sojourn in the West, I feel I can only comply. Perhaps
you will consider traveling down from Boston during
my stay in New York. I will extend congratulations in
person to a most distinguished new Congressman!

On a similar topic, there is every belief that Dakota
Territory will be admitted to the Union as the thirty-
ninth state. Governor Gilbert Pierce, through the urg-
ings of my associates here, has offered to appoint me
the first Senator from Dakota. I am, of course, quite
honored; however, after brief consideration, I have de-
clined the offer. I no longer hear the sirens' call to a ca-
reer in politics, much as I expressed to you when last we
met in February. You will no doubt be disappointed by
my decision, but there it is. I am quite content here in
the West.

Roosevelt set his pen aside. He studied the last paragraph at length, wondering if his old friend might find the words cavalier in tone. Lodge was campaigning night and day to win election to Congress, and he had all too casually refused a seat in the Senate. Still, however much Lodge disagreed with his decision, he thought his friend would easily read between the lines. He might return to New York to celebrate Christmas with his family, but for no other reason. His refusal to seek a fourth term in the New York legislature was no different than his rejection of appointment to the Senate. His interest in politics was nil.

The last line he'd written caught his eye. There was no obfuscation in saying he was content in Dakota. On the other hand, there was an omission, for anyone reading it might construe as well that he was at peace. Though his intent was not to mislead, his selection of words, intentionally or otherwise, had probably done so. Whatever peace of mind was, and the definition seemed to him increasingly obscure, he knew he hadn't found it. He was content in general, with Elkhorn and his writing, with the life of a rancher and his frequent hunting trips. Yet however much he deceived others, he never deceived himself. He was not at peace.

Nor was he willing to brood on it. He took up his pen and finished the letter to Lodge, three pages of newsy observations on the association, his future plans for Elkhorn and the Maltese Cross, and the fellowship he'd found among other ranchers. He ended with a witty recounting of how, after badgering him for a milch cow, Erma Sewall and Irene Dow had convinced him to buy chickens and build a henhouse. He now awakened to the crowing of a rooster, whose amorous feats with the hens resulted in eggs for breakfast. Domesticity, Roosevelt noted wryly, had come at last to Elkhorn.

The envelope was addressed and sealed in time for supper. He walked through the house and found Sewall and Dow seated in the parlor, waiting to be called into the dining

room. Dark was falling across the land, and coal-oil lamps
lighted the parlor in a buttery glow. The stone fireplace
blazed with logs, tongues of flame leaping into the chimney.
Sewall looked up from reading the *Badlands Cowboy*.

"Says here," he said, tapping the newspaper, "you're
gonna be our new senator when we get statehood. Or least-
ways, there's a movement afoot to make it so."

"Indeed?"

Roosevelt had brought the latest issue with him from
town, but he hadn't yet read it. He took the paper from Sewall and quickly scanned a boxed editorial on the front
page. Amos Packard, the young publisher, was in fine form:

> We take occasion to remark that Theodore Roose-
> velt's record as a public man is above reproach and
> that he is a vigorous Republican of the progressive
> school. This young political Hercules has already
> got Western Dakota in his pocket, and we are reli-
> ably informed that Governor Gilbert Pierce will
> appoint him to the post of Senator upon statehood.
> We could think of no man better equipped for the
> job than the titanic Mr. Roosevelt.

"I'm surprised at Packard," Roosevelt said. "He should
learn to check his facts before going to print."

"What's wrong with it?" Sewall asked. "Are you sayin'
the governor didn't offer you the job?"

"No, insofar as it goes, that part is correct. Packard
failed to mention that I declined the offer."

"When was this?"

"A week ago, at the association board meeting. I made my
position quite clear, and I'm sure Packard was so informed.
Which accounts for why he didn't request an interview."

"How's that again?" Sewall said. "Why wouldn't he
want to interview you?"

"Because it is a conspiracy," Roosevelt said with an
amused smile. "One engineered by my chief drumbeater,
Gregor Lang."

"What's Lang got to do with it?"

"Lang and Gudgell called on the governor and secured his support. They assumed I would be amenable to the idea. I was not."

"Huh." Sewall was confused. "Don't sound like much of a conspiracy."

"No, I meant the editorial," Roosevelt said. "After I declined the offer, Lang convinced Packard to write something positive in tone. He hopes people will read it and pressure me to change my mind."

"But you don't aim to be pressured?"

"As I said, I've made my position clear."

Dow appeared bewildered. "Mr. Roosevelt, you don't mind my askin', why would you refuse? I'd think you'd be honored to be a senator."

"Honored indeed," Roosevelt said. "Or more to the point, honored to be asked."

Sewall frowned. "So why'd you turn it down?"

"Adam, I am out of politics. Nothing could sway my thinking on the subject. I much prefer Elkhorn to public life."

"If that's the case, how'd you end up head of the Stockgrowers Association? How'd you get involved chargin' the Marquis with murder?"

"Hardly an apt comparison," Roosevelt said. "Certain things are done out of moral obligation. Perhaps a sense of duty."

"Yeah, but you could've refused," Sewall retorted slyly. "You could've let somenbody else head the association. You could've let somebody else put the law on de Mores. You could've just stayed here at Elkhorn—out of public life."

"Are you trying to draw me into debate?"

"No, sir, I'm sayin' you're a leader and, on top of that, you *like* to lead men. You generally don't have to be asked to take charge."

Roosevelt chuckled. "You make me sound quite the martinet. Perhaps I should have sought a career in the army."

"Or the Senate," Sewall said evenly. "You weren't

meant to herd a bunch of cowhands or chase horse thieves. You've got bigger things to do in life."

"You should be in league with Gregor Lang. I'm sure he would welcome another conspirator."

"Maybe I'll offer my services. We might just get you to see the light."

"I follow no light but my own, Adam. And it led me here to Elkhorn."

"Suppertime!"

Erma Sewall called from the doorway. The men followed her into the dining room with a sense of an argument postponed. She and Irene scurried back and forth from the kitchen with a platter of steaks and an array of steaming dishes from their summer garden. Amy served the men coffee, and once she sat down, Roosevelt engaged her in a conversation on the tactics of avoiding being spurred on the way to the henhouse. The rooster, nicknamed the Assassin, invariably ambushed her when she went to collect eggs. She considered the bird her mortal enemy.

After supper, Roosevelt shrugged into his mackinaw and went outside. A large meal often made him feel sluggish, and the crisp night air served to restore his vigor. The sky was dark as ebony, dotted with bright, winking stars to the points of the compass. He walked to the edge of the porch, hands stuffed in his pockets. Off in the distance an owl hooted its plaintive cry.

Roosevelt was still troubled by his verbal exchange with Sewall. He'd left the house as much to escape further debate as to take the night air. Sewall knew him too well and had easily seen through his tissue of excuses. Turning his back on politics was simply another instance of turning his back on the world. He did not seek responsibility, nor the leadership of men, and as he dwelled on it, his mood became darker. His eyes were drawn to the cottonwoods by the river.

The last time he'd seen them was there by the river. Often, particularly in moments of deepest despair, he willed them to come again. Yet he knew it was not within his power to summon spirits from the beyond. Just as he knew Alice and his mother were out there even now. Waiting. Waiting . . .

Their presence, so keenly sensed, gave him pause. He wondered if they approved of anything he'd done since leaving New York. The ranch, his new life in the West, his withdrawal from anything that reminded him of his past life. He no longer chided himself for believing in haunts or apparitions or some ephemeral existence beyond the grave. He just wanted to know why they were waiting. . . .

To hear at last what they were here to say.

EIGHTEEN

Thanksgiving was celebrated in the midst of an arctic storm. The weather was so fierce that the cowhands had been confined to the bunkhouse for the past three days. Elkhorn was gripped in the stillness of a frozen tundra.

The crew was invited to Thanksgiving Day dinner at the main house. Bud Ledbetter, the bunkhouse cook, volunteered to work with Erma Sewall and Irene Dow in preparing the meal. Roosevelt, who treated harsh weather with indifference, had trekked out to a shelterbelt of woods and bagged four wild turkeys with his shotgun. The birds were being baked two at a time in the kitchen oven.

Dinner was scheduled for one o'clock. The cowhands waited in the bunkhouse, playing checkers and a popular card game called euchre. Sewall and Dow settled into the parlor, absorbed in reading books, while Ledbetter and the women, assisted by Amy, bustled about the kitchen. Roosevelt retreated to his study, where logs snapped and crackled in the stone fireplace. The warmth from the fire slowly melted the ice on the windows.

For the past three days, watching the storm rage, Roosevelt had become fascinated with the effects of a blizzard on the landscape. Early that morning the overcast skies had cleared and the valley glittered like a sea of frosty diamonds beneath a winter sun. Yet his interest was not in sunny skies but rather in the bleaker aspects of a storm that virtually paralyzed creatures, man and beast alike, as well as the land. He set himself the task of capturing it on paper, a prose poem that might be worked into his book. He entitled the piece "Winter Weather."

> When the days have dwindled to their shortest, then all the great northern plains are changed into an abode of iron desolation. Furious gales blow down from the north, driving before them clouds of blinding snow-dust, wrapping the mantle of death round every unsheltered being that faces their unshackled anger. They roar in a thunderous bass as they sweep across the prairie; they shiver the great brittle cottonwoods, and beneath their rough touch the icy limbs of the pines that cluster in gorges sing like the chords of an Aeolian harp. The still, merciless cold that broods over the earth like the shadow of silent death seems even more dreadful in its gloomy rigor than in the lawless madness of the storms. All the land is like granite; the great rivers stand still in their beds, as if turned to frosted steel. In the long nights there is no sound to break the lifeless silence.

Roosevelt sat back, pen in hand, scanning the lines. He thought the composition was fairly structured for a first draft, but it nonetheless needed work. Perhaps expanding it somewhat to include a finer sense of the barren wastes of ice and snow, and the brutal cold that numbed a man to the bone. It occurred to him that he hadn't adequately depicted the river, which was as starkly symbolic of winter as the land. He rose from his desk and walked through the house.

Sewall was dozing in a chair, a book open across his lap. Dow scarcely glanced up, mesmerized by the derring-do in an adventure by James Fenimore Cooper. Roosevelt crossed the parlor, intent on a more analytical examination of the Little Missouri. The blaze from the great fireplace had left the windows partially frosted, and the view eastward from the house was one of raw chaos. He committed the sight to memory.

The arctic conditions had frozen the river solid. Then, as the storm blew out and the sun rose high, the river current broke through the middle of the ice pack. Huge floes tore loose, grinding and grating, swept aside to form jagged battlements along the banks on either side. The result was a gorge of ice ten feet tall, upstream and downstream, for as far as the eye could see. The dark waters of the river swirled through the gorge like obsidian roiling against white rock.

Dow closed his book and moved across the room. "Wild as it gets," he said, nodding out the window. "Never saw nothin' like that back in Maine."

"By Jove it's so!" Roosevelt chortled. "A man must come West to see such a sight."

"Mr. Roosevelt, the way you talk, anybody'd think you like these storms."

"We have been treated to winter at its most majestic. I look upon it with awe."

"Well, one thing's for sure," Dow said. "Weather like this makes it rough on cows."

"Cattle are hardy brutes," Roosevelt said, motioning off into the valley. "They gather in canyons and ravines, on the lee of the wind, and ride it out. Far sturdier than we puny men."

"Well, sir," Dow remarked with a slow smile, "I have to say I feel plumb puny when I step outside."

Roosevelt was in a chipper mood today. The storm somehow invigorated him, and he was reminded that life had its brighter moments. On October 27 he had turned twenty-five, though in darker moments he sometimes felt twice that age. Erma had baked him a birthday cake, and his adopted family laughingly watched him blow out the candles. Today was another day of celebration, and he thought Thanksgiving was properly named. A time to give thanks for the good things in life.

The clock on the mantle chimed one. As if on cue, the cowhands trooped over from the bunkhouse, cinched in their mackinaws and puffing frost. Bob Hallett and Dutch

Wannegan led the way, followed by Sam Jeeter and Oscar Dixon. Roosevelt met them at the door and they crowded into the parlor, stamping their feet and flapping their arms. Hallett rolled his eyes.

"Colder'n a witch's—" He stopped, remembering there were women in the house, and glibly altered the curse. "Yessir, colder'n a witch's big toe."

Sewall roused himself from his chair. "Bob, if it gets any colder, we'll be breathin' icicles. You boys ready for turkey and the fixin's?"

"Shore are," Jeeter said. "Don't recollect last time I had turkey for Thanksgivin'."

"Mr. Roosevelt's treat," Sewall said with a smile. "He went out in the blizzard and shot our dinner."

Roosevelt took a bow. "Gentlemen, I do believe we are in for a feast. Happy Thanksgiving!"

Amy appeared in the doorway of the dining room. Her cheeks were flushed with excitement as she called them to dinner. Erma and Irene, assisted by Bud Ledbetter, brought in four turkeys packed with stuffing and topped with wild plum sauce; mashed potatoes and bowls of gravy; and loaves of bread baked that morning. Every chair in the house, plus a couple of kitchen stools, had been collected to set enough places at the table. When they were all seated, Sewall said grace, thanking God for the bounty of the land and the good health of all at Elkhorn. The men chorused, "Amen."

Roosevelt, wielding a long kitchen knife, went around the table and carved the turkeys with deft strokes. The cowhands, who knew little of etiquette and less of napkins, watched the women for pointers. Dishes were passed, everyone loading their plates, Amy claiming two turkey legs and the others up for grabs. Conversation revolved around the weather, and there was general agreement that winter had come on too soon, too hard. For dessert, Erma served an angel food cake with white icing, and a berry cobbler. The men scraped their plates clean.

After dinner, the cowhands extolled praise on the

women. Most of them had never set foot in the main house, and they were at some pains to thank Roosevelt for the invitation. As they gathered their coats and hats, he stood at the doorway, shaking hands, again wishing each of them a happy Thanksgiving. When the men were gone, he took seats with Sewall and Dow in the parlor while the women and Amy busied themselves clearing the table. A few minutes later, as Roosevelt engaged Dow in conversation about *The Deerslayer,* there was a knock at the door. Sewall crossed the room and admitted Bob Hallett.

"Figgered I'd best tell you," Hallett said. "Took a walk to work off dinner and went down to have a look at the river. Somebody's stole Mr. Roosevelt's boat."

Roosevelt kept a two-seater rowboat to paddle across the river for an occasional hunting trip. Because of the ice floes, the boat had been dragged ashore and tied to a tree. Sewall had checked on it late yesterday afternoon.

"Maybe the river got it," he said. "Way that ice shifts, it wouldn't surprise me."

"Wasn't the river," Hallett told him. "Somebody cut the rope clean in half."

Roosevelt threw on his coat and hat. "I'll have a look myself."

Sewall and Dow grabbed their mackinaws off the wall pegs by the door. With Hallett in the lead, they followed Roosevelt down the clearing to a stand of cottonwoods. The ice jam towered above their heads, a frozen wall crowded close to the riverbank. On the snow-packed ground, there was a shallow imprint from the hull of the boat. The rope, knotted around the base of a tree, had been severed.

"No question of it," Roosevelt said. "The knot is frozen to the tree and impossible to get loose. They had little choice but to cut the rope."

"Nobody'd steal a boat at night," Sewall observed. "That current's too strong to try pushin' off in the dark. I'd say they took it right about daylight."

A broad crevice in the wall of ice opened onto the river.

Dow pointed out skid marks in the ice. "Dragged it in there," he said with a puzzled frown. "Who'd steal a boat in this kind of weather?"

"Red Finnegan," Hallett said with some certainty. "One of John Eaton's crew told me Finnegan and his boys have been rustlin' a cow or two at a time. Eaton warned 'em to clear out or face the music."

"When was this?" Sewall asked.

"Day before yesterday."

Jack Finnegan was a redheaded Irishman who owned a homestead bordering Eaton's range. He'd built a crude cabin and lived there with his cohorts, Earl Burnsted and Walt Pfaffenbach. They were disreputable characters, with no known means of support, and suspected of small-time rustling. John Eaton had apparently grown tired of losing a cow or two now and then.

"Why steal a boat?" Dow said curiously. "They could've skipped the country on horses."

"Not in this weather," Hallett allowed. "Horse wouldn't get ten miles in this snow without breakin' down. Then you'd be afoot and frozen stiff in no time."

"Yeah, the boat makes sense," Sewall said. "They was probably scared Eaton would show up when the storm blew out. So they took to the water."

"And they're headed downriver," Hallett added. "Current runnin' that fast, nobody could row upstream."

"Good thinking!" Roosevelt said vigorously. "We shall undertake pursuit as rapidly as possible."

Sewall groaned. "It's only a boat, Mr. Roosevelt. A polar bear wouldn't go nowhere in this cold."

"Adam, I will not tolerate thieves, even for a boat. If Finnegan can travel, so shall we."

"Well, appears to me, we've got ourselves a problem. Like Bob said, horses won't get us very far. And they've stole the boat."

"You and Will are handy with tools. Couldn't you build river transport of some fashion?"

"Yessir," Sewall said wearily. "I suppose we could

knock together a flatboat from logs. More on the order of a
raft."

"Bully!"

"Course, even if we start now, it won't be ready till tomorrow mornin'. That puts Finnegan a day ahead of us."

"Better late than never seems the appropriate axiom. I
shall go prepare my kit for the hunt."

Roosevelt flashed a mouthful of teeth in a broad grin.
His shoulders squared, he marched off at a purposeful
stride toward the house. Sewall let loose a long sigh and
Dow stared out at the river. Hallett wagged his head.

"All for a *boat*?" he said. "Don't hardly make sense."

Sewall grunted. "Does if your name's Theodore Roosevelt."

"Yeah, why's that?"

"'Cause nobody else has ever done it."

"What the devil you talking about?"

"Red Finnegan."

"What about him?"

"He's gonna wish he never stole that boat."

The Little Missouri was unlike other rivers. Downstream
was in the wrong direction, winding north by northeast instead of south. The current was drawn ever northward to
empty into the mighty Missouri, one of the largest rivers
on the continent. There was a sense of gravity gone askew.

Their third day out the weather was bitterly cold. The
temperature was below freezing and a raw wind whistled
down from the north. Their campsite was in the lee of a bluff,
with the raft beached and secured to a tree. As the sun edged
over the horizon, they hunkered about a small fire, soaking
up warmth. Breakfast was fried bacon, hardtack, and coffee.

"We've come a far piece," Sewall said, bacon grease
dripping down his chin. "I figure somewheres around a
hundred miles."

"Certainly that," Roosevelt agreed. "Perhaps a bit farther."

They were dressed in mackinaws and heavy shirts, scarves wrapped around their necks. Their bedding was wool blankets tucked inside sheets of canvas to ward off the cold. The fire warmed them, but every word was spoken in a puff of frost. They ate in silence a moment.

"Think we're gonna catch 'em?" Sewall said. "What with a day's head start, they might've got away by now."

Roosevelt munched a bite of hardtack. "Do you agree they could not take to land?"

"Not likely they'd try it on foot. Cold as it is, they'd freeze stiffer'n a brass monkey."

"So they have no choice but to continue by boat. The nearest town on the river is Mandan."

"How far is that?"

Roosevelt set his coffee cup aside. He took a map from inside his mackinaw and spread it on the ground. From landfall last night he roughly estimated their position at the moment. Using his thumb and forefinger as a caliper, he measured the distance to where the Little Missouri flowed into the Missouri. From there, tracking southeastward along the Missouri, he measured the distance to Mandan. His eyes narrowed behind his spectacles.

"A hundred miles to the Missouri," he said. "Another two hundred miles down the Missouri to Mandan."

"Nine or ten days by boat," Sewall said woodenly. "And they'll still be a day ahead of us."

"Perhaps we'll yet overtake them. If not, when we reach Mandan, Sheriff Bullard will assist in the hunt. I am resolved to see this through."

"No choice anyway," Dow interjected. "We'd never make it back upstream to Elkhorn. Not against the current."

Sewall climbed to his feet. "Guess we might as well go ahead and go. The day's not gettin' any younger."

Their camp gear was soon stowed aboard the raft. A crude affair fashioned of logs, the raft was some twelve feet wide by twenty feet long. The logs were lashed together with rope, and tar pitch had been used to seal the gaps watertight. Sewall stood at the stern, steering with a rudder he'd fashioned from planed boards. Dow muscled against the current with a long pole from the bow.

Roosevelt periodically spelled Dow with the pole. For now, he took a seat amidships, cushioned by their bedrolls. A brassbound chest stocked with provisions sufficient to last them a week was lashed to the logs. All of the men carried pistols, and their rifles were wrapped in canvas and secured to one side of the chest. Sewall, who was the better boatman, never left the rudder.

Three days ago, when they departed from the ranch, Roosevelt had selected Sewall and Dow to accompany him on the hunt. They were experienced rivermen, having plied the waterways of Maine by boat and canoe for most of their lives. The race to overtake the thieves required a crew who could master the turbulent Little Missouri; were they to swamp the raft, they would almost certainly succumb to the frigid waters and exposure to the cold. Survival left no margin for error.

The women had seen to their supplies. The brassbound chest was packed with slabs of bacon, hardtack, beans, a can of ground coffee, and cooking utensils. Included as well were matches in a waterproof tin, dry socks, and extra ammunition for their weapons. Bob Hallett, who was the top hand and second only to Sewall, had been left in charge at Elkhorn. His orders were to notify the sheriff if the men hadn't returned in two weeks.

The sun rose higher in a cloudless sky as they shoved off from the riverbank. The glare was blinding as streamers of light bounced off the ice packs along the western shoreline. Beyond the shore, the snow-crowned buttes stood like forlorn sentinels guarding a bleak and frozen wasteland. Deer were frequently seen watering where ice jams separated and left clear spots on the river; but the men dared not fire, even though they were famished for fresh meat. A gunshot in the crystalline winter air would travel for miles and perhaps alert the men they pursued. It was a risk they could not chance.

Roosevelt took a copy of *Anna Karenina* from the chest.

Even on a manhunt, and he'd known the chase might be prolonged, he couldn't resist bringing the book. He considered it Tolstoy's finest novel, and though he'd read it before, he was still entranced by the story of star-crossed lovers and the heroine's tragic end. He thought it was in many ways superior to Dostoyevsky's Russian classic *The Brothers Karamazov.* A patriarch contending with obstreperous sons was somehow less engrossing than young lovers doomed by circumstance and fate. He read through the morning, warmed by an arctic sun.

"There's your boat!"

Sewall's warning was delivered in a hissed voice. Roosevelt snapped the book closed as the raft rounded a dogleg bend in the river. Not fifty yards ahead, along the western shoreline, the rowboat was beached on a patchy stretch of riverbank between two ice floes. Beyond the boat, on higher ground, smoke drifted skyward from a thick grove of cottonwoods. As Sewall swung the raft around, Roosevelt scrambled to uncase their rifles from the canvas wrapping. Dow poled furiously toward the shore.

"Look alert," Roosevelt whispered. "They are most surely armed."

The raft bumped into the riverbank beside the boat. Dow hopped off with a mooring rope and looped it around a large boulder. Roosevelt passed out the rifles once they were ashore, then took the lead up the snow-crusted slope. A few moments later they topped the crest and paused, fanning out on a line. Directly ahead, in the stand of cottonwoods, a man sat hunched over a campfire. His back was to them, and there was no one else in sight. They moved forward, rifles at the ready.

"Do not move!" Roosevelt said sharply. "We have you covered."

The man twisted around, his hand clutching at a rifle on the ground. Then he saw them, their rifles pointed at his chest, and he slowly raised his hands. They recognized him as Walt Pfaffenbach, one of the men who worked for Red Finnegan. His mouth crooked in a befuddled grimace.

"Sonovabitch," he said blearily. "Where the hell'd you spring from?"

"Never mind that," Roosevelt said, glancing about the campsite. "Where are Finnegan and Burnsted?"

"Why, we done run out of vittles. They went off huntin' and left me to watch the boat. Now I've got myself captured."

"How long have they been gone?"

"All mornin' jest about," Pfaffenbach said. "We et the last of our grub and it was hunt or starve to death. Red was hopin' to see a deer."

"Which direction did they go?"

"Off to the west there."

Roosevelt quickly assessed the situation. "Will, relieve him of his weapon and bind his arms behind his back. Adam, you come with me."

The country to the west was rolling prairie studded with ravines. A thicket of sagebrush, heavily covered with snow, bordered the edge of the tree line. Roosevelt and Sewall moved through the cottonwoods and crouched down behind the screen of brush. Hidden from view, they were able to peer through spotty gaps in the brush and keep watch. They settled in to wait.

To their rear, obscured by the trees, Dow fed the campfire, and smoke spiraled above the branches. As the day wore on, they envied Dow the warmth of the fire; they were unable to move for fear of revealing their position, and the cold slowly seeped into their bones. Finally, with the sun slanted toward the westward buttes, they heard voices in the distance. The sound of two men talking gradually drew closer.

"Gawddamn country," one man grouched. "Helluva note when you can't even shoot a rabbit."

"Well, we gotta do something, Red. I'm so hungry I could eat my boots."

"Lemme know how it tastes."

"Hands up!"

Roosevelt stepped clear of the brush. Sewall was at his side, their rifles trained on the men. Red Finnegan and Earl

Burnsted stared at them in stunned disbelief. Finnegan quickly recovered, and started to raise his rifle.

"Careful now!" Roosevelt ordered. "We've no wish to kill you."

A tense moment slipped past as Finnegan weighed his chances. Burnsted abruptly dropped his rifle on the ground, and Finnegan, with a muttered curse, was only a beat behind. They raised their hands overhead.

"Gawddamnit anyway," Finnegan said sourly. "Never figgered you'd come after us. You must set some store by that boat."

"I care nothing for the boat," Roosevelt informed him. "But I very much detest a thief. You men are under arrest."

"Well, what the hell, I been in jail before. Hope the food's better this time."

"You will shortly find out, Mr. Finnegan."

Sewall relieved the men of their pistols and knives. They were marched back to camp, where Dow waited with Pfaffenbach. After their arms were bound with rope, Finnegan and Burnsted were seated by the fire. Sewall motioned to Roosevelt and walked off into the trees. His look was somber.

"We've got a problem," he said. "We only brought food enough for ourselves. How're we gonna feed them?"

"There is adequate for tonight," Roosevelt noted. "Tomorrow I shall replenish the larder with a deer. We will do fine."

"Those boys were out all day and didn't see any game. Let's hope you have better luck."

"Those boys, as you call them, strike me as poor hunters. We will have venison for breakfast."

"What then?" Sewall asked, still concerned. "We're a long way from anything that resembles a jail. You said Mandan's a couple hundred miles downriver."

"Adam, you worry too much," Roosevelt said confidently. "Will can handle the boat by himself, and you and I shall transport the prisoners on the raft. I foresee no great difficulty."

Sewall was on the verge of arguing the point. A journey of two hundred miles on open water in the dead of winter seemed to him something more than difficult. But then, on second thought, it occurred to him that Roosevelt was right. Mandan, however far, was their only option.

He hoped to hell it didn't snow again.

NINETEEN

Roosevelt was mounted on a roan gelding. He rode be-hind a lumbering wagon driven by Ike Miller, a cow-hand for the Diamond C ranch. The three prisoners, bound hand and foot, jounced along in the back of the wagon. They rolled into Dickinson on December 2.

The odd little convoy drew stares from people on the street. Dickinson was some forty miles east of Medora, lo-cated on the Northern Pacific line. The town prospered by virtue of the railroad and served as a trade center for outly-ing farmers and cattlemen. The main thoroughfare was crowded with shops and stores.

A few doors down from the bank, Roosevelt spotted the town marshal's office. He rode forward, motioning Miller to bring the wagon to a halt. Finnegan, Burnsted, and Pfaf-fenbach glanced at him, then craned their necks for a look at the local jail. He dismounted from the roan gelding, looping the reins around the hitchrack. He walked back to the wagon.

"Ike, I shouldn't be long. We've come so far, let's not take any chances now. Keep a sharp eye on our prisoners."

"Yessir, Mr. Roosevelt." Miller patted the six-gun strapped on his hip. "They mess with me and I'll shoot their ears off."

"I'm sure you will."

Roosevelt liked the man's spirit. He and Miller had shared an adventure over the past three days, traveling almost fifty miles across open range. During the day, Miller drove the wagon and Roosevelt rode behind, his gaze never far from the prisoners. At night, with a large campfire blazing, they spelled each other at two-hour intervals, standing guard. Miller seemed willing to shoot on the slightest pretext.

The journey to Dickinson had been nothing short of happenstance. The day after capturing the men, Roosevelt and Sewall manning the raft and Dow in the boat, they had floated past the eastern foothills of the Killdeer Mountains. On the riverbank they spotted a Diamond C cowhand, out checking on the herd after the storm. Once ashore, they explained their predicament and requested assistance from the Diamond C. The cowhand rode off toward ranch headquarters.

Early that afternoon Bill Cameron, owner of the Diamond C, showed up with a wagon. His outfit was closer to Dickinson than Medora, but he knew of Roosevelt's record in the Badlands. Cameron arranged for a wagon, driven by Ike Miller, to transport Roosevelt and the prisoners to the railhead at Dickinson. At Roosevelt's request, Cameron arranged for another wagon to haul Sewall and Dow and the rowboat on an overland trek to the river crossing opposite Elkhorn. They would be back with their families in a couple days.

Cameron provided Roosevelt with rations and the loan of a saddle horse and assured him that Ike Miller was just the man to help guard prisoners. Dickinson was almost due south of the Diamond C, some fifty miles distant, with a relatively easy crossing at the Knife River. Over the course of the trip, Roosevelt found that Miller was good company, reliable, and, like most cowboys, antagonistic to thieves of any nature. By the time they reached Dickinson, the prisoners were relieved to see the last of Miller. They knew he would have welcomed an excuse to unlimber his pistol.

"I shan't be long," Roosevelt said now. "Do you know the marshal's name?"

"John Odell," Miller replied. "Only marshal Dickinson's ever had."

"I'll just have a word with him."

Roosevelt crossed the boardwalk. The marshal's office was a Spartan affair, with a battered desk, a potbellied stove, and a padlocked rack for long guns. To the rear, through a heavy door, was a small lockup with two barred cells, both now empty. The man behind the desk was stoutly built, with a handlebar mustache and the welt of an old scar over his left eyebrow. He looked up as Roosevelt came through the door.

"Mornin'."

"Good morning," Roosevelt said. "I am Theodore Roosevelt, deputy sheriff of Billings County. I have prisoners who require lodging for the night."

Odell stood and extended his hand. "Heard of you, Mr. Roosevelt. That 'barefoot and bareback' story with the horse thieves was a corker. Made quite a name for yourself."

"Thank you." Roosevelt accepted his handshake. "I have three men in custody and I would appreciate you holding them overnight. I plan to take them to Mandan tomorrow."

"What's the charge?"

"Theft."

"Cows or horses?"

"Neither," Roosevelt said. "They stole my boat."

"Boat," Odell repeated somewhat dubiously. "I don't recollect anybody ever gettin' arrested for stealing a boat. How'd you wind up in Dickinson?"

Roosevelt briefly recounted the manhunt. As he told of the days on the river and the trek from the Diamond C ranch, Odell's mouth fell open. He ended with a wave of his hand.

"We were fortunate," he said. "Had it snowed again, we might never have caught them."

"Let me get this straight," Odell said, clearly astonished. "You chased them three days on the river—all for a boat?"

"Indeed we did."

"Well, that's the damnedest story I ever heard. Have to say, you're hell on thieves, Mr. Roosevelt."

"I'm flattered you think so," Roosevelt said. "Will you be able to detain these men for me?"

"Why, sure," Odell said. "Won't be no trouble at all."

"What time is the morning train to Mandan?"

"Nine o'clock."

"Perhaps you will be so kind as to loan me three sets of manacles. I will return them on my way back to Medora."

"Hell, I'll loan you a deputy, if you want. Wouldn't hurt to have somebody along on the train."

"Excellent idea," Roosevelt said. "I appreciate your assistance, Marshal."

Odell followed him outside. Miller hopped down from the wagon seat and helped unload the prisoners. They were led into the office, still hobbled by their bonds, and Roosevelt cut the ropes with a sheath knife. The marshal put Finnegan and Burnsted in one cell and Pfaffenbach in the other. He couldn't resist an amused smile.

"Guess you boys won't be stealin' no boats again."

"World's plumb gone to hell," Finnegan said, flopping down on a bunk. "Who'd 've thought a shitty little boat would land you in the pokey?"

"Bub, you're just lucky you stole it from Mr. Roosevelt. Some men would've hung you."

Odell closed the door to the lockup. "They're in for the night," he said to Roosevelt. "I'll have 'em ready for you bright and early."

"I wonder if you might recommend a hotel, Marshal."

"Only got one and that'd be the Dixon House. Down in the next block."

"Then I shall see you at eight in the morning. Once again, thank you for your courtesy."

"Don't think nothin' of it, Mr. Roosevelt. Pleasure's all mine."

Roosevelt went out. As he crossed the boardwalk, Miller finished tying the roan gelding to the rear of the wagon. He pulled Roosevelt's Winchester from the saddle scabbard and walked forward.

"You'll be wantin' that," he said, handing over the rifle. "Reckon I'll head on out."

"Won't you stay the night?" Roosevelt said. "I'd thought to put you up at the hotel and buy dinner. It's the least you deserve for all your efforts."

"Obliged, but there's still plenty of daylight and I've got a ways to go. I'd sooner sleep under the stars anyhow."

"Ike, I wish there were something I could do. Your help was most invaluable and very much appreciated."

"Wouldn't have missed it for all the tea in China, Mr. Roosevelt. I'll be tellin' this story round the bunkhouse the rest of the winter."

"Allow me to thank you, then." Roosevelt pumped his arm with a firm handshake. "You are welcome at Elkhorn any time you ride our way."

"Maybe I'll see you one of these days."

Miller climbed into the wagon and drove off. Roosevelt watched after him a moment, wondering again at the casual courage of men who put themselves in harm's way with no reward asked or expected. He thought it spoke to the spirit of Westerners, singular in their willingness to lend a hand even when it involved danger. They were, he told himself, a breed apart.

Downstreet, Roosevelt turned into a mercantile store. He'd worn the same clothes for the last week, and he felt not just grubby but odoriferous. The clerk who waited on him apparently shared the view, standing at a discreet distance and all but pinching his nose. Roosevelt bought a flannel shirt, wool trousers, a fresh set of long johns, and a straight razor. He walked out with his Winchester in one hand and the package under his other arm.

The Dixon House hotel was plain but comfortable. Roosevelt took a room on the second floor and paid extra for a rubber bathtub and hot water. A porter lugged the bathtub to his room and then made several trips with pails of steaming water and a bar of yellow soap. After stripping

off his old clothes, Roosevelt spent the next hour luxuriat-
ing in the tub, scrubbing himself from head to foot. Once
he'd finished, he changed into his new long johns, moved
to the mirror over the washstand, and shaved off a week's
growth of whiskers. He felt clean for the first time since
leaving Elkhorn.

Downstairs again, dressed in his new shirt and trousers,
he went into the dining room. Noontime was now over, and
the waiter took his order for four eggs, a tenderloin steak,
fried potatoes, and buttermilk biscuits. He swigged coffee
until the waiter returned with a heaping platter, then tore
into the food with unrestrained gusto. His mouth was
stuffed with steak when two men stopped at his table.

"Mr. Roosevelt?"

"Yes."

"I am Cecil Hollister, mayor of Dickinson, and this is
Judge Webster Starr."

"Gentlemen." Roosevelt swallowed the bite of steak.
"How may I help you?"

"Would you mind if we joined you?"

"Not if you don't mind watching me eat. I haven't had a
decent meal in a week."

"So we understand," Hollister said as the men seated
themselves. "Marshal Odell told us about your capture of
the thieves. Damn risky business."

Roosevelt spread jam on a biscuit. "I rather enjoyed it
myself. Apart from the monotonous diet, of course."

"Yes, of course," Judge Starr said agreeably. "Mr.
Roosevelt, we know the governor supports you as the first
senator from Dakota. We gather from newspaper stories
that you are reluctant to accept the appointment."

"That is correct."

"Entirely understandable," Hollister said with oily sincerity. "A man who has served in public office as long as
you might feel the need for a quieter life. Even the life of a
rancher."

"That is correct as well."

"Nevertheless," Starr announced in a sonorous voice.

"Every man has an obligation to serve when duty calls. Particularly a man of your remarkable capabilities, Mr. Roosevelt."

The men were alert to his reaction. Roosevelt glanced around the room, expecting to find Gregor Lang hidden in some dark corner. He thought Lang must be traveling the country beating the drum for a candidate who refused to campaign. Before he could reply, Mayor Hollister leaned forward, elbows on the table. His tone was almost righteous.

"You are the man for the job," he said solemnly. "We support you, the town of Dickinson supports you, all of Dakota supports you. We are here to convince you that you have been called."

Roosevelt cut another bite of steak. He popped it into his mouth and chewed thoughtfully, as though weighing the import of their words. But he was wondering how he might say no yet again. Say it with finality.

So clearly that all of Dakota would hear.

The train ground to a halt outside the depot. A light snow was falling and Medora seemed oddly tranquil beneath a powdery white veil. Winter was a time of quietude in the Badlands.

Roosevelt stepped off the caboose. As a deputy sheriff, his badge pinned to his shirt, he'd hitched a ride yesterday evening on the overnight freight train from Mandan. He waved to the brakeman as he crossed the depot platform.

Yesterday he had delivered his prisoners to Sheriff Bullard at the Billings County jail. A quick hearing was arranged in Superior Court, and Finnegan, Burnsted, and Pfaffenbach had been arraigned on charges of grand theft. The court docket was crowded, and the judge had offered leniency if they waived a jury trial and pleaded guilty. They were sentenced to a year in the penitentiary.

Roosevelt was pleased with the outcome. A year in prison seemed to him satisfactory punishment for stealing a boat. But upon departing Mandan his mind had turned to the breakfast discussion with Mayor Hollister and Judge

Starr in Dickinson. Last night, in one of the crew bunks on
the caboose, he'd wrestled with the matter of how he might
discourage further overtures of political office. He had decided on a public statement.

On the way uptown, he caught people staring at him as
he hurried along the street. He was still carrying his Winchester, for there was no other way to return it to Elkhorn.
It occurred to him that a man walking about town with a rifle was an unusual sight, even for Medora. Everyone knew
him by now, and gossip would soon spread about Roosevelt
stalking the streets loaded for bear. He was chuckling about
it as he turned into the office of the *Badlands Cowboy*.

A printing press clattered at the back of the room. Amos
Packard was talking to one of the pressmen and glanced
around as the door swung open. He thought Roosevelt
looked every inch the Westerner, packing a holstered Colt,
a Winchester gripped in one hand, his Stetson creased from
wear. A far cry from the Eastern dude who had arrived in
Medora only nine months ago. Packard walked forward
with a smile.

"Hail the conquering hero! You return draped in laurels,
Mr. Roosevelt."

"Do I?" Roosevelt said. "Conquest is in the eye of the
beholder, Amos. What am I accused of now?"

"The story came in over the wire," Packard replied.
"Your intrepid pursuit of armed and dangerous thieves
along a river clogged with arctic ice floes. You are now the
stuff of legend."

"Stuff and nonsense would be more to the point.
Finnegan and his half-wit thugs are hardly the brigands of
Western lore. I doubt Ned Buntline would consider them
worthy material for a dime novel."

"No, but he might well consider you. A plains stalwart
to rival Buffalo Bill."

"Good Lord, I shudder at the prospect."

Roosevelt leaned his rifle against Packard's desk. He removed his pince-nez and wiped away the smear of
snowflakes with a handkerchief. He clipped the spectacles

onto the bridge of his nose and started to deliver his lecture. Packard beat him to the punch.

"We're just going to press," he said. "I'm glad you showed up, because I wanted a personal interview. The story out of Mandan is that Finnegan and his bunch received a year in prison."

"Yes, that's so," Roosevelt affirmed. "They pled guilty and were sentenced on the spot. Justice, in this instance, was served swiftly."

"Are you satisfied with the sentence?"

"Judge Oscar Horton asked me that very question before he offered them leniency. I told him I would prefer ten years, but one would suffice. There was, in the end, no violence attached to the crime."

"So they offered no resistance when you captured them?"

"Actually, they had little choice but to surrender. We took them quite unawares."

"You caught them with their pants down?"

"Yes, in a manner of speaking. And I insist that you give Adam Sewall and William Dow their just due in this affair. They were the very marrow of our expedition."

"Dow and Sewall," Packard repeated, jotting the names in his notepad. "I suppose Sheriff Bullard was even more impressed than before. His newest deputy gets his man again."

"You make far too much of it," Roosevelt said. "In fact, I suggest we move on to an interview of a different nature. I came here straightaway for that very purpose."

"What is the topic of the interview?"

"Politics."

"I knew it!" Packard whooped. "You've changed your mind, haven't you? You're going to accept the post of senator."

"Quite the contrary," Roosevelt said. "I wish to lay this matter to rest without the slightest equivocation. Are you ready . . . ?"

"Yes," Packard said, his pencil poised. "Although I don't think I'm going to like it."

"You may quote me as saying that there are no circumstances, now or in the future, under which I would accept appointment as Dakota's senator. The decision is final, and no longer open to discussion."

"Are you willing to be quoted as to why?"

"I have retired from politics," Roosevelt said emphatically. "I do not seek public office, nor will I entertain nomination to any post. And please inform your readers"—he paused, crafting the quote in his head—"while I am honored by their support, I wish the campaigning to cease. Theodore Roosevelt is a cattleman, not a candidate."

Packard looked up from his notepad. "I'm truly sorry to hear it, Mr. Roosevelt. Your decision is Dakota's loss."

"No man is indispensable to any endeavor. Dakota will do quite nicely without me in Washington."

"Just for the record, I believe we would do far better with you."

"Amos, we shall never know!"

Roosevelt's teeth snapped in a jack-o'-lantern grin. He collected his rifle, nodding to Packard, and walked out the door. He was immensely pleased with himself and confident now that his friends would halt their behind-the-scenes campaign. Newsprint, for most people, was the embodiment of literal truth.

On the street, he again turned uptown. Headquarters for the Northern Pacific Refrigerator Car Company was in the next building, and as he moved along the boardwalk the Marquis de Mores and Jake Paddock stepped out the door. He was upon them in the same moment they saw him. They stopped in his path.

"Lookit here, armed to the teeth," Paddock said, eyeing the rifle. "Out chasin' badmen are you, Deputy?"

Roosevelt stared at him. "I believe you're the only one left, Paddock. All your cohorts are on the run."

"Talk tough now that you're wearin' a badge. One of these days I'm gonna clip your wings."

"To my face, or in the back?"

"You goddamn—"

"Enough!"

De Mores broke in, silencing Paddock with a look. His gaze shifted back to Roosevelt. "There is much talk of your latest adventure, M'sieur Roosevelt."

"In my experience, talk has little currency."

"Are you saying the story is unfounded?"

"No, I am not," Roosevelt said pointedly. "You may read about it in the newspaper."

"Of course," de Mores said with a bogus smile. "Will I read as well that you are to be our senator?"

"No doubt you will be disappointed to learn otherwise. I'm sure you are one of my most ardent supporters."

"*Certainement.* You have become the most dashing figure in the Badlands. Our Beowulf in buckskins, ever in search of dragons."

"Sarcasm profits neither of us, Marquis. However, as you may imagine, I await your murder trial with eager anticipation. Good day."

Roosevelt stepped around them. As he continued along the boardwalk he could feel their eyes burning holes in his back. He knew de Mores and Paddock were infuriated by his meddling, that he'd convinced the authorities to bring murder charges. Yet the brief exchange of insults gave his spirits a lift. A man was known best by his choice of enemies.

Downstreet, he turned into Ferris's store. The topic of the manhunt was unavoidable, and he was forced to satisfy the storekeeper's curiosity with the more salient details. That done, he requested a loan of the saddle horse Ferris kept stabled at the local livery. He planned to spend the night in his room over the store and ride on to Elkhorn tomorrow. Ferris readily agreed to let him have the horse.

Upstairs, he spent the balance of the morning penning letters to Bamie and Henry Cabot Lodge. The date was December 5 and his plans were to depart in ten days for Christmas in New York. *Hunting Trips of a Ranchman* was completed, apart from minor revisions, and he penned a letter as well to his publisher. When he went out at noon-

time, he stopped by the post office and mailed the letters.
He ate a leisurely lunch at the Metropolian's dining room.

Roosevelt was already thinking about his next book. He
wasn't as yet sure about the subject matter, but he knew he
would one day write another book about his experiences in
the Badlands. With that in mind, he devoted the afternoon
to writing a chronological account of the manhunt for Red
Finnegan and the boat thieves. He was particularly intent
in lauding Sewall and Dow for their valiant efforts in seeing justice done. He credited them and their raft for over-
taking the culprits.

That evening, he returned to the Metropolitan for dinner. The hotel was all but empty during the winter months,
and he was thankful the dining room remained open for occasional travelers. The only other eatery in town was Murphy's Café, which was notorious for greasy food and a
limited menu. He treated himself to a blood-rare steak,
topped with fried onions, and finished the meal with a
large chunk of chocolate cake. He was pleasantly stuffed
as he drained a last cup of coffee.

Nightfall came early in the winter. The snow had
stopped, and when he walked back to his room the street
was deserted except for the saloons at the lower end of
town. He stoked the fire in the wood-burning stove and selected a copy of *Don Quixote* from the small library he
kept in the room. Cervantes was one of his favorite writers;
he admired the Spaniard's incisive wit and quick insights
into the human condition. He never tired of the addled nobleman who tilted at windmills. . . .

Sometime later, he was startled awake. He straightened
his chair, surprised he'd fallen asleep, and realized the fire
had gone out in the stove. As he closed the book and placed
it on the desk, a faint rattling noise attracted his attention.
He remembered locking the door, and when he turned he
saw the doorknob rotate, then slowly fall back into place.
The only windows were on the street side, and it occurred
to him that whoever was on the stairwell landing couldn't

see into the room. His gun belt was on the desk, where he'd dropped it after returning from supper. He pulled the Colt.

"Yes?" he said in a sharp voice. "Who's there?"

Footsteps pounded down the outside stairs. Roosevelt crossed the room, unlocked the door, and threw it open. He glimpsed the shadowy figure of a man jump off the boardwalk into the street. He moved onto the stairwell landing.

"You there!" he shouted. *"Halt!"*

The man spun around, his arm raised. Too late, Roosevelt realized he was framed in a spill of lamplight from the room. The gun in the man's hand spit flame, and a slug splintered the doorjamb beside Roosevelt's head. He brought his Colt to bear, thumbing the hammer, and fired a quick snap shot. The window in the store across the street shattered into shards of glass.

The man sprinted off down the street. Roosevelt's first instinct was to chase after him, but he knew it would be a fool's play. Hunting an armed man in the dark was reckless business, an invitation to ambush. And he'd used up his luck for one night with the bullet in the doorjamb. He should be dead.

Roosevelt moved back into the room. He locked the door and stood staring at the Colt in his hand. For the first time in his life he'd fired on another man, and he knew the man's name. He couldn't prove it because it was too dark to identify his assailant. But the angry exchange on the street that morning resonated in his mind. He still heard the words.

Jake Paddock had tried to clip his wings.

TWENTY

A heavy snowfall cloaked New York in a mantle of white. Roosevelt arrived aboard the Chicago Limited the afternoon of December 20. The train pulled into Grand Central Station shortly after three o'clock.

Roosevelt was attired in suit and tie, with a top hat and his fur-collared overcoat. When he stepped off the train, he was overcome by a sense of dark remembrance. Ten months and five days ago he had stepped off another train, hurrying to the bedside of his wife and mother. The memory, even now, gripped at his heart.

There was holiday gaiety all about him as friends and loved ones greeted passengers from the train. Roosevelt tried not to watch, for a moment wishing he'd ignored Bamie's entreaties and stayed in Dakota. The crowd slowly thinned out, and he waited on the platform until a porter appeared with his luggage from the baggage car. He led the way into the main terminal.

The vast amphitheater was swarming with people. Roosevelt looked at the massive vaulted arches and the towering stained-glass windows as if seeing them for the first time. His eyes were drawn to the ceiling, where the constellations of the zodiac were wrought in gold on a blue background. He slowed, staring upward, then stopped, and the porter almost bumped into him. His gaze traveled over the ceiling.

"Real nice, isn't it?" the porter said. "Lots of people stop their first time through here."

Roosevelt might have been deaf. He stared at the airy colossus of the ceiling as though looking into a vision of the beyond. His Dutch heritage and his upbringing in the Presbyterian church taught eternal life and heaven in the hereafter. Yet Alice and his mother had appeared to him any number of times, and he suddenly wondered why they were trapped in limbo, denied eternal life. The transmigration of souls lifted the spirit into the afterlife, and yet they were still earthbound, still with him. Were he to reveal what he'd seen, he would be thought crazed, and perhaps, in a way, he was. No sane man claimed communion with ghosts.

"Mister?" the porter said, inspecting the strange cast of his features. "You all right, sir?"

Roosevelt got hold of himself. "Yes, quite well, thank you. I became distracted."

"Yessir, like I said, people do."

The porter led him to the Forty Second Street exit. Outside, after whistling up a hansom cab, the porter stowed his luggage in the boot. Roosevelt overtipped him for his trouble, then gave the address to the driver and climbed into the cab. Snow was still falling and Roosevelt was reminded of the dense fog that enveloped the city the night he'd rushed home for a final moment with Alice and his mother. He recalled that he hadn't accepted the reality of the situation and even later, at their bedsides, head bowed in prayer, he believed they might be spared. Yet, in the end, prayer and hope changed nothing. Mortality was a heartless arbiter.

The streets were jammed with shoppers. Here and there, Salvation Army brothers and sisters stood huddled in the snow, trumpets blaring, voices raised in Yuletide carols. Wreaths with red bows hung from lampposts, and storefronts were decorated with colorful displays celebrating the holiday season. In the window of one store Roosevelt saw a life-size figure of Saint Nicholas, with a long white beard and a peaked cap, garbed in a billowing smock and carrying a bag stuffed with toys. As the cab trundled past the store, he remembered he had gifts to buy, a duty forgotten until now. Hard as it might be, he had to get himself in the Christmas spirit.

A short while later the cab rolled to a halt before the mansion at 6 West Fifty Seventh Street. After paying the driver, Roosevelt crossed the snowy sidewalk, mounted the steps, and rapped the door knocker. Harold, the family manservant he'd almost forgotten, greeted him warmly and then went to collect his bags from the cab. Bamie hurried into the vestibule as he removed his coat and hat and dropped them on a chair. Her eyes were alight with happiness and she threw her arms around his neck. She kissed him soundly on the cheek.

"Oh Teddy!" she exclaimed in a quavering voice. "I've missed you so, dearest brother. Welcome home."

Roosevelt put on a cheery smile. "I must say you haven't aged a day. You look positively splendid."

"You always were the flatterer. Did you have a nice trip?"

"By George, I've seen nothing but snow from Dakota to New York. No one need worry about a white Christmas this year."

"I can't believe you are here." She took his arm, walked him toward the parlor. "Corinne and Elliot are coming for dinner this evening. They are so anxious to see you."

"Bully!" Roosevelt said, squeezing her arm. "I'm interested to hear all their news."

A blue spruce Christmas tree enlivened the parlor. The tree was decorated with shiny glass bulbs, ornaments dangling from branches, and a winged angel affixed to the crown. As they started through the door, Bamie suddenly stopped. She clapped a hand to her mouth.

"Oh my goodness! What am I thinking, rushing you in here. You'll want to see Baby Lee."

Roosevelt appreciated her kindness. The child's full name was Alice Lee, but in her letters Bamie always re-

ferred to the girl as Baby Lee. She somehow sensed her
brother would be pained by the sound of his departed
wife's name. Roosevelt himself had come to think of his
daughter as Baby Lee.

Bamie led him upstairs to a nursery at the rear of the
house. Though he made no comment, Roosevelt was
thankful that the child had been moved from the suite of
rooms where his wife had died. A nanny, an older woman
with gray hair, was seated in a chair as they entered the
nursery. She knew Roosevelt was arriving today, and after
a quick smile she discreetly left the room. Bamie gently
closed the door.

Roosevelt approached the crib. The baby was asleep, a
thumb in her mouth, and he was amazed at how much
she'd grown in his absence. Her cheeks were chubby and
rosy, her downy hair reddish gold in color, and a tiny foot
arched from beneath a light blanket. He stared down at her,
his throat dry, gripped by an emotion so overpowering he
dared not speak. He saw in her all that he'd lost those many
months ago. And it broke his heart yet again.

"Darling Baby Lee," Bamie said tenderly. "She is the
very picture of her mother."

"Yes," Roosevelt managed. "So alike."

The strange voice woke her. She popped the thumb out
of her mouth, staring up at him, and cooed in a soft voice.
Her eyes were blue as larkspur, and reflected there Roosevelt saw born again his sunny Alice. The baby waved a
chubby little hand, as if beckoning him closer, and smiled
a winsome smile. Her eyes drank him in.

He knew then he would love her forever.

The morning was sunny and clear. Overnight the snow
squall had rolled out to sea, leaving the city to shovel out
from the storm. Traffic had reduced the streets to a dingy
slush.

A fire crackled in the grate. Roosevelt was seated at the
desk in the study, reviewing his manuscript one last time.
He was scheduled to meet with his publisher that afternoon

and felt compelled to subject the book to a final critique. He thought it read well.

Shortly before ten o'clock he turned the last page. A fiery ember exploded in the fireplace, distracting his attention from the book. His gaze went from the fireplace to the bookshelves and he was somehow reminded that the room had once been Greatheart's study, his father's study. The entire house was haunted with memories, and yet it seemed curiously foreign, an artifact of a past life. Here only a day, he longed to return to Elkhorn.

Last night, unable to sleep, he'd lain awake reflecting on the vicissitudes of life. He had enjoyed dinner with Corinne and Elliot, but their talk of society balls and Wall Street coups seemed to him somehow jaded, oddly stale. Bamie had planned a Christmas Day celebration, with all the Roosevelt family members gathered around the tree, exchanging presents and good cheer. Corinne and Elliot, to honor their brother's homecoming, were throwing a New Year's Eve party, and the guest list included all of Roosevelt's New York friends. Yet his thoughts, as he lay awake last night, were back in Dakota. He felt distanced from what mattered most.

There was but one heartening aspect to his visit. He had found in his daughter what he thought he'd lost forever, the capacity to open his heart and love again. For a brief moment, restless and wakeful in the night, he'd considered taking Baby Lee and her nanny with him to Elkhorn. But just as quickly, unable to ignore the reality of the situation, he knew the rough life he led in the West was no place for his daughter. Even more telling, Bamie would be devastated by the separation, for it was obvious that she now saw herself as the baby's mother. He concluded he would just have to visit New York more often.

There was a light knock on the door. Harold, who doubled as a butler, stepped inside. "Mr. Lodge has arrived," he said. "Shall I show him in, sir?"

"Yes! Yes!" Roosevelt almost leaped from his chair. "Hurry right along, Harold."

By their exchange of letters Henry Cabot Lodge had

agreed to a quick visit. With Christmas in the offing, he could allow only one day away, and he'd come down by train late yesterday evening. He planned to stay the night and return to Boston early tomorrow morning. Harold ushered him into the study with a slight bow.

"Cabot!" Roosevelt rushed forward with an outstretched hand. "Dee—*lighted* to see you, old man."

"As am I, Theodore." Lodge smiled affably, exchanging a warm handshake. "You've been much too long in the Wild West."

Tall and patrician, Lodge was attired in a cutaway coat with long tails and a silk vest. His first impression was that Roosevelt had never looked more robust and vital, with the ruddy features of an outdoorsman. Life in the West clearly agreed with a man born to aristocracy and educated at Harvard. Roosevelt motioned him to a leather armchair before the fireplace.

"I must say, you look quite fit, Theodore. Herding cows is apparently a healthy vocation."

Roosevelt laughed. "I've spent more time of late on my book and pursuing thieves. I believe I wrote you I'd been commissioned a deputy sheriff."

"Yes, as a matter of fact," Lodge said. "Rather an exciting life for a literary fellow. Have you completed the book?"

"I deliver it to my publisher this afternoon."

"Perhaps I should write another book. I've certainly nothing to show for my political efforts."

"No fault of your own," Roosevelt said earnestly. "You were the victim of a Democratic landslide."

"Theodore, I fear for our country with Grover Cleveland as president."

Late in October, five days before the election, James G. Blaine, the Republican candidate, had committed an unpardonable error. During a speech in New York, he had accused the Democratic Party and Grover Cleveland of supporting "rum, Romanism, and rebellion." Giddy over the lapse of judgment, Cleveland's national headquarters telegraphed the quote to newspaper editors across the country. By election eve, Blaine's credibility had evaporated among prohibitionists, Catholics, and Southerners, three blocs of voters no candidate could afford to lose. Grover Cleveland was elected the first Democratic president since before the Civil War.

"We follow divergent paths these days," Lodge said. "I lose an election for Congress and you refuse an appointment to the Senate. Has the Wild West so captivated you, Theodore?"

Roosevelt was saddened that his closest friend had been humiliated at the polls. He searched his mind for a way he might explain his own cavalier attitude toward politics. At breakfast that morning, he had read an unusual and somewhat astonishing article in the *New York Times*. He thought it might make the point.

"I read an article in the *Times* this morning," he said with a rueful shake of his head. "There are forty thousand horses in New York, and every day they deposit four hundred tons of manure and twenty thousand gallons of urine on the streets. Imagine that if you will."

"Hardly surprising," Lodge remarked. "Apart from streetcars, every vehicle in the city is horse drawn. What does that have to do with politics?"

"Not politics alone, Cabot. Until I returned, I had forgotten the noxious stench that pervades the whole of New York. I compare it to the sweet, clean air of Dakota, and I cannot wait to be gone. I have found a life there that I far prefer."

"And does that life exclude public service?"

"Yes, in large degree," Roosevelt said. "I shall never again run for political office."

Lodge was silent a moment. "Theodore, I find myself amazed to say that I envy you. Few men are able to replicate what you have in Dakota. Perhaps I should join you on your ranch."

"You would be most welcome," Roosevelt said with a

chuckle. "Although I must admit, I cannot picture you as a cowboy. I do rather poorly at it myself."

"We can discuss it at dinner tonight."

Lodge was staying at the Waldorf-Astoria and Roosevelt planned to pick him up at eight o'clock. Their dinner reservation was at Delmonico's, a restaurant frequented by New York's social elite. For now, Roosevelt steered the conversation away from politics and on to literary matters. He intended to put a proposal before his publisher for a new book.

He tried it out first on Lodge.

The traffic on Fifth Avenue was chaotic. The broad thoroughfare, north to south, was jammed with wagons and carriages of every description. All of them were horse drawn.

The air festered with the stench of New York. A ripe blend of rotting garbage, horse manure, and noxious coal smoke pouring from chimneys. Roosevelt was in a hansom cab, on the way downtown to meet with his publisher. He wrinkled his nose, reminded of his remark earlier to Lodge, overpowered by the pungent smell of the city. He longed for the crisp fresh winds of Dakota.

G. P. Putnam's Sons, Roosevelt's publisher, was located off Union Square. He arrived shortly before two o'clock, carrying his handwritten manuscript in a cardboard box. A secretary ushered him into the office of Malcolm Weatherby, the senior editor and his principal contact with the publishing house. Weatherby was a slender man, with a look of birdlike alertness, thick spectacles perched on the end of his nose. He greeted Roosevelt effusively.

"The laureate of the West!" he said, offering a delicate handshake. "So wonderful to see you again, Theodore."

"Thank you, Malcolm." Roosevelt took a chair before the desk. "Your encouragement in our correspondence has been most welcome."

"And your adventures in the West sound positively Homeric. Have you brought me a masterpiece?"

"In all modesty, I believe it is rather well done. Of course, I await your opinion."

Roosevelt handed over the box. Weatherby removed the lid and quickly scanned several pages. *The Naval War of 1812*, Roosevelt's first book, was a scholarly work and had by now achieved textbook status. *Hunting Trips of a Ranchman* was lyrical in tone, with lush descriptions of the Badlands and a sense of personal relationship between hunter and hunted. Weatherby glanced up with a look of piqued excitement.

"Splendid," he said, peering over his glasses. "You have a marvelous command of the language, and the public so wants a fresh view of the Wild West. I have every confidence it will become a best seller."

Roosevelt preened. "A writer basks in the approval of his editor, and at the risk of appearing presumptuous, I would like to propose a new book. A biography."

"On whom?"

"Thomas Hart Benton."

"Senator Benton?" Weatherby asked. "The expansionist?"

"Indeed!"

Roosevelt warmed to the subject. He'd given much thought to the project, and his overview was one of unrestrained enthusiasm. Thomas Hart Benton had been born in North Carolina, migrated to Tennessee, and served as an officer under Andrew Jackson in the War of 1812. A Westering man, he later moved to Missouri and was elected to the U.S. Senate in 1812. His career in Washington spanned thirty years.

Benton was a strong proponent of Manifest Destiny. He believed America was destined by divine providence to expand its national domain from sea to sea. His vision was based on the grandeur of a continent as one nation, and he advocated an American Pacifica encompassing the lands from Baja California to the Bering Strait off the shores of Alaska. His efforts were the foundation for the Homestead Act of 1862.

"Thomas Hart Benton," Roosevelt went on, "personi-
fied the very spirit of the West. He was a man of courage,
honor, and patriotism—American to the core."

"Yes, he was all that," Weatherby agreed. "How would
you present him in an historical context?"

"Senator Benton was a statesman, but more important,
he was the spokesman for Westerners. He articulated their
beliefs and longings on a world stage, with all the tenacity
of a snapping turtle."

Weatherby was struck by a quick and incisive insight.
He thought Roosevelt's love of the West and philosophical
view of Manifest Destiny rivaled that of Thomas Hart Benton. He felt confident Roosevelt would author an engrossing biography.

"Very well, Theodore," he said. "I'll have a contract
drawn and sent round for your approval."

"Bully!" Roosevelt said stoutly. "I'll begin writing upon
my return to Dakota."

"In the meantime, I've arranged an interview with the
New York Times. Never too early for publicity on your new
book."

"I shall be delighted to speak with the *Times*."

"Also, I've arranged an appointment with a photographer for tomorrow morning. By chance, did you bring any
of your hunting paraphernalia with you?"

"Not by chance," Roosevelt said. "I had much the same
idea myself for a picture on the flyleaf of the book. I
brought the gear I normally use on a hunt."

"Excellent," Weatherby said. "Avery Shaw of the *Times*
is waiting for you in the conference room. Drop back by
when you've finished the interview."

"Certainly."

Roosevelt walked down the hall. Avery Shaw was seated
at a round conference table, a cigar wedged in the corner of
his mouth. He knew Roosevelt on sight, as did almost
every reporter in New York. They exchanged a handshake
and Roosevelt seated himself at the table. Shaw took out
his notepad.

"You don't mind my saying so," he said, "you're something of an anomaly, Mr. Roosevelt. A politician who spurns public office."

"Interesting choice of words," Roosevelt observed. "I do not spurn public office, Mr. Shaw. I simply chose not to run."

"Yeah, I heard that from a couple of sources. You could have had a fourth term in the legislature. Why'd you turn it down?"

"I have a ranching enterprise in Dakota Territory. It occupies all my time."

"Well, that's an anomaly, too. The Associated Press reported you'd been offered the Senate seat when Dakota gets statehood. Care to comment?"

"No comment is necessary," Roosevelt said. "I am a rancher without political aspirations."

"Why is that?" Shaw probed. "Not many men would refuse appointment to the United States Senate."

"I understood our interview was for the purpose of my book. Have I been misinformed?"

"No, I'll do a bang-up article on your book. I just thought politics would make an interesting side issue."

"Nothing is more interesting, Mr. Shaw, than stalking bighorn sheep."

Roosevelt told him the story. Then he described the harsh splendor of the Badlands and the serenity of Elkhorn. Shaw took copious notes and asked questions typical of a city dweller whose knowledge of wildlife was limited to the zoo at Central Park. But Roosevelt was all too aware that he hadn't sidetracked the reporter on the issue of politics. The article would be on a New York politician who—inexplicably—was now a Western hunter. The anomaly was the angle.

The next morning Roosevelt appeared at the studio of Victor Trevelyan, the foremost portrait photographer of the day. He carried a valise with his Western garb and a gun case for his Winchester; after a perfunctory handshake, the photographer hustled him into a dressing room. A short while later he emerged wearing fringed buckskins with a colorful kerchief knotted at his throat. A large sheath knife hung from the cartridge belt cinched around his waist.

"*C'est magnifique!*" Trevelyan exclaimed, his hands to his mouth. "The scout of the plains!"

"Hardly," Roosevelt said, wondering what he'd gotten himself into. "These are merely my hunting clothes."

"Yes, but you look formidable!"

Trevelyan was a fussy little man with a beak of a nose and a wispy goatee. Against a lighted wall he had arranged a backdrop of fake trees, a cerulean sky, bunchgrass, and papier-mâché flowers. He posed Roosevelt before the backdrop as though staring off into distant plains, the Winchester clasped in both hands. Trevelyan stepped back, inspecting his artistry, and made a face.

"Do you mind?" he said, removing Roosevelt's pince-nez with a deft touch. "Spectacles dilute the image we seek to create."

Roosevelt started to object. Trevelyan motioned him quiet with a flutter of hands and retreated from the backdrop. He slipped behind his camera, a bulky affair mounted on a tall tripod. After peering through the lens, he held a flash pan overhead. His voice was soft, almost caressing.

"Please do not move—and *voilà!*"

The flash pan exploded in a flare of light. Roosevelt felt somehow diminished, caught in a moment of posterity that was contrived and, without his glasses, somehow bogus. The photograph might impress Eastern readers, but it was not genuine. Nor was it the man he'd become in the Badlands.

He longed to be gone from New York.

TWENTY-ONE

A hard winter chill was upon Elkhorn. By day the valley glittered with snow, and at night the trees creaked and groaned under brittle frost. The river was once more frozen over, rigid and still, like a long, rumpled bar of blue steel. Wolves traveled the ice in darkness as though it were a wilderness road.

Roosevelt sat at his desk in the study. Logs blazed in the fireplace, and his gaze was fixed on the wall. He was well into the second chapter of the biography, and he was trying to imagine Thomas Hart Benton's emotions during a pivotal battle in the War of 1812. His desk was littered with research books, but something was missing in the dry, scholarly prose. He was searching for the spirit of the inner man.

The image was just beyond his grasp. He stood, pacing about the room, attempting to strike the spark of inspiration. His eye fell on the desk calendar, marked at January 15, and he was reminded again that it was now 1885. He had returned to Elkhorn only a week ago, with the sense of an inmate fleeing an asylum. The memory of the New Year's Eve party hosted by Corinne and Elliot was still fresh and painfully raw. An evening he wouldn't soon forget.

All his old friends were there. They were at pains not to mention Alice or his mother and yet treated him somewhat like an oddity from a circus. The conversation revolved around his curious withdrawal from politics and what they saw as his eccentric retreat to the wilds of Dakota. When he tried to explain, he ended up feeling like the caricature of a batty Easterner who'd thrown it all over to run off and play cowboy. He greeted the New Year by leaving the party shortly after midnight.

Two days later he left New York. His one regret in departing was that he couldn't take Baby Lee along. Over the holidays, he had grown to treasure her in much the same way he'd idolized her mother. Perhaps because he doted on her so, the strangest aspect hadn't become apparent until his return to Elkhorn. He felt closer to Alice and his mother at the ranch than he had in the New York mansion. He sensed their presence, their nearness. Patiently waiting . . .

"Mr. Roosevelt."

"Yes." His reverie broken, he turned to find Dow in the doorway. "What is it, Will?"

"Adam asked that you come out front. We've got trouble."

"What sort of trouble?"

"It's Steve Mahan," Dow said. "Somebody's beat him to within an inch of his life."

Steve Mahan was a small rancher. He and his partner, Isaac Hooper, had taken over the homestead of Red Finnegan after he was sentenced to prison. They were formerly cowhands for John Eaton, and with Eaton's blessing they'd bought twenty cows and stocked their outfit in the dead of winter. Their cabn was five miles upriver from Elkhorn.

Roosevelt followed Dow through the house. Sewall and the women had seated the young rancher in a chair at the dining room table. His mackinaw and hat were on the floor; his face looked as though he'd been savaged by a bear. There was a deep gash over his left eyebrow, his nose was broken, and two of his front teeth were missing. Erma and Irene were sponging his wounds with a damp cloth. Amy watched with round-eyed horror.

"Here now," Roosevelt said, appalled by the sight. "What on earth's happened?"

"We don't know," Sewall said. "He rode in half-dead and fell off his horse. Will and me lugged him inside."

Erma dabbed gently at his mouth. His left eye was swollen shut and his arms hung limply at his sides. "He's hurt terribly," she said. "It's a miracle he stayed on a horse this far."

Roosevelt stooped down. "Steve," he said softly. "Can you hear me?"

Mahan groaned, his mouth working in a bloody maw. His good eye rolled open and he blinked, trying to focus. "Mr. Roosevelt?"

"You're at Elkhorn," Roosevelt said. "Are you able to talk?"

"Yeah. . . ."

"Who did this to you?"

"I . . ." Mahan struggled for consciousness as the women tended to his wounds. "Men . . . three men."

"Did you know them?"

"Only one."

"Do you know his name?"

"Bonner." Mahan drew a ragged breath. "Dave Bonner. Works for Paddock."

"Was that why they beat you?" Roosevelt asked. "Were they trying to force you to sell your land?"

"Said next time they'd kill . . ."

"Kill you?"

"And Isaac." Mahan tried to sit straighter, his good eye blinking wildly. "You've got to go take care of Isaac. He's hurt worse'n me."

"You needn't worry, we'll look after your partner. Just relax now, let these ladies look after you."

Roosevelt nodded to Erma and Irene. He motioned to Sewall and Dow, then led them from the dining room into the parlor. His mouth was set in a tight line.

"Will, I want you to take Jeeter and ride to Mahan's cabin. Bring Isaac Hooper back here."

"Yessir."

"And tell Bob Hallett I wish to see him."

Dow grabbed a coat and hurried out. As he ran toward

the bunkhouse, Sewall turned to Roosevelt. "What are you aimin' to do?"

"We have a name," Roosevelt said. "The first place to look for Bonner and these other hooligans is in Medora. We might well find them in company with Paddock."

"Why'd you send for Hallett?"

"I intend to ask him to accompany me. I may require assistance in making the arrests."

Sewall looked offended. "Why wouldn't you ask me instead of Hallett?"

"Your place is here," Roosevelt said simply. "You are the foreman of Elkhorn."

"And if you get yourself killed, you know I'll take care of the ranch. Isn't that what you're sayin'?"

"No harm will come to me, Adam."

"Says you," Sewall said querulously. "You keep chasin' off after thieves and such and the odds are gonna run out. You might go once too often."

Roosevelt shrugged it off. "I am the deputy sheriff and the head of the Stockgrowers Association. I could hardly ask someone to go in my place."

"Why not? Let them put their necks on the line for a change. You can't police the whole Badlands."

"A man who accepts responsibility cannot shirk his duty. You should know that, Adam."

"And you should know you can't do it all by yourself."

"Point taken." Roosevelt was silent a moment, thoughtful. "Very well, I shall stop by the Eatons' and request their assistance. Does that satisfy your concern?"

"Only about halfway," Sewall said. "You're still gonna be in the thick of it."

"Yes, but we may finally have the opportunity to bring down Jake Paddock. And with him, the Marquis de Mores."

"They're set to stand trial in a couple of months. Aren't you satisfied to get 'em hung for murder?"

"I much prefer a bird in hand. Who knows what will happen at their trial?"

Bob Hallett rapped on the door and stepped inside. "You wanted to see me, Mr. Roosevelt?"

"Yes, Bob, I do."

Roosevelt quickly explained the situation with Steve Mahan and Isaac Hooper. He went on to relate his intention of arresting those responsible for the beating. He held Hallett's gaze.

"I'm asking you to volunteer," he said. "If you prefer not to become involved, then simply say so. I will understand."

"Why me?" Hallett said. "Why not one of the other boys?"

"I believe you will stand fast in the event of trouble."

"You reckon there's gonna be gunplay?"

"Quite possibly," Roosevelt replied. "These men may very well resist arrest."

Hallett nodded. "I'm all for nailin' Paddock's hide to the wall. You can count on me."

"Thank you, Bob. Would you saddle Manitou for me and a horse for yourself? I'll collect my gear."

"Yessir, meet you at the corral."

Ten minutes later they rode south from Elkhorn. The weather was bitterly cold, a sharp wind blowing down out of the north. They were bundled in heavy mackinaws, scarves pulled over their faces, their hands protected by fur-lined gloves. The snow was glazed with a thin sheet of ice, and they held their horses to a walk. Hallett finally broke the silence.

"Been thinkin' about something," he said. "Why you reckon Mahan came to us and not the Eatons? Wouldn't have been much farther to their place."

Roosevelt's breath was a puffy vapor over the top of his scarf. "The men who beat him apparently headed for Medora. He was wise to ride in the opposite direction."

"When Dow came to get Jeeter, he said Hooper was busted up pretty bad. Hope they get there in time."

"Did they leave immediately?"

"Yessir, quick as Jeeter got his coat."

The sun was out, and all around them the land glim-

mered with a layer of frosty snow. The horse herd, apart
from those kept in the corral, was allowed to run free in the
winter. Horses were smarter than cows, and Roosevelt saw
a small band pawing through the snow to feed on the stem-
cured grass covering the ground. Farther along, he spotted
a bunch of cows huddled in a ravine, gnawing listlessly on
stumps of frozen sagebrush. He turned to Hallett.

"Why is it the cows never learn from the horses? Simple
observation should teach them how to uncover the grass."

"They're born dumb," Hallett said. "Only critter
dumber'n a cow is a sheep. No explainin' it."

"I wonder we don't lose more stock during the winter."

"Well, folks are always sayin' how God watches over
fools and the feeble. Guess that includes cows."

Late that afternoon they rode into the Slash E headquarters. None of the Eaton brothers was married, and their log
house smelled of stale clothes and saddle gear. John, Paul,
and Charlie gathered around a cluttered dining table as
Roosevelt recounted the events of the day. He outlined his
plan to attempt the capture of the three ruffians.

"I mean to arrest them," he said. "Your assistance would
be most appreciated."

"Why, hell yes," John readily agreed. "Steve and Isaac
was good hands, elsewise we wouldn't have helped 'em
start their ranch. When you aim to tackle this bunch?"

"Tomorrow," Roosevelt said. "Assuming, of course, we
find them in Medora. If you have room, Bob and I will
spend the night here."

"Got lots of room," John said. "Me and Paul will go
with you into town come mornin'. Charlie can stay here
and look after things."

"Jesus H. Christ!" Charlie complained. "How come you
and Paul get to have all the fun?"

"'Cause you're the pup of the family and I don't want
you gettin' shot. Let's hear no more about it."

"Still ain't fair, and you damn well know it."

Roosevelt was amused with the byplay. John was the
eldest at thirty, with Paul twenty-eight, and Charlie the

youngest at twenty-four. He understood John's reasoning and he sympathized with Charlie for being left out. Yet he thought it the right decision.

The pup of the family should never be put in harm's way. Someone had to be held back to carry on the bloodline. Particularly if things went wrong.

Charlie was the odd man out.

The sky was overcast, threatening snow. A blustery wind howled out of the northwest, rattling windowpanes as it swept through town. Medora appeared locked in a frozen tableau.

Roosevelt forded the river by the railroad trestle early the next afternoon. Strung out in a line behind him were John and Paul Eaton, with Hallett bringing up the rear. Stiff with cold from five hours on the trail, they rode past the railroad depot. Their mustaches were white with frost.

Upstreet, they reined to a halt in front of Ferris's store. After tying their horses to the hitchrack, they trooped inside, suddenly buffeted by a wave of heat. A large potbellied stove in the center of the store radiated warmth, though the store itself was empty of customers. They stood stamping cold from their feet.

Joe Ferris came around the counter. His clerks were stocking shelves at the back of the store and they paused, watching steam pour off the men's thawing mackinaws. Ferris was taken aback to see Roosevelt and the Eaton brothers in town on a Friday, especially with a storm brewing. But he thought he knew why they were here, and it wasn't to order supplies. Their business was about men and the law.

"Good afternoon, Joe," Roosevelt said, ice rapidly melting off his mustache. "It appears we've brought you another storm."

"Yessir, it does," Ferris acknowledged. "Way the sky looks, it'll likely hit before nightfall. Maybe sooner."

"Then I daresay we've arrived just in time. We are here seeking information."

"Oh?"

"Do you know Steve Mahan and Isaac Hooper?"

Ferris nodded. "They trade with me."

"Yesterday they were subjected to a brutal beating by three men. One of those men is named Dave Bonner."

"Yessir, I know."

'You *know*?" Roosevelt was openly surprised. "How would you know?"

"It's all over town," Ferris said. "Bonner and his boys rode in last night and went on a drunk. They've been braggin' about it."

"Bragging on it in public?"

"Well, don't you see, liquor loosens a man's tongue. They're right proud of themselves."

"What have they said?"

"Spoutin' off about how they whipped Mahan and Hooper. Claimed it was over a card debt."

Roosevelt arched an eyebrow. "Are you referring to a gambling debt?"

"That's the story I get," Ferris affirmed. "Bonner says Mahan lost fifty bucks in a poker game and wouldn't pay up. So he took it out of his hide."

"Tommyrot! Bonner attempted to coerce them into selling their homestead. Mahan told me so himself."

"Nobody believes Bonner and his boys. They're out-and-out scoundrels."

"The other two men, what are their names?"

"Roy Ellis and Ed Lawton."

The heat in the store was too much for heavy clothing. Roosevelt shrugged out of his mackinaw and tossed it on the counter. "Joe, I am naturally curious," he said. "Do these men work for Jake Paddock?"

"That'd be my guess," Ferris said. "You remember Frank Miller and Quincy Moore?"

"Yes, of course. The men who were involved with de Mores and Paddock in the murder of George Luffsey. They disappeared before we could arrest them."

"Word has it they hightailed it for California. Anyway, a

month or so later, Bonner and his boys started hangin' out at the Alhambra Saloon. They're evidently real tight with Paddock."

"What does that mean?" Roosevelt asked. "Are you saying they work for Paddock?"

"Don't rightly know," Ferris admitted. "Only tellin' you what I hear on the grapevine."

"And what is that?"

"Bonner and his boys are reported to be horse thieves and gunmen. Rumor has it they skedaddled out of Montana to keep from gettin' hung. They've been regulars at the Alhambra ever since."

"One thing's for damn sure," John Eaton interrupted. "Mahan didn't lose no fifty dollars at a poker table. Him and Hooper saved every nickel they earned to buy cows. I know, 'cause they bought 'em from me."

"Like I said," Farris remarked, "Bonner and his boys are general no-accounts and drunk half the time. Nobody believes their story."

"Don't matter anyhow," Eaton said gruffly. "What they did to Mahan and Hooper was just short of murder. You think they're in the Alhambra now?"

"Most likely," Ferris said, glancing at a clock behind the counter. "They practically live there, what with the whores and whiskey. Probably crawlin' out of bed about now."

Eaton looked around. "What are we waitin' for then? Let's waltz in there and arrest the bastards."

"I think not," Roosevelt said in a firm voice. "If we corner them in the Alhambra, they may very well fight. I will not risk any of you being killed."

"Yeah, I'd vote for that," Eaton said. "So how do we go about it?"

Roosevelt walked to the large plate-glass window at the front of the store. For several moments, lost in thought, he stared off down the street. He finally turned back to Ferris. "Joe, do you know these men on sight?"

"Yessir, sure do," Ferris said. "They've been in the store any number of times. Waited on them myself."

"Would you be willing to assist in their arrest?"

"I'd count it an honor, Mr. Roosevelt."

"Excellent!" Roosevelt said, clapping him on the shoulder. "If your theory is correct, Bonner and his men are just starting their day. As you put it, just crawling out of bed."

"Night owls like that, their mornin' generally starts in the afternoon."

"Which means they will want breakfast. And Murphy's Café is only a few doors from the Alhambra. Correct?"

"Yeah, that's where the sporting crowd usually eats."

Roosevelt pointed out the window. "Both the butcher's shop and the barber's shop are directly across the street from the Alhambra. Do you think we might secure the cooperation of the owners?"

"Mr. Roosevelt, you're the deputy sheriff. I tend to doubt they'd turn you down."

"Very well," Roosevelt said, turning to face the men. "John, you and Paul will be stationed in the butcher's shop. I will be in the barbershop with Joe and Bob. Follow my lead in whatever happens." He looked from man to man. "Understood?"

The men nodded agreement. Ferris and one of the clerks slipped outside, pulling rifles from saddle scabbards, and hurried back inside. After the men checked their weapons, Ferris led them through the stockroom to the rear door. They proceeded down the alleyway, crossed the intersecting street, and moved into the next block. The Eaton brothers waited until Roosevelt spoke with the butcher, then entered the shop by the back door. Roosevelt, Ferris, and Hallett entered the barbershop.

Roosevelt had his badge pinned on his mackinaw. The shop was empty except for the barber, who was seated in a chair reading the *Badlands Cowboy*. He knew Roosevelt and, after listening to a brief explanation, put on his coat and left by the rear door. The men moved to the front of the shop, standing in the shadows, away from the window. Hardly more than ten minutes passed before the door of the Alhambra swung open and Paddock stepped outside.

He was followed by three men who looked hungover, shoulders slouched, hands stuffed in the pockets of their coats. They turned east along the boardwalk, toward Murphy's Café.

"That's them," Ferris said. "Bonner's the one behind Paddock. The other two are Ellis and Lawton."

Roosevelt moved through the door. Hallett followed him outside, the butt of his rifle tucked into his shoulder. They stepped off the boardwalk into the street.

"Halt!" Roosevelt shouted. "You men are under arrest."

The command brought the four men around. As they turned, the Eaton brothers came through the door of the butcher shop, their rifles trained on the men. There was a prolonged moment of silence as Paddock and the other three stared into the muzzles of the rifles. Roosevelt wagged the snout of his Winchester.

"Drop your gun belts," he ordered. "Do it slowly and very carefully."

"What the hell's this?" Paddock demanded. "Ain't nobody here charged with nothin'."

"The charge is extortion, conspiracy, and assault and battery. Do not make it worse by resisting arrest."

"Roosevelt, you're off your rocker. Who we supposed to have assaulted?"

"Steve Mahan and Issac Hooper," Roosevelt said. "Since it was at your orders, you are equally quilty."

"Hell I am." Paddock turned to the three men with a hard stare. "I never ordered you boys to do nothin'—did I?"

"Not a damn thing," Bonner said, as if on cue. "And Mahan welched on what he lost at poker. We was just tryin' to collect a debt."

"Come now, Bonner," Roosevelt said sternly. "Paddock will sacrifice you to save himself, and no qualms about it. Why lie to protect him?"

"Who you callin' a liar?" Bonner bristled. "I done told you the truth about the whole thing. Ain't that right, boys?"

Ellis and Lawton obediently nodded agreement. Roosevelt briefly deliberated whether or not they could be convinced to change their story. But then, just as quickly, he saw that by implicating Paddock they convicted themselves on the assault charge. Bitter as it was, he realized he was stymied.

"Paddock, you may step aside," he said. "Of course, I may yet return to arrest you. Assuming these men come to their senses."

"You might try arrestin' me once too often, Roosevelt. Don't push your luck."

"Move along before I arrest you now."

Paddock glanced at the men, then walked toward the Alhambra. Roosevelt motioned to them with his Winchester. "Drop those gun belts," he said. "I will not tell you again."

The men unbuckled their gun belts. "Goddamn law," Bonner grumped. "Where you takin' us, anyway?"

"To jail, where you belong."

The men were marched to the railway depot. There was an evening train to Mandan, and Roosevelt planned to be on it with his prisoners. He thought Hallett could accompany him and, once the men were bound hand and foot, there would be little risk of escape. His one regret was that Paddock wasn't along for the trip.

Honor among thieves seemed to him an unintended irony.

TWENTY-TWO

A formation of Canadian geese winged northward against a cloudless sky. The date was March 30, and rivers and streams overflowed their banks with the melt-off of winter snow. Spotty patches of emerald grass dotted the flatland prairie.

The morning train from Medora chugged eastward beneath a noonday sun. With a stop in Dickinson, the trip to Mandan usually consumed four hours, and the train was on time. There were three passenger coaches, with an express car behind the tender, and the engineer held the throttle open. Cinders from the smokestack floated on the wind like fiery hornets.

Roosevelt and Dutch Wannegan were in the last passenger coach. Wannegan was seated by the window, and Roosevelt sat facing the forward door. His deputy's badge was pinned to his jacket, and his ivory-handled Colt, snugged in a crossdraw holster, was in plain sight. They were on their way to Mandan for the murder trial of the Marquis de Mores and Jake Paddock. The trial was set to begin in Superior Court tomorrow morning.

The forward door opened as the conductor came through the vestibule. Roosevelt momentarily stiffened, his hand touching the butt of the Colt, until he saw that there was no one behind the conductor. De Mores and Paddock were riding in the middle coach, and he feared there might be some last-minute attempt on Wannegan's life. Early that morning, at the depot in Medora, there had been a tense moment as he waited to see which coach de Mores and Paddock would board. He knew without asking that Paddock was armed.

Dutch Wannegan was the key prosecution witness. Tom O'Donald, the only other eyewitness to the shooting, had vanished from Medora soon after recovering from his wound. After hiring Wannegan as a cowhand, Roosevelt had kept him quarantined on Elkhorn for nearly eight months. He had done so in the knowledge that if Wannegan went into Medora, he would almost certainly be killed. Paddock might yet try it, and Roosevelt had appointed himself Wannegan's bodyguard. His hand never strayed far from his pistol.

De Mores was no less vindictive. He made no secret of his belief that Roosevelt, by hiring and protecting Wannegan, was intent on persecuting him for a crime he had not committed. In an interview with the *Badlands Cowboy,* the Marquis had been quoted as saying; "The purpose of the murder charge is to destroy my business enterprise and remove me from the cattle trade. The man behind it is none other than Theodore Roosevelt." De Mores' vitriolic remarks left little doubt as to his perception of the upcoming trial. He considered Roosevelt his personal enemy.

The antagonism of De Mores and Paddock was fueled by more recent developments. Only last month, three weeks after their capture, Dave Bonner, Roy Ellis, and Ed Lawton had been brought to trial. Steve Mahan and Isaac Hooper testified about being viciously assaulted on their ranch, and Roosevelt corroborated their statements. The defendants steadfastly refused to implicate Paddock but were nonetheless found guilty and sentenced to two years in prison. The conviction was yet another black eye for de Mores and Paddock at the hands of Roosevelt. Thus far, he had defeated them at every turn.

The train pulled into Mandan shortly after one o'clock. The second-largest town in Dakota, Mandan was located on the western shore of the Missouri River. Directly across

the river was Bismarck, the territorial capital and half
again as large. Mandan was the county seat for Billings
County and a trade center for farmers and cattlemen on the
vast prairie stretching westward from the river. Town
boosters were quick to boast that the Lewis and Clark expedition had wintered there at the original Mandan Indian
village in 1804. The tribe, though few spoke of it, was virtually wiped out by smallpox, the white man's first import.

Roosevelt delayed getting off the train. He waited until
he saw de Mores and Paddock walk by on the platform and
then led Wannegan off the coach. The railroad station was
crowded, and they fell in behind a knot of passengers, trailing de Mores and Paddock at a distance. The accused men
were still free on bond, and the court had ordered that they
surrender themselves to the sheriff the day before the trial.
Outside the depot the town spread north and south along
the banks of the river. Roosevelt paused on the street.

"Dutch, I'll leave you here," he said. "We have reservations at the Grand Hotel on Front Street. I will meet you
there within the hour."

"The Grand Hotel," Wannegan repeated, looking
around at the busy streets. "Whereabouts you headed, Mr.
Roosevelt?"

"I want to make sure our friends go directly to the sheriff's office. I shan't be long."

"You reckon I got time for a drink? I don't rightly remember the last time I was in a saloon."

"By all means, have yourself a drink. But don't make me
come searching for you. I expect to find you at the hotel."

"Yessir, one drink'll do me fine."

Roosevelt hurried off after de Mores and Paddock.
They were a block ahead, waiting at a corner as an electric
streetcar clanged through the intersection. That morning,
in Medora, he'd thought he might have to take them into
custody and escort them to Mandan. But they were under
fifty thousand dollars' bond, and de Mores apparently had
no intention of forfeiting such a sum. They made the train
with time to spare.

Uptown, Roosevelt noted that their pace slowed as they approached the courthouse. There was no conversation between them, and he could well imagine their thoughts at the prospect of being incarcerated. Judge Oscar Horton, who presided over the Superior Court, had ordered that they surrender and be placed in jail by two o'clock. Given the evidence, Roosevelt was confident today would be the last day they walked the streets as free men. He followed them into the courthouse.

The sheriff's office was on the ground floor. De Mores and Paddock went through the door, unaware that Roosevelt was only a few paces behind. The room was airy, with windows looking across the river to Bismarck, and two deputies sat at desks. Seth Bullard's private office was in the far corner, and he saw them enter and halt before one of the deputies. He moved forward into the outer office.

"Deputy Roosevelt," he said, looking past them. "See you got 'em here on time."

De Mores and Paddock glanced around. Their faces registered first surprise and then anger. "Roosevelt, you amaze me," de Mores said. "Did you think it necessary to skulk along behind us?"

"Not at all," Roosevelt said lightly. "I simply made sure you didn't lose your way."

Paddock snorted. "Where's the pet monkey you been guarding? Finally let him off the leash?"

"Have no concern about Mr. Wannegan. You shall see him in court tomorrow."

"Full of lies, no doubt," de Mores huffed, turning away. "In any event, Sheriff Bullard, we surrender of our own volition. No credit falls to Roosevelt."

"Depends on who's talkin'," Bullard said. "Either one of you gents armed?"

"I am," Paddock replied, handing over his pistol. "Never know who you're gonna meet on a train."

"All right, here's the drill," Bullard said. "The jail's down in the cellar and you both get your own cell. No visitors except for your lawyer."

"Our attorney is Alfred Payne," de Mores noted. "I expect him to call on us this afternoon."

"I'll send him along the minute he shows. Now this here's Deputy Johnson and Deputy Manyrd. They'll take you down to the jail."

Johnson took de Mores and Manyrd took Paddock. The deputies marched them out of the office and down the hallway, toward the rear of the building. When the door closed, Bullard turned to Roosevelt. Bullard's walrus mustache lifted in a smile.

"Them two hate your guts," he said. "I wonder they haven't killed you before now."

"Someone tried," Roosevelt said. "An inch closer and we wouldn't be talking today."

"Too bad you missed when you fired back. Would've saved us puttin' Paddock on trial tomorrow."

"Quite frankly, I would rather see him hanged. A bullet would have been too quick."

"You ever seen a hangin'?"

"No, I have not."

"There's a science to it," Bullard said with a trace of awe. "We hire a hangman out of Minneapolis, and he weighs 'em on a beef scale to determine the length of the drop. Snaps a man's neck like a matchstick."

Roosevelt nodded. "Paddock deserves whatever the law allows."

"What about the Marquis?"

"De Mores is a victim of his own greed. Paddock is simply an evil man."

"Are you sayin' de Mores ought not be hung?"

"Not at all," Roosevelt commented. "Greed is hardly a mitigating factor in a trial for murder. De Mores is equally guilty."

Bullard considered his newest deputy something of an enigma. Roosevelt was unquestionably a man of action and yet, at the same time, a philosopher of sorts. Bullard often thought it an odd combination.

"Well, anyway," he said. "First thing we have to do is get 'em convicted. Wannegan all set to testify?"

"Indeed he is," Roosevelt confirmed. "There will be no equivocation when he takes the stand. He will make an excellent witness."

"Where is Wannegan, anyway?"

"I'm meeting him at the hotel."

"Guess you'd better bring him back here. Titus Warren's the county attorney, and he'll be prosecuting the case. He wants to review Wannegan's testimony."

"I'll attend to it immediately."

Roosevelt hurried off to the hotel. He returned a short while later with Wannegan and escorted him to Warren's office on the second floor. Warren first reviewed the details of the shooting and then spent the balance of the afternoon rehearsing Wannegan's testimony. By the end of the day, Warren was satisfied the case was ready for trial.

Early that evening, Roosevelt took Wannegan to the hotel dining room for dinner. Wannegan was accustomed to bunkhouse fare, and he marveled at the selections on the menu. He ordered braised duck with orange sauce and tore into it like a kid at a birthday party. The duck, which seemed to him an exotic treat, somehow reminded him of another matter. He paused with a chunk of duck breast on his fork.

"Mind if I ask you something, Mr. Roosevelt?"

"Go right ahead."

"There's talk around the bunkhouse," Wannegan said. "Some of the boys allow you're fixin' to go off huntin' grizzly bears. Anything to it?"

"Yes, I leave the end of the week," Roosevelt remarked. "Grizzlies are somewhat scarce in Dakota, so I'm traveling to Wyoming. Why do you ask?"

"Just wonderin' why you're so keen to hunt grizzly. I've heard they're tough critters."

"Indeed, the fiercest creature on the continent!"

"Heard they eat men for breakfast real regular."

Roosevelt grinned. "And there is the answer to your question, Dutch. I am intrigued with hunting something that might eat me. What better sport?"

"Don't sound much like sport to get yourself et."

"Yes, but you see, the very uncertainty of it is the point. Not unlike gladiators in Roman times."

Wannegan popped the bite of duck into his mouth. He felt a sense of loyalty and gratitude toward Roosevelt, for he'd found both a sanctuary and a home at Elkhorn. He was convinced as well Roosevelt was brave beyond reckoning, almost immune to fear. But he had to agree with the boys in the bunkhouse.

A man who'd pick a fight with a grizzly was plumb peculiar.

Superior Court was on the second floor of the courthouse. By nine o'clock the next morning the benches were packed with spectators, drawn by the sensational nature of the trial. They were there to see the French nobleman charged with murder.

The newspapers had been full of the case for the past week. There was speculation, particularly in editorials, that the Marquis de Mores had called in political chits at the highest levels. His business dealings with the Northern Pacific and the railroad's influence at the territorial capital seemed the only reasons he'd been granted bond for seven months. Little was said of Jake Paddock, for Dakota was overrun with gunmen and his role in the affair was that of a hired hand. The star attraction was the Frenchman.

De Mores and Paddock were seated at the defense table. Their lawyer, Alfred Payne, was short and slight of build, with sleek hair, muddy eyes, and a pencil-thin mustache. He had been quoted in newspapers as saying the Marquis was an innocent man, persecuted by business rivals in Medora for personal gain. Payne looked like a fighting cock ready to be pitted.

On the opposite side of the courtroom, Titus Warren, the county attorney, was seated at the prosecutor's table.

He was a fleshy man, with an ample paunch, a gold watch chain tight across his vest. Directly behind him, on the other side of the balustrade, Roosevelt and Wannegan were seated in the first row of benches. Sheriff Bullard stood by the wall near the jury box.

"All rise!"

The bailiff's command brought the spectators to their feet. Judge Oscar Horton, presiding over the trial, entered from his chambers at the rear of the room. He mounted the bench, seated himself in a high-backed chair, and took out his spectacles. He nodded to the bailiff.

"This court is now in session," the bailiff said loudly. "The docket concerns *The Territory of Dakota versus Antoine de Mores and Jacob Paddock,* herein charged with murder in the first degree. Be seated!"

The crowd resumed their seats. Judge Horton adjusted his spectacles, waiting for everyone to get settled. He was an imposing man, with salt-and-pepper hair and sharp features. His eyes were magnified behind the glasses, and his look left no doubt as to who was in charge. He addressed the attorneys in an orotund voice.

"Are you gentlemen ready to proceed?"

Titus Warren got to his feet. "The prosecution is prepared, Your Honor."

"The defense is prepared," Alfred Payne echoed. "And may I say it's an honor to be in your courtroom, Judge Horton."

"Thank you, counselor." Horton nodded to the bailiff. "Bring in the jury."

The bailiff opened a door at the rear of the jury box. Twelve men filed in from a waiting room and settled into their seats. Under Dakota statute, jurors were impanelled from a standing list compiled by the county tax assessor. The first twelve men on the list, along with two alternates, had been called to jury duty.

Warren presented the opening argument for the prosecution. He painted a picture of a land-grabbing foreign nobleman whose ruthless tactics ended in a treacherous ambush and murder. Payne, in his statement for the defense, declared the charges baseless, the insidious work of business rivals bent on destroying the accused. He labeled it "persecution" of the rankest sort.

Judge Horton ordered the prosecution to call its first witness. Dutch Wannegan was sworn in by the bailiff and took a seat on the witness stand. Warren first elicited testimony about the threats made in an effort to force Tom O'Donald to sell his ranch. He then moved to the subsequent arson of an equipment shed, the rifle assault on the ranch house, and O'Donald's confrontation with Paddock in the Alhambra Saloon. He finally went to the matter of the ambush.

"You were taken unawares," he said. "You were fired upon without warning by men laying in ambush. Is that correct?"

Wannegan bobbed his head. "Yessir, we shore was."

"Are the men who fired on you in this courtroom today?"

"The Marquis de Mores and Jake Paddock, sittin' right over there. The other two was Frank Miller and Quincy Moore."

"What was the result of the rifle fire?"

"Me and Tom was wounded pretty bad. George Luffsey, the other fellow that worked for Tom—he was killed."

"Did you see who fired the shot that killed Luffsey?"

"No, sir, I didn't see much of nothin'. We was ridin' along, and there's all this shootin', and next thing you know, I'm on the ground. Got plugged in the leg."

"Tell us now . . ." Warren paused for emphasis. "Did you, or O'Donald, or Luffsey at any time fire your weapons?"

"No, sir," Wannegan responded. "Way it happened, we never had no chance. They just shot us down."

"And without warning, unable to defend himself, George Luffsey was murdered. Is that your testimony?"

"Yessir, cold-blooded murder, that's what it was."

"No further questions."

Alfred Payne approached the witness stand. "Quite a fanciful tale, Mr. Wannegan," he said with a mocking smile. "The man you worked for, Tom O'Donald, where is he today?"

"Don't know," Wannegan said. "Tom took off when he was able to travel. Told me he was scared."

"But you didn't take off, did you, Mr. Wannegan? Why is that?"

"Well, Mr. Roosevelt hired me on at his ranch, Elkhorn. I figgered I was pretty safe out there."

"You're speaking of Theodore Roosevelt?"

"Yessir."

"And Roosevelt hired you to keep you around and bring forth your testimony here today. Isn't that so?"

"Objection!" Warren said. "Calls for an opinion."

"I'll allow it," Judge Horton ruled. "You may answer the question, Mr. Wannegan."

"I reckon so," Wannegan said. "I'm the only one left."

"Precisely!" Payne thundered. "O'Donald, the alleged injured party, refused to appear in this courtroom today. So we have only your word for what transpired. Correct?"

"Yeah, I guess."

"Isn't it a fact that you and your friends fired first?"

"No, we never fired at all."

"Isn't it a fact that you were present at the Alhambra Saloon when O'Donald threatened the lives of Mr. de Mores and Mr. Paddock? Isn't that true?"

"Maybe Tom did, but it was only 'cause—"

"Indeed he did," Payne interrupted. "And isn't it a fact, after the initial exchange of gunfire—when you were attempting to fire again—Mr. de Mores stopped his men from firing on you? Interceded and *saved* your life!"

"Wasn't like that." Wannegan appeared rattled. "They was fixin' to shoot and—"

"And Mr. de Mores mercifully spared your life. Except for his intervention, you wouldn't be here today. Isn't that the God's honest truth?"

"Well, yeah, I reckon he stopped 'em."

"I have no further questions, Your Honor."

Roosevelt was next called to the witness stand. After he was sworn in, Warren led him through the aftermath of the shooting. He testified that his investigation indicated a plot resulting in an ambush, the murder of one man, and the attempted murder of two others. Roosevelt went on to say that he requested the sheriff travel to Medora to arrest the assailants uncovered by his investigation. Warren thanked him for his testimony and turned him over for cross-examination. Payne approached with a sardonic expression.

"You speak of *your* investigation, Mr. Roosevelt. Were you a law officer at the time?"

"No, I was not," Roosevelt said. "I acted in my capacity as president of the Stockgrowers Association."

"Of course you did," Payne said sarcastically. "And you offered Wannegan a job for no other reason than your civic duty. So that he might testify in this trial. Correct?"

"I did so in the cause of justice."

"Well, sir, in the cause of justice, speak to the jury now. Your relationship with Mr. de Mores might fairly be characterized as antagonistic. Isn't that true?"

"We are not friends," Roosevelt said. "Any adversarial feeling stems solely from de Mores."

"Isn't it a fact that you opposed Mr. de Mores for the position of president of the Stockgrowers Association?"

"The fact, counselor, is that he nominated himself for the position. I neither opposed nor endorsed him."

"So you say." Payne cast a rueful look at the jurors. "You have publicly expressed the opinion that Mr. De Mores is a harmful influence on the cattle trade. And your purpose in this entire affair is to drive him from business. Isn't that so?"

"No, it is not," Roosevelt said, restraining his anger. "You are twisting facts to serve your own ends. Everything you imply is false."

"I will allow the jury to decide who speaks false, Mr. Roosevelt. You may step down."

Roosevelt felt the jurors' eyes on him as he returned to his seat. Yet, for all his anger, he grudgingly admired

Payne's talent for deception. Sheriff Seth Bullard was called to the stand and recounted his interrogation of both Tom O'Donald and Dutch Wannegan. Prosecutor Warren then brought him to the critical issue.

"Sheriff, did you have occasion to speak with Dr. Horace Stickney? The physician who attended O'Donald and Wannegan?"

"Yessir, I did," Bullard said. "He also told me the dead man, Luffsey, had been killed by a single gunshot wound to the throat."

"I see." Warren nodded thoughtfully. "And did Dr. Stickney say anything to indicate he had examined the weapons of O'Donald, Wannegan, and Luffsey?"

"Yessir, he said their guns had not been—"

"Objection!" Payne shouted. "Hearsay is not admissible, Your Honor."

Warren looked to the bench. "Dr. Stickney was unable to be here today, Your Honor. He is the only physician in Medora, and he could not desert his patients. Surely there is no reason to question the word of Sheriff Bullard."

"Not to the point," Payne interjected. "Prosecution had ample time to arrange for Dr. Stickney's appearance. No one may speak for him."

Judge Horton stared down from the bench. "Objection sustained," he said. "Jury will disregard Sheriff Bullard's last remark."

Roosevelt knew the case had been seriously damaged. By the court's ruling, the jury could not admit into evidence that the victims' guns had never been fired. He watched as Warren tried to salvage something by having the sheriff rehash Wannegan's testimony. But the repetition clearly had little effect on the jurors. The prosecution rested its case.

Payne mounted a spirited defense. Jess Hogue, owner of the Alhambra Saloon, was brought in to verify the threat made by Tom O'Donald. Paddock was next, attired in a freshly pressed suit, and he proved to be a credible witness. He testified that he feared for his life and, rather than an ambush, the purpose was to capture O'Donald and his crew. He went on to say that O'Donald had fired first and he and his men had returned fire only in self-defense. Under Payne's coaxing, he argued that if he was in fact guilty of murdering Luffsey, he could have eliminated any witnesses by killing O'Donald and Wannegan. Prosecutor Warren was unable to shake his testimony on cross-examination.

De Mores was the last witness. His manner was forthright, and as if coached, he occasionally directed his answers to the jurors. His testimony, point by point, mirrored the fabricated story just elicited from Paddock. Payne carefully wove a tapestry of distorted facts and illusion. He finally came to the pivotal questions.

"By Wannegan's own admission—*his* testimony!—you ordered your men not to fire and thus saved his life and the life of Tom O'Donald. Is that correct?"

"Yes, it is," de Mores said with great sincerity. "I wished these men no harm. None at all."

"So you spared their lives," Payne intoned. "And then, rather than leave them to die of their wounds, you transported them to the doctor's office for medical care. Isn't that so?"

"I could do nothing less under the circumstances."

"One last question on this unfortunate affair, Mr. de Mores. Why has Theodore Roosevelt conducted a vendetta against you? Can you think of a reason?"

"I cannot," de Mores replied in a wounded voice. "I have always treated Mr. Roosevelt with the utmost respect. I considered him my friend."

"A friend filled with envy and spite, and the determination to destroy you. Would that be a fair statement?"

"Objection!" Warren said. "Solicits an opinion."

Payne walked away. "I have no further questions, Your Honor. The defense rests."

De Mores maintained his composure under cross-examination, never once deviating from his story. In closing argument, Warren attempted to reconstruct a picture of ambition and greed so pervasive that it led to murder.

Payne rebutted the argument by portraying an image of a man who spared the lives of his enemies only to be persecuted by an embittered and envious rival in the cattle trade. The trial had lasted three hours and twenty-eight minutes, and Judge Horton turned the case over to the jury. He then recessed court for lunch.

The jury returned at two o'clock, after a quick lunch and forty-three minutes of deliberation. All the parties to the action were recalled, and a crowd of spectators hastily filled the courtroom. Judge Horton asked the jury foreman to read the verdict aloud.

" 'We the jury,' " the foreman read from a scrawled form, " 'find the defendants, Antoine de Mores and Jacob Paddock, not guilty.' "

Roosevelt was not surprised by the verdict. The tenor of the trial, from beginning to end, led him to believe justice would not be served. As he rose to leave, with Wannegan at his side, de Mores turned and looked at him with a cold, implacable stare. There was no triumph in the look but rather a hard, loathsome malice. Their eyes locked for a moment, then Roosevelt moved into the aisle. He walked from the courtroom.

On the street, Wannegan seemed somewhat dazed. He shook his head like a bull hooking at cobwebs. "How the hell'd they get off?" he said. "Murder a man and the jury turns 'em loose. Don't make sense."

"I believe it's called misdirection," Roosevelt said. "Magicians divert the attention of the audience with one hand while performing a trick with the other. Alfred Payne is a clever lawyer."

"I ain't followin' you, Mr. Roosevelt. What'd he do?"

"Why, he made me the villain of the piece, Dutch. He convinced the jury that I was conducting a personal vendetta against de Mores. He pulled a rabbit from a hat."

"Still don't make a lick of sense. Where we headed in such a hurry?"

"There is an afternoon train to Medora and I intend to be on it. I have seen quite enough of Mandan and magicians."

Roosevelt strode off toward the train station. He thought the trial was nothing short of a travesty, a perversion of the judicial system. Duplicity and guile ruled the day, and murderers would celebrate victory in Mandan tonight. Yet vindication often bred rage in such men. A thirst for revenge.

He knew he hadn't heard the last of the Marquis.

TWENTY-THREE

Dawn slowly merged with the light of day. The buttes to the west were scarlet and burnt orange, the bottomland studded with silvery aspen. A woodpecker hammered on a tree in the distance.

The campsite was along the banks of the river. Five horses, hobbles on their forelegs, grazed across a tawny meadow. A buckboard loaded with supplies was parked nearby, the rear end covered with a tarp against the night dampness. The rushing waters of the stream were turbulent with winter melt-off from the high country.

Merrifield squatted by the fire. He was cooking thick slices of bacon while biscuits from last night warmed in a Dutch oven. Roosevelt sat opposite him, watching as the bacon sizzled and curled, sipping coffee from a tin cup. Nate Lebo, their hunting guide, turned from the river with a bucket of water and walked back to camp. He hunkered down across from Merrifield.

"Nothin' like a hot breakfast," he said, rubbing his hands against the heat of the fire. "Glad your mama taught you to cook."

"Good thing she did," Merrifield said. "We'd starve to death if we had to eat your cookin'. Never saw a man so helpless around a fire."

"Well, the thing is, I was hired on to show you where the grizz' lives. Never said I was a cook."

Roosevelt smiled. "I admire a truthful man, Nate. You have no other concern than to put me in front of a grizz."

"Don't you worry 'bout that," Lebo said. "We gonna find you a big one."

"How much farther to the Bighorns?"

"Mebbe six, seven days."

Merrifield had recommended Lebo for the hunt. A gaunt man, dressed in greasy buckskins, Lebo was something of a legend in the West. Originally a trapper, he had later served as a scout for the army and later still as a hunting guide for wealthy Easterners and foreign nobility. He was French-Canadian, transplanted to the West over two decades ago, and his specialty was bears. He was the man who knew where the grizz lived.

Roosevelt had invited Merrifield to accompany him on the hunt. He thought Merrifield deserved some time off, and a top hand had been left to oversee the Maltese Cross. They had departed three days after the murder trial in Mandan, and today was their sixth day on the trail. They followed the Little Missouri southwestward, and Lebo estimated they had crossed into Wyoming late yesterday. Their destination, the Bighorn Mountains, was now due west.

Their little caravan averaged something over twenty miles a day. The buckboard slowed them, but for a long trip Roosevelt preferred whatever amenities possible for camping. Merrifield drove the buckboard, which was loaded with victuals, rifles and shotguns, bedrolls, and camp gear. The Bighorn Mountains were some three hundred miles from the Maltese Cross, and Merrifield had outfitted them for a trek of four weeks. The only supply point in the wilderness was an army post in the foothills of the Bighorns.

Roosevelt had brought Manitou, his most reliable mount, on the trip. There were horses as well for Lebo and Merrifield, a stocky draft horse to pull the buckboard, and a packhorse. By day, Lebo and Roosevelt ranged out ahead, selecting a route through a land broken by tributary streams and rocky gorges. Roosevelt kept the camp supplied with fresh meat by downing prairie chickens, sage hens, and an occasional deer. Lebo often remarked that he'd never eaten so well on a hunting trip.

Seated around the fire, the men heaped their tin plates with crisp bacon and sourdough biscuits warmed in the Dutch oven. Lebo, like many trappers and mountain men, believed that grease possessed medicinal properties and warded off many ills. He dabbed his biscuit in the frying pan, soaking it in bacon fat, and wolfed it down with relish. As he ate, the dinge of dawn faded to daylight, and he kept glancing off to the northwest. He poured another cup of coffee when he'd cleaned his plate.

"Weather's buildin'," he said. "Don't like the looks of what's headed our way."

The day was overcast, the silty light bleak and leaden. To the northwest, the skies were dark with a towering mass of slate gray clouds. A freshening wind was chill with the scent of moisture.

"Doubt it's snow," Merrifield said. "What is it now, first week in April? Not too likely we'll get snowed on."

"Why godalmighty!" Lebo hooted. "I seen snow in May, never you mind April. Cold so bad it'd freeze your balls."

"Sure, ever' now and then," Merrifield conceded. "But like I said, it ain't all that likely."

Lebo swigged his coffee. "Still don't care for the looks of them clouds. We might be better off to hole up right here."

"I've no wish to delay," Roosevelt said. "I prefer to reach the Bighorns with all dispatch."

"Them bears'll still be there. We get caught in a howler and you'll wish you'd stayed here. Another day ain't gonna make no difference."

Roosevelt studied the sky a moment. "I think not," he said at length. "Let us push on and see how the day progresses. We can always take cover."

Lebo snorted. "Ain't too much cover out on the plains. We'd play hell hidin' under a rock."

"Nate, I do believe you are a worrywart."

"Well, don't you see, that's why I'm still kickin'."

Lebo fussed and grumbled, but he knew he'd lost the argument. After they finished breakfast, Merrifield scoured the cooking utensils while Roosevelt secured the bedrolls and Lebo saddled Manitou and his own mount. The stocky draft horse was then harnessed to the buckboard, and Merrifield's saddle horse and the packhorse were tied to the rear. They struck camp under a lowering sky.

Their course was westward from the river. The terrain gradually changed from buttes and ravines to rolling plains. From the southern headwaters of the Little Missouri to the Bighorns there was more than a hundred miles of tallgrass prairie. The vast expanse of land, millions of square acres, was largely uninhabited. A few scattered ranches dotted the country, but there were no roads, no trails, no sign of man. The emptiness stretched onward into an infinity of grass.

Roosevelt and Lebo were perhaps a mile in front of the buckboard. Except for occasional dips in the prairie, Merrifield was able to keep them in sight across the grassy tableland. Somewhere around midmorning they rode over a low knoll and spotted a small herd of antelope in the distance. A stiff wind spanked their cheeks from the northwest and the sky was the color of charred pewter. Roosevelt reined to a halt.

"Tell me, Nate," he said, staring at the distant antelope. "What do you estimate the range?"

"Too dang far for me," Lebo said, squinting with one eye. "But if I had to guess, I'd judge it's mebbe four hundred paces. You gonna take a shot?"

"I believe I will."

"Waste of powder."

"You never know until you try."

Roosevelt dismounted. Over the winter he'd ordered a Winchester Model 76 through the gunsmith in Medora. The rifle was lever action, chambered for the .45–75 cartridge, with a massive slug of 350 grains. A folding leaf sight had been installed on the stock, slightly to the rear of the hammer, and was graduated out to a thousand yards. Winchester advertised it as a rifle for big-game hunters.

Lebo watched from his saddle. Roosevelt took a seat on the knoll, raising the leaf sight, and cranked the knob up to four hundred yards. After levering a cartridge into the chamber, he estimated the drift of the wind and braced his elbows on his upright knees. He sighted on a buck ante-lope, holding slightly high for good measure, and feathered the trigger. The rifle boomed in a cloud of smoke.

"Jumpin' Jehoshaphat!" Lebo whooped. "You done kilt the sonovabitch!"

The buck lay sprawled on the ground while the other antelope bounded across the prairie. Roosevelt stood, star-ing into the distance, hardly able to believe he'd made the shot. He jumped into the saddle, still holding the rifle, and gigged Manitou into a lope. Lebo pounded along beside him, and a minute or so later they skidded to a halt before the fallen buck. A wide splotch of blood glistened just be-low the shoulder.

"Would you look at that," Lebo said in an awed voice. "Got him clean through the heart."

Roosevelt stared down with a toothy grin. "Nate, I be-lieve we will have antelope steaks for supper."

"By God, that's one to write home about. Never saw nothin' like it."

Lebo dismounted and pulled out his sheath knife. Still shaking his head and talking to himself, he began gutting the buck. A short while later Merrifield rolled up in the buckboard, and Lebo recounted the shot with the boister-ous air of a man who couldn't quite credit his own eyes. Roosevelt listened, frankly amazed by his marksmanship, grinning the entire time. Lebo tied the carcass on the side of the buckboard.

Roosevelt and Lebo were so enthused by the once-in-a-lifetime shot that they'd lost track of the weather. Merri-field pointed off to the northwest. "Storm's movin' fast," he said. "We'd best find ourselves some cover."

The sky was black and ominous. As Roosevelt and Lebo mounted, dark clouds boiled out of the northwest at frightening speed and raindrops began pelting the ground. Within moments the skies opened in a deluge and sheets of blinding rain soaked them as if they'd been dipped in a pond. The wind shrieked and moaned, gathering in intensity, suddenly buffeting them at gale force. The rain gusted almost level before the impact of the wind.

Lebo spurred his horse into a gallop. He motioned southward, and Roosevelt on Manitou and Merrifield in the buckboard thundered along in his wake. The wind abruptly went frigid and the skies split with hailstones double the size of pigeons' eggs. The men held the reins in one hand and the other arm before their faces, warding off the hammering blows of the rock-hard hailstones. Lebo led them into a craggy gully perhaps ten feet deep and half again as wide.

Roosevelt and Lebo quickly dismounted. Merrifield hopped out of the buckboard and grabbed the noseband to steady the draft horse. They hugged the windward side of the gully, heads ducked low as hail continued to pound the earth in a rattling, icy torrent. The roar of the wind slowly diminished, followed by a last pummeling of hail, and the towering black clouds drifted off to the southeast. A moment later the sun burst through, almost at its zenith in a clear sky of azure blue. The plains were carpeted with snowy, glittering hailstones.

"Good thing we found shelter," Merrifield said in a bemused tone. "That stuff could've brained a man to death."

Lebo rubbed a knot on his forehead. He'd been struck by a hailstone and the bump was already turning purple. "Mebbe you'll listen next time," he said, glowering at Roosevelt. "Told you we should've holed up by the river."

"Come now, Nate," Roosevelt said with a jocular smile. "What's a little hail compared to the shot I made today? I shall remember it all my life."

"Yeah, me, too." Lebo winced, exploring the knot on his head. "This thing as big as it feels?"

"What do you think, Bill?" Roosevelt asked jovially. "Has it spoiled Nate's looks?"

"Nope," Merrifield said, deadpan. "Wasn't nothin' to spoil."

Lebo muttered something to himself. He swung into the saddle and led them out onto a prairie bright with hailstones. Roosevelt was already composing notes to be entered into his journal that night. The shot of a lifetime and a freakish storm. A rare day.

His best yet on the plains of Wyoming.

The Bighorn Mountains rose in a majestic column beneath a hazy sun. Towering skyward, with elevations above thirteen thousand feet, the fluted spires sometimes touched the clouds. A light snow had fallen overnight and the land was dusted in white.

A deer hung from a stout limb on a tall pine. The camp was situated in a mountain meadow at seven thousand feet, the air crisp and bracing in the morning sunlight. Smoke from the fire drifted on a wayward breeze, and waters from a rapid brook tumbled musically over a rocky streambed. The horses were tied to a picket line in the trees.

The men were lounging around the fire. Merrifield and Lebo were discussing the doe hanging from the tree and how certain choice cuts might be prepared for supper. Roosevelt was cleaning his Winchester .45-75, running an oily patch secured to a piece of string through the barrel. He lightly oiled the breech, worked the lever several times, and lowered the hammer. After inspecting his handiwork, he removed cartridges from his gun belt and loaded five rounds into the magazine. He darted an impatient glance at Lebo.

"I am ready to hunt," he said shortly. "Do you have some notion of when we might be on our way?"

"Pretty soon," Lebo said without any sense of urgency. "That lazy ol' grizz ain't gonna be out for a while yet. We got time."

"How can you be so certain of his habits?"

"'Cause I been trackin' him for two days. Know him pretty good by now."

"Do you?" Roosevelt said. "Then why haven't I had a shot?"

"Ol' bears're smart bears," Lebo explained. "But we're gonna be little bit smarter 'n him today. He'll come to feed."

Late yesterday Lebo and Roosevelt had tracked the bear through a broad ravine. By the size of the paw prints Lebo knew it was a boar grizzly and estimated its standing height at ten feet or more. They had lost the tracks on a patch of shale just before dusk and abandoned the hunt for the day. Downslope from the shale, near the mouth of the ravine, they stumbled upon a buck deer and Lebo had shot it without hesitation. He'd left the carcass as bait for the grizzly.

Roosevelt was anxious to kill his bear. Five days ago, they had arrived at Crazy Woman Creek, which flowed through the foothills of the Bighorns. The supplies were off-loaded from the buckboard and afterward, using diamond-hitch pack saddles, loaded onto the two spare horses. Lebo then led them on a two-day trek into the Bighorns, climbing ever higher, until they reached the mountain meadow. The forested terrain, he declared, was where the grizz lived.

The first day had been spent in setting up their campsite. Roosevelt shot a deer to replenish their larder and, after dressing it out, hung it from the pine tree. The following morning, Merrifield stayed back to tend camp, and Roosevelt and Lebo undertook the hunt. Lebo found sign almost immediately, and for two days they had tracked the largest boar grizzly in the surrounding countryside. But Roosevelt's patience for stalking only stretched so far. He was ready to meet the bear.

"How long must we wait?" he asked. "When do you expect our bear will come to dine?"

Lebo squinted at the sun. "Mornin's not his time," he

said. "That ol' devil come out when the sun's high. No hurry."

"Perhaps he might take breakfast early today. Wouldn't it be prudent to stake out the bait?"

Merrifield chuckled. "Nate, there's no need talkin' when Mr. Roosevelt sets his mind. He ain't one to sit and twiddle his thumbs."

"No indeed," Roosevelt announced. "I've traveled much too far to idle by a campfire."

"Never pays to rush a grizz," Lebo said. "Don't recollect I've told you the hunter's prayer. Mebbe now'd be the time."

"Very well, what is the hunter's prayer?"

"Oh Lord, help me kill that grizz, and if you don't help me, Oh Lord, don't help the grizz."

Roosevelt smiled despite himself. "Quite to the point," he said. "In another life, you might have been a court jester. Now, shall we be on our way?"

Lebo scrambled to his feet. He gave Merrifield a sly wink and collected his rifle from where he'd leaned it against a tree. Roosevelt was waiting at the edge of the camp, rifle in hand, and Lebo led him north into the forest. He thought he'd never seen a man so keen to kill a bear.

Neither of them spoke as they moved steadily northward. The sun arced higher in the sky, and an hour or so later they approached the ravine where the deer carcass had been left overnight. Lebo walked along a ridge studded with trees, planning to stake out the bait from an elevated shooting position. He finally stopped at an ancient pine that overlooked the mouth of the ravine. Roosevelt halted at his side.

"I'll be damned," Lebo said coarsely. "That ol' grizz ain't as lazy as I figgered."

Roosevelt stared down into the ravine. The deer carcass was ripped open from shoulder to flank and half-consumed. He shook his head. "We're too late," he said. "Our bear has been here and gone."

"Yeah, guess you was right about him takin' breakfast early. Course, it don't matter, 'cause he ain't gonna get away."

"Why not?"

Lebo pointed with a thorny finger. The overnight dusting of snow was still fresh on the ground. Huge paw prints, double the handspan of a man, were visible even from a distance. The tracks led up the slope on the opposite side of the ravine. The top of the ridge was covered with trees.

"Lost him there yesterday," Lebo said, still pointing. "Where all that rocky ground climbs into the timber. Mr. Bear didn't figger on it snowin'."

Roosevelt looked at the far ridge. "Do you believe he's over there now?"

"Oh, sure, he's there. Got himself a bellyful of fresh meat and crawled off for a snooze. He's bedded down somewhere in them trees."

"Well then, we follow the tracks and find the bear. Is that it?"

"Just keep sayin' the hunter's prayer once we get into them trees. You remember how it goes?"

"Lord, don't help the grizz."

"Not today, nohow."

They clambered down the ridge, moving past the mangled deer carcass. The paw prints pressed through the dusting of snow, still distinct despite the growing warmth of the sun. Lebo licked his forefinger and held it to the air.

"Wind's in our favor," he whispered. "Walk quiet and no talkin' from here on. Don't want to rile ol' grizz."

Roosevelt merely nodded, eyes alert behind his spectacles. Lebo led the way up the slope, following the broad imprints in the snow. The tracks meandered through the trees, skirting clumps of brush, generally on a line to the west. A short distance into the timber, the tracks disappeared into an overgrown thicket of podgy young spruces. The branches of the trees were heavily tangled in a dense barrier.

Lebo pushed through the ticket, snow cascading off the

branches in a powdery screen. He suddenly froze, one arm holding the limbs apart, and hissed beneath his breath. He motioned Roosevelt forward, moving aside to create an opening, his eyes fixed straight ahead. The bear, disturbed by their passage through the thicket, rose from a bed of boughs not ten yards away. Roosevelt stepped into the clearing.

The grizzly reared up on his hind legs, his massive shoulders casting a shadow over the men. The hair bristled on his neck, and he bellowed a ferocious roar, batting the air with his paws. As Roosevelt raised his rifle, the bear dropped to all fours, still snarling, and charged across the clearing. Roosevelt caught the sights, aware that he had time for only one shot, and aimed for the head. He tripped the trigger and fired, the Winchester recoiling in a streak of flame. The grizzly collapsed in midstride, plowing snow with its broad snout.

Neither of the men moved for an instant. Then Roosevelt slowly lowered his rifle, staring at the bulk of the fallen giant. Not three yards from where he stood, the bear was sprawled in a furry pile, spikelike claws gouged in the earth. Lebo eased past, cautious even now, and halted a few feet from the grizzly. His mouth popped open.

"Goddamn," he said with an astounded look. "You got him right between the eyes. Dead center!"

Roosevelt appeared equally astonished. "I tried for a head shot. It seemed the only way to stop him."

"Well, sir, that's damn fine shootin'. You done got yourself a monster grizz. Bastard's big as a house."

"By George, I'll not soon forget this day! You have no peers as a guide, Mr. Lebo."

Lebo grinned. "Told you I knew where the grizz lived."

Early that afternoon they returned to camp. Lebo recounted the story of the hunt to Merrifield with all the histrionics of a thespian striding about a stage. Roosevelt was cast as the hero of the tale and accepted Merrifield's congratulations with what little modesty he could muster. The balance of the afternoon was spent at the site of the

kill, where Lebo and Merrifield skinned the grizzly for a
rug to be displayed at Elkhorn. The packhorse, skittish all
the while, reluctantly hauled the bloody hide back to camp.

By sundown, with the hide stretched on an improvised
rack, the men gathered around the fire. Merrifield roasted a
haunch of venison on a spit and baked a fresh batch of biscuits in the Dutch oven. Lebo produced a pint of whiskey
from his pack, which he'd brought along for just such an
occasion. He and Merrifield sloshed whiskey into their tin
cups, and Roosevelt accepted their toast with a cup of coffee. Over supper, Lebo related tales of other bear hunts but
none to top what he had seen today. He bragged on Roosevelt's shot as though he'd made it himself.

Later that night, after finishing the bottle, Merrifield
and Lebo crawled into their bedrolls. Roosevelt was still
energized by the day's hunt and wondered if he would
sleep at all. A full moon rose over the mountains, and he
decided on a walk to tire himself out. On their first day in
camp, while he was off hunting deer, he had come across a
spot of singular beauty. He thought it might look even
more memorable in the moonlight.

A short distance from camp, a sheer outcropping of
rock overlooked a forested valley. Off to the west, the
snowcapped peaks of the mountains glittered in the buttery
glow of the moon. Roosevelt walked to the edge of the cliff
and stood gazing out across the limned splendor of spires
reaching for the heavens. He wondered if some ancient
tribe of Indians, or perhaps fur trappers, had stood there
before him and marveled at the serenity of the wilderness
under a full moon. He somehow doubted it was ever more
magnificent than tonight.

Something caught his eye off to the left. He turned from
the outcropping and saw Alice and his mother on the verge
of the tree line. His heart thudded in his chest as he
watched them move closer, shrouded in gossamer raiments
and luminous in the moonlight. They approached to within
a few feet, nearer than ever before, hovering as though in

flight, their arms outstretched. Their eyes held him in loving embrace.

Teddy.

Alice spoke, her voice at once sad and endearing. Her lips seemed not to move.

You hold us with you, Teddy. We cannot leave your world while you still grieve.

Roosevelt stared at her, desperate that she might hear him. Yet, for all he struggled, he could not find his voice. His mother lifted her hand, almost touched him.

Alice and I are happy, Theodore. You must let us go.

Alice smiled, the sunny smile so magical in memory. He tried to speak to her, but again his voice failed. Her eyes held him lovingly, intently.

Life is before you and your way will be clear. We wish to leave you now, Teddy. Give us peace.

Roosevelt realized he was terrified to let go. Even now, when they finally spoke to him, he wanted nothing more than to keep them close. Yet their words were a catharsis and he felt somehow cleansed of sorrow. Not a release but rather a way to live with the memory. He nodded, his eyes misty, and in that instant . . . let them go.

Sweet Teddy, we will always be with you. We love you so.

Alice smiled one last time. His mother's features were somehow beatific, and they slowly moved away, a vision still. Then, as though he'd blinked, their images faded into the moonlit trees. A gentle breeze touched him like a final sigh.

He knew they were gone forever.

TWENTY-FOUR

Spring was upon the land. Wildflowers sprinkled brightness like prisms of glass across the emerald grasses of the valley. The buttes rose monolithic from the valley floor, blazed in vermilion and ocher against the western sky. Sunlight danced with motes of dust where cattle grazed near the river.

Roosevelt rode into Elkhorn the afternoon of May 1. He was leading the packhorse, burdened under the weight of the bearskin from his Wyoming hunt. Yesterday, south of Medora, Merrifield had gone on to the Maltese Cross to prepare for spring roundup. Nate Lebo had parted with them several days earlier, off to Montana in search of new adventures. He was still talking about the shot that killed the grizz.

On the long trip from Wyoming, Roosevelt had undergone a startling transformation. The final night in the Bighorns, those final moments with Alice and his mother, had a profound impact on his view of the world. At some visceral level, he believed they had watched over him until he was emotionally healed, and only then was he able to hear their voices. He felt he'd crossed a mystic threshold, lost to them in time but still joined in spirit. He was at last restored in mind, ready for life.

Will Dow met him at the corral. "By golly, Mr. Roosevelt, seems like you weren't never comin' back. How was your trip?"

"Quite a good hunt," Roosevelt said, motioning to the packhorse. "I've brought home my grizzly."

"Looks like you got yourself a big one."

"Yes, we finally have a trophy worthy of Elkhorn. Would you carry it to the house for me, Will?"

Dow untied the bundle from the packhorse. He staggered under the weight, hefting it onto his shoulder, and followed Roosevelt to the house. Sewall saw them through the window, alerting the women with a shout, and they were met at the door by Erma and Irene and young Amy. Their greeting was warm and joyful, and Roosevelt felt somewhat like a soldier returned from distant wars. He had Dow spread the bearskin on the floor before the fireplace.

On the way back from Wyoming, Nate Lebo had cured the hide with a mix of deer brains and ash. The underside was velvety soft, and the furry outer coat covered so much of the floor that furniture had to be moved aside. Sewall paced it off, shaking his head, and the women marveled at the size of the creature. Roosevelt, with little urging, acted out the hunt, stalking about the parlor, his features grimaced in the snarl of a charging grizzly. The shot between the eyes left them agog with wonder.

The women finally went off to the kitchen to prepare supper. Dow excused himself, still admiring the bearskin, and went out to unsaddle Manitou and the packhorse. Roosevelt and Sewall seated themselves in the parlor, and Sewall reached down to rub the grizzly's furry pelt. He again wagged his head.

"That's a lotta bear," he said. "Sounds like you had yourself a pretty frisky time."

Roosevelt chortled. "As our cowboys are fond of saying, I wouldn't have missed it for all the tea in China. How are things here at Elkhorn?"

"Well, believe it or not, we've done real fine in your absence. I'm no cowboy as yet, but I've got the hang of things."

"Has a date been set for spring roundup?"

"Week from today," Sewall told him. "We'll start the same place as last year. Up on the Hash Knife range."

"When you say 'we,'" Roosevelt asked with a jesting smile, "are you referring to yourself?"

"I suppose I'm cowboy enough to work roundup. Course, they'll likely put me with you to wrestlin' calves."

"There is no ignominy in working the branding fires. Unless, of course, one has no skill with a rope."

"I just suspect we'll get all the ignominy we can swallow."

"Yes, but it is an honest day's labor," Roosevelt said genially. "I came straightaway here from the Maltese Cross. How are affairs these days in Medora?"

"Guess you haven't heard, then."

"Heard what?"

"Jake Paddock's dead."

Roosevelt appeared shocked. "Am I correct in assuming it was not a natural death?"

"Anything but," Sewall said. "A cardsharp came through town, and him and Paddock got into it over a poker game. They settled it with guns."

"And he killed Paddock?"

"Dead as a mackerel."

"What happened to the cardsharp?"

"Held everybody at gunpoint and backed out of the Alhambra. Walked straight to the train station and hopped a freight headed west. Nobody's heard of him since."

"What greater irony," Roosevelt said thoughtfully. "To escape the hangman's noose and be killed in a gunfight. Paddock must have been the most surprised of all."

Sewall grunted. "Him and the Devil probably talk about it every day."

"Of course, that does not account for the Marquis de Mores. He escaped the noose no less than Paddock."

"That reminds me, you got a letter from de Mores. It's with the other mail in your study."

"I can't imagine any good reason he would write me. When did the letter arrive?"

"Few days after you left for Wyoming. Will picked it up with the mail when he was in town."

"I believe I'll just have a look."

Roosevelt walked back to his study. A stack of mail was on his desk and he riffled through the envelopes. There were two letters from Bamie, one from Henry Cabot Lodge, and one from Republican Committee headquarters in New York. The letter from de Mores was farther down in the pile, but his curiosity was whetted by the one from Republican headquarters. He tore open the envelope.

The letter was signed by John Abernathy, chairman of the Republican Committee. Abernathy, with considerable hyperbole, offered Roosevelt the nomination for mayor of New York. He congratulated Roosevelt on *Hunting Trips of a Ranchman*, which was still on the best-seller list throughout the East. Because of the book's success, the *New York Times* had published a series of articles depicting Roosevelt's adventures in Dakota Territory. The series cast Roosevelt in a heroic role, thwarting horse thieves and murderers, halting depredations by hostile Sioux warriors, and building a cattle empire in the wilderness. The articles sensationalized Roosevelt into a mythic figure.

Abnernathy was nothing if not pragmatic. His letter went on to say that publicity from the articles had made Roosevelt the talk of New York. The series reviewed as well Roosevelt's distinguished career in the New York State Legislature and his reputation as a forthright reformer. The Republican Party, Abernathy wrote, believed that Roosevelt's nomination as mayor would result in victory over the latest Tammany Hall stooge. He urged Roosevelt to accept the nomination and return forthwith to begin campaigning for office. He requested a reply by May 15.

Roosevelt's immediate reaction was one of ambivalence. He thought the offer a great honor, but he felt he'd found a renewal of spirit and soul in the Badlands. Then, too, there was the matter of the new life he'd made for himself in Dakota, the personal satisfaction derived from operating a cattle enterprise. He placed the letter aside and

opened the one from de Mores. His features twisted in a
scowl as he scanned the lines:

> *Dear Roosevelt,*
> *A gentleman in all honor cannot overlook an insult. You*
> *have been very active against me, as has been reported*
> *in the newspapers. To acerbate matters, you were re-*
> *sponsible for a false charge of murder being lodged, and*
> *supported Mr. Wannegan in his perjurious testimony at*
> *trial. You have cast yourself as my enemy, and I demand*
> *satisfaction in an honorable manner. Among gentlemen*
> *such matters are settled quite directly. I await your reply.*
> *Very truly,*
> *Antoine de Mores*

The letter was dated April 3, three days after de Mores'
acquittal for murder. Roosevelt was by then on his way to
Wyoming, and as he read the letter he regretted not having
responded sooner. His anger mounting, he promised himself de Mores would have to wait no longer for satisfaction.
He walked through the house to the parlor, where Sewall
was seated on the sofa. He waved the letter.

"What temerity!" he barked. "De Mores has challenged
me to a duel!"

"Duel?" Sewall repeated blankly. "Why would he do a
fool thing like that?"

"I have insulted his honor as a *gentleman*. He demands
satisfaction."

"You mean to ignore it . . . don't you?"

"No indeed!" Roosevelt said furiously. "I will not be
bullied by a Frenchman."

Sewall got to his feet. "Look here, no sense flyin' off the
handle about things. You're just mad because he slipped
loose on that murder charge."

"Yes, I am hopping mad, and with every reason. The
man would vex a saint!"

"Well, don't let that cloud your judgment. You gotta
calm down and act sensible."

"Unless I accept the challenge, de Mores will brand me a coward. I will not have it."

"So you're gonna run off and get yourself killed? You ask me, that's just plain dumb."

"No one asked you," Roosevelt informed him. "And besides, who says de Mores is the better man? I am not without some skill at arms."

Sewall let out a gusty sigh. "Just because you killed a grizzly don't mean you're a gunfighter. Think about it overnight and you'll see I'm right."

"I plan to spend the night at the Eaton ranch. I shall call on de Mores tomorrow morning."

"You're actin' the fool here, and you know it."

"Thank you for your vote of confidence."

Roosevelt walked out of the house.

Medora was somnolent under a warm spring sun. A dog lay sprawled in sleep near the train depot, and the street was all but empty of wagons. Horses stood hip-shot outside a few of the saloons.

Roosevelt rode into town shortly before the noon hour. He kept his eyes straight ahead as he went past the newspaper and the Northern Pacific Refrigerator Car Company. The last thing he wanted was Amos Packard hounding him for an interview, and he wasn't quite ready to call on the Marquis de Mores. Yet his mood was somewhat improved from when he'd left Elkhorn.

Last night, at the Eaton ranch, the three brothers had been both concerned and electrified by his news. John, the eldest, was troubled that Roosevelt, regardless of his proficiency with weapons, might come to a bad end. Paul and Charlie were wildly excited by the very idea of a duel and grilled Roosevelt for the details of how such affairs were conducted. After considerable discussion even John agreed on the central point at issue. There was no choice but to accept the challenge.

Upstreet, Roosevelt reined to a halt before Medora Hardware & Emporium. He stepped down from the saddle,

loosened the girth, and left Manitou tied to the hitchrack.
As he crossed the boardwalk, he tugged at his gun belt, settling the holstered Colt firmly on his hip. Inside the store,
one of the clerks was waiting on a customer and the other
was rolling a keg of nails in from the back room. Joe Ferris looked up from a stack of invoices spread over the
counter.

"Well, Mr. Roosevelt," he said with a grin. "When'd you
get back from Wyoming?"

"Just yesterday," Roosevelt said. "I wanted to be here in
time for spring roundup."

"How'd your bear hunt go?"

"Splendid! I bagged what our guide called a 'brute of a
grizz' and brought his hide home. We now have a bearskin
rug at Elkhorn."

"Glad you're back in one piece," Ferris said. "Have you
heard the news about Jake Paddock?"

"Adam Sewall told me," Roosevelt acknowledged. "I
understand Paddock was killed by a cardsharp."

"Turns out he was slicker with a gun than he was with
cards. Way I heard it, Paddock accused him of cheating,
and one thing led to another. He beat Paddock to the draw."

"Perhaps Paddock was not the gunman everyone
thought."

"Thing is, you never know about these cardsharps. Doc
Holliday and Luke Short travel the gamblers' circuit pretty
regular, and nobody's ever beat them with a gun. Paddock
braced the wrong man."

"Justice, like God, works in mysterious ways. One
might say this gambler was an instrument of the Lord."

"Yessir, he might've been," Ferris said. "Never thought
of it like that just exactly, but it makes sense. The Lord sure
wouldn't side with Jake Paddock."

Roosevelt glanced at the clerks. "Joe, I wonder if we
might speak in private."

"Why, sure thing, Mr. Roosevelt."

Ferris led the way to the storeroom and closed the door.
Roosevelt fished de Mores' letter from inside his jacket

and handed it over. "If you will, read this," he said. "Then I have a favor to ask."

A moment passed as Ferris read through the letter. He paused, looking up at Roosevelt, and read it again. His expression was grave.

"Do I get this right?" he asked. "The Marquis is callin' you out?"

"Exactly," Roosevelt replied. "Although he has challenged me to a duel, which is the European way of doing such things. I would like you to be my second."

"What's that mean, your 'second'?"

"There is a certain protocol to these matters. Each of the men involved has a second, someone who protects his interests during the affair. You would ensure that it is conducted properly."

"Are you sayin' you intend to accept the challenge?"

"Honor demands that I do so."

"Honor be damned!" Ferris said gruffly. "The Marquis likes to brag he killed two men in duels back in France. One with a pistol and the other with a sword. You want to be the third?"

"I appreciate your concern," Roosevelt said. "However, I feel bound to respond to the challenge. I see no other option."

"Why, hell yes, there's an option, Mr. Roosevelt. You just ignore him and don't do nothin'. It's as simple as that."

"I will not be intimidated by his reputation. Nor will I have my name sullied because I failed to respond."

"You'd get yourself killed to save your name?"

"I've no wish to debate the matter, Joe. Will you serve as my second?"

"Yeah, I suppose," Ferris said reluctantly. "Still think you're makin' a mistake."

"I will keep you apprised of how things progress. And thank you most sincerely for your assistance."

"Just wish't I could've talked you out of it."

"No one could do that, Joe."

Roosevelt went back through the store. On the street, he

moved along the boardwalk past the hotel and entered the offices of de Mores' company. He gave his name to a secretary and waited while the man knocked on a door at the rear of the room. A moment later he was ushered into de Mores' private office.

"Well, Roosevelt—" De Mores rose from behind his desk. "I gather you have been off bear hunting in Wyoming."

"That is correct," Roosevelt said, halting before the desk. "Your letter was waiting upon my return to Elkhorn. I am here to respond."

"So you are."

"As the challenged party, I believe I have the choice of weapons. Isn't that the protocol?"

"Yes, it is."

"I choose shotguns."

"Pardon me?"

"You heard correctly," Roosevelt said. "Shotguns, at twenty paces."

"You are insane," de Mores said truculently. "We would both be killed."

"That is a distinct possibility."

"Gentlemen do not settle affairs of honor with shotguns. It is not . . . civilized."

"Neither is dueling," Roosevelt said. "However, by your own admission, the rules are quite clear in such matters. I have the choice of weapons."

De Mores frowned. "These affairs are traditionally resolved with pistols or swords. Why would you choose shotguns?"

"I will not permit you to escape alive. Buckshot at twenty paces removes any advantage you might have with other weapons."

"You are willing to die in order to kill me. Is that it?"

"I believe you are confused, Marquis. You are the one who insisted on a duel."

De Mores waved it off. "I will not agree to shotguns. You go beyond the bounds of propriety."

"Let me understand," Roosevelt said. "Are you withdrawing the challenge?"

"Only if you apologize."

"Apologize for what?"

"All you have said and done to slander my reputation. The murder charge in particular."

"No, I will not apologize," Roosevelt said firmly. "You are responsible, even though you may not have fired the shot. A man was killed."

De Mores did not reply. Though he would never admit it, he knew he bore the ultimate responsibility for the ambush and murder. He knew as well that he would be killed in any contest with shotguns. The prospect was not acceptable.

"Very well," he finally said. "I withdraw the challenge."

"Then our business here is finished."

"Roosevelt, we are gentlemen and there is no reason for us to be at odds. I offer you my hand in friendship."

"No, I think not," Roosevelt said, ignoring his outstretched hand. "I do not wish to be your friend."

"Why must we be adversaries?" De Mores seemed genuinely baffled. "We are of the aristocratic class, you and I. Why do you oppose me?"

"Were I to answer that, I would merely insult you again. Good day, Marquis."

Roosevelt walked from the office. De Mores resumed his chair behind the desk and sat staring at the door. He almost wished he'd agreed to shotguns, for he felt some odd sense of loss. Not so much a loss of reputation as a loss of esteem.

The esteem of the one man he respected. A man who knew the meaning of honor. A man . . .

Too honorable to compromise.

Medora de Mores loved the springtime. Her passion, apart from her husband, was her flower garden. She could hardly wait for the first rose of summer. Yet wait she must.

Wildflowers bloomed in profusion in the spring. But her

delicate roses, awaiting the heat of summer, were still a month away. Shortly before noontime, she left her gardener to tend the rosebushes outside what she secretly regarded as her château in the Badlands. She hurried into the house.

Upstairs, she removed her gardening dress as she sat down at the dressing table. She fluffed her hair, which she wore in the fashionable upswept style, and applied the faintest dab of rouge to her cheeks. Then she slipped into a fitted gown that accentuated her stemlike waist and sumptuous figure. She inspected herself a moment in a full-length mirror, satisfied with her appearance. She rushed out of the bedroom.

De Mores entered the vestibule as she came down the stairs. He dropped his hat on a side table and moved forward. "How charming," he said, taking her hands. "You look ravishing, my dear."

"Thank you, Antoine." She kissed him lightly on the cheek. "I am so happy you approve."

"No man is more fortunate than myself."

Barring imperative business matters, de Mores always came home for lunch. Today the cook had prepared one of his favorite dishes, veal scallops sautéed in a light wine sauce. After seating Medora in the dining room, he took his place at the opposite end of the table. The butler served them from steaming platters, then disappeared into the kitchen. De Mores sampled the veal.

"Excellent," he said appreciatively. "Cook has outdone herself again."

"She is a treasure," Medora agreed brightly. "And how was your morning?"

"Actually, I wonder that I have any appetite at all. Theodore Roosevelt called on me not an hour ago."

"Oh?"

"Yes, he responded at last to my challenge."

Medora had argued strongly against issuing the challenge. She was confident her husband would prevail in a duel, but she'd thought it a mistake to further antagonize

Roosevelt. She had supported de Mores through the murder trial and afterward breathed a sigh of relief when Jake Paddock was killed in a barroom dispute. She felt it was time to repair their struggling business enterprise. Pride and old-world duels were luxuries they could not afford.

"So?" she asked anxiously. "Did Mr. Roosevelt accept your challenge?"

"Roosevelt would never refuse," de Mores said. "As was his right, he exercised his choice of weapons. Imagine my astonishment when he chose shotguns."

"Shotguns!" Medora dropped her fork, aghast. "You can't be serious."

"I assure you Roosevelt was quite serious."

"And what did you do?"

De Mores suddenly lost his appetite. He pushed his plate aside, unable to meet her gaze. "I refused," he said in a humiliated voice. "I withdrew the challenge."

"You did?" She could hardly believe it. "Does that mean there will be no duel?"

"Yes, that is exactly what it means. I have disgraced myself in the eyes of honorable men."

"Oh, Antoine, sweetheart, think of it as a blessing. You really didn't want to kill Theodore Roosevelt . . . did you?"

"Life is one great paradox, hmmm? I wanted him as a friend and instead he became my albatross. Nothing has gone right since he returned to Dakota."

Medora thought her husband sometimes misread the tea leaves. Their business affairs were in tatters because he was more of a visionary than a businessman. He was a dreamer who lacked the acumen to make his grand schemes a reality. Yet she loved him still.

"Don't despair," she said gently. "Father has promised me he will finance your business at least through the rest of the year. I know you will find a way to make it succeed."

"Yes, of course," de Mores said without conviction. "Although I grow weary of your father's charity. I have no talent for begging."

"I will do the begging for you, my sweet."

"And perhaps we will yet make a success of it."

De Mores had never found an object more worthy of worship than himself. His closest relationship, real or imagined, was born of the mythical Narcissus. For all that, he adored Medora, and decided not to tell her that he was already looking at other ventures. He'd read in business journals of opportunities with vast potential in other countries. India, in particular, appeared quite promising.

"You know—" He pulled his plate back and cut a slice of veal. "I believe our little talk has restored my appetite. You always were an elixir, my dear."

Medora beamed. "And you were never more gallant, *mon cheri*."

TWENTY-FIVE

Roosevelt forded the river by Chimney Butte early that afternoon. The Maltese Cross lay quiet beneath a brassy sun, and cattle grazed across the prairie. A lone horseman topped a ridge far to the south.

Smoke drifted from the cookshack as Roosevelt rode into the compound. He dismounted by the corral and tied Manitou's reins to a fence rail. Merrifield came through the door of the cookshack and walked forward with a look of mild surprise. He nodded to Roosevelt.

"Didn't expect to see you back so soon. How's things at Elkhorn?"

"Never better," Roosevelt said. "Adam Sewall tells me roundup will start next week. Are we ready here?"

"Yessir, we're in pretty good shape. I've got the boys out scoutin' the rough country off to the west. Figured we'd see where the herds drifted over the winter."

"How many men will you send north for roundup?"

"Likely be four, includin' me. I was just talkin' with the cook about what supplies we need to order. I'll have somebody take the list in to Ferris."

"Excellent idea."

Merrifield wondered where the conversation was headed. Only two days ago, upon their return from Wyoming, Roosevelt had dropped him off at the Maltese Cross. Clearly, Roosevelt had ridden on to Elkhorn, and now he was back again. Something didn't rhyme.

"You're gettin' around," Merrifield said, his curiosity aroused. "What brings you out this way?"

"I need a message delivered," Roosevelt said. "I plan to visit Gregor Lang, and I want one of your men to ride to Elkhorn. Have him inform Sewall where I've gone."

"I'll take care of it soon as the boys get back. You don't mind my askin', why would Sewall be worried over your whereabouts?"

"I had a bit of a problem with the Marquis de Mores. I wouldn't want Sewall to be concerned."

"What sort of problem?"

Roosevelt quickly explained the situation. As he talked, Merrifield listened with a look that alternated between amazement and consternation. Roosevelt ended by relating the events in Medora that morning. His features were sober.

"De Mores has no liking for shotguns."

"Hell, I'd guess not," Merrifield said, still shocked himself. "Where'd you come up with that notion?"

"A calculated bluff," Roosevelt admitted. "I thought perhaps it might be one step too far for de Mores. I had no wish to fight a duel."

"You reckon that ends it?"

"I daresay the Marquis has had his fill of me. His so-called honor could not stand further ridicule."

"Why, you think the story'll get around?"

"Ferris and the Eaton brothers will see to that. By tomorrow, it will be public knowledge."

"Yeah, you're right," Merrifield agreed. "You gonna tell Lang?"

"Yes, I suppose I will," Roosevelt said. "Although that is not the purpose of my visit. I have other matters to discuss with him."

"Well, he's gonna be tickled pink when he hears about de Mores. Never was any love lost between them two."

"I'd best be on my way. Perhaps I'll return tomorrow and spend the night."

"We'll be lookin' for you, then."

Roosevelt rode south along the river. He was glad Merrifield hadn't asked his reason for visiting Gregor Lang. There was confusion in his own mind as to the purpose; he hadn't yet fully explained it to himself. The confrontation with de Mores seemed to him an ending of some sort, rather than wiping the slate clean. But he was uncertain what it meant and even less certain of what came next. He felt he needed advice.

There was, as well, the matter of Alice and his mother. Their final words, admonishing him to get on with his life, had somehow crystallized his love for Baby Lee. Whether healed or simply scarred over by time, the grief he'd once borne seemed to ebb the night Alice and his mother departed his world. All the way back from Wyoming, he'd tried to reconcile how the cleansing of grief opened the heart to renewed emotion. He kept thinking his daughter awaited him in New York.

Over a year ago he had fled New York in an attempt to outrun anguish and sorrow. Dakota had become his sanctuary and the Badlands a place to forge a new life. Yet he'd come to realize that a man never really outran his past or himself. Old dreams and a lifetime of aspirations, once thought buried, were not easily supplanted by the pursuit of solace in a distant land. The nomination for mayor of New York left him ambivalent and deeply confused but nonetheless intrigued by the prospect. He felt oddly like a warhorse alert to the sound of bugles.

The sun went down in a splash of orange and gold as he rode into the Yule ranch headquarters. Lang was not expecting him, and the family had already gathered around the table for supper. But a visit by Roosevelt, even unannounced, was an occasion for celebration in the Lang household. Gregor Lang welcomed him at the door while young Linc went to unsaddle his horse, and Edith set a place for him at the table. Throughout the meal, they peppered him with questions about his expedition to Wyoming and the fabled Big Horns. He vigorously related the tale of how he'd shot the grizz.

"Dead center!" he exclaimed, a finger between his eyes. "The brute dropped dead at my feet."

"Holy Hannah," Linc breathed, his eyes round with wonder. "Weren't you scared when he charged you, Mr. Roosevelt?"

"Frightened out of my wits," Roosevelt said expansively. "Although I didn't realize it until after he was on the ground. My knees were knocking like castanets."

"Oh, you're funnin' me," the boy said with a crooked grin. "I'll bet you weren't *that* scared."

"Of course he wasn't, laddie," Lang said humorously. "The bear was the one who was frightened, and never with better reason. He was facing Theodore Roosevelt."

Edith laughed gaily. "I think your father is right, Linc. The bear should have run the other way."

"By Jove!" Roosevelt chuckled out loud. "Now wouldn't that have made a story!"

After supper, Edith shooed the men into the parlor. Linc, with only mild protest, was dragooned into helping her clean the table. The windows were open and a light breeze fluttered the curtains as the men seated themselves. Lang tamped tobacco into his pipe and fired up in a haze of smoke. Roosevelt patted his stomach.

"I am stuffed," he said with a contented sigh. "Were I here more often, Edith would make a fat man of me."

"You visit too seldom," Lang said, gesturing with his pipe. "We'll be talking about your bear for a long while to come. What other news do you bring?"

"A trifle of sorts on de Mores."

"Oh, what's he done now?"

Roosevelt recounted the events of the day. When he finished, Lang gave him a strange look. "You sometimes amaze me, Theodore. Did it occur to you that your bluff might not work?"

"I felt rather confident," Roosevelt said. "De Mores thinks of shotguns as a peasant's weapon. Quite beneath his dignity."

"And if he had agreed to stoop that low?"

"Fortunately for me, he was as I judged him."

"Fortunate indeed." Lang puffed a wad of smoke, his gaze penetrating. "So, then, you rode all this way to tell me of your encounter with de Mores—?"

"Actually, no."

Roosevelt removed his pince-nez, rubbing the bridge of his nose. He was thoughtful a moment, still not certain how to begin. He finally replaced his glasses, looked up with a shrug.

"Upon my return to Elkhorn, a letter was waiting from the Republican Committee. I have been offered the nomination for mayor of New York."

"I see," Lang said. "And you are tempted, is that it?"

"Gregor, I have mixed feelings," Roosevelt confessed. "Tempted, yes, but with great ambivalence."

"Why is that?"

"Well, first off, it would mean leaving Dakota and all I've found here. On the other hand, by accepting, I would be reunited with my daughter. I've grown to miss her terribly."

"Perhaps there is a middle ground," Lang suggested. "You could accept the Senate appointment and spend a good part of your time in the East. The best of both worlds."

"I considered that," Roosevelt said. "No one knows when Dakota will become a state. A year, two years? Perhaps more."

"And you could be mayor of New York this year?"

"Yes, if I accept the nomination."

"I've often wondered how long it would take."

"How long what would take?"

"Theodore, you were destined for a larger role in life. Dakota could never hold you."

Roosevelt stared at him. "To be quite frank, part of my ambivalence has to do with politics. As you know, it's not all wine and roses. There is a seamier side to the political arena."

"Every coin has two sides," Lang reminded him. "Sir Richard Steele was one of the great philosophers of eighteenth-century England. He once wrote: 'The noblest motive is the public good.'"

'Yes, I believe that as well."

'Why, of course you do, Theodore. You are a reformer, a progressive in every sense of the word. You were meant to lead people by your very example."

"Lead them where?" Roosevelt said. "Does government always serve the public good?"

"There is no higher calling," Lang insisted. "Men of great integrity are drawn to government service like a nail to a magnet. Otherwise mankind itself would perish."

Roosevelt was momentarily distracted. Unbidden, he heard again Alice's words deep in the wilds of Wyoming. *Life is before you and your way will be clear.* He was overcome with the sense that her words had brought him to this instant in time and a decision. His gaze shuttled back to Lang.

"So you believe I should accept the nomination?"

"Why would my opinion matter one way or the other?"

"Yours is the only opinion I respect in the Badlands. I suppose I'm looking for validation of my own . . . assessment."

Lang was silent a moment. "I recall you are familiar with Sir Walter Scott."

"Of course," Roosevelt said. "A splendid writer and a gifted poet. I particularly admire his *Ivanhoe*."

"I'm rather partial to his narrative poems. A verse from *Marmion* has always reminded me of you. Would you like to hear it?"

"I would indeed."

> " 'His square-turn'd joints, and strength of limb,
> Show'd him no carpet knight so trim,
> But in close fight a champion grim,
> In camps a leader sage.' "

"Well, Gregor—" Roosevelt blinked behind his pince-nez. "You flatter me far too much."

Lang puffed his pipe. "Go to New York and accept the nomination. You are the 'leader sage' the people so desperately need."

Edith and Linc came in from the dining room. The expressions on the faces of the men were so intense that she thought she'd interrupted some weighty discussion. "Aren't we serious tonight," she said lightly. "Have you two solved the problems of the world?"

"Hardly the world," Lang said with a wry smile. "Only the most important city in America."

"Well, for goodness' sakes, then, tell us!"

"Theodore is about to become the next mayor of New York. Aren't you, Theodore?"

"Yes—" Roosevelt grinned like a bulldog. "I just believe I will."

Lang laughed. "No doubt whatever, eh?"

"No, Gregor, no doubt at all."

Spring roundup was set to begin tomorrow. The men trooped into the Metropolitan an hour or so before the usual noontime crowd. Their features were somber, and they moved through the lobby like a funeral procession. None of them wanted to attend the meeting.

Roosevelt was waiting in the dining room. He was departing on the noon train, and he'd called an emergency board meeting of the Stockgrowers Association. The board members filed through the door, John Eaton and Luther Gudgell, followed by Jack Simpson and Gregor Lang. They took seats around the table.

The past four days had been a hectic time for Roosevelt. After returning to Medora, he had telegraphed the Republican Committee, accepting the nomination for mayor. He'd then gone on to Elkhorn and back again to the Maltese Cross, settling arrangements for management of the ranches. His last official act was to leave the Stockgrowers Association in good hands.

"Gentlemen," he said, nodding around the table. "Thank you for coming on such short notice. I know you are busy preparing for roundup."

"Too bad you won't be with us," Simpson said. "All the boys was waitin' to hear your bear story."

"Have Bill Merrifield tell it in my place. He can spin quite a yarn around a campfire."

"Not hardly the same," Eaton said dourly. "We'd sooner hear it from the horse's mouth, except the horse is runnin' off to New York. Why you wanna be mayor of that pesthole?"

"Why, John, I thought you knew me better," Roosevelt said in a jocose tone. "I cannot resist the opportunity to orate my views on pestholes. New York provides the perfect stage."

Gudgell snorted. "Yeah, but who's gonna keep the Marquis on the straight and narrow? You're the only one that ever boxed his ears."

"Damn right," Simpson added. "Everbody's heard how he turned piss-willie about duelin' with shotguns. You plumb put him in the shade."

Roosevelt stilled them with an upraised palm. "I have confidence you men are equal to the task. Collectively, you are the power in Medora, not the Marquis. Never forget that he must dance to your tune."

Gregor Lang smiled to himself. He reflected that it was Roosevelt who had formed the association and instilled in the men seated here today a sense of law and order in a lawless land. Lang was pleased that he'd had some small part in shaping Roosevelt's journey into the future. He thought New York was about to see lightning uncorked from a bottle.

"Now, on to business," Roosevelt said. "With my departure, the board will require a fifth member. I suggest Mike Boyce of the Three Seven outfit. He's a steady man in a tight situation."

The vote was unanimous. "Excellent," Roosevelt said, nodding his approval. "As my last official act, I bring you now to the matter of electing a new president. The floor is open to nominations."

"Who's your choice?" Gudgell asked. "We'll vote for whoever you pick."

"Only kings appoint their successor," Roosevelt said.

"You have a responsibility to elect your own president. That is the democratic way."

"Look here," Simpson said forcefully. "You're the one that put the association together, and before you hightail it for New York, you oughta pick the best man for the job. Ain't that right, boys?"

There was a loud murmur of assent. Roosevelt glanced at Lang, and in that instant the Scotsman knew he would not be selected. "Very well," Roosevelt said to the group. "If it were left to me, I would choose John Eaton. He's tough, he's smart, and he will bring solidity to the board."

"Godalmighty," Eaton said, ducking his head. "I didn't come here lookin' for no job."

"Perhaps not," Lang said. "But as Theodore just noted, a tough job requires a tough man. I propose we make the vote unanimous."

Simpson laughed. "John, that puts you on the firin' line with the Marquis. Hope to hell you can fill Roosevelt's boots."

The meeting was adjourned with Eaton installed as president. The men rose from their chairs and stood waiting by the door. Eaton, their newly elected leader, suggested that they accompany Roosevelt to the train station. The ranchers nodded agreement, but Roosevelt came around the table and stopped before Eaton. He extended his hand.

"I dislike farewells," he said. "Besides, Merrifield and Sewall insisted on seeing me off. I could hardly refuse my new partners."

"Well, then," Eaton said, pumping his arm. "I reckon we'll say good-bye here."

"No, John, not good-bye. I shall return from time to time, and you may depend on it. The Badlands will always call me back."

Roosevelt went down the line, shaking hands and offering a parting comment to each of the men. Lang was the last in line, standing nearest the door. Roosevelt clasped his hand.

"Gregor, I am indebted to you far more than you know. Thank you for your wise counsel."

"No thanks necessary, Theodore," Lang said warmly. "I merely confirmed what was so very apparent. You were ready to move on."

"I am nonetheless indebted."

Roosevelt led the way into the hall. The ranchers moved past him, waving a last farewell, and went out the street door. Merrifield and Sewall were waiting in the lobby, Amos Packard of the *Badlands Cowboy* at their side. The editor nodded with a rueful shrug.

"I really hate to see you go," he said. "There won't be anything worth reporting without you around."

"Somehow I doubt that," Roosevelt said amiably. "A go-getter like you will always find a newsworthy headline."

"Well, the lead story in the next issue will be about you running for mayor of New York. How about a quote?"

"I plan to run on a platform of removing the Tammany Hall rascals from the public trough. You may quote me as saying I will prevail at the ballot box."

"New York's gain is our loss, Mr. Roosevelt. You'll be missed in the Badlands."

"No more than I shall miss the Badlands, Amos. The pyramids of Egypt pale by comparison."

"By golly, there's my headline!"

They walked toward the door, followed by Merrifield and Sewall. Joe Ferris was waiting outside, and Packard shook Roosevelt's hand, then hurried off. Ferris looked glum as a bloodhound.

"Just wanted to say good-bye," he said. "Everybody in town's sorry you're leavin'."

Roosevelt chuckled. "I suspect the Marquis de Mores does not share your opinion."

"Yeah, things are gonna be a little tame with you gone. We got used to your fireworks."

"Let us hope I have the same effect in New York. Fireworks are very much needed there."

"You'll win it in a landslide, Mr. Roosevelt. I'd bet money on it."

"I thought you weren't a gambling man."

"Yessir, but I know enough to bet on a sure thing."

"Then I shan't let you down, Joe."

After a final handshake, Ferris turned back toward his store. Roosevelt, with Merrifield and Sewall at his side, set off in the direction of the train station. He was reflective, lost in a moment of introspection, genuinely touched by the sentiments of so many friends. Yet he thought that they no longer needed his fireworks, as Ferris had expressed it, or for that matter, a torchbearer in the fight for law and order. Medora was now their town.

Nor was he concerned about Elkhorn and the Maltese Cross. Over the past few days he had revised the management contracts with Merrifield and Sewall. For all intents and purposes, they were now partners in his ranching enterprise. They were to receive 25 percent of the yearly profits and a monthly salary to be applied against their share of the operation. The arrangement ensured they would be working in his best interests to augment their own stake. The more he made, the more they made.

The noon train squealed to a halt outside the depot as they walked through the waiting room. Roosevelt already had his tickets, and his luggage had been checked with the stationmaster earlier that morning. He thought he'd timed it perfectly, for if there was anything he hated more than farewells, it was lengthy farewells. The conductor stepped down from the lead coach, and several passengers began boarding. Roosevelt turned to Merrifield and Sewall.

"Mind you now," he said briskly. "Take good care of *our* cows. I expect a handsome profit."

"Well hell," Merrifield mumbled, suddenly at a loss for anything to say. "Don't know what we're gonna do without you on roundup, Mr. Roosevelt."

"Why, you will have Adam to break in at the branding fires. Isn't that so, Adam?"

Sewall nodded. "I aim to take over your title as champion calf wrestler. I'll make a cowboy yet."

"Bully!" Roosevelt laughed heartily. "I always knew you were a Westerner in spirit. Time has proved me right."

"Yeah, I guess I'm here to stay."

Roosevelt unbuckled his gun belt. He rolled it up and handed the holstered Colt to Sewall. "Keep this for me," he said with a wry smile. "I rather doubt I'll need it in New York."

"Good thing, too," Sewall said. "You'd likely scare off the voters."

"All aboard!"

The conductor's cry brought them around. There was no time for further words, and they shook hands with the warmth of men who had formed a bond that would last a lifetime. Roosevelt hurried across the platform and boarded the rear coach as the engineer engaged the driving wheels. The train lurched into motion.

Sewall and Merrifield stood there, unwilling to turn away just yet. As the train gathered speed, the door at the back of the rear coach popped open. Roosevelt stepped onto the observation platform and raised his arm in a final salute. His teeth flashed in his nutcracker grin.

He looked like a man with worlds to conquer.

EPILOGUE

Theodore Roosevelt returned again and again to the Badlands during his lifetime. A terrible blizzard in the winter of 1886 all but destroyed the cattle industry, and he sold his ranching enterprise to a consortium of cattlemen. Yet he was always welcome at Elkhorn.

In one of his few setbacks, Roosevelt was defeated in the mayoral election of New York City. The defeat did nothing to temper his indomitable spirit or his commitment to public service. He went on to reform the Civil Service Commission in Washington and later served as Police Commissioner of New York City. In 1897, he became the U.S. Assistant Secretary of the Navy; with the outbreak of the Spanish-American War in 1898, he resigned his post in Washington to lead the Rough Riders to victory at San Juan Hill in Cuba. He was elected governor of New York in 1899 and Vice President of the United States in 1900. When William McKinley was assassinated, Roosevelt became president, and he was elected in his own right in 1904. He occupied the White House for almost eight years.

During his presidency, Roosevelt enforced the Sherman Anti-Trust Act against business monopolies, championed the rights of the "little man," originated the "big stick" policy to enforce the Monroe Doctrine, and established America as a world power. His greatest legacy was in land conservation, creating five national parks, thirteen national forests, sixteen national bird refuges, and fifteen national monuments, including the Grand Canyon. He was awarded the Nobel Peace Prize in 1906 for mediating an end to the Russo-Japanese War.

Pres. Theodore Roosevelt visited the Badlands for the last time in 1903. The people of Medora and hundreds from throughout the Dakotas assembled to greet him in the town hall. His speech to the crowd was reflective, delivered as a man rather than a president. He told them what was in his heart.

"I am, myself, at heart as much a Westerner as an Easterner. The time I lived here among you was unquestionably the happiest time of my life. I am proud, indeed, to be considered one of yourselves."

Roosevelt was larger than life, one of the most beloved figures in American history. Mount Rushmore, the national memorial in the Black Hills of South Dakota, was completed in 1941. On its face are carved the immense sculptures of George Washington, Thomas Jefferson, Abraham Lincoln, and Theodore Roosevelt. He died in his sleep at Sagamore Hill, the family estate, the night of January 6, 1919. Vice President Thomas Marshall, one among his legion of admirers, wrote an epitaph befitting the man.

Death had to take him sleeping. For if Theodore Roosevelt had been awake, there would have been a fight.